WILD
SALVATION

A NOVEL BY
ALFRED STIFSIM

T W O D O T ®

GUILFORD, CONNECTICUT
HELENA, MONTANA

A · TWODOT® · BOOK

An imprint of Globe Pequot, the trade division of
The Rowman & Littlefield Publishing Group, Inc.
4501 Forbes Blvd., Ste. 200
Lanham, MD 20706
www.rowman.com

Distributed by NATIONAL BOOK NETWORK

British Library Cataloguing in Publication Information available

Library of Congress Cataloging-in-Publication Data

Names: Stifsim, Alfred, author.
Title: Wild salvation : a novel / Alfred Stifsim.
Description: Guilford, Connecticut : TwoDot, [2022] |
Identifiers: LCCN 2021039034 (print) | LCCN 2021039035 (ebook) | ISBN 9781493064243 (hardcover) | ISBN 9781493064250 (epub)
Subjects: LCGFT: Western fiction. | Novels.
Classification: LCC PS3619.T5385 W55 2022 (print) | LCC PS3619.T5385 (ebook) | DDC 813/.6--dc23
LC record available at https://lccn.loc.gov/2021039034
LC ebook record available at https://lccn.loc.gov/2021039035

The paper used in this publication meets the minimum requirements of American National Standard for Information Sciences—Permanence of Paper for Printed Library Materials, ANSI/NISO Z39.48-1992.

CONTENTS

Contents

PROLOGUE

JOHNSON WOKE TO THE SOUND OF KEYS JINGLING ACCOMPANIED BY A rusty mechanical click. He tipped his hat back just enough to see the sheriff's white-knuckle grip on the bars of his cell door.

"You did it! I know you did it!" the sheriff's voice boomed. "Lucky for you, seeing as how no one else was there, court o' law can't prove that you did it." Lip snarled under his thick mustache, he stared Johnson down for a long moment before finally swinging open the heavy metal door. "I suggest," he drew out his words in a serious tone, "you get far from here fast as you can. Frederick Boyd is her father. He'll be sure to come after you soon as he hears, and I've half a mind to join him."

PART I

Chapter 1

Western Missouri
April 1876

The countryside was vast and open, an ocean of green prairie grass rippling like waves in the wind, stretching over the land until it touched the cloudless blue sky. In it, a road cut deep into the plain. Its two wagon ruts raced parallel to each other for miles over the rolling hills and disappeared into the distance of the great blue yonder. Between the ruts, a thin strip of trodden grass struggled to grow, yet spring wildflowers blossomed along the outer edge of the road, occasionally trampled under hoof as they strained outward in their greed for more sunlight.

Thousands had traveled the dirt blemish cut into the prairie grass as they ventured west in search of new lives, but their presence was unseen by the late morning. Idle, the well-worn path drew silence, yet the music of the plain abounded; the call of a killdeer accompanied by the song of a young child.

Two bare feet trudged along the ground away from a small sod house sitting alone like a dirt island in the sea of grass. "Eeny, meeny . . . miny, moe." The little blond girl sang in pauses between carefully placed steps, stumbling along as she wandered down the hill.

Her patchwork dress told a story of hardship and the struggle for survival on the frontier as it dragged through the prairie. Slightly too long, its frayed threads were dirty and green from being stepped on time and again.

"Catch a nigger by his toe." The girl joyfully repeated the opening to the nursery rhyme. Another pause, only this time in contemplation over the words for the next verse.

Peee peeee! The sound of a killdeer flying overhead quickly diverted her attention. Nose pointed in the air, she stared into the great open sky. Lost in its brilliant color, she was captured by the moment. A soft wind picked up, blowing the girl's blond locks across her face, breaking her trance. Remembering the song, the missing words came to her, "If he hollers!" Eagerly, she approached the bottom of the hill, "let him go! Eeny, meeny, miny, moe!" *Thump!* Cross legged, the girl came down in a decisive motion at the edge of the road and began picking wildflowers. She plucked individual petals, placing them in her lap for safekeeping, each color in its own neatly stacked pile. Her song began again, "Eeny, meeny, miny—"

"*Watch out!*"

The voice called out as a stagecoach careened over the hill. Behind it dragged a long trail of dust that raised high in the air as the stage raced along the dirt path. The driver clung from the side of his seat while several passengers hung out of the windows attempting to assist him. Blood stained the man's shirt as the horse team raged forward in a violent sprint. Wide eyed, the little girl scrambled to her feet, tripping on her dress and tumbling directly into the path of the oncoming stage.

Paralyzed by fear, the young girl lay in the road, tears streaming from her eyes. A terrified cry escaped her as the out-of-control team drew closer. Closing her eyes, she squealed as she felt pressure and tasted dirt as she rolled over the ground; the clomping of hooves and screams of passengers passed as quickly as they had arrived.

"It's alright; it's alright." A calming voice came through the darkness of her firmly closed eyelids. "You're gonna be alright now."

The girl was slow to open her eyes. She was shaken but in the bright sunlight a blurry figure came into focus. She had never seen a person with a dark face before and her curiosity about the man erased the terror she had clung to so deeply moments earlier. He helped her stand and she smiled at him with glee.

"See? There you go. Everything's just fine," Johnson said, reassuring her. "Now, let's see if we can't find where you come from."

Brushing himself off, he looked around then picked the girl up in his arms. Dust lingered in the air. The stage hadn't been stopped on its rampage and disappeared down the road and over the crest of the next hill. With the girl in his arms, Johnson stared after its trail. For a moment he pondered the fate of the passengers then returned his attention to the girl.

"Which way?" he asked.

The girl stretched out a hand to point out the direction from which she had traveled. He glanced quickly to the east where the stagecoach had appeared, recalling the yells of the passengers and the cloud of dust as it tore through. As he stared, he wondered how he always managed to end up in such tangling circumstances. All he wanted was to get to the next town without any trouble. What would he do if he couldn't find any family looking for the girl nearby? Holding the girl firmly in his arms, he stepped a worn boot across the deep rut of the road and began to climb the hill on the other side.

Johnson had heard that the West was vast and wild. The frontier of American civilization. A place where any man could find freedom. Freedom to get good work, freedom from the status quo, freedom from your past, maybe even from the color of your skin. Runaway stagecoaches and saving little girls wasn't what he'd had in mind. He just wanted the chance to be his own man.

You'll find your freedom, he thought to himself, *one thing at a time. Gotta get this girl safe.*

"Nigger! You get yer hands off o' her!" A woman appeared at the top of the hill. Hard eyed and slinging a shotgun, she was unmistakably the girl's mother.

In his surprise, Johnson was barely able to catch his balance to avoid tumbling back down the slope.

The girl exploded in tears as she cried out for her mother.

"You let her go!"

"Hold up now! She's just a little shook—"

"*Now!*" the woman yelled, pulling back the hammer on the shotgun.

"Whoa, whoa, whoa! No need for trouble!" Johnson yelled as he set the girl on her feet.

Running to her mother, the girl gripped one of her legs so tight it looked like she'd never let go.

"You best git from here and leave my family alone!" she said, tears in her eyes, shaking the shotgun.

"Look, I was just tryin' to help her out," Johnson explained, hands raised.

"Maybe you was, maybe you wasn't. Don't matter now! You go on and git before I change my mind and decide to take you into town to let the marshal decide."

"Alright, I'm leavin', I'm leavin'," Johnson said, hands still raised. Mindful of how he moved, he backstepped then quickly turned and headed down to the road.

That's exactly the kinda trouble you need no part of! he thought to himself. *Problem's off your hands now.*

Reaching the bottom of the hill, Johnson picked up his pack from the spot he had dropped it before running to save the girl.

I know she's worried about her child, but damn. Maybe I can't find freedom from everything.

Saint Andrews, Indiana
March 1876: One Month Earlier

Frederick Boyd's formidable figure stood in contemplation, silhouetted in the center of a large arched window overlooking the river. From his vantage point the man could view the riverboat empire he had created. Family meant everything to him; family *was* everything he had. He made sure those in his family were brought into the business and placed in positions of power. They were trained to understand the inner workings of every aspect of the business. No one could be trusted like family, and he could not bear the thought that when he was gone, his cutthroat competitors might slither their way into *his* business, *his* family. Not that he had any qualms about merciless ambition, but he would do everything in his power to protect what he had built. He had worked too hard, too long, and he would abide no threats. A threat to family was a threat to business, no matter how large or insignificant. He would protect his family, and when he could not, he would ensure justice was carried out for his family.

A puny balding man with wire-framed glasses quietly entered Boyd's study, carrying himself in a manner that suggested a lack of self-worth.

"*Er-hmm*," he cleared his throat. "Mr. Boyd, I've assembled the usual party of local men. There has been no sign of him."

"You've talked with *all* those negros working the docks?"

"Yes sir, as usual many of them seem . . . reluctant to say anything."

"I hope you haven't caused too much damage."

"No sir, nothing anybody will care about. Just roughed up some men, and . . . 'redecorated' a few of their establishments."

"And he was nowhere to be found?"

"He may have already left the city."

Boyd turned to the man and stared at him with malice in his eyes. "Get me Allan Pinkerton."

Western Missouri
April 1876
From atop the hill Johnson could see the entire town. Though he figured he'd probably be able to see the whole town even if he wasn't on the hill. There wasn't much to it. The old road he had followed since Missouri ran straight through, and he could see a few taller buildings sitting on either side. Five buildings in total, not counting the smaller establishments and houses dotting the outer edges of town. He wasn't even entirely sure what town it was, but he hoped it was New Pittsburg. That would mean he had finally made it out of Missouri and into Kansas.

It had been a long journey that always seemed to grow longer, almost as if he were running a race in which the finish line was continually moving farther and farther ahead of him. He was tired. Not the normal kind of tired that could be fixed with a couple extra hours of sleep, but the kind of tired that eats at a man until it seemed as if his very soul were going to decide that it had had enough and find a place to lay him down for good.

Johnson removed his hat to wipe the sweat from his forehead. He took a long swig of water from his canteen. Removing his right boot, he sat down in the grass and began to massage his foot. *I'm gonna have to find a better way*, he thought, *all this walkin' is too much.*

Both his feet ached terribly. Back East he had heard tales about how some of the Indians would supposedly walk for thousands of miles across all kinds of landscapes: canyons, deserts, mountains. After this, though, he questioned the truthfulness of such claims. He had never even seen canyons, deserts, or mountains, but his heels burned so badly after a few hours of walking in the grass that he had to start stepping funny to try and alleviate the pain. That started hurting the sides of his feet after a short while, too, until he almost couldn't take it anymore. He'd resigned to the idea that he was just going to have to get used to it. Unless he could pay for a stage or get a horse, his poor feet were doomed to ache, and he had very little money. *No* money, to be exact. If he couldn't find a job in this town, he'd be in trouble for sure.

Johnson was used to the city. Much of what he'd experienced so far was entirely new to him and if he was going to make a successful life for himself out West, he knew he'd have to learn everything he could. The one thing he was certain of from all the tales and stories he'd heard about the West was that success was built on reputation, and reputation was all about what you knew and how well you knew it.

Don't get too ahead of yourself, he thought, checking himself, *you gotta make it to that town first.* Slipping his boot back on with a grimace, he finished his water, grabbed his pack, and headed down the hill.

Hours later, he stumbled into the outskirts of town. By then it was late afternoon and the temperature had gotten significantly hotter. He hadn't realized how much farther he had to travel, and like a fool, he'd already drank the rest of his water during his stop on the hill.

Parched, he'd spotted the stable for the stagecoach a few miles out from the town and knew there would be water there to keep the horses fresh for the next leg of their journey. In his thirst he could only focus on the thought of cool water down his throat. When he arrived he didn't care to ask. Johnson plunged his face deep into the horse trough and took in water so fast that it went down the wrong pipe. Throwing his head back, he began to cough violently as he lay in the mud.

"My god," came an old man's voice, "you must be greener than all the goddamned grass in Kansas!"

Johnson finished hacking up the last bit of water from his lungs and stared up at the man. Long, stringy white hair hung from his head paired with the thick white stubble that grew on his pale face.

"What—what town is this?" Johnson asked through gasping breaths.

"Flatridge," the man quickly replied, hands firmly placed on his boney hips.

Johnson gulped. "New Pittsburg?"

"Few miles west."

"Saw a—a runaway coach," Johnson said, finally catching his breath.

"Oh yeah," the old man said, lighting up like he was remembering a story from his younger years. "Got attacked by bandits. Got all the valuables from the passengers before the teamster decided to be a hero. They shot him as he was pulling a gun he had hidden under the seat. Passengers said it spooked the horses and they took off running." His voice turned solemn, "Teamster didn't make it though."

The old man put out a hand and helped Johnson to his feet. He was short but had a grip strength that took Johnson by surprise.

"I'm guessing you need a place to stay tonight."

"What makes you say that?"

"Well, you didn't come in on that stage, and I don't see your horse anywhere. Means you walked, and I wouldn't expect a man who just walks into a town he doesn't even know the name of to have planned his accommodations accordingly."

"I suppose that's a healthy observation," Johnson said.

"And seeing as how you walked into a town you don't know the name of, I would also hazard a guess you don't have much in the way of capital neither."

"I'm willin' to work for a room."

"Oh, you're gonna work," the old man said, "but I can't guarantee a room." He opened the barn door and motioned toward the hayloft.

Johnson pushed his hat up with one hand and scratched his forehead.

"Don't worry. I'll feed ya," the old man said.

Johnson paused to think. "Deal." He held out his hand with a smile.

The old man shook it with a big, toothy grin. "Burt Griffin."

"Johnson."

"Well, Mr. Johnson, I'm glad to have you. Been a long time since I've had any good help around here. I sure do need it and you look like a hard-working boy. C'mon. I'll show you around."

Burt worked for the Douglass & Kinney Stagecoach Company. The relay station he managed was for the coaches traveling through to Wichita. "This is the only road that goes west from here. Since we're right on the border of Missouri, mine is the first stop in Kansas," Burt said as he walked Johnson through the barn. "Due to such a favorable location, we get a decent amount of traffic, pioneers and sod-busting types, people moving west looking to start new lives. As more folks came through, plenty stayed and Flatridge grew up." Burt stopped at the last stall. "Now you're mostly gonna be in charge of mucking the stalls, feeding, and tending to anything that needs fixing." The old man talked so fast Johnson had a hard time keeping up with what he was saying.

"When do I start?" Johnson asked.

"Right now," Burt said, handing him a pitchfork.

That night Johnson stared at the stars through large cracks in the roof.

I'm probably gonna have to fix those, he thought to himself as he laid on the floor of the loft. The hay wasn't as uncomfortable as he had expected, but the loft was hot from the rising warm air. *Finally made it out West and it's plenty exciting already*, he thought as he drifted into unconsciousness.

Chapter 2

Saint Andrews, Indiana
March 1876

The river was wide. So wide that for many years opportunistic men helped turn it into a bustling thoroughfare for goods, services, travel, and warfare. America had gained its independence and expanded its boundaries through wars with England, Mexico, and several Indian nations. Pioneers settled westward, stretching the ever-expanding American frontier, and a great war had raged among the states, tearing the country in two, its resolution a lingering wound poorly sewn together like a patchwork flag left to dangle in the wind.

All the while, the river tycoons gained wealth and notoriety as barons in the central regions of the country. They built their empires in port cities that dotted the banks of the country's great waterways with locks and piers, forever putting their stamp on the nation. The waterways of the United States of America had become so interconnected that one could board a riverboat on the Ohio River in Pittsburgh or Cincinnati and arrive in New Orleans by way of the Mississippi in what seemed to be no time at all.

Johnson knew he had only so much time to flee Saint Andrews before a mob of angry white men would be after him. What he didn't know was how he would be able to afford any form of swift passage out of town. Having gathered what few possessions he had to his name, he wandered the docks by the river, scrambling to find Jimmy Perkins.

Jimmy was a coworker of his on the docks, and one of the few people he had gotten to know since coming to town a few weeks earlier. Luckily for Johnson, he was the right person to know in a tight situation.

Jimmy was a fixer. He knew how to get things, and he knew how to make things—and people—disappear quickly. As Johnson wandered the busy riverfront, he visited popular locales, stopping familiar faces to ask for Jimmy, but no one seemed to know where he was. A sickening pain gnawed at Johnson's stomach. He knew if he didn't find a way out of town that night, he was done for sure.

To his surprise, Jimmy found him. Tightly clasping his arm from behind, Jimmy yanked him into a side alley.

"Boy, what do you think you're doin'?" He pinned Johnson to the wall behind him as he carefully poked his head around the corner.

"Lookin' for you!" Johnson replied.

"Well, it looks like I found *you* an' I wasn't lookin' that hard. Think how easy it'll be for those white folks ta find ya," Jimmy said. "Lucky I found ya first. You're in trouble now, so ya better get smart." Still holding Johnson's arm in a tight grasp, Jimmy pulled him further down the alley behind a tall brick building.

"I knew to go lookin' for you; that's smart."

"Yeah, but you was dumb enough ta talk to the whole damn town about it. Now they're gonna be comin' after my ass lookin' for you!"

"How will they know? I didn't talk to any white folks."

Jimmy stopped, pushed him against the wall again, and looked him dead in the eyes. "Let's get one thing straight. If you think some of these other black men won't sell you out, you got another thing comin'," he said in an angry whisper. "It's not their fault. They don't got much in the way of options. It's help an' be left alone or be difficult and things get more difficult. There's big money behind gettin' you, and big money don't forget." He turned to look down the alleyway they came from. "*Your* damn fool ass is lucky I ain't decided to forget. Now come on."

It was a dreary, cloudy day and the air smelled of wet dirt. Rain had fallen periodically throughout the afternoon and Johnson's feet and pant legs were soaked from stepping through the puddles of the poorly drained alleyways. As they moved, Jimmy kept constant vigilance. He well expected to receive a visit from some of the thugs who had become all too familiar with the citizens of the lower part of town. Too often when someone needed to be "persuaded" to sell his shop and move out of the city, they would be there to personally deliver the message. In this case, a person of interest needed to be found and that required more manpower than the usual brute squad had available. He knew that as the search extended, professionals would soon be brought in.

They kept up their pace, navigating the maze of backstreets. At one point, they ran past the back entrance to a butcher's shop, almost knocking the butcher over as he exited. Jimmy ducked as the butcher hauled a large bag down the back step.

"Goddammit!" the man yelled, dropping the bag.

They didn't stop to help as the contents spilled over the ground and the butcher cursed them down the alleyway.

Jimmy knew every passageway and was always careful at each corner they approached. It was as if a map of the city was seared into his brain, and he knew where they would be most vulnerable to interception.

The thought of being dragged away and lynched made the sick feeling in Johnson's stomach grow even worse. It was not uncommon for groups of angry white people to take it upon themselves to dispense their idea of justice on a black man in the streets, especially when they felt like their official justice system had failed in its duty.

"You know how to get me outta here, right?"

"I know a place you'll lay low for a while."

"You don't understand; I gotta get out. Tonight!"

"Ain't no free tickets outta town," Jimmy said, putting a finger to Johnson's chest. "You're gonna have to give me time—"

They froze at the sound of footsteps in an alleyway behind them. Water dripped from the rooftops in the stillness. The footsteps passed.

"I don't have much time!"

"You don't have much choice! This mess is outta the box. It ain't goin' back in!"

Jimmy lead him in several directions. Sometimes they took an alley several blocks north or south out of their way to get one or two blocks west. It was inconvenient, but they were in a dangerous situation and neither man desired the consequences of an ill-timed chance.

Finally, the two men stopped at an alley that opened onto a main street. They approached with caution. Across the street Johnson could see what looked to be a burned-out building sitting at the edge of the riverfront. The roof had partly caved and most of the upper windows were smashed, but the main structure stood solid. It was three stories of charred red brick and although the top two stories were boarded up, from the first floor a sign hung over the door—*Commercial Storage*.

"Almost there," Jimmy said, "we just gotta make it to that building."

Squatting low, they edged to the end of the alley.

Rain began in a light mist. The men paused. Voices and sounds of a struggle carried from a short distance down the road. Johnson's stomach turned.

Jimmy pressed his face to the wall, wet brick shoving against his cheek as he carefully inched to the corner of the building, just far enough to see the commotion. Four men surrounded a fifth, pushing and shoving him around the circle. The clouds had brought the late afternoon into an early nightfall, and the streetlights had yet to be ignited. The street was barely illuminated by the few buildings that had lit windows and a lantern one of the four men held. They pushed the man they were harassing to the ground.

"I told you I don't know anything!" he yelled, using his arms to protect his face from anticipated blows.

"Hear that?" their fat leader said, giving him a hard kick to the side, "This darkie say he don't know nothin'."

The man cringed in pain and rolled onto all fours.

"Funny how they never seem ta know nothing, even though they all know each other," replied another man who proceeded to stomp on his hand.

"Please," the man winced, "I really don't know."

"Fine then," the fat leader delivered another kick to his stomach. "You lucky we gotta check out dis ol' warehouse. Don't suppose you know if that ol' negro is in?"

"No," he replied through gritted teeth.

"Well, fine then!" the fat leader said again. "Git outta here!" he yelled, with a kick to the man's backside as he got up and ran away. "C'mon boys. We check that place out right now. Let's check all the alleyways 'round here, too."

Both Johnson and Jimmy froze as the men walked in their direction. They could hear their footsteps splattering on the wet ground as they approached the corner. Silently, Jimmy moved his hand toward a knife in his boot. He glanced at Johnson, who responded with a nod. The sick feeling had turned into a tight knot. Blood raced through his body as his heart throbbed. The sky opened, and rain beat down on them.

"Hey!"

Both men felt their hearts skip.

"Hey, you!" the fat leader yelled, right at the edge of the alleyway. "C'mere, *boy*, we wanna talk to ya."

Another man had appeared farther down the street, grabbing the attention of the four thugs. Realizing their intent, he immediately turned to flee. In pursuit, the men ran right past the alley, unaware of the two crouched figures.

Neither man spoke. They didn't even look to make sure it was safe to cross the street for fear of missing their opportunity. They sprang from the alleyway and into the street as the rain tried to beat them into the ground. Eyes fixed on the building opposite him, Johnson had never run so hard in his life.

When they reach the other side of the street, Jimmy ushered him to the side door. He slid it open and they ducked in, out of the rain. Jimmy slammed the door shut. His hands shook as he tried to secure the lock; it took him several tries before he was successful. From behind them, another door swung open with a loud thud. Startled, they both turned and pressed against the wall. An old man with patches of curly white hair held a lantern. They relaxed, almost collapsing as the adrenaline began to wear off.

"What took ya so long?" the old man asked. "Them men been roaming the streets for hours."

He wore overalls with no shirt underneath, and his large belly stretched the buttons so that his dark skin was displayed between the holes in the denim. "Nobody cares about us when shit goes down at the docks, but soon as some white girl gets involved, the white folk suddenly wanna start solving every crime in the neighborhood."

"They ain't tryin' ta solve shit," Jimmy said as he pointed to Johnson. "They're lookin' for this one here, and they'll be back soon so we gotta get him hid!"

"Dammit, I shoulda known—" *Thump! Thump! Thump!*

"Ol' man, I know yer in there!" the fat man bellowed through the front door. "We don't want no trouble—just wanna talk." The pounding persisted as the other men began to join in. "Ol' man!"

"Go! Both of ya. I'll deal with them," the old man whispered as he turned and shut the door. "Goddammit imma comin'!"

"C'mon, help me move this," Jimmy said as he tugged at a large wooden cargo box. Johnson quickly jumped in to help.

Each individual box was labeled and ready for shipment. The whole room had been stacked with them. The ceiling was high, and the walls extended back for what looked to be a few hundred feet—enough to create a significant amount of storage space or a good place to hide in a pinch, Johnson realized. The two men pushed another box with "soap" painted on the side against a stack at the back wall that was several rows wide and about fifteen feet high. Jimmy began to climb and to Johnson's surprise, swung open the lid on one of the highest boxes against the wall.

"Hurry!" he whispered and motioned Johnson to follow.

He scrambled after him and could see that inside the box, a ladder reached down to a crawlspace below the floor. Johnson descended the ladder. Darkness came over him as Jimmy closed the top of the box above them and secured the hatch.

—◆—

"Do y'all really think I'm stupid enough to do a thing like that?" the old man said to the group of men from behind the front counter. "I got enough problems to worry about as it is. I don't need y'all coming here, causing a ruckus and threatening to raise my rent."

"Jus' remember who that rent go to every month."

The old man scowled. "Can't hardly forget with you in here reminding me all the damn time."

"For good reason, an' if you ever own this ol' burnt-out hunk o' shit, you'll only have ta see us when we come collect protection money," the fat leader said with a wicked grin.

"I ain't seen nobody tonight, so go on ahead and bother some other poor soul!"

"OK, but you make sure ta come tell us if ya happen ta see that darkie. Maybe ya rent'll go down a lil' bit."

All four men laughed and proceeded to knock over a barrel of flour by the door on their way out. Its powdery white contents spilled over the floor and filled the room with dust. Rainwater seeped through the doorway and turned the flour to a sticky paste.

The old man was tired and considered making some dinner before cleaning it up or returning to the back room to check on the men in the hidden chamber.

"Should just leave 'em down there in the dark," he said to himself. "Let 'em rot."

He grabbed a broom and dustpan, then sat on a crate next to the overturned barrel and exhaled, staring at the mess.

—◦—

The lid to the trapdoor creaked as light spilled down into the chamber. "Jim, you got yourself into some real shit this time," came the old man's voice.

"Why don't ya come down here and we'll talk about it," Jimmy joked as he climbed the ladder.

"Goddammit, I ain't got time to be doing this anymore. You said we'd be done."

"You an' I both know things ain't changed much since we was hidin' runaway slaves down there," Jimmy said as he stepped from the ladder, taking the old man's hand. "Difference is, back then we had a lot more guests comin' through. So, way I see it, ya actually got more time for this than ya used ta have," he said with a smile.

"Fuck you. Go on, do what you gotta do."

Johnson waited for what seemed like several hours alone in the dark. He tried to focus his thoughts positively but had very little to choose from and sunk into the fear that the next face he'd see open the trapdoor wouldn't be a welcome one. He tried to sleep but his mind raced with thoughts of his own death. He wasn't safe and he wouldn't feel safe until he was far from Saint Andrews. He might never feel safe again.

The trapdoor opened above him. He flinched in the light.

Jimmy's voice echoed down. "C'mon up. It's 'bout time for ya ta go."

Relieved, Johnson moved toward the ladder. As he climbed out of the hole, he realized there was another man with Jimmy.

"This here is Abraham," Jimmy said. "He's gonna get you a job on the *Queen Bellamy* shovelin' coal."

Clouds began to break as the rain finally ceased. Luminescent spheres reflected off the surface of the water as riverboats passed. The three men scrambled in the darkness to a small dock at the water's edge where a worn-out rowboat was securely tied. Johnson and Abraham each boarded the boat, grabbing hold of an oar as Jimmy untied the rope.

"Thanks for this," Johnson said. "I won't be able to repay you."

"You don't have time ta worry 'bout that," he replied. "Do your best ta stay alive an' we even."

Johnson's face went blank as the weight of his situation struck him. He'd been so focused on escape that his mind hadn't settled on what he was escaping from. Death.

Not the adrenaline-fueled fear of death he and Jimmy tried to flee through the sodden backstreets of Saint Andrews, but the true concept of death. His life ceasing to exist. Panicked, Johnson stared at Jimmy as he stood on the dock, rope in hand.

"How do I stay alive?"

Jimmy smiled as he pushed them from the dock and tossed him the rope. "Watch ya back, learn ta fight, be careful who ya trust," he said as if these were attributes all men carried easily. "Abraham'll get ya down ta New Orleans. After that, I'd head west if I was ya. Lotta space out there for a man to make a new life. Freedom's out there; ya just gotta go an' get it."

Johnson's mind raced. Overwhelmed by fear and fatigue, for the first time that evening, he wished he wasn't in a hurry to get out of the city. He'd spent so much time worrying about escape that he hadn't even considered what he would do next if he did. He struggled to focus on Jimmy's words and wished he'd taken the time to find a few more moments to get some advice that wasn't shouted to him last minute from a dock. Instead, he had to watch Jimmy disappear into the darkness as he rowed with a man he didn't know, slowly weaving through the illuminations floating across the water.

The dim flicker of candles shrouded the room in half-light. A lone desk stood as a centerpiece for the space flanked by bookshelves containing notable volumes by Tocqueville and Darwin. Two large chairs upholstered in red leather sat on either side of the ornate wooden desk, and a large glass bottle containing the finest brandy rested on its surface flanked by two crystal glasses. It was a set with the intent for serious business. The whole room hosted quiet anticipation as shadows danced across the walls. The silence ended as two men approached, their muffled discourse becoming clearer as they progressed from down the hall.

Well dressed with a neatly manicured mustache, Frederick Boyd opened the door and ushered his counterpart through. Bearded, this man's features were sharp with lips held in a permanent grimace. Each man occupied one of the red leather chairs, and Boyd fixed the bearded man a drink.

"Thank you for agreeing to meet with me personally, Mr. Pinkerton," Boyd said as he poured.

Pinkerton raised his hand to signal the amount in his glass was enough. "I'm always willing to assist a man of your stature. It's tragic, what happened to your eldest daughter, and it certainly doesn't reflect well on your character."

Boyd hunched over, put his hand to his forehead, then slammed his fist hard on the surface of the desk. The finely crafted oak piece hardly gave notice to the assault. "I want that black bastard brought to me!"

A twisted smile curled Pinkerton's lips. "I assure you, Mr. Boyd, I'll assign some of my best agents to the task."

Flatridge, Kansas
June 1876

Johnson woke to the crash of thunder and realized that he was soaked from the rain. He quickly grabbed a bundle of hay and made his way below where the horses were kept. Restless from the storm, they stirred at his approach. Attempting to calm them, he whistled as he passed and laid a hand on those that would let him as he walked to the end of the stable.

He unlatched the gate to the last stall. Mildred, Burt's old mule, was kept there.

"Looks like it's you and me again," Johnson said as he ran his hand over her side.

The mule kept still, indifferent to his presence. He laid the hay in the back corner then sat against the wall, tipping his hat to cover his face before swiftly falling back asleep.

Chapter 3

Flatridge, Kansas
June 1876

Burt Griffin's morning began with the sound of incessant pounding, a hammering from somewhere above him. He sprang from his cot in the back of the station office and scrambled out the door in a fluster, shirt untucked and misbuttoned. Eyes trained to the roof of the station, he saw nothing.

"Where is that goddamned racket?" he yelled to himself, running around back.

Thwack, thwack, thwack, thwack, thwack. . . . Thwack, thwack, thwack.

The noise grew louder as he approached the stable. He looked up at Johnson nailing random scraps of wood to the roof. He was shirtless, wearing nothing but tattered boots over his long johns. His muscular torso glistened in the sunlight as sweat dripped from his skin.

"Oooooooh no!" Burt yelled, "if you're gonna fix it, fix it right!"

Catching his breath, Johnson stood on the roof, hands to his hips, staring down at the pale old man. "This is the only spare wood laying around. 'Sides, you're not the one who has to sleep in the barn. Why do you care?"

"Because it's *my* barn, and if you're going to the trouble to cause all this racket, I'd rather you not have to do it again anytime soon!"

"Well, I just spent all mornin' draggin' all this up here."

"And you're gonna drag your ass back down here so you can go buy some new wood to do it all again!"

Johnson gave a frustrated curse and began prying the scraps of wood from the roof, tossing them to the ground in a heap.

"What happened to your clothes?" Burt asked, looking around the yard.

"Gettin' 'em washed," he replied, pointing the hammer to the wash-tub boiling over the fire. "Had to sleep with Mildred again."

"Did you make breakfast yet?"

"Haven't had time."

Burt paused, watching him work in the sticky, early morning heat. "Well, come on down. You can finish that later. I'll make you something to eat."

The two men spent the rest of the morning sitting around the fire eating biscuits. After breakfast, Johnson hurried to get his shirt washed and hung. His pants were already drying, hanging from a line he had stretched from the barn to the back of the station building. He wanted to finish as quickly as he could, as an eleven o'clock stage was due soon. Preferring to avoid unnecessary contact with passengers whenever possible, Johnson found the best way to accomplish this was to keep to his work in the barn when they arrived.

Burt whittled a stick while Johnson scrubbed away at the shirt.

"You sleep with that old mule enough I'm surprised you waste time with washing that," Burt said, staring down at his whittling stick.

Johnson wrung out the shirt and got up to hang it on the line. "You could let me sleep in the station. Wouldn't be a problem then."

"Heavens no! You smell like horse shit. Don't need you stinking up the place and scaring off all the passengers!"

"Oh, I forgot you were running such a high-class establishment. Maybe if my boss saw fit to let me occupy its fine accommodations I wouldn't have to sleep with the damn mule."

"You couldn't afford the surcharge."

Johnson shot him an annoyed glance, then got up to prepare fresh stalls for the day's stage.

Anymore, most passengers preferred to stay at the Flatridge Inn, but Burt, being the seasoned professional that he was, still insisted that accommodations in the station be available at a moment's notice.

Johnson really didn't mind the barn all that much. *Though it would be nice not to constantly smell like horse shit*, he thought to himself as he laid hay on the stable floor.

When the stagecoach arrived, it was in commotion. From inside the barn Johnson could hear its stampede and he ran to the door as the teamster gave a loud whooping yell. The team raced into the station and the teamster, with a Winchester laid across his lap, pulled the horses to a halt. Jumping down, he hurried into a defensive position behind the coach, readying the rifle. A practiced stillness took the man. He waited attentively as he looked out over the plain, scanning the hills for movement.

Wind rippled through the grass, the presence of danger absent. With the realization that no threat was imminent, he turned to explain his actions to a harried Burt Griffin, who had run back inside to grab his own rifle as the stage approached.

"Bandits. Saw 'em early an' sent off a few warnin' shots. They gave us good chase for a tick," the teamster said as Burt arrived, breathing heavily.

Burt set his rifle down and shook the man's hand. He had a red mustache and red hair to match, which was covered by a large hat with the brim folded up in the front. He wasn't tall but had a confident stature as he turned his attention back to the stagecoach.

"Everyone a'right?" he yelled to the passengers as he opened the door.

"Couple of ruffled feathers, but we'll be fine," said a woman with brown hair fashioned into a bun on the top of her head. She was in her late twenties and exuded an air of dignity that gave her a commanding presence. Burt immediately composed himself, setting his rifle against the wheel of the stage. Taking her hand, he led her from the coach to a set of wooden steps.

"Welcome, ma'am. Glad you're OK," he said as he introduced himself. "I assume a lady of your stature prefers to lodge at the inn?"

"That would be most appropriate, Mr. Griffin. Thank you." She hiked up her green dress to avoid dragging it through the mud. "I assume this town has all the proper amenities?"

"Yes, ma'am. You'll hardly notice any difference from your usual conveniences."

"I highly doubt that," she said with an arrogant smile as she sat in the shade of the station's front porch.

While Burt and the teamster helped the other two passengers down and unloaded their luggage, Johnson harnessed Mildred to the carriage.

"We had a long night, so I hope your lazy ass is ready to do some work today," he said to the mule, talking to himself as much as to her. Leading her out of the stall, he closed the gate. "You better be on your best behavior," he joked as he walked the mule out of the barn.

Despite all the horses that came through, the old mule was the most reliable animal they had at their disposal. Her temperament was agreeable, rarely did she act up or give him any trouble, and despite her age, she was still remarkably sturdy and strong willed. She reminded him of Burt in that way. Both were beyond their better years but worked hard and never seemed to quit. What they had lost in physical ability, they made up for with experience and sheer willpower. But Johnson suspected that Burt had only just started to become a shadow of his younger self over the past few years, whereas Mildred seemed like she had always been slow. Not that it mattered. Slow or not, she never failed in her duty when called upon, no matter how long it eventually took.

Once the mule was ready, Johnson brought the carriage around front, in front of the stagecoach, and saw the woman in the green dress. He did his best not to look at her as he pulled close, but she stared at him from the porch, following his movements with her head so there was no mistaking the object of her attention.

Johnson was unnerved by the woman's beauty. So much so that his body wanted to run away from her in every direction at the same time. In that moment he wanted to keep driving. He wished he could explain to Burt later that he'd had something else more important to do. Instead, he brought Mildred to a halt and pretended not to see the woman as he climbed down.

"Thank you, sir," she said, her brown eyes and red lips perfectly accented by her dress.

With a polite nod, he attempted to walk past, trying to avoid her gaze and move toward Burt and the teamster, who were talking with the other passengers. Before he could pass, she quickly turned to him with a light step.

"I'm sorry," she said with an inviting tone. "I don't believe I caught your name, Mr.—?"

He was blunt. "Johnson."

"You are Mr. Griffin's servant, is that correct?"

"I'm my own man," he replied in a stern voice. "Burt's hired me to work if that's what you mean."

"Yes, of course you are," she replied apologetically.

"Ma'am," Johnson said, tipping his hat and attempting to end the conversation there.

"I do apologize, but I am afraid I'm a bit flustered from our trip," she continued, fanning herself. "It is rather warm here this time of year, isn't it?"

"Seems it."

"It would be so delightful to have a nice bath."

"I'm sure they'll be able to accommodate you at the inn."

"And will you show us to the inn?"

"No, ma'am, my work's right here."

"Oh, well, what a shame. Maybe we shall see each other again sometime before I depart, Mr. Johnson." She smiled coyly before pulling the skirt of her dress tight around her bottom as she climbed onto the front seat of the carriage.

Relieved the conversation had ended quickly, Johnson exhaled then turned to make his escape before she decided to say anything more. It would've been a lie to say he wasn't curious about her forwardness, but his experience with women was mixed and troublesome. He knew well enough to be careful just talking to a white woman. An encounter with a white woman was the whole reason he'd ended up here in the first place. Besides, over the years, he often misunderstood most women's intentions anyway and concluded that they were mostly beyond his comprehension. It was not his intention or in his best interest to get caught up in a relationship with any woman, least of all with a woman like this. Keeping his distance had kept him safe this far, and he saw no reason to wander off into dangerous territory now.

The other two passengers finished talking with Burt and climbed onto the back seat of the carriage.

"We can get the horses if you'd like to take the passengers to the inn for a drink," Burt told the teamster as Johnson approached. "I'm sure you could do with a bit of relaxation."

"That'd be much appreciated," the teamster said as he kicked the mud off his boots and made his way to the carriage. He climbed up next to the woman in the green dress. His shaggy red hair made the drawstrings on his hat look like they were growing out of his earlobes.

"A'right folks, let's get ya to a nice comfy room," he said, clutching the reins as they took off into town.

As they headed for the inn, Burt and Johnson unharnessed the horses, leading them into the pen. "That's an independent woman," Burt said, grabbing the reins of the first horse. "Fact that she's out here all alone means she's not afraid to go and get what she wants."

Burt liked to talk a lot about everything and nothing at all and prided himself on his ability to assess people. Mostly, Johnson ignored him when he started on about people, despite his observations usually being correct.

"Now, that teamster, he probably fought in the war," Burt went on. "A man who acts cool in the face of danger has seen some shit."

Johnson removed his hat and wiped the sweat from his brow. Storm clouds from the previous night had broken well before dawn, leaving the afternoon clear.

"Oh, by the way," Burt remembered, "I got a letter yesterday. I'm gonna have to go back East in a few weeks."

"What for?"

"Stage business. It's not that important. I'll need you to take care of things while I'm gone."

"That somethin' you think I'm ready for?"

"Well, I don't really have any other choice, do I?"

Johnson furrowed his brow. "Thanks for the confidence."

One by one, they moved the horses from the coach into the stable. They tried to hurry as the animals were quickly growing ill-tempered. The combination of the heat and being pushed so hard over the last few miles of their journey had put them in a poor mood. One horse was having a rough time of it, delivering an impatient kick to the horse directly behind it as soon as Johnson unharnessed him.

"Whoa there, fella. Feelin' a bit ornery," he said, trying to calm him down.

He led the horse into the pen without any problems, whistling to keep its attention, but as soon as they turned toward the stable, it began to put up a fight, jerking and turning as it tried to escape Johnson's hold.

"Dig your heels in!" Burt yelled as the horse reared back on its hind legs, trying to break his grip.

Johnson struggled to bring it back under control, but the more he tried, the harder it fought back.

"Come on now, we were doin' alright," he said in an attempt to calm it.

The horse whinnied and they slowly danced in a circle as it pulled and hopped to its left, kicking out its back legs as it did so. They turned in the pen and the reins dug into Johnson's hands as he held tight trying to show his authority.

"Dig in your heels!" Burt yelled at him again.

The horse sensed it was gaining the upper hand. This time it began walking back, jerking its head side to side. Johnson held on as tight as he could and leaned back, trying to dig his feet into the ground, but as the horse pulled backward, Johnson's worn-out boots couldn't find enough purchase against its strength. His feet slid through the mud while he held the lead. Suddenly, the horse dipped its head and lunged forward, throwing Johnson's balance off. He tumbled backward, hitting the ground as the horse reared back on its hind legs again.

Stunned from the fall and empty of breath, Johnson gasped as he stared at the two front hooves raised above him. He scrambled out of the way as they slammed into the mud. Johnson clambered to his feet and ran to the fence as fast as he could.

"Ahhhhahahaha!" Burt was beside himself with laughter. "You still got a lot to learn!" he said, hunched over.

"Thanks for the help," Johnson replied, walking past him.

"Oh, it was my pleasure!" he quipped, gripping his sides.

Johnson walked past the remaining horses still harnessed to the stagecoach and into the road, turning toward the main strip of the town.

"Wait, where are you going?" Burt yelled. "We still have work to do."

"To get that wood for the barn," Johnson replied without looking back, "and maybe a drink."

It was midafternoon by the time Johnson walked past the welcome sign marking the official limits of town.

Welcome to Flatridge
Please Leave All Firearms with the Town Marshal

He laid his hand on it, running his fingers through a few of the routed-out letters, and made sure to cross to the other side of the street to avoid walking past the marshal's office. Another round of ominous clouds was building to the west, creating an eerie orange light as the sun dipped low behind them. As he slowly walked along the row of buildings, he moved past townsfolk without speaking. He rarely came to town for anything but work and didn't make much conversation when he did. Mainly because many of the townsfolk seemed disinterested in making conversation with him. He found it was easier to keep to himself. He didn't trust anyone anyway.

The hardware store was located in a building on the other side of the street directly across from the inn. Mildred and the carriage were out front. He gave the old mule a quick pat on her nose then, throwing a glance down the way, crossed the road. A large covered wagon belonging to a family of pioneers who'd passed him on his way into town was parked outside the hardware store, and they ushered their children behind the wagon as he approached. He disregarded them entirely as he stepped up to the wooden walkway.

"How can I help you, Mr. Johnson?" the clerk greeted him as he walked through the door. Mr. Portnoy was one of the few people in town Johnson had any familiarity with. Due to the regularity of Johnson's visits, it couldn't be avoided. The clerk was a short, balding, Jewish man who wore round bifocals that clung to the end of his nose.

"Need some planks to patch a roof, and probably a few fresh nails."

The shop was small, sharing the building with a barber and the general store, which flanked it on either side. Mostly, it sold farm equipment, but Johnson was usually able to get what he needed whenever he had repairs to make.

Portnoy adjusted his bifocals. "Well, unfortunately we're running low on supplies. I can sell you a few planks, but we don't have any nails. Last storm cleaned us out."

"Any idea when the next shipment is?"

"Not 'til next Tuesday."

"How many planks do you have?"

"'Bout five or six, but only half are in any decent shape. Like I said, we're cleaned out. How badly do you need them? You could try New Pittsburg."

"Damn," Johnson cursed. Hands on his hips, he thought for a second. "I guess I'll go ahead and take the planks now."

"Certainly," the clerk replied.

Staring down his nose through the circular frames, he made a few quick scribbles on a sheet of paper then disappeared into a back room, leaving Johnson alone in the front of the store. While he waited, he paced the shop, examining the different tools for sale. Repair parts for a plow were on display for the season. Next to them was a shovel. Grabbing it, he briefly mimed digging a hole in the floor and was in the process of returning it to its place when the flash of polished metal caught his eye.

Curious, he turned and there it was. A pristine six-shot revolver was on display behind the counter. His heart raced at the thrill of owning something so exciting and powerful.

Johnson continued to stare at the gun as Mr. Portnoy returned with a stack of five wooden planks, his gaze focused on the requisition sheet. "I assume this goes on Burt's account? You have a saw, right? Because I—" Looking up, the clerk realized what had captured Johnson's attention. "Beauty, isn't it?" he said with a grin. "She's brand new. Smith & Wesson Model 3, .44 caliber. Obviously though, around here you can't have it loaded, but I'm sure it could come in handy for a man such as yourself."

"I couldn't afford the cartridges," Johnson said, eyes fixed on the revolver, tracing its every line and curve.

The clerk grabbed the gun, handing it to him with a smile. Johnson felt powerful as he gripped it in his hands. Holding it out straight, he stared down the barrel. It felt good. He imagined himself as Kit Carson fighting off Indians on the frontier. He knew he had to have it, and he began to find good reasons for why he needed it. Bandits and wild animals—and men. Men who harbored ill will. Men who might want him dead.

Johnson left the shop carrying the bundle of wood in both hands, adding up figures in his head, poring over ways he could earn the $17 needed for the revolver.

He crossed the street, walking over to the carriage and loading the wood into the back. Scratching his head, he stared up at the facade of the Flatridge Inn. For a town the size of Flatridge, the inn was a huge structure: three stories. The bottom level was a bar and restaurant, and the top two floors contained rooms for both guests and permanent residents. A long balcony stretched across the face of building on the second floor from which hung a giant cloth sign that said "Flatridge Inn."

Although the sensation of holding the revolver had felt good, its grip over him waned the moment he decided to get a drink instead.

Liquor's more affordable, he told himself as he stepped through the swinging doors.

"I got rights!" yelled a black man to the bartender as soon as Johnson walked through the doorway.

A tall white man grabbed the black man from behind and began to drag him away from the bar.

"Let me go! Bastard!" the black man yelled as he stomped and dragged his feet, trying to break loose.

Another man stepped in to assist and they both lifted the black man up by his armpits and carried him toward the entrance.

"You bastards!" he yelled again at the two white men, "I got rights!"

"Maybe so," the bartender yelled, "but ya ain't got no money! Get 'im outta here boys!"

Wide eyed, Johnson realized he was blocking the doorway and nervously fumbled out of the way as the two burly men barreled toward him, forcefully sending their charge out the double doors and rolling into the street. Landing facedown in the mud, he rose and brushed himself off in humiliated fashion. Johnson watched the man walk away. Shoulders slumped, he turned into the alley and out of view.

"You!" the bartender yelled.

Pointing to himself, Johnson was startled by his stern, heavy voice. The two big white men were now standing in front of him.

"You got money?" the bartender asked.

Johnson was quick to produce a coin from his pocket. Satisfied, the bartender nodded to the two white men, who sat down. The atmosphere of the room returned to an air of relative normalcy after the afternoon's spectacle had ended.

Walking with caution, Johnson took off his hat and set it upside down on the bar.

"Uh, one for now," he said apprehensively as the bartender turned to him with a tight glare.

He watched, on edge, as a shot glass was set out and the bartender poured brown liquid into it from a clear glass bottle, spilling some as it overflowed. Johnson laid the coin on the counter before grabbing the glass. The bartender picked it up and examined it with a scowl, like he expected it to be fake, then exhaled from his nose and turned away. Relieved, Johnson turned to scan the room.

It was a large open space. The row of rooms on the second floor opened to a balcony overlooking the restaurant below, and a large staircase led directly down to the bar, which was separated from the restaurant by a wooden railing. Several patrons in the restaurant enjoyed dinner as a man at the front of the room played "Arkansas Traveler" on an accordion, and waitresses moved in and out of the kitchen like bees entering and exiting a hive as they delivered the food to each table.

Noticing a group of men huddled around a table in the back corner playing cards, Johnson fingered another coin in his pocket. It wasn't uncommon for a man to win more than $17 in a single hand if the cards were right. It also wasn't uncommon to lose everything when your opponents insisted on a chance to win it back. Despite this, he still entertained trying his luck.

Then he noticed a strange-looking man at the table. Johnson's muscles tensed. Something about the man didn't sit right, yet he couldn't put his finger on it. Staring hard, he saw something clinging to the man's jacket. He squinted firmly as he tried to make it out—a badge! Johnson quickly downed his shot and turned back to the bar.

"One more to go," he ordered, holding up a finger and placing the hat back on his head.

"Yer not leavin' already, are ya?" a voice came from behind him.

Nervous sweat poured from his body.

"This one's on me," the stagecoach teamster slurred his words ever so slightly as he appeared next to Johnson and leaned into the bar.

Johnson took a breath to relax. Focused on the commotion between the men when he'd walked in, he hadn't even noticed the teamster drinking at the end of the bar. His anxieties were slightly allayed by the sight of the man.

"Bartender! We need another!" The teamster poked the bar as he said it. ·

"You paying or is he?"

"I am!" the teamster said.

Setting out two more glasses, this time with less hostility, the bartender began to pour.

"Men like us, me 'n' you," the teamster said, wrapping an arm around Johnson's shoulder, "we're born a different breed."

As he spoke, his every word smelled as if a whiskey still were hidden somewhere deep within his gut.

"No, no!" he yelled to the bartender as he began to cork the bottle. "I meant two more, two more!" He turned back to Johnson, giving him a wink and a nod, "Takes a lot ta go through what we been through."

Confused, Johnson had no idea what he meant, but returned the gesture with a small two-fingered salute anyway. He regretted it, as it sent the man into a tirade of drunken chatter.

"Ya know, rich men wanted a war and they got it, but they didn't have ta fight it," he said, taking his first shot.

He paused, staring through the bottom of his glass as the accordion hummed over the drone of background conversation and silverware scraping plates.

Snapping out of it, he looked up and pointed a shaky finger to Johnson's drink, "Don't forget yers."

Johnson raised it to him, downing it in a quick gulp and slamming it on the bar.

31

"*Ah-ha!*" the teamster sloppily pushed him another with a grin.

"Appreciate it," Johnson said with a nod.

"Rich men in the South, they made ya do all they work for 'em," he continued. "Then rich men in the North made men like me," he stuck a thumb to his chest, "poor and penniless, fight ta free ya. Free all the niggers!"

Johnson shifted uncomfortably. The teamster took notice.

"Oh, I don't mean no offense. Ya see, I ain't got no problems with, uh, negros."

"That's good to know, considerin' present company," Johnson replied.

The teamster gave him another grin and went on, "I grew up in Kentucky, grew up with y'all."

"That so?"

"Yep, most people was scared if y'all got yer freedom, good jobs would get took by negros fer cheap pay. Not me though. I knew you people was jus' poor like the rest o' us."

Slowly, Johnson shook his head and smiled. "Oh yeah, if we weren't poor, we wouldn't have any problems."

"Hey," the teamster replied, hands out, palms up, "people like us, though, we got it rough."

"Damn straight," Johnson said, half sarcastically lifting his glass to him. The man crashed his into Johnson's, making a loud clinking noise before they both drained them. The burning liquid began to loosen Johnson as it flowed to his head.

"All these goddamned rich folk—they think they can jus' buy it all!" the teamster spat in revelation.

"Ain't too far from the truth, I'd guess," Johnson replied. "Rich men already seem to own this whole damn country."

"They do own it! An' there's nothin' we can do."

"A man can always keep movin'."

"How far can he move?" the teamster asked. "The scourge of westward freedom is ever present. The great frontier wanes daily under the stress of an ever-expandin' nation. People pioneerin', rich men prospectin', takin' up all the land."

"They can't take it all, not possible. There's too much."

"They can an' they will," the teamster said with disdain. "I fought in the war, ya know? My name is written down on a piece a paper somewhere, Rex T. Bowen. Some cocksucker offered me $300 ta go in place o' his son. And know what?" he sounded increasingly regretful. "I did it."

Rex stared at the wall as if he could see through it like glass, visualizing something haunting him on the other side.

"Bodies everywhere," he said soberly, "not together. In parts and pieces. Thousands of men ordered to march across that field, only to be blown apart in artillery fire. The officers didn't care; they just kept orderin' more an' more. Southern men fightin' northern men. All for rich men's gain. They said we was doin' it for the Union. Marchin' day in, day out through the heat an' the rain. Men dyin' from sickness, men dyin' from fightin', comin' home ta nothin'. Turns out it was all fer slaves. Some people who might not've been rich in money, but rich in superior moral character, decided good men had ta die for the black man's freedom. Don't get me wrong! Glad ya got yer freedom, just wish it happened another way."

"Don't know if it coulda happened another way," Johnson replied.

Rex leaned against the bar with his elbows. "Probably right," he said, hands clasped, staring down as if in prayer.

"Is that why you came out here?" Johnson asked. "To get away from the war?" From the corner of his eye, Johnson watched the man with the badge exit the room and ascend the stairs. He felt relief.

"Nah, came out here after," Rex replied. "Tried ta go back ta my fields, but they was ruined from bein' unattended. Tried ta start over, but I got too antsy, couldn't stay still."

Moved by their new liquor-fueled companionship, Johnson ordered two more shots and handed one to Rex. "To the rich bastards who own it all!"

Rex smiled through the thick red bristles on his face. "Damn them all ta hell!"

Both men cheered as they finished their drinks, laughed themselves into a stupor, and ordered more. The background noise began to fade due to both their drunkenness and the departure of other patrons, and they talked away the late afternoon and into the evening.

By the time it grew dark outside, most everyone had vacated the restaurant except for a few men still playing cards. Johnson and Rex had relocated to a table in the dining area, as standing had become problematic under the weight of their heavy drunkenness.

"Life has a way of slowly tryin' to take everything away from you," Johnson said, looking down at his hands. "I suppose it's up to us to hold on to as much as we can before it's gone for good."

He brought his eyes back to Rex, who was staring at what he was sure must be some kind of mirage.

Rex spoke in a mumble, holding his gaze steady at the wall. "Men like us, we need freedom, but there's only so much time to find it. . . . We gotta be free. . . ."

At that, he rose from the table and silently walked out into the night.

The two bar doors kept swinging well after his exit, as if an invisible presence moved them in his absence. Johnson stared past them into the darkness, listening to their slow creak as they moved back and forth.

"Mr. Johnson," a woman's voice broke through the air, "what a surprise to see you again so soon."

His heart leapt as he turned to see the woman from the stage descending the stairs. After a full day's events, he had almost forgotten about her. Now she had caught him off guard in his drunken state.

"May I join you?" she asked.

His previous coldness thawed by liquor, he couldn't bring himself to object. She approached in sweeping, graceful steps and took the chair closest to him, adjusting the skirt of her dress as she sat down. Oil lamps along the walls doused the large room in half-light, casting a soft glow on her face as she stared at him.

She was quick to confront him. "You didn't ask me for my name earlier, Mr. Johnson."

"Johnson's fine."

"My name, Johnson. Aren't you curious to know it? You are quite unrefined, aren't you?"

"Uh, I suppose. Miss—?"

"Herston. Margret Herston," she replied, lightening up as she said it.

She had changed clothes since their first encounter. Now she wore a royal blue dress with white lace around the neck. Her hair was down with braids that wrapped around the back of her head.

"Now that pleasantries are out of the way, tell me Mr. Johnson—I'm sorry, *Johnson*—" she corrected herself, "what brings you to a town like this?"

Her every word was to the point, and as she smiled her brown eyes worked hard to pierce what remained of his reluctance to speak with her.

"Work, I suppose. Just tryin' to . . ." he trailed off, catching himself before he revealed too much.

"Don't be afraid. I won't bite," she said with a laugh. "How about I go first? I have come out West, all the way from Boston, because I've aspirations to be a writer." Her words were full of joyful excitement. "There have been many great women writers, you know: Harriet Beecher Stowe, Isabella Bird, Louisa May Alcott. . . ."

Johnson's stare was blank. Ignorant to the words she spoke, he could feel the warmth of embarrassment in his cheeks.

She shot him a reasonable smile. "I see I've gotten carried away. I shouldn't have expected you to be familiar with these names."

"I don't mean any disrespect," he replied, suddenly finding himself not wishing to offend her.

"Not to worry. All in all, I have come to write about the experience of the western frontier before it's gone forever!" Her face lit up as she fantasized about the prospect.

"That's a lot to write about, I suppose. So far, I've only made it as far as Kansas."

"Yes, but it seems a different world from where I am from. So much more . . . uncivilized," she said with a smile.

"Boston might be a fancy big city, but people are always the same."

"People might be far more different than you give them credit."

Unconvinced, Johnson pursed his lips. "Maybe, but in the end, they all want the same things."

"And what do you want?" she asked.

Johnson paused, shifting in his seat to avoid her gaze.

"You work in the stable, correct? Is that all you do?" her voice softened as she spoke.

"No, ma'am," he replied. "I gotta make a run to New Pittsburg in the next few days. And I fix things up around the station. . . ."

Politely, she interjected, laying her hand on the table in front of him. "I'm sorry. You mistook my meaning. What I meant to say was do you have another job?"

"Oh, no. I only work for Burt. I work hard and he's treated me well. Hadn't really thought about another job 'til . . ." Again, he trailed off, remembering how he'd felt while holding the revolver in his hands, the smooth lines and cool finish.

"Until?" she repeated, reeling him back to the present with a raised eyebrow.

"Oh, uh . . ." His eyes fell on Margret, who, he noticed, had smooth lines of her own. The curves of her body were perfectly complemented by the dress, her plump, rosy lips beaming as she leaned in so close he could smell her perfume.

She placed a hand on his thigh. "Do you have a woman here in Flatridge?"

Warmth filled his face as his heart rate quickened. "N-no, ma'am," he said. "I-I should be goin' though. It's gettin' late."

"But we've only just gotten acquainted," she replied, squeezing his thigh lightly, "and I suppose I'll be leaving in the morning on the coach to Wichita. So if we are to become more familiar, we haven't much time."

He stood quickly, stumbling as he tripped over his chair. "I probably need to get back." Johnson's eyes shot to the bartender, who stared at him with ire as he polished a glass.

"Probably? You don't sound so sure," Margret said. She ran her hand along the neckline of her dress and spoke in a tone of unbridled seduction. "You've had quite a lot to drink, and I would feel horrid if something awful were to happen to you on your way back."

Mouth dry, no words found him. Johnson stood unmoving, captured under the weight of the moment, gazing heavily into her brown eyes.

"I think it would be much safer if you stayed here tonight."

Heart racing, Johnson's chest burned. He ached to take Margret to bed. He wanted to feel her warmth. "I can't." Clenching his fists, it took everything he had to turn and walk away.

"It was good to meet you, Mr. Johnson."

He paused in the doorway, Margret's voice cutting through him. With a half pivot, he turned to acknowledge her farewell with an uneasy look.

"Though I am regretful you've decided you couldn't stay any longer," she said.

Nodding, Johnson turned and stepped through the swinging doors of the bar. His thoughts raced as he stood on the walkway.

Idiot! You know better. Johnson pounded on his chest. *Shoulda never let it get that far with a white woman. Or anyone!*

Johnson's heart pounded as he scanned the street and allowed his eyes to adjust to the darkness. To his surprise, Mildred was still out front, harnessed to the carriage, content as ever. Rex, though, was nowhere within his immediate view.

Where'd that drunken fool get off to? he worried as he ran down the walkway to the nearest alley. Searching behind crates and barrels, he expected to find Rex passed out in the seclusion of a drunken piss, but there was no sign of the man.

Johnson moved to the middle of the street and in a low hiss began calling, "Rex!" Not wishing to stir any sleeping townsfolk, he cupped his hands to direct the sound, "Rex!"

Walking up and down both sides of the strip, he turned toward each alleyway, to no avail. A cold wind picked up and blew hard, giving him a chill as he stood in the middle of the street. Lightning lit the clouded night sky, and he ducked, covering his head out of reflex, startled by a thunderclap.

Sorry, Rex, he thought to himself. *You're on your own.*

He ran back to the carriage as fast as he could, hoping he could get back in time to beat the storm. Untying Mildred, he quickly hopped into the front seat—"*Oof!*"

The body of a passed-out man already occupied the spot.

"Goddammit, Rex," Johnson said, attempting to get him upright. "We don't have time for this!"

Sitting up, Rex immediately slumped over to the other side, almost falling out of the carriage.

"C'mon now!" Johnson yelled, grabbing him by the shoulder of his shirt as he pulled the man upright again.

Wrapping his right arm around Rex's waist, he held him steady then slid a hand under the man's armpit, awkwardly grabbing the reins. Right when Johnson got Mildred moving in the direction of home, another bolt of lightning struck the sky.

At another time and place, perhaps he would've found humor in the situation: two drunken men and an old mule struggling to get only half a mile out of town, racing a violent storm. A more accurate representation of his life couldn't be easier to find. His mind drifted to the alternative that had been presented to him: the warm body he left behind at the inn. Thunder crashed, and Johnson ducked his head low.

Neither Rex nor the mule seemed to notice.

She may have been steady, but Mildred was also slow, and no matter how fast the storm approached or how much Johnson pushed her to go faster, she traveled at the same pace. Large drops of rain started to fall, hitting the ground with a heavy pat. The wind blew harder, the contrast between the warm air and cold gusts brought a shiver up Johnson's back.

"Almost there," he told himself, knowing the other man couldn't hear and the mule didn't care.

In the distance he saw the shapes of the station buildings. The flashes of lightning lit them up bright like a beacon, showing him the way home.

Thunder and lightning struck at the same time that they pulled in front of the station. Johnson dropped the reins and hurried to the other side of the carriage, hoping to get there before Rex fell out. He didn't make it. The man slumped to the ground like he was boneless.

The rain came down full force in cold drops. "Shit."

Rex weighed far more than he looked. Johnson struggled to lift the man from the mud. Taking a deep breath, he hauled him up around the waist with all the strength left in his tired, drunken body, waddling them both through the station door and loudly grunting as he moved past the office.

"How are you always making a racket whenever I'm trying to sleep?" Burt said, appearing behind the counter.

Johnson cursed at him, mumbling through stressed breaths. "Can sleep through a storm, but ya wake up if someone walks through the fuckin' door."

"Nah," Burt replied. "Was already awake, but you're being goddamn loud!"

Johnson ignored him as he strained to pull Rex into the next room.

"Hurry up with that. You still gotta get the mule back to the barn," Burt's stern voice came from the other room. "And when you're done with that, you can go ahead and sleep in here tonight."

Johnson gave a worn-out chuckle as he dumped the drunken stage-coach teamster on a cot. Untangling the man's soaking wet hat from around his neck, he set it on his head, covering his face, and walked out to deal with Mildred.

The wind blew so hard as Johnson led the old mule through the big doors of the barn that it penetrated the cracks of the walls and caused his lantern to flicker. Thunder crashed, and he whistled his familiar tune to the horses as he walked to the end of the row. When he approached the last stall, something was sitting in the corner where he slept on rainy nights. Hand on his hips, a large grin spread across his face as he moved closer to find a brand-new pair of boots and leather gloves.

"Burt, you sure have an interestin' way."

Chapter 4

The next morning Johnson woke with a pounding headache. Wiping the sleep from his eyes, he realized once again that Rex was nowhere to be seen, the wet cot next to him empty. He sat up and stretched his whole body, yawning deeply as he did so, and rubbed an ache in his right shoulder. Remembering the boots, he beamed as he sat up and slipped them over his feet. He lunged and stomped, testing them as he walked around the room. They fit a bit snug, but that was a good thing, since any good pair of leather boots would have to break in. Filled with confidence, he stood tall and broad shouldered as he walked outside to meet the day with pride despite his pounding head.

There was a chill to the morning and for once clouds lingered in the sky after the storm. He hadn't slept late but was surprised Burt hadn't made a point to wake him. It was obvious that someone had gone into town early; the wet mud showed fresh tracks in the road. Whether it was Rex or Burt, he couldn't tell. Staring down the road, Johnson paused as a cry echoed through the air.

From behind the barn, he heard yells of, "*Yah! Hee-ya!*"

He walked around back, and there was Rex with a rope in his hand, swinging it in circles high above his head. "*Yah!*" he yelled as he threw it out in front of him, lassoing a fence post.

"Take long to learn that?" Johnson asked, leaning against the fence.

"Not too terribly long," Rex replied. "How 'bout ya make some fresh coffee, an' I give ya some tips?"

"Alright, but we ain't got any good coffee," Johnson replied, "so I don't want you to think I'm cheatin' ya."

"Can't be that bad. What d'ya got?"

"Just some old grinds cut with chicory."

"Well, I've had better. Jus' need somethin' for the achin' in my head."

Johnson agreed and walked over to start a fire. His head throbbed even more as he blew on the kindling to stoke the small flame. Leaning back, he rubbed his temples, pushing fingers up under his hat. He was glad it was a cloudy day and he didn't have the bright sun beating down on him as well.

"New mud pipes?" Rex asked, coiling his rope as he walked up.

Johnson questioned him with a blank stare. "Huh?"

"Yer boots."

"Right," Johnson looked down and rubbed a spot of mud off the fresh brown leather. "Yeah, the old ones weren't doin' the trick."

"Well, no sense in shinin' 'em now," Rex replied, giving him a heavy pat on the back and smiling, "gonna get 'em broke in raight after I have mah coffee."

While they waited for the water to boil, Rex showed him how to tie a knot for the lasso and started in on a few basic tips for maneuvers.

"It's about momentum and release," he said as he displayed how to grip the lasso to keep the knot from slipping shut as it swung around in the air. "Yer not throwin' it like a ball, jus' lettin' it go." With a quick action, he motioned the process of slinging an invisible rope toward the fire. "Ya wanna follow through," he explained. "Ya want the rope stiff, too. Stationary targets is one thing, but ta catch a horse or cow, yer loops gotta be wider than a whore ya paid a half-dollar!"

"Think you can teach me to shoot, too?" Johnson asked, his mind slipping back to the revolver.

Rex smiled. "One thing at a time. Let's focus on ropes first."

Once the coffee was ready, they each poured a cup and wandered back over to the barn for some practice. It didn't take Johnson long to realize he had a natural talent for the skill, but he could tell that he would need a lot of practice before he'd be roping anything that moved. Swinging the rope in his left hand high above his head, he released it straight, only just missing the fence post he was aiming for.

"Lookin' good," Rex told him as he sat on the fence sipping his coffee. "Yer form's raight, now jus' keep yer head straight when yer lookin' at the target."

"How'd you learn?" Johnson asked as he pulled the rope back.

"Same way yer learnin' now. An ol' negro cowboy taught me on a fence post," he said, setting his coffee on the fence. "I drove cattle in Texas fer a few seasons, so I had ta learn quick. It's a sink-or-swim business drivin' cattle. Ya either got it or ya don't. Ain't a lot o' patience for a cowhand that don't know how ta learn."

Johnson readjusted and began circling the lasso around his head again.

"Head straight," Rex said, as he focused.

He kept his neck tight and released the rope from his grip. It sailed through the air, this time dropping perfectly around the fence post.

"Now reel 'em in an' pull tight!" Rex yelled.

Johnson pulled the rope hand over hand until the loop closed tight around the post. He took a powerful stance and leaned back. Immediately, he could feel the difference in his new boots. The thick heel grabbed the mud as he dug them in, almost as if his feet were rooted to the spot.

"There you go!" Burt yelled, walking up from the front of the station. "Next time I tell you to dig in your heels, you won't have any excuses!"

Burt wasn't alone; two other men were in tow. One of them was the town marshal.

During the few months Johnson had spent in Flatridge, he had yet to personally encounter the marshal. He'd only seen him from a distance, yet it was inevitable in a town the size of Flatridge that eventually they would cross paths. The marshal was slightly shorter than Johnson and overweight. Johnson thought he looked even more pathetic up close; his thin blond hair was slicked back in a poor attempt to cover a bald spot. For the most part, the marshal's job consisted of collecting firearms from town visitors. Johnson had never paid a visit to the station before. Another man moved beside the marshal. Johnson didn't know this man but immediately recognized him. His pale white skin contrasted with the black clothes he wore and a metal badge was visible on his jacket. Johnson fought hard against the instinct to run as they approached.

"Ya say it's these two here, Burt?" he shouted, pointing two fingers toward Johnson and Rex.

Visibly annoyed, Burt chose to ignore him.

"I could tell it's them, by the way you was talking," the marshal panted as he walked.

"Boys, this here is Mr. Cole Charles," Burt said, introducing the man. "He's been sent here to investigate and, hopefully, put a stop to all this pesky business with bandits."

Cole Charles's long, greasy black hair was parted down the middle, and as he put his hands to his hips, the words "Pinkerton National Detective Agency" glinted on his badge.

"Gentlemen," he paused, stretching his neck forward and staring both men in the eyes, "Burt here tells me you've dealt with the Jester Wells gang personally." His voice was an eerie rasp and his dark eyes tore deep into the men.

Nervous sweat ran down Johnson's back, but he did his best to avoid looking away as the man shifted his burning gaze between them.

"The who?" Rex asked.

"That's what the papers are calling these stagecoach bandits," Burt replied. "Makes them sound flashier. Sells better, I guess."

"Precisely, Mr. Griffin," Cole Charles said. "Their leader, Jester Wells, is a vicious criminal who has proven to be devoid of any and *all* moral character. He has now killed three people while robbing stagecoaches owned by the Douglass & Kinney Company and stolen nearly $1,000 worth of money and property. I am hoping the two of you will provide me with information that could help me stop this man and his group of miscreants."

"Burt says you two both seen the bandits," the marshal said.

"Bradley, I swear you might be the dullest person this side of the Mississippi River," Burt berated him loudly in his long-winded manner. As the argument between the two men got heated, Rex intervened to keep them from coming to blows.

Cole Charles focused his stare solely on Johnson. His dark eyes studied him with intensity as they drifted down to the rope in his hand.

"I didn't actually see any bandits," Johnson said bluntly. He figured it best to come straight out with what he knew. That way the detective could get what he wanted and leave.

"What did you see then?" Cole Charles asked.

"Runaway stage with the teamster shot."

"Can you elaborate?"

"I just told you what I saw."

"And where were you when you supposedly saw this?"

"'Bout ten miles east of town."

"This happened when?"

"Dunno, few months ago."

He pulled a handbill from his inside jacket pocket and unfolded it for Johnson to see. It displayed the face of a ragged-looking man with a detailed description of his crimes below the picture. "Are you certain this man wasn't present?" he asked.

"I said I didn't see any bandits," Johnson replied.

"You're certain?" he asked again.

"I'm certain," Johnson replied, irritated.

Sensing his frustration, an impish grin crossed Cole Charles's face. "I am curious, could you read what this says right here about Wells for me?" He pointed a finger to the few lines of text printed at the bottom of the page.

"Read it yourself," Johnson replied through gritted teeth.

"I'd rather have you read it for me," Cole Charles said with a spiteful chuckle. "Why don't you humor me?"

"I'll pass."

"You're not much of a talkative man, Mr. Johnson, though I guess that's no particular surprise either," Cole Charles said, his eyes boring into Johnson's.

"Guess not." As Johnson stared back at the Pinkerton agent, his fear and frustration became a slow-burning anger deep in his gut. Neither man blinked for several seconds as they became locked in a battle of wills.

"You half-wit!" Burt yelled, still going at the marshal. "It's a wonder you've made it this far!"

The marshal huffed, "I know yer just trying ta get my red up fer kicks!"

"And you're dumb enough to go for it every time, aren't ya?" Burt yelled around Rex, who had stepped between them to end the quarrel.

"Alright now, let's settle this down 'fore it gets outta hand," he said, keeping them at arm's length.

"Before it gets out of hand? If the marshal had three hands, he's so useless he still wouldn't know how to get anything out of them!" Burt replied.

"OK, that's enough!" Rex interjected before the marshal had a chance to respond and pushed Burt several feet away in a final attempt to end the conflict.

"Ah, not worth my time getting into it with someone so weak between the ears," Burt said, turning away.

"Fine," said the marshal, "we got business ta take care of *anyhow*."

Still riled, the two men walked away kicking at the ground and angrily mumbling to themselves. Taking a deep breath, Rex adjusted his hat, satisfied Burt and the marshal had avoided physical conflict, but as he looked back toward the barn, he realized the stare down taking place between Johnson and the Pinkerton agent and again acted quickly to avoid another escalation.

"I thought we was talkin' 'bout bandits," he said.

"We are," Cole Charles replied, his eyes still locked with Johnson's.

"Well, I definitely saw 'em."

"Do tell then, Mr. Bowen." Cole Charles turned to him.

Johnson fumed. Turning away in frustration, he stared out at the plains, hands on his hips, trying to calm himself. He took a deep breath. It surprised him how easily he'd let himself be provoked. He could tell this was a dangerous man and knew he'd foolishly let Cole Charles get the better of him.

"What exactly did you see?" Cole Charles asked Rex. "I need you to be specific. I want details."

"Well, I was drivin' the coach into Flatridge," Rex said, putting his hand to his chin with a reflective look as he recalled the incident. "Probably close ta where he said he seen his coach. As soon as we caught the bottom of the hill, they closed in on us."

"Really? And what course of action did you take?"

"High tailed it outta there."

"They gave chase?"

"Yes, sir, but I saw 'em early an' got enough shots off ta get away."

"Did any of your bullets hit?"

"Couldn't tell ya. Didn' stick around ta find out."

"Did any of these men come close enough for you to see their faces?"

"Not too close, but it wouldn'ta made no difference. They wore bandannas."

"This happened yesterday, correct?"

"Yes, sir."

"Thank you for *your* willingness to cooperate with this investigation, Mr. Bowen," he said as he cast a sharp glance toward Johnson.

"Yeah, uh, thanks," the marshal repeated, still flustered from getting worked up with Burt. "Now we was wonderin'... that is, if uh ... to say if, you—"

"I believe what the good marshal is trying to express," Cole Charles interrupted, "is that we have devised a plan to catch Jester Wells and his associates. For this purpose, we require the assistance of a few capable men who will, of course, be rewarded fairly; $20 to each man upon Wells's capture." He turned to Rex intent on a solicited response. "Mr. Griffin has already agreed to come. Would you join with us Mr. Bowen?"

"Well," Rex said slowly, "I'd help ya, but I'm already obligated ta take this coach outta town today." He pointed to the stagecoach parked in front of the barn.

"That shouldn't be a problem," Cole Charles said. "The Douglass & Kinney Company has authorized me to make good use of any persons in their employ, diverting them from their regular duties if necessary."

"That's true," Burt said. "He's got a letter signed by Mr. Douglass himself. They want this bandit business cleared up soon as possible."

Johnson wanted nothing to do with either of the men involved in the investigation and was still heated from his conversation with Cole Charles, but as soon as he mentioned the $20 reward, the prospect of getting enough money for Mr. Portnoy's revolver blunted his sharp reservations.

"I'll help," Johnson said eagerly, surprised by how quickly the words jumped out of his mouth.

"Boy, do you even know how to shoot a gun?" the marshal asked.

"No, but I can drive," he replied.

"That's true," Burt replied. "He can handle even the big coaches."

Cole Charles looked at Johnson with new interest. "Have we crossed paths before, Mr. Johnson? Something about you seems vaguely familiar to me."

Johnson tensed, regretting drawing so much attention to himself.

"Yeah, boy, you got a look about ya," the marshal said, taking a step toward him and looking him up and down. "I ain't seen you around here much. Maybe you an' me need ta have a little longer talk down at the jail before we make any decisions."

"Jesus, if he looks familiar it's because he's been working for me for the past few months, Bradley," Burt spouted in irritation. "Maybe if you got out of your goddamned office once in a while you'd actually know what was going on in this town!"

"Now, Burt, I don't need no more disrespect from you today, just trying ta do my job," the marshal replied with a frustrated tone.

"*Ha!* Trying."

"I assure you, Marshal Bradley, there is no need to bother Mr. Johnson with any unnecessary accusations. I was making a simple observation," Cole Charles said, drawing out his final word, holding his hands between the two men. "But I will be forthright with you, Mr. Johnson. Much is at stake for this mission. If you choose to come with us, I am not accountable for your life." His dark eyes were motionless as he stared at him.

Rex interjected, "Wait, what about the passengers? They expect ta leave today."

"They already know about the delay," Burt replied.

"But I didn't say I was goin'," said Rex.

Cole Charles turned to him, pushing a strand of greasy black hair behind his ear. "It would be unfortunate if you chose not to assist us, Mr. Bowen. But regardless, we require the use of your stagecoach, and this, I assure you, you have no choice about."

Johnson kept silent, cursing himself in his head for the lack of self-control he'd shown throughout the entire encounter. Not wishing to draw further inquiry, he tried to remove himself from the conversation by gathering his rope.

Cole Charles's eerie voice stopped him. "Mr. Johnson, if you are serious about your offer of assistance, we gather at the jail in one hour."

Johnson nodded but said nothing. He struggled to sift through the flood of thoughts racing around his mind.

"For the life of me I cannot figure out how that idiot Bradley has kept his job as town marshal," Burt said as Cole Charles and the marshal disappeared around the front of the station. "Did you see the way he sucked on that man's teat? His family tree was probably a goddamned shrub. Wouldn't last a day in Dodge. I'll tell you what . . ."

As Burt continued his rant about the incompetence of the marshal to Rex, Johnson leaned back against the fence and examined the fibers of the rope, pulling it through his gloved hands. Helping Charles was a risk. He knew that, and he wasn't keen on rubbing shoulders with any lawmen, but he knew this wasn't just about the money or the gun. It was a feeling that had slowly been eating at him ever since he stepped out of the hardware store. The feeling of power, of control. Having that extra bit of control over his own life that he felt he'd never had before. *But was it worth the risk?*

"No sense in daydreaming," Burt's voice broke his concentration, "we better start getting those horses hitched up and ready to go."

Johnson turned, raising an eyebrow at Rex. "Well, what do you say?"

Hand on his hips, Rex shot a glance to the hills east of town. "I suppose $20 ain't too bad."

——◆——

"I don't trust negros," Cole Charles said to the marshal while pacing the room. "Especially arrogant ones like that." His thoughts drifted back to something Burt had said. That Johnson had started working for him only a few months ago.

Bradley looked up from the game of solitaire he was playing at his desk. "He don't have ta go wit' ya. You can find somebody else—"

"With *us*, Bradley."

"What do ya mean 'us'? As town marshal, I agreed ta help ya raise a posse. I didn't say nothin' 'bout going. My job's here. Protectin' the town."

"I'm sorry, marshal, but we don't have any other choice. There simply aren't enough available men. You are going to have to accompany us," Cole Charles said as he walked behind his desk.

Flipping through his cards, Bradley had nothing to play in his hand. "No, I don't think I'll be going," he said.

Coming up beside Bradley, Cole Charles pulled the two of spades from one of the rows and placed it neatly on the ace at the top. "I don't think you heard me clearly, marshal," he said in a chilling tone. "You are coming with us."

In one swift motion, he pushed Bradley's chair backward against the wall and drew his gun, shoving it hard into the marshal's round belly—*click.* "I know that you were a deserter during the war and have worked hard to hide that fact." His hand gripped the marshal's shirt collar. "So, you'll do it, or I'll turn you over to the US government."

The marshal winced. "Alright, alright, please don't hurt me. I'll go."

"That's better. I'm glad we were able to come to an amicable agreement."

———

The front of the jail was covered with wanted posters, some of them so faded it was hard to discern who was wanted or why. Johnson pulled up in the stagecoach with Rex seated beside him, the picture of Jester Wells glaring at them. There was a deep scar on his cheek, and his arrogant smirk dared them to chase after the $250 reward. The gray clouds still hung low in the sky, threatening rain at any moment. The wind picked up, blowing cool air through the town. The front door of the jail opened as Cole Charles and the marshal exited the building, rifles in hand.

"We'd better make this quick!" Burt yelled out the window of the coach. "I'm sure Bradley is in a hurry to get back to his cards." To his surprise, the marshal didn't respond and instead opened the door to the coach and took the farthest window seat in the back. He stared out as if he were riding to his doom.

"What's got into him?" Burt asked, gesturing at the marshal as Cole Charles walked past.

"I couldn't tell you. Marshal Bradley has been real quiet ever since we got back," he replied. He turned and walked to the driver's seat to address Johnson. "The plan is simple. Drive east along the road; hopefully we pose an easy enough target, drawing Wells's attention. Not too fast, the idea is to make them think you're surrendering. We'll be in the back lying in wait." He turned to Rex. "Mr. Bowen, you're with us," Cole Charles said, signaling for him to join the other men inside the coach. "Remember, Mr. Johnson, if things go badly, you're on your own." His cold eyes burned into Johnson as he said it, almost as if he wished it to happen. Then he turned and climbed into the coach.

Rex climbed down from the front seat, pausing as he got to the ground. "If they do show, don't be no hero. Jus' play it safe, an' we'll take care of the rest." He pulled a knife from his belt and handed it to him. "But jus' in case it gets down to it, take cover an' do what ya gotta do."

The signs in the town moved restlessly, trying to escape the storefronts they hung from as a burst of wind caught hold of them. Johnson got down from his seat and double-checked all the fittings on the harnesses.

The horses recognized this was a change from the regular duties they were tasked. Chuffing and neighing, they sensed they were about to be driven into a state of high risk, feeding off the tense energy of the men they carried. Once around to the other side of the coach, Johnson stared hard eastbound down the road. The grassy slopes rippled as the gusts tore through the open land.

"Don't get too caught up," Burt said, sticking his head out of the window. "Just keep your head on straight and you'll be fine."

"Easy for you to say," Johnson replied as he climbed into the front seat. "You're not the one who gets shot at first."

Loaded up, Johnson gave a "*yah!*" and snapped the reins.

They took off in a bold sprint as the stagecoach pulled forward, traveling west through Flatridge. The small concentration of buildings gave way to the open plains at the outskirts of town. Gray sky surrounded them as Johnson took in the moment. He felt the leather in his hands and the rumbling of the coach beneath him as the horse team ran. Drawing them into a wide curve, he righted the team back eastbound, and as they came through town again, their rumble over the soft ground drew the attention of the townsfolk, who stared as they went by.

On approach to the inn, Johnson caught a glimpse of bright crimson. He turned to look, and there was Margret, standing tall on the second-floor balcony, hair blowing in the wind. Motionless, she neither waved nor signaled acknowledgment in any way as they approached, following only with her eyes. "*Yah!*" Johnson yelled again, picking up speed as they raced past. He didn't look back, keeping his gaze focused on the rolling hills ahead.

"I'll be damned if this works," Burt said as he stared out the window at the people going by. "It's so goddamned obvious what we're doing, those bandits are probably halfway to Dodge by now."

"They always want more, Mr. Griffin," Cole Charles said, meticulously checking over his rifle. "I've yet to meet a bandit who has died of old age."

"I'd reckon ya see ta that personally," replied Rex.

Cole Charles's eyes narrowed as he glared back at him. "Remember, gentlemen," he said, "we want to give them the chance of surrender first. They're worth more *alive*."

Rex huffed and stared down at the floor as he knocked dirt from his boots with the butt of his rifle.

Never afraid to push the issue, Burt spoke up. "Do you really think those men will let you take them alive? They know their fate if they're brought in. Hung by the neck until dead. No, if we find anyone out there on the wrong side of the law, get ready for a fight."

Cole Charles was quick to reply. "Mr. Griffin, I am well aware of the crisis of conscience that men like this face at a time of despondence, and it does not concern me. What does concern me is that there is a whole network of bandits and outlaws in the West, and any one of them may have important information to divulge that might be useful to a future investigation."

Burt laughed. "Ha! Like they'd talk to you even if you could get them back alive."

"I have my ways." Cole Charles drew out the words in a deep, grim tone.

Marshal Bradley kept silent but began to look increasingly pale, sitting with his eyes fixed out the window. Hands trembling, he swallowed hard as he fumbled to drag a pocket comb through his thin hair.

Johnson slowed the team as they approached the first hill and began to climb. Cool in his vigilance, he kept a sharp eye on the horizon, watching for any movement. He was surprised by how calm he felt. His heart was beating fast, not out of fear, but excitement. It was unexpected. Filled with eagerness as they approached the crest, he carefully checked the adrenaline coursing through his body, focusing on the road and the potential dangers that lay ahead.

The gray clouds ahead of them grew darker as the hidden sun moved farther west along the sky. With steady patience, Johnson kept his composure, but the presence of bandits remained unseen in the late afternoon.

"Looks like your bandits took a day off," Burt said as he rubbed a sore spot from sitting for so long. "We should probably get back. Bradley's about to piss himself."

For the first time since they'd left, the marshal turned away from the window and looked at the other men. "Has ta be more'n two hours by now." He sounded like a worried child. "Maybe we should get back to town."

"I will decide when it is time for us to turn back," Cole Charles said, "and I say we'll be out here as long as it takes." The men were shifted to one side as the coach hit a large bump. "I thought that boy said he could drive!" Cole Charles yelled, pushing himself away from the marshal.

"With Rex here, he's the best damn driver available!" Burt yelled. "Not his fault the road's for shit!"

"Well, he better come good when the time comes," Cole Charles replied.

"I'd trust that boy with my life," Burt said to reassure him.

"That doesn't mean I trust him with mine," Cole Charles replied darkly, looking back out at the plains.

Whistling as the stage drove along, Johnson approached the top of another hill. Killdeer let out their shrill calls as they circled, attempting to draw attention away from their nests in the grass. The stage slowly descended again, and the harness jingled as the horses trotted down the hill.

On the valley floor, a lone tree grew in the distance. He fixated on it, wondering what allowed it to survive when so many others did not. *Crack!*

A single shot of gunfire echoed across the valley. In a heartbeat, Johnson snapped to his left. Two riders sprinted toward him, rifles in hand. Off to his right, three more approached in a dead heat.

"*Yah!*" he yelled, leaning forward as the horses jumped into a hard gallop. Their muscles pushed and strained as they moved, their manes flowing as they ran.

"Looks like you were right, after all," Burt said, cocking his rifle.

"I knew Wells couldn't resist," Cole Charles said eagerly, a devilishly satisfied smile on his face.

Each man readied, trying to hold himself steady amid the bumping and rattling of the speeding stagecoach. The marshal was sweating so profusely that it became visible at his armpits and along his suspenders that ran down his shirt. Rex pulled the hat from his head, letting it hang from his neck. Using his thumb and forefinger, he brushed his red mustache down, then took hold of his rifle, gauging the riders approaching from his side.

As Johnson whipped the reins hard, pushing the horses onward in a whirlwind race, two more shots rang out, whooshing over his head. The bandits began to draw in closer, enough for him to see the red bandannas wrapped around their faces. He knew he couldn't outrun them even if he'd wanted to. Looking to his left, another bandit took aim, but as he was about to fire, a gust of wind took his hat. *Crack—Crunch!* A shot flew in from the right and buried itself into the coach.

"Goddammit!" Burt yelled. Brushing splinters from his hair, he stared through the hole above the door, connecting it to its exit point on the other side.

"Not long now," Cole Charles said calmly, keeping his eyes focused on the riders to the south of them. "Five total. Wait for my signal."

Rex gave him a nod and ducked down, keeping his face from easy view of the window.

When the bandits finally closed at fifty yards, they fired their rifles high in the air, all at once in a loud barrage. At that, Johnson pulled the stage to a halt, almost throwing himself and the men in the back forward.

The bandits halted. Silence took over the landscape.

Johnson could hear his heart beating in his head as he watched the masked men surround the stagecoach with rifles aimed. Another cool gust rippled down the valley as everything went still.

"Alright!" Johnson yelled, breathing heavily, "I'm done!" Dropping the reins, he held his hands in the air.

"Get down and start walking toward us!" the muffled voice of the bandit closest to his left carried across the distance. Slowly standing, hands still raised, he turned to step down.

"Don't try anything foolish now!" the men in the coach heard the voice say as they kept still. Pressed tight and low against the walls, they held their breaths.

"That's good right there! On yer knees!" the voice said. "Alright now, we're coming up. We don't wanna have ta hurt nobody!"

As they waited, the sound of horses rustling through the tall grass came closer.

"*Alive*," Cole Charles hissed as he scanned the faces of the other men. "We wait for them to get close, then on my signal."

Hands raised, cold damp from the ground seeped into Johnson's pants as he kneeled several yards away. Cautious in their approach, the five bandits closed in around the coach. The man who'd done the talking holstered his rifle as he rode up and pulled out a revolver. Looking down at Johnson, he said nothing as he pointed it to his head and pulled back the hammer. Johnson didn't turn to look up at him. Silent, he held his head straight and kept still as the four remaining bandits approached the stagecoach.

"No need ta hide," said one of the men through his bandanna, "This'll be quick an' easy an' y'all be on yer way soon enough!"

Lying terrified on the floor, Bradley began shaking so violently his rifle repeatedly rapped against the wooden door, making a loud knocking sound. Quickly, Rex kicked out his foot and tightly pinned the marshal's hands under the gun. "*Mrgh*," he groaned, biting back the the pain of crushed fingers.

"Sounds like they's a little scared," said another voice no further than twenty feet away. "Everything's gonna be just fine. Boys, ya know what ta do."

Three of the mounted bandits held rifles steadily trained on the windows, while the fourth dropped to the ground with a jingling thump.

"A'right folks, here's how this works," he said, slowly walking up to the right side of the coach.

Eyes hidden from view below his hat, Johnson carefully surveyed his man.

"I'm gonna walk y'all out here one by one, put ya in a line."

Burt swallowed hard, tightly gripping his rifle.

"We're gonna go ahead an' take anything ya got that's pretty or shiny."

Cole Charles took a breath and scowled in concentration.

"Anybody tries anythin' funny, my associates here gonna cut 'em down quicker than they was brought into this world."

Rex removed his foot as tears began streaming from Bradley's eyes.

"Game's up. No more hiding," the man said as he put his hand to the door of the coach.

As he opened the door, Bradley pulled his rifle's trigger, sending a shot ripping through the man's chest.

"*Ahhhh!*" The man went down screaming as he gripped the bloody wound, kicking his legs and pressing himself hard into the ground.

Taken by surprise, the mounted riders wildly fired into the coach, setting the scene for a chaos of gunfire.

Rex rose to shoot one of the remaining two men on the right, hitting him deep in the gut.

"Goddammit!" Cole Charles yelled as he and Burt fired at the two men on their left through smoke and splinters.

Realizing the ambush, the man guarding Johnson turned and fired at the stagecoach. Johnson grabbed the knife Rex had given him, jumped up, and stabbed the man in the leg, pulling him from his horse.

Crack—pop—bang! Gunshots rang out as the two men rolled on the ground, each struggling to gain the upper hand. Johnson's muscles strained as the man grabbed at him, trying to pry the knife away. The red bandanna slid down his nose and Johnson clawed at his face as they thrashed on the ground. Twisting, the man rolled on top of Johnson and grabbed his throat. Slowly, the knife in Johnson's hand was turned toward his own gut.

"Don't let him get away!" Cole Charles yelled as he hobbled out of the coach. The last mounted bandit had decided his best chance for survival was to make a run for it. Rex and Burt fired several shots as he turned his horse around and dashed off. Furiously, Cole Charles limped his way into the trampled grass and took a deep breath, aiming his rifle steadily at the man. The echo of the gunshot carried across the valley.

The horse slowed as its rider fell to the ground in a heap.

Shaking under the weight of his opponent, Johnson landed several weak punches with his free hand to the side of his opponent with no effect. He felt like his eyes were going to burst as he stared at the bandanna hanging from the man's chin. The suffocating grip was becoming too much. He was running out of air.

Johnson summoned all his strength and delivered a sharp knee to where he'd stabbed the man in the leg.

"*Ahhhh!*" the yell rang out.

Shifting in just enough time for the knife to plunge into the ground beside them, Johnson punched the man in the face and threw him off.

"That should be enough, Mr. Johnson," Cole Charles said, standing above him, rifle aimed at the bandit.

Chapter 5

Rain fell as they collected the bodies. The blood of the first man who was shot spilled into the muddy road, mixing with the pooling rainwater. It took them several minutes to find the body of the last man, since his horse had wandered far from where he'd gone down, but they found him facedown in the grass with a bullet hole through his back.

Cole Charles stared at the handbill as he stood over the laid-out bodies. He crumpled the piece of paper and threw it to the ground. "This is why I said I wanted them alive!" he said, rubbing his brow.

"Well, we got one alive, didn't we?" the marshal replied with a renewed sense of liveliness.

"But none of these men is Jester fucking Wells!" Cole Charles yelled as he kicked the one surviving bandit.

"*Oof!*" the man uttered in pain as he fell to his side, hands tied behind his back.

"I said wait for my signal!" Cole Charles scolded the marshal. "And you fired at the first chance, you cowardly oaf! Now we have only one man to connect us to the whereabouts of Wells! One man!" Exhausted by his outburst, Charles winced in pain as he leaned against one of the large spoked wheels of the stagecoach.

"And what exactly were you going to do if we had waited? Politely ask them to stand down?" Burt asked, nursing the gunshot wound in his arm. "We'd likely have a damn sight more bullet holes in us if we did it your way. Hate to say it but the marshal probably saved all our asses, and that's the last thing we need, 'cause now Bradley is gonna chalk up bandit killer to anything in a five-foot earshot," Burt said, making light of their situation. "His walls will think he's killed a hundred men by tomorrow morning."

Cole Charles had nothing to say. He was in worse shape than Burt and, with the adrenaline wearing off, had nearly exerted what energy he had left. He'd been shot clean through his right shoulder, but another bullet was lodged deep in his thigh. Amazingly, Bradley and Rex came out of the altercation unscathed. The same could not be said for one of the bandit's horses. It had taken a stray bullet and Johnson found it lying on its side, struggling to breathe.

"Only one thing ta do," Rex said, walking over to him holding out a rifle. "You'd better make it quick."

"Why me?"

"Said ya wanted ta learn how ta shoot. Gotta show ya can handle what needs ta be done," Rex replied.

Johnson grabbed the gun from Rex's hand and turned toward the dying animal. Squatting low over the horse, he stared into its eye as it lay suffering in the grass. He wondered what kind of thoughts, if any, the animal might be thinking at that moment. Did it understand what he was about to do? Solemnly, he gave it a quick pat then stood up, placed the barrel of the rifle to its head, took a deep breath, then pulled the trigger.

He immediately understood why Rex had insisted that he take care of the horse, and it gave him a new perspective on his desire to own a gun. The horse was dead, easily put out of its misery with the pull of a trigger. Just as easily as the four men who were laid out on the ground. Johnson was surprised he wasn't dead. If the man who was guarding him had decided to shoot him in the head and ride off, he surely would've gotten away clean. But now, to his relief, that man was at the mercy of Cole Charles. Johnson hoped that since Cole Charles finally had one of his bandits in hand, he would be too distracted to turn his focus toward any suspicions he might have about him.

As far as Johnson knew, he wasn't a wanted criminal like Jester Wells. While passing through the different cities and towns on his journey, Johnson had been stopped enough times by lawmen who felt he "looked suspicious" to know there were no handbills with his face on them, yet he'd had enough run-ins with bounty hunters and private detectives to know he was still wanted back in Saint Andrews. So far, Cole Charles was not one of those men, and Johnson was tired of running. He had traveled so far to escape the specter of his past—farther than he'd ever thought he would travel in his lifetime. Now with Cole Charles around, he again was faced with the realization that he might have to keep running. Yet as he watched the disturbing man strain to climb into the stagecoach on his wounded leg, Johnson questioned whether the Pinkerton even had it in him to finish the job he'd been hired to do, let alone to come after him.

While Cole Charles, Burt, and the marshal rested in the coach safely out of the rain, Johnson and Rex loaded the corpses of the four dead men onto the luggage rack on the roof. Carefully they secured the bodies as raindrops washed the dirt and blood from the dead men onto the outside walls of the stage, coating it in the carnage of their skirmish.

"Not sure how ta feel about tha' new coat o' paint," Rex joked.

"I guess your passengers will have to make do," Johnson replied.

"I've seen worse," Rex said. "Shoulda seen the carts full o' arms an' legs durin' the war. 'Nuff ta give a man a lifetime o' nightmares."

Johnson wasn't sure how to respond to such a statement and was relieved to see Rex didn't seem fixed on it as he helped lift the last body. He tried to imagine how many men came back from the war missing limbs and wondered how different their encounter with the bandits was from actual warfare. Their fight had been quick, but was it enough to make him start seeing ghosts the way Rex did? He wasn't sure.

"I suppose we could give the local undertaker some competition with that load," Rex said as Johnson climbed back down.

"Think I'd rather drive a stage instead," Johnson replied with a smile.

"Ya got a lot ta go 'til yer good as me!" Rex replied with a haughty laugh.

Sitting in the coach, Burt shot the marshal an annoyed look. "Bradley, why aren't you out there helping them?"

"Broke ma hand in all the action," he responded, holding it up with his other hand.

"Broke your—Rex broke your hand because you were shivering like a goddamned baby before anything even happened!"

"I saved us all! Ya said so yerself!"

"And I'm already starting to regret it!"

Cole Charles groaned loud enough for them to hear as he leaned back and closed his eyes, trying to distract himself from the pain in his leg.

"Don't let him fall asleep until we can get a doctor," Burt said to the marshal, breaking away from their quarrel.

"I assure you, Mr. Griffin, I will be fine," Cole Charles said through gritted teeth. "But I would like to suggest that Mr. Bowen take one of the horses and ride ahead."

"That's probably not a bad idea," Burt said, examining his arm.

Johnson and Rex loaded their captive, who was tied up and gagged with one of the red bandannas, into the coach next to Burt, who held the man's revolver at the ready.

"No sudden moves." Burt poked it into his side.

"Yeah, don't get too cozy," the marshal said with a laugh. "I've gotta nice cell for you soon as we get back."

"Please just shut up, Bradley," Cole Charles said, eyes closed and heavily breathing. "I would prefer it if we could make this a quiet ride back."

Once the horses were rounded up, Rex readied one to ride back to Flatridge so he could alert the doctor. The rain died down along with the daylight as he mounted the horse.

"Don't worry too much 'bout gettin' back in a hurry," he said as Johnson tied the other horses to the back of the stagecoach. "Burt ain't too bad off, an' you don't owe that Cole Charles fella nothin'." With that, he took off with a "*he-yah!*" and quickly descended into the oncoming dusk.

Slowly, Johnson climbed the front seat of the stage and started the team toward town.

~∙~

Somewhere on the Kansas plains
June 1876

"I warned him," said the gravelly voice of a man shrouded in the darkness as he reclined away from the fire. "Maybe the rest of you fools'll listen to me next time I say it's time to lay low fer a while!"

"Jester, we knew you was right. Wouldn't've made it this long if you wasn't always right," said another man across the fire. "You know you can trust us."

"I thought I could trust Dan," Jester Wells said, leaning into the fire's glow to reveal the deep scar across his cheek. "Now he's probably fucking dead, and if he ain't, he will be soon enough! Question is, how much information did he rat out on us before he died?" *Click.* The sound of the hammer pulled back on his revolver brought every man to attention. "Maybe I should just tie up all the loose ends right here and now," he said, slowly panning the revolver across the fire.

The crackle of the burning wood was the only sound in the camp. No one spoke a word as Jester stared at each man with wild eyes. *Click.* "Bahahahaha." He laughed like a madman as he put the gun away, taking a long swig of whiskey.

In relief all the other men joined in the laughter. Jester leaned back again, away from the firelight.

"Ah, we knew ya didn't mean it," said the man across the fire.

"No, I did mean it," Jester said from the darkness. "I'll kill every one of you if I have to."

Several hours of darkness had fully set in by the time Johnson pulled the stagecoach up to the jail where Rex and the doctor waited.

"How we doin'?" Rex asked as Johnson jumped down.

Burt interjected. "I've been worse," he said, stepping out of the coach before Johnson had a chance to respond. "Be better once we get this patched up. Come on Doc, let's get to it."

Walking to the door, Burt motioned for the doctor to follow him into the building as Cole Charles stumbled down the steps of the stagecoach, almost collapsing as he got to the ground. The doctor ran to his aid, catching him before he fell and propping him up as he helped him walk into the building.

Behind them, Marshal Bradley paraded their bandit captive at gunpoint and beamed at the idea that he would have an audience as he put the man in one of his cells. Johnson and Rex stood back and watched in silence as the strange procession unfolded and quickly disappeared through the front doorway of the building.

"Well, looks like ya didn't have too much trouble then," Rex said with a dose of heavy sarcasm. Walking over to inspect the coach, he stuck a finger through one of the bullet holes from their firefight.

"Just a few bumps along the way," Johnson replied with a smile. "Ya find the doctor OK?"

"Yeah, he was sat down with his family fer dinner, so I don't suppose he was too happy 'bout the call, but he came accordingly."

"Hope ya weren't waitin' too long."

"Nah, played a few hands with the doc while we waited. He ain't a half-bad poker player. Hope he's a half-decent doctor at least. Didn't seem too keen on bein' around Burt though."

"Well, it's no easy task dealin' with a man like Burt sometimes," Johnson replied. Eyeing the bloody heap tied to the top of the coach, he said, "I suppose we'd better get those down."

"Yeah, and if I'm gonna take these passengers outta here tomorrow mornin', we better get the horses back sooner rather than later."

"Alright," Johnson said, "let me check in on Burt then we can get going."

Johnson took the steps up to the jail, put his hand on the door, and stared through the bars on the windows. These bars weren't for keeping men in—a cell door did a good enough job of that—these bars were for keeping men out. Specifically, they were for keeping out angry men who weren't satisfied with the way the justice system worked and thought it might be far more prudent to take the law into their own hands. He wondered how likely it would be that Cole Charles died of his wounds after walking through the door. *It would make things a lot easier.*

The jail wasn't a large building, but it seemed even smaller from the inside. Split into two sections, three cells built of iron bars were in the back, each with one cot and enough standing room for a few men. A thin, six-foot half-wall separated them from the front of the building, dividing the space between captive and captor. An entryway connected the two halves of the room and opened to the right of the marshal's desk, which was placed in the center of the room. A large gun cabinet was to the left of the desk along with a few extra chairs for visitors.

As Johnson entered, Burt was sitting at the desk, leaning back, feet propped up while Bradley helped the doctor operate on Cole Charles's leg in the cell farthest left. The bandit was placed in the cell farthest right with the empty cell between them. Eyes closed, the bandit tried to sleep through the groans and yells erupting from Cole Charles as the doctor dug for the bullet.

"We're gonna go ahead and take the stage back," Johnson said to Burt, who had a fresh strip of gauze tied tight around his arm; a small red spot was bleeding through. "You comin' back with us?"

"Nah, doctor isn't finished with me yet, just did a quick patch. He's probably hoping I bleed out, so he doesn't have to deal with it," Burt replied. "You go on. Come get me with Mildred when you're done."

Cole Charles groaned loudly.

"Rex is plannin' on leavin' tomorrow. You still want me to—"

"Fuck!" Cole Charles screamed in pain, startling the bandit awake. Both men paused as the marshal ran past them and out the front door at the behest of the doctor.

Johnson turned back to Burt. "You still want me to go to New Pittsburg tomorrow?"

Burt threw him a stern look. "Just because you don't have to sleep in the barn anymore doesn't mean you don't have to finish fixing the roof."

"Fine, but I'm sleepin' in again."

"Fine by me. Stage doesn't leave 'til eleven anyway. Just make sure to have everything ready on time. These people are already pissed off enough being delayed a day; I don't want them delayed one more minute." Burt paused for a second, staring at Johnson in silence. "I know I don't express it as such, but it means a lot to have you around here. Not sure what I'd do without you."

"You seemed to be doin' just fine before."

"You'd think it," Burt replied.

Johnson gave him a grin as Burt pulled open the top drawer of Bradley's desk and grabbed the deck of cards.

"I guess I'll be back ta check on ya in 'bout an hour."

Burt gave him a nod and began laying out a game of solitaire.

When Johnson opened the door to leave, Bradley rushed back in with a bottle of whiskey in his hands. He tripped on his way to the doctor, dropping the bottle, which rolled across the floor and clattered to a halt against the bandit's cell door.

The room fell silent as the man sat up in his cot. Staring at the marshal, he extended his hand and slowly pulled the whiskey bottle through the bars.

"D-d-don't ya get any . . . uh . . . any ideas now," Bradley said, drawing his revolver.

"The name is D-D-Dan," the man said, uncorking the bottle, "and marshal, you ain't got nothing to worry about. I wanna be your friend."

Taking a swig from the bottle, he replaced the cork and held it through the bars grinning. Bradley remained frozen to the spot, revolver shaking in his hand.

"Come on now, marshal," he said, waving the bottle. "Just trying to be helpful."

Bradley inched up to the cell. Giving him a look of reassurance, the bandit grinned again as the marshal slowly wrapped his fingers around the bottle, taking it from his hand.

"See? No harm, no foul."

"Can we please hurry!" the doctor yelled. "The longer this takes, the harder it will be!"

Johnson turned and walked out the door.

Rex leaned against the wall outside smoking a cigarette. The four dead men were now laid out on the ground in front of the walkway.

"That didn't take long," Johnson said, motioning to the bodies.

"Easier ta get 'em down than up."

"Guess ya don't have to worry about showin' thieves and murderers any dignity."

"Not in my book."

"Fair enough. Let's go."

Sounds of agony erupted as the two men climbed onto the front seat of the stagecoach and took off. As they turned the coach around at the west end of town, lively music drifted from the glow of the Flatridge Inn, in heavy contrast to the hellish scene at the jail.

The station was dark when they arrived, so Johnson lit a lantern and hung it in the barn while they worked.

"Ya know, if ya ever get tired o' shovelin' shit, there's good money drivin' cattle," Rex said, unhitching one of the horses. "Ya got what it takes, just gotta jump on a crew in one of the cow towns down in Texas."

"I dunno," Johnson replied. "Not sure what use I'd be."

"Ya ain't too bad with horses. Could start out takin' care of them, work yer way up. Ya'd be at least on the drags in no time."

"I suppose it's worth a thought. I only just got settled, though. Not sure if I'm ready for another change."

"Only reason I'm sayin' somethin' is 'cause I been thinkin' 'bout it myself. Season's 'bout ta start gettin' into full swing, and I'm sure we could hop on one of the late crews easy enough."

The possibility of becoming a cowboy excited Johnson. The thought of living free on the wild range, away from any towns and most folks, absent from any problems—*and* people—that might try to follow. He almost considered telling Rex yes right then until he remembered what Burt had said to him back at the jail.

"I don't think I could do that ta Burt. He's done me a favor givin' me this job. I owe him a lot and he really needs my help around here."

"Jus' think it over. I'll be back through in two weeks. We can talk more 'bout it then."

As Rex put the last horse in its stall, Johnson harnessed Mildred to the carriage and pulled her around to the front of the barn. "You comin' with me?" he asked as Rex walked out.

"Gonna pass." He yawned and scratched the stubble on his face. "Been a crazy fuckin' day and there ain't nothin' special ta see. Besides, I'm raight tired. Think I'll just be turnin' in." Stretching his back, he turned away and began walking toward the station before slowly raising his right hand to him. "G'night."

"See ya in the mornin' then," Johnson said as he snapped the reins and got Mildred moving.

The clouds began to break, allowing the white light of the thick crescent moon to shine down, lighting the road. As Johnson made his way back to the jail, he mulled over Rex's offer. His stay in Flatridge was his longest since fleeing Saint Andrews, and in that time, not a single traveler from out of town had showed any interest in him until Margret tried to get friendly. Then the next day, Cole Charles showed up, prodding around as if he were looking for more than just bandits. That didn't sit right with him. Could Margret's advances have been a ploy to catch him in a vulnerable state?

What if she's trying to trick me? he wondered. *What if they're working together?*

Then he remembered. Cole Charles *had* been at the inn while he was drinking with Rex!

What about Rex?

Johnson paused as he pulled up to the jail again and sat in silence for several minutes, staring out at the town before shaking his head.

No, it's been a long day. You're letting it get to you.

The only reason Rex and Margret were still in town was because Cole Charles needed the stagecoach. Cole Charles was the only one worth worrying about. If it wasn't for his investigation, they'd have moved on by now.

They'll both be gone by tomorrow. She'll be gone after tomorrow.

Johnson gathered his thoughts as he climbed down and walked to the doorway. It was quiet inside. The previous sounds of anguish had ceased, and only a dim glow shone through the windows.

The marshal had passed out in his chair snoring, mouth wide open. Johnson gathered that the doctor had taken his leave awhile before he returned; Burt was passed out in the middle cell between Cole Charles and the bandit, Dan.

Johnson walked into Burt's cell and stared at Cole Charles on the other side of the bars. He looked horrible. His face was sunken and had almost no color. He lay motionless on his back, right arm in a sling. Johnson turned to wake Burt, but before he could, a pale hand quickly grabbed his arm through the bars. His body went cold.

Cole Charles muttered, "The sooner you get out of here, the sooner I can get back to sleep."

His eyes were closed, his face positioned straight upward toward the ceiling. For a second, Johnson thought he might even still be asleep.

Johnson brushed his hand away and was about to loudly curse the man when Burt rose in a stupor.

"Can't you keep it down?" he said groggily.

"C'mon Burt, let's go."

He carefully ushered the old man out of his cell, helping him as he stumbled through the doorway. Before they exited the room, he took one last glance at Cole Charles, who continued to rest, unmoved from his position.

The sooner you're gone, the better, he thought as he helped Burt shuffle out the front door.

—⁓—

The air was still in the emptiness of the late night. Cole Charles lay on his cot in pain, his thoughts centered on his son's eighth birthday, which was soon approaching. He let out a slow breath. Despite the pain he was in and how much he wanted to be there for his son, he needed to find Jester Wells. And then there was Johnson. Every Pinkerton agent west of the Mississippi had been ordered to be on the lookout for a negro who had been on the run these past months. He needed to investigate him further.

Cole Charles always finished a job. His tenacity made him a top agent; his methods always produced quick results. Turning his head, he narrowed his eyes and stared through the bars at the bandit, Dan, who slept motionless with his back to the room. Cole Charles quietly rose from his cot and paused to listen for sounds of movement, the loud snores of the sleeping marshal the only noise that carried over from the other side of the wall. He watched for several seconds as the man's body expanded and contracted with each slumbering breath, and he began counting them in his head.

One in, one out. Two in, two out. . . . He started over once he reached ten breaths.

After several minutes, he began to mimic the marshal's breathing pattern then steadily limped from his cell, slowly counting breaths to keep pace and suppress the burning pain in his shoulder and thigh. Approaching the entryway, he paused again to hug the wall while listening to the marshal's snores. Gradually stretching his neck through the entrance to the front room of the jail, he examined Bradley slumbering in front of his desk: leaning back, hands at his sides, mouth wide open. Cole Charles stared hard at the top left drawer of the desk, the drawer where the keys to the cells were kept. He moved around the wall in silent determination as he crept toward the desk. Standing only inches from the marshal, he could smell the man's rotten breath as he leaned over, stretching out his good hand.

Snooooore!

Caught off guard as the marshal let out the extra boisterous snort, Charles flinched and searing pain radiated from the bullet wounds. Reeling in pain, he gave everything he had to keep from collapsing to the floor. It was several minutes before he could regain his composure and again focus all his energy into suppressing his agony.

With deep breaths, he resumed counting, *one in, one out . . .*

His breathing controlled again, the purple of early dawn began creeping in through the windows. He worked quickly, reaching out to slide open the wooden drawer and wrapping his entire hand around the ring of keys to keep them from jingling together and alarming the marshal.

"Wake up," Cole Charles whispered, crouched in front of Dan's cot.

To his surprise, Dan's eyes sprung open. "I got nothin' to say to you. Where's the marshal—"

"Shhhhhhh," Cole Charles replied, pressing the barrel of his revolver to Dan's lips. "I see no need to bother Bradley while he's sleeping."

Dan closed his eyes. "You ain't gonna shoot me. I'm unarmed. So I don't believe we have anything to discuss."

"Oh, I think you might have something to discuss with this," Cole Charles forced his sling hand over Dan's mouth and jammed his revolver hard into the knife wound in the bandit's leg.

"*Mhhhhhhh!*" came Dan's muffled yell.

Cole Charles pressed harder.

"*Mhhhhh—mhhhhh!*"

"What was that?" he asked as Dan's eyes watered. A broken look crossed the bandit's face as he stared up, shaking his head. "I'll need you to keep it down; remember the marshal."

"*Bhh-ghh,*" Dan vocalized in a display of cooperation.

Slowly, Cole Charles released pressure on the leg, while keeping his hand tight over Dan's mouth. "Now then, it seems that you are interested in speaking with the marshal. Is that correct?"

Without making a sound, Dan nodded his head yes.

"Well, I might be even more help to you than Marshal Bradley. In fact, I'm the best friend you could have right now, and I'm willing to make you a deal. How about this? If you tell me what I want to know, I don't shoot you, and just to be nice, I'll make sure you go free."

Again, Dan nodded his head vigorously.

Cole Charles balanced on his good leg as he leaned back against the wall of the cell, his revolver still trained on the bandit. "Why wasn't Jester Wells with you at the robbery?"

Dan grabbed his injured leg and winced. "Jester always lays low for a while when things get hot. I shoulda gone with him, too. Instead, I started my own crew, and now I'm here."

"Does Jester take to a regular hiding place?" Cole Charles asked.

Dan shook his head. "No hideout; just keeps moving. He knows the land better than just about anyone. Taught me a thing or two about navigating these parts after I joined up with him."

"And how long ago was that?"

"I dunno. A few months? Came up from Arkansas."

Cole Charles's eyes widened slightly. "I don't suppose you'd know anything about the negro man who gave you that wound?"

Dan scoffed. "I know if I ever see him again once I get out of here, I'm likely to kill him."

"While in Arkansas did you hear anything about money for the capture of a negro fleeing Saint Andrews? He may have escaped via steamboat."

Dan sat up with excitement. "Oh wait, I might've heard something about that. A lot of money if it's true. You think it's him?"

Cole Charles held his lips tight in thought.

"How's about I help you catch him, and we split the pot fifty-fifty?"

An amused grin grew across Cole Charles's face. "And why would I need your help?"

Dan smiled back at him. "Because I'll tell the marshal everything we've talked about if you don't. Fool like him will probably ruin your chance—Wait! You said—*No!*—"

Bang! Bang!

The marshal woke in alarm at the gunshots and fell out of his chair. A loud ringing echoed in his ears. Scrambling to gather himself, he crawled to the wall behind his desk and pressed his back tight against it as he drew his gun with a shaky hand.

"W-what's goin' on now?" he yelled out, his mind still in a haze of sleep. "I-I-I mean, there's no need for trouble. Just put the gun down an' no one has to get hurt!" He had no intention of trying to subdue anyone. He just hoped to give himself enough time to make a run for the front door.

"Unfortunately, Marshal Bradley, it is too late for that." Cole Charles's voice came from the other side of the room.

"What do ya mean?"

Slowly, Cole Charles limped through the entryway. He meticulously looked over his revolver, towering above the marshal, who was crouched on the floor.

"I made the mistake of trying to interrogate the prisoner alone. He tried to grab my weapon. I had no other choice but to put him down."

The marshal squirmed toward the opening in the wall and peered through the bars of the cell where Dan's body lay bloodied on the floor.

"Christ in heaven."

Chapter 6

Thump! "Time to get up," Burt said as he kicked Johnson's cot.

Eyes shut, Johnson could feel the mugginess of the morning air as he turned his back to the sound of the old man's voice. "You said I could sleep in."

"Changed my mind," Burt replied in the gravelly voice he used for giving commands. "We probably should've done this a lot sooner."

"*Mrgh,*" Johnson uttered in frustration at being woken so early. "Done what?"

Too curious to insist on catching a few extra minutes, he sat up, rubbed his face, and opened his eyes. Burt stood in the doorway holding a rifle in each hand.

"It's far past time you learned to shoot. I put you in danger and you got lucky. I won't have that on my conscience."

"You didn't put me there; I asked ta go."

"Beside the point. It was a damn fool idea and I think we both know it."

"I ain't a fool."

"I didn't say you were, goddammit!" Burt replied frustrated. "Do you wanna learn or not? 'Cause there's plenty of other things I could have you doing around here!"

"No! I'm gettin' up! I'm gettin' up!" Johnson said, afraid he might ruin his chance.

"Well hurry up then. I'm tired of standing here."

Johnson scrambled from his bed with excitement, grabbing his pants and shaking them out to remove the thick layer of dirt that had accumulated over the last two days. Standing on his right leg, he quickly slipped the left through the pants, but as he pulled the other leg in, his foot caught the belt and sent him down in a lumbering fall to the floor.

Burt gave a heavy sigh. "Maybe we should've started with a lesson about getting dressed."

"I just woke up!"

"Well, if you can manage to get your shirt on without any problems, I'll be around back."

The last remnants of a colorful dawn were transitioning into a clear blue sky, and the loud *ts-ts-ts-ts* of the cicadas radiated from the few small trees in the area as Johnson emerged from the station. Dressed and ready, he could see that Burt had set up a makeshift shooting range of old cans and bottles outside of the barn. Sitting amid the backdrop of the rolling hills, they lined the far fence about twenty yards from the front of the horse pen where Burt stood impatiently.

"I see you managed to get your boots on your feet and your hat on your head. If you had mixed those up, we'd have been in real trouble," he said as Johnson approached.

"I was half asleep! You were having plenty of your own troubles after I woke ya last night—"

Burt cut him off. "We're not here to talk about last night. If you want to reminisce, do it on the way to New Pittsburg later. We've only got so much time before that stage has to leave."

"Right," Johnson said. "Let's get to it." He bent forward, reaching out for one of the two rifles leaning against the fence.

"Hold on now," Burt said, swatting his hand away. "There's more than just picking up a gun and shooting. We're going to go over the basics."

Johnson stepped back and stood attentively, waiting for instructions as Burt turned aside.

"OK, now pick it up. But don't even think about putting your fingers near that goddammed trigger until I say so!"

Johnson gave him a nod as he tried to focus, prepared to commit every part of this introductory lesson to memory.

"First things first," Burt said, taking the other rifle in hand and lifting it to his shoulder. "Make your feet about shoulder's width apart from each other with your left foot forward."

Johnson did so.

"Now grip the handle with your right hand, but don't touch the trigger."

"But I'm left-handed," Johnson replied.

Burt cursed. "Ah, Christ. Then do the opposite. Switch your feet, too."

Johnson did so, awkwardly shuffling his right foot about a half-step forward.

"There you go; that's good there."

Lifting the rifle, Johnson reached for the barrel with his right hand when Burt suddenly slapped the rifle down with his own.

"My finger's off the trigger!" he replied defensively.

"Don't care. Until you're ready to fire, you keep that thing pointed at the ground," Burt said. "Now watch me." In one smooth motion, he lifted the rifle and tucked the butt of the gun into his right shoulder. "You want to lean into it because it is going to kick."

Burt angled forward ever so slightly, creating a powerful stance with the positioning of his feet, his whole body working together to ensure the weapon became a deadly extension of himself. Johnson watched attentively as the old man gave instruction.

"Sight your target up," he said, standing completely still. "Take a breath and slowly let it out, then just *ease* on the trigger."

Bang! At the other end of the pen, a can on the far left went flying through the air, falling into the grass and stirring several killdeers as it landed. Smoke wafted from the end of the rifle as Burt stared down his next target. This time he shattered a dirty glass bottle.

Relaxing, he leaned back and lowered the rifle toward the ground again in one smooth motion. "Takes practice, but that's all there is to it."

"You mean standin' right and breathin's all you need?"

"No, practice. If you're ever in sticky situation, you don't have time to think, just feel. Your body has already got to know what to do, and the only way it will is if you practice. You could be a natural shot, but when a man is running you down from a few yards, you'd better be damn sure you've got more than good aim."

"My turn?" Johnson asked.

This time Burt nodded. "Aim for the one on the right."

Johnson slowly readied his rifle, doing everything in his power to imitate Burt's actions as best he could.

As he stared down the barrel at the can, Burt coached him. "Sight it and breathe."

Taking a deep breath, Johnson focused, slowly letting the breath out as he moved his finger to the trigger with the can in his sight. *Bang! Crunch!* The shot hit just to the right of the can, ripping through the fence post and taking out a large chunk of wood, which sent splinters shooting through the air.

"Not bad!" Burt laughed. "Don't worry about putting holes in that old fence. You can fix it later."

Johnson gave him a dry glance.

Burt returned it with his old grin. "I still see twelve targets out there. Stage leaves at eleven."

Cracking a smile, Johnson looked out across the horse pen, raised the rifle, and sighted down the barrel again. *Bang!*

Johnson managed to score a few hits before he had to quit and start readying the coach for Wichita. Although he wasn't a poor shot, he wasn't a great one, either, but that didn't discourage him. Soon he would have the revolver, and he was determined to practice every morning until he was so well drilled that he could comfortably hit any target set in front of him. He fantasized about making trick shots. Hopping around and upbeat as he pretended to be a gunfighter, he whistled to the horses as he led them out of the barn and hitched them to the stagecoach. But his good mood dampened.

Johnson fully expected Rex to appear and double-check everything before he'd finished, yet as he harnessed the last horse, Rex was still nowhere to be seen. The longer Johnson waited, the more he worried that Rex had gotten drunk. Too drunk to get back. It wouldn't have been the first time one of the teamsters had done so. If the departure was late, Burt would be furious. Johnson decided that the best way to avoid receiving any outrage was to get a jump on his work cleaning the empty stalls.

The muggy air in the barn was stale with the smell of horse shit and old hay. The remaining horses sniffed and snorted, alert to his presence as he moved past them with his pitchfork in hand. The gate to the last stall creaked when he pulled it open. He always started in the back, shoveling out each stall one by one and working his way forward. In his mind, working them in that order helped to push the smell to the front of the barn and out the door. He wasn't certain if it made any difference, but he was a person of habits. Once he found a way to get the job done, he preferred to stick with it.

Every few minutes, he could hear the horses outside stir. Each time, he expected Rex to walk in shortly thereafter. Each time, Rex failed to appear. After finishing the rear stalls, he decided to take a break. Leaning against the wall, Johnson wiped his brow before looking around and sniffing the air. He wasn't sure if the humidity in the barn had gotten worse, but it felt worse and didn't help the smell. Conscious of the comments Burt made regarding his odor, Johnson wondered if he had enough time to rinse off before he had to leave for New Pittsburg. Though he knew it was only a joke, the idea of offending strangers with his foul smell still bothered him. The more he thought about it, the more determined he became to make sure he would have time for a rinse.

"Rex should've been here by now," he said to himself, worrying something wasn't right. No sooner had he finished the thought when he heard the horses stir again, only this time he heard another sound as someone approached the barn.

"If the stage is late, I'm not the one takin' the blame!" a voice yelled. Johnson stepped from the stall when he heard the slow squeak of the barn door.

Johnson expected Rex to strut in, a grin on his face and the smell of liquor on his breath. To his alarm, it was not Rex. The silhouette of a strange figure appeared and paused before making his way forward.

Cole Charles slowly hobbled through the doorway.

Johnson's throat became dry. He had expected it to take several days, if not a week, for Cole Charles to walk again under his own strength, let alone leave the confines of the jail. Last night, the man looked like he had one foot in the grave. Yet here was, pale and dark as ever, more a manifestation of death's ally than one of his victims. Johnson wished he were someplace else. Somewhere not alone with Cole Charles standing between him and the only exit.

"Mr. Johnson, how did I know I would find you out here?" he said, smiling without looking amused.

"Lucky guess."

"It would seem," Cole Charles replied darkly. He craned his neck to peer into an adjacent stall. "You certainly keep like company."

"You implyin' somethin'?" Johnson gripped the handle of the pitchfork.

Cole Charles sneered. "Nothing your smell hasn't already."

The old building creaked, filling the void of silence as each man stared down the other in the dim light of the stable. Taking a deep breath to compose himself, Johnson turned a half-step, making sure to keep the man in his view.

"You got a reason ta be here? 'Cause I got work to do."

"I have your payment from yesterday," Cole Charles replied, extending his hand.

Johnson paused. He straightened and turned back toward Cole Charles. His heart raced. This uncomfortable moment was something of his own making. He had gotten involved with the business of a dangerous man, and now here he was.

Taking another deep breath, he leaned the pitchfork against the wall. The whistle of air navigating the cracks of the building increased as the wind picked up outside. Dust swirled through the beam of sunlight that shone through the open barn door as Johnson cautiously approached, his slow footsteps marked by the sound of shuffling hay as he made his way to where Cole Charles stood. Not wishing to get any closer than necessary, he stopped short, holding his palm out to receive the money. Cole Charles's eyebrow twitched as he lowered his hand to Johnson's, releasing a small handful of coins.

Johnson's blood boiled. "You lyin' bastard!" he yelled, stepping back. Clutching the money tightly in his fist, he waved it at Cole Charles. "Is this supposed to be some kinda trick?!"

Cole Charles made no movement in the face of Johnson's displeasure and replied with his usual dark calmness. "I will not be disparaged like some common fool, Mr. Johnson. I am not the marshal and I do not take lightly to insult."

"What do you call this, then?" Johnson yelled.

"That is your cut."

"My cut! Then what'd Burt and Rex get?" Johnson replied furiously.

"The same amount, I assure you."

"We were promised $20 each!"

"Yes, $20 was the agreed-upon reward for capturing Jester Wells," Cole Charles replied, a sharpness in his tone hinting at the worn cracks in his cool demeanor. "Did you capture Jester Wells? No, you did not!"

"Well, I sure didn't risk my ass for $5 neither! I want my fair share!"

Cole Charles erupted in fury. "I'll give you your fair share of something warmer if you really feel the need to press the issue!" he yelled, laying his hand to his gun belt. "Those men were only worth $15 each! I don't need some entitled negro to tell me what's fair! I would pay you nothing for them if I could!"

Click.

Johnson froze at the sound of a revolver's hammer cocking back.

Cole Charles ceased his hate-filled outburst.

"I believe that since the man has been paid, ya best get on ta more important business." Rex's voice came from behind Cole Charles as he walked in, revolver drawn. "Ya said so yerself; that Jester Wells character is still out there jus' waitin' ta get caught."

Cole Charles spoke no words as he glared at Johnson. He slowly moved his hand from his waist and backed away.

"Until next time, Mr. Johnson," he said with a renewed calmness in his voice.

"I appreciate your intervention, Mr. Bowen," he said, turning to Rex, whose gun hand trailed his every movement. "These types of negotiations do have a way of getting heated. I wish you safe travels on your journey to Wichita." With that, he turned and limped off.

Johnson's muscles relaxed, but his heart still raced, and his hand ached. Looking down, he realized the coins had pressed deeply into his palm as he clutched them in his fist. He recounted the money then cursed loudly.

"That Cole Charles sure seems ta have it out for ya," Rex said, slipping his gun into its holster as he stepped out of the sunlight and into the barn.

"I couldn't tell you why," Johnson lied, knowing Cole Charles wasn't the first person and wouldn't be the last to treat him in such a way. "I try not to worry about it."

"Well, he's a strange sort anyway, that fella."

"Sure," Johnson replied, aware that Rex didn't understand how he was feeling. "C'mon," he said, still frustrated, "if we don't have that stage ready in time, who knows what Burt's gonna do."

Johnson put on a good face while they finished with the stagecoach. Walking around it with Rex to ensure everything was secure, he burned deep inside. He had risked so much for basically nothing. Under normal circumstances, he would have been pleased to have an extra $5, but he felt like he had lost more than just the revolver. He'd known it was a stupid idea to do anything but avoid Cole Charles from the moment he saw him, yet he went against his better instincts, hoping he might come away from this gamble with a better sense of control over his life. Instead, he felt even less safe than he had before.

"Ya alright?" Rex asked. "Look like yer lost."

"Yeah, I'm fine," he lied again. "Jus' tired. Woke up early."

Rex laughed. "Not too early. Ya sure seemed ta be sleepin' like a baby when I got up."

Johnson shot him half a grin then turned back toward the barn. He wasn't going to wait around for Cole Charles to kill him. No, Johnson would prove he still controlled his life. When he left for New Pittsburg later that day, he wouldn't be returning to Flatridge.

Chapter 7

"We'll see each other again soon," Rex said as he climbed onto the driver's seat of the stagecoach, "jus' steer clear of ol' Cole Charles. He's more trouble than he's worth."

"Trust me," Johnson said as he raised his arm and shook Rex's hand, "that shouldn't be a problem."

"Goddammit, if we aren't at that inn to get those passengers in ten minutes, I'll tell Cole Charles you're both hardened criminals wanted for robbing me of my better senses!" Burt shouted, leaning out the window of the coach. "I was hoping you'd have already left for New Pittsburg by now, but clearly someone here is on a different schedule!" He stared down at Johnson. "Soon as you get Mildred and the carriage together, you come meet me."

Johnson gave a quick nod. "I gotta rinse off first."

Burt's white whiskers became even more visible as his pale face turned bright red with anger. "How about I get you set up with a bubble bath at the inn while we're at it?" he yelled, eyes widened in frustration. "It's gonna be damn near nightfall before you even get back as it is! Get the mule and don't dawdle! Now can we please get this goddamned thing moving?"

"Sure thing, boss," Rex replied with a heavy dose of sarcasm, giving Johnson a wink and a smile. With a quick "*he-yah*," he got the team moving.

Johnson stood on the station's front porch as the stagecoach lurched forward. All the clomping, creaks, pops, and jingles that resulted from the immense amount of stress and energy required to move such a great mechanism went with it.

"See ya in a couple o' weeks!" Rex shouted, throwing him a wave from the driver's seat as the coach picked up speed.

The bullet holes and bloodstains were prominent in the light of the midday sun as the stagecoach bounced along a rough patch of the road on the way to pick up its load of passengers who would likely find no comfort or amusement in its appearance.

Johnson drew a heavy breath, still worked up by all the emotions surrounding the past few days finally coming to a head with Cole Charles. As he watched the stage blend into the distance, the image of Margret standing alone on the balcony, scarlet dress blowing in the wind, pushed its way into his thoughts. He tried to dismiss it, but it played over again in his mind. It became the only thing he could think of. She was rich and educated, why was she so interested in him? He groaned, scratching vigorously under his hat. As he walked around the back of the station to rinse himself off, he wondered if he'd ever meet a woman like that again.

It didn't take Johnson long to pack. He grabbed whatever dry goods he could, stuff he didn't think Burt would immediately notice had gone missing: oats, some flour, salt, and a few pieces of jerky. Along with the food, he filled an extra canteen and put it in his pack. He would have grabbed a rifle and some ammo, but the cabinet where they were kept had been locked. For a moment, he entertained the idea of looking for an extra key but knew better. Burt wouldn't have been so careless, and he'd already wasted so much time that the old man probably already suspected something wasn't right.

"I promise I'll take good care of you," he said to Mildred as he hooked her to the carriage. "Burt'll be just fine without you."

The old mule displayed her usual indifference as he put a hand to her nose. Deep down, he did feel guilty for stealing the only animal at the station that Burt actually owned, but he didn't see any other good option. Rex had said he would be back in two weeks, but two weeks was too long. As he'd already seen firsthand, it didn't take much to cause a delay for a day or two. On top of that, there was no guarantee Rex meant what he'd said about going to Texas. Friendly as he was, Johnson had known the man only a couple of days and wasn't willing to risk his life on the chance he would act on a passing conversation. Climbing onto the driver's seat, he considered leaving the $5 he'd gotten from Cole Charles as payment for the mule but ultimately decided he would likely need it somewhere along the trip.

If only I had a gun.

As he pulled out of the station, Johnson mulled over his plan. He would go into town one last time and talk to Burt as if nothing were out of the ordinary. That way he could buy some time before he knew anything was wrong. After that, he was free to go almost anywhere he wanted.

Not much of a plan, he thought as Mildred slowly pulled along. He wasn't sure where he'd go, but he wasn't all too worried about it, either. He just had to get away from Cole Charles. *Maybe I could still go to Texas.*

Texas was appealing to him. He wasn't as confident about his chances of becoming a cowboy without Rex, but surely there were plenty of other things he could do that might allow him to prove himself enough to work his way onto a cattle crew.

Texas. . . . Then the realization hit him. *Where* is *Texas?*

Johnson's chest tightened as the eagerness of his decision to leave was overcome by dread.

He didn't know where Texas was! He didn't even know what was west of Kansas! As he tried to recall everything he knew about other places in the West, there was an empty space in his mind.

His heart raced as he approached the town's welcome sign, which now felt as if it were sending him toward the unknown. Was he taking a bigger risk by leaving? What was out there for him beyond Flatridge?

Without thinking, his body went stiff and sweat began to pour from under his arms as the carriage rolled past the jail. Head straight, he didn't dare to even peek from the corner of his eye to see if Cole Charles or the marshal were nearby; he just stared ahead, focused on the now desperate uncertainty that awaited him at the other end of the town.

You're almost there; you're almost there. Johnson repeated it over and over again in his head to calm himself.

Three new families of pioneers loaded supplies in front Mr. Portnoy's hardware store as Johnson pulled up to the inn. Burt was sitting alone on a bench outside. Johnson could tell the old man was fuming. He scowled at Johnson.

"What took you so goddamn long?" Burt said. "I should make you start sleeping in the barn again!"

"Mildred was getting ornery," Johnson lied, knowing it was a poor lie at that. "She—"

"Goddammit, I don't have time for excuses. Here."

Burt stretched out his arm and handed him $5.

Johnson stared at him in confusion.

"It's for the wood," Burt said, as if speaking to a child.

"Oh, right."

"And one more thing," Burt said. Walking back toward the doorway of the inn, he called to someone within the bar, then pointed straight at Johnson.

Johnson drew a deep breath and held it. *Burt knows! He really has turned me in!* His head began to spin as he stared into the darkness behind the double doors at a figure walking forward.

This is it, he thought solemnly.

Taking hold of one of the small swinging doors, Burt scowled at him again as he pulled it open.

Johnson froze.

Margret emerged wearing a light blue dress and carrying a white lace parasol that matched the white lace on her dress.

He exhaled.

"Ms. Herston has decided to stay in town a few more days and requested to go with you to New Pittsburg," Burt said, clearly trying to hide the frustration in his voice.

"Quite right, Mr. Griffin. I've heard it's a lovely place and would like to see it," she said, directing a smile toward Johnson. "I hope I'm not a bother?"

Johnson swallowed, but his throat was dry. "*Um,* n-no, ma'am," he replied in a weak voice.

"Speak up, boy! Don't be rude to our guest," Burt said, helping Margret onto the seat next to Johnson. "I apologize, ma'am, and I assure you it's no bother. Mr. Johnson will take excellent care of you."

She pulled her lips into a tight smile. "Oh, I am certain of that."

"Wonderful," Burt replied. "Better hurry now, Johnson. We wouldn't want to keep our guest out past nightfall."

"Right," Johnson said, trying to avoid Margret's gaze.

Snapping the reins, Johnson's mind spun as the mule slowly drew the carriage forward.

As they moved beyond the west end of town, the church bell tolled, signaling the approach of noon. They passed a small graveyard where a preacher carefully trimmed the grass growing around three wooden crosses stubbed into the dirt. Johnson was not a religious man, and though the thought crossed his mind, it didn't seem right to pray for help with what he was doing. He was taking off with his boss's mule and now even considering how to leave a woman stranded in the next town. What other choice did he have?

She'll be fine, Johnson reassured himself as he labored over what to do. *It's not anywhere dangerous. Burt will be mad, though.*

As the yards around the sod houses at the outskirts of town gave way to the open plains, he tried to think of ways he could separate himself from Margret for long enough to take the carriage and get out of town. Perhaps he should suggest a visit to the bakery. Or maybe there was a dress shop? It would give him the perfect excuse to leave her unaccompanied while he pretended to visit the hardware store. He cringed at the thought of what Burt would say when he found out. *Why are you so nervous about Burt? You'll never see him again,* he reminded himself.

"You're awfully quiet," Margret said, pulling him from his thoughts.

Sitting beside him under the lace umbrella, she shifted the parasol to rest on her right shoulder. "I must say, Mr. Johnson, that I am truly grateful to you for letting me accompany you," she said in an elegant voice.

"Wasn't much my decision," Johnson said.

"Nevertheless, here we are together, and the ride is rather long, so it seems life has presented us with the perfect opportunity to continue becoming better acquainted."

"I feel like we're already the right amount acquainted," he replied. He tried to focus on anything except Margret's presence as he drove: birds, the clouds, grass, the mule. Hopefully, she would recognize his discomfort with the conversation.

"But I am still curious to know more about you," she replied.

"What's there to know?"

"Precisely, Mr. Johnson. You tell me. Each person is the history of their own unique experiences."

"That so?"

"Absolutely! Tell me, how long have you lived in Flatridge?"

"Dunno, a few months, don't see why that matters."

"Why wouldn't it matter?"

"'Cause I live there now. Why's it matter how long it's been?"

"Well, where are you from?"

"East, I suppose."

Clearly frustrated with the lack of depth in his answers, the gracefulness in her voice broke. "Mr. Johnson, I am from 'back East,' and where I am from, I assure you, a man has enough common sense and manners to know when he should properly indulge a woman! Now, are you going to be a real man who'll treat me like a proper lady, or would you rather sit there silently and continue to act uncivilized?"

Johnson gave no reply but to stare straight ahead.

Margret exhaled. "I'm sorry," she said, softening her tone. "I often forget proper etiquette doesn't come naturally out here."

"Look, I was well-oiled the last time we talked, and you knew it."

"Yes, but wasn't there a part of you that wanted to talk to me?"

"I shoulda left as soon as you sat down," Johnson said coldly.

"Please, Johnson, indulge me," she replied with her enticing smile.

"I wouldn't want to upset a lady such as yourself with my *uncivilized* behavior," he replied.

Pausing, she took a breath through her nose and slowly exhaled. "I apologize for making such harsh comments, but a person can better oneself only by facing their undesirable truths, not hiding from them."

"Ah, and the truth is?"

"As I've stated, I have come west to write. What better subject for my writing than the betterment of the lowly negro frontiersmen? Taming the West by bringing him into the fold of modern American society!"

"Who said that's what I wanted?" he asked. "Did ya ever consider some men might come west to escape all that?"

"But I can help you. I have helped many negros become great credits to your race!"

"And how's that?" Johnson asked in a dry tone. Her comments began to strike a chord within him.

"I've taught them to read!" she said with excitement, oblivious to Johnson's rising frustration. "You will never truly get anywhere unless you can read. I often helped our servants read back home, you know. Of course, Father always said it was a waste of time, but many of them have become quite impressive—"

"So now I'm just some poor, uncivilized nigger who can't read?" Johnson angrily snapped. "Well, I suppose you're just some uppity bitch who thinks she's got a right to say whatever she wants!"

Margret was aghast. "Excuse me?"

"Don't play dumb. You just wanna use me to look good for some high-class rich folk! 'Look at the poor nigger; he'll never be anything without white help!' No thanks. I don't aim to be your pet. It's none of your damn business why I'm here and what I plan to do, so if I don't feel like associatin', that's my business!"

An uncomfortable warmth moved through his body as he realized how harsh he had been. He shouldn't have spoken out, but he couldn't hold it in any longer. In doing so, Johnson had put himself in the most dangerous of situations. If Margret wanted to, she could tell the first white person they saw in New Pittsburg that he'd done just about anything to her, and they'd believe it.

Still, it was satisfying to truly speak his mind for once. He felt as though part of a considerable weight had been lifted from him. He couldn't take it back now, so there was no use dwelling on it. Calming down, he sat up straight and proud. Looking ahead past Mildred, he snapped the reins with vigor despite knowing that the mule would not go any faster.

Margret was completely taken aback. Rarely was she spoken to this way, and she therefore had no inherent reaction to his remarks but to stare at him, mouth agape. Caught between anger and embarrassment, she was at a loss for words. She turned to stare at the grassy landscape, brooding as she watched the prairie slowly inch by.

They sat in silence for a long time with the creak of the carriage and the rustle of the grass the only noticeable sounds as they drove on. All the while, Johnson's thoughts were on planning his escape. *Maybe I could leave her here on the prairie before she can say anything.* He glanced at Margret out of the corner of his eye. *No. She can walk faster than Mildred.* He had to hope she wasn't so angry that she'd do something rash.

Out to the west, dark clouds formed a gloomy veil on the horizon, and the day's humidity seemed to increase.

As Margret sat, she continued to mull over what Johnson had said to her. The more she thought about it, the angrier she became until her injured pride eventually overtook her embarrassment. Confident she had been wronged, she sat up straight, intent on reclaiming some of her dignity.

"Mr. Johnson!"

Startled by the sharpness in her voice, he nearly jumped from his seat. "*Wha* . . . yes?"

"You had no right to placate or expel some greater frustration at my expense solely out of some perceived feminine inferiority, and I demand an apology!" Margret stared down her nose at him like a queen. She closed the parasol and laid it across her lap as she awaited his reply.

Johnson tilted his head quizzically. Maybe this was his chance to make it right. "Look, I'm not entirely sure what you just said, but what I said, I shouldn't have. I . . . I'm sorry."

"No."

"No what?"

"I do not accept that."

"Fine with me," he replied, satisfied with continuing in silence as he awaited the angry white mob that was sure to be his fate.

"So maybe it is true, then? Are you just some *uncivilized* nigger?"

Johnson's blood boiled. Was she trying to push him? "What's your problem, lady?"

"You, Mr. Johnson!" Margret snapped again. "To put it bluntly, I am insulted by the way you have treated me. I have yet to treat you with any such ill will nor have I given you any reason to treat me as you have. But it seems you have no respect for a woman in that regard."

Johnson furrowed his brow at her. It was as if she had suddenly begun speaking a different language. "I still don't follow what you're gettin' at."

Margret exhaled to calm herself. As she gathered her thoughts, she carefully pondered how to phrase what she was trying to explain to him. "Would you have acted similarly if I were a man?"

Johnson paused as he thought about her question. "I guess. I suppose I forgot my manners. A lady shouldn't get treated like that."

"We are definitely permitted a certain courtesy, but that is not what I mean."

"Well, what do you mean then?"

"I mean, do you go around bellowing at other men when you feel the slightest bit affronted or is it just your temperament to act that way toward women?" Margret stared at him, eyebrows slightly raised as she waited for his answer.

Johnson gripped the reins tighter. She had triggered something he hadn't considered before. He realized that he did feel more comfortable and freer to say what he wanted to her. *Why?* It was because he wasn't afraid of Margret because she was a woman. Not only that but he felt he had no right to be afraid of her. After all, she was just a woman. What was there to be afraid of? "If I'd said it like that to a man, it would probably start a fight. Maybe worse."

"But because you don't fear the same retribution from me, I deserve to be spoken down to?"

"What about you speakin' down to *me*? I bet you don't go around assumin' white men can't read."

Margret's face softened as she realized her own miscue. "Maybe we can both afford each other a little more respect."

Johnson slowly nodded. "I am sorry for losin' my temper," he said, snapping the reins. He meant it, even if he still meant what he'd said.

"Thank you, Mr. Johnson."

Johnson exhaled in relief. Despite every instinct that told him to stay away from her, no matter how hard he tried, Johnson was still intrigued by Margret, even though she could get him into trouble.

No sooner had he come to that conclusion than she again turned to him, breaking the silence. "Would you prefer it better if I were a negro girl?"

Johnson again was at a loss for how to respond. "What does that have to do with all this?" he asked, uncomfortably scratching the scruff on the side of his face.

"Don't worry, honey, I like all girls," replied an unfamiliar voice.

"*Aheee!*" Margret screamed as two men on horseback appeared on either side of the carriage, guns drawn.

Caught up in their argument, they hadn't noticed the men. Snapping to attention, Johnson pulled Mildred to a halt.

"I apologize. We didn't particularly mean to eavesdrop on you-all's conversation. It's just that once you've heard it—well—it's hard ta unhear."

Raising his hands, Johnson glared at the man who rode up next to him.

"I'm Atlas. This here's my associate J. T.," the man said, pointing his revolver at the other man next to Margret, who trembled uncontrollably.

"You ain't gotta tell 'em our fuckin' names, Atlas!"

"Don't matter none," Atlas smiled, knocking Johnson's hat off his head and onto the ground with his gun. "They're coming with us."

Chapter 8

Distant thunder crashed, but no rain fell as Johnson and Margret sat tied together, blindfolded on the back of Muriel. The bandit named J. T. rode a few yards ahead of them, pulling the mule's lead.

"Why we always gotta split up and travel so far?" J. T. complained as he watched the lightning dance on the dark horizon. The open prairie offered no cover from the coming storm for miles.

"Jester might be ornery, but he ain't had a plan go bad yet," Atlas replied, riding alongside him.

"Ornery ain't the half of it. Ever since he got the syph real bad, he's seemed plumb mad."

"Nah, he'll be better soon. You'll see," Atlas said, assuring him. "He's been using that mercury from the doc we robbed. Supposed to cure it right up."

"We'll see about that—goddamn! Can't this fuckin' mule go any faster?" J. T. jerked on the lead.

"Stop your complaining! It's gonna take most o' a day's ride regardless."

"Well, I'm startin' ta think we oughta jus' shoot 'em an' be done with it."

"So, we just went ta all that trouble for nothing?" Atlas said, frustrated. "I thought you wanted the woman!"

"I did—still do. Let's have her and be done with it," J. T. replied, pulling out his revolver and turning his horse back toward Mildred.

Click. Atlas drew his own revolver in response. "You go ahead an' put that away now."

"You ain't gonna shoot me," he replied, taking out his knife to cut Margret loose.

"No! No! No! No!" Margret screamed as he grabbed her arm.

"Let her go!" Johnson yelled.

"Shut up, darkie. Ain't nothin' you can do about—"

Bang! Atlas fired a shot into the sky.

J. T. ducked and released Margret.

"I said they're coming with us!"

"Fuck sake, Atlas!"

"She's Jester's now. If you wanted her, you should've had her when we had the chance."

A loud bout of thunder broke nearby as its lightning bolt lit the dark sky.

"I'll get you anyway, little bird," J. T. whispered in Margret's ear. "And I'll make sure you get yours, darkie!"

Removing his revolver, he swung the butt hard into Johnson's gut before placing it into his holster and turning his horse back toward Atlas. Johnson doubled over in pain, pulling Margret with him.

"Are you OK, Mr. Johnson?" Margret asked as she helped him lean back.

"I'll be fine."

"I said no talking!" Atlas yelled as another streak of lightning lit the sky.

"What could they possibly want with us?" she whispered.

"I know what they want with you. Couldn't tell ya why I'm still here."

She began to sob. "I'm so scared. I don't know what to do."

"Just try ta stay cool. I'll think of something," he said, trying to calm her.

He was scared, too, and there was no way of escaping the two men. If he could keep Margret alive and safe long enough to reach their destination, hopefully a better opportunity might present itself.

As they rode, muscle strains and aches in Johnson's lower back and groin began to pain him from sitting bareback on Mildred for so long. Margret's hands had been tied around his waist. She had grabbed Johnson's hand when J. T. tried to pull her down, and she had yet to release her grip. She held on so tight that his hand had gone numb. He was certain it would not feel much better when she finally let go.

They rode on for what seemed like hours. The blindfolds and the darkness brought on by the storm clouds that covered the sky made it difficult to accurately gauge how much time had passed. Johnson assumed night had fallen, but all they could tell was that the storm was getting worse, the wind, thunder, and lightning picking up. He wondered how long it would take passing strangers to report the abandoned carriage or Burt to decide that they had been gone too long and come looking. Would a search party even come to the rescue of a black man and a woman with no kin this side of the Mississippi? Even if it did, it seemed unlikely that help would arrive in time. Burt might even assume they had decided to room in New Pittsburg to wait out the storm until tomorrow.

"That's the meeting spot down there!" Atlas yelled over the strong winds. "J. T., you set up camp. I'll get them down."

"What? Don't trust me?" J. T. replied with a laugh.

"No, I fucking don't. Now put down around them trees over there and start gathering up some wood."

J. T. handed Mildred's lead to Atlas then slowly rode toward a patch of sycamores lining a small stream.

The winds blew hard. The smell of rain was in the air.

"Alright now, I'm going ta get you-all down for the night, you hear me?" Atlas said as he rode up to them. Both Margret and Johnson nodded in reply.

"Good. Now, lucky for you, you brought your own food. Otherwise you would've had ta go without," he said, lifting the pack of food Johnson had brought as he led them toward the trees. "I'll get you fed, then I don't want ta hear a fucking sound from you two the rest of the night!"

Again, they nodded to show their willingness to comply.

J. T. was collecting branches and twigs and chasing blowing leaves to start the fire as they approached. He had tied his horse to a low branch and placed his saddle on the ground to the left of his small kindling pile. Riding past him, Atlas took Margret, Johnson, and Mildred several yards to the right of where the fire was intended to be and secured Mildred's lead to the trunk of a small tree.

"What are ya tryin' ta have tonight?" J. T. asked, lighting the fire.

"Beans," Atlas replied unenthused.

"Beans it is, 'cause beans is all we fuckin' got! *Hehe!*" J. T. said, half in song.

While J. T. delighted in getting the fire going, Atlas untied the rope around Johnson and Margret. He held her by the waist as she swung her right leg over the mule and lowered it to the ground.

"Careful now," Atlas said with a twisted smile, groping Margret's breast as he helped her down, sitting her next to one of the trees.

"Hey there, little bird," J. T. called from the fire with a grin.

Turning back to Johnson, Atlas yanked him down and his right leg caught on Mildred's back. He fell to his side before his left foot touched the ground.

"Come here," Atlas said, dragging him away from the mule. "Eat this and keep it quiet." He shoved a cut of Johnson's own jerky into his hands. Turning back to the fire, he sniffed the air. "How those beans?"

"Ain't done yet."

"Well, what's taking so long? I'm starving!" Atlas replied, putting a piece of jerky in his mouth.

"I don't give a rat's ass. You can eat 'em cold. I'm gonna wait."

Atlas groaned. He stood for several minutes staring at the fire as he chewed on the tough piece of dried meat, listening to the thunder.

As Johnson lay on his back eating the only food he'd had in hours, he tried to gauge his surroundings. He could tell the two men were to his right, but Margret had been so quiet he had no idea where she was. It occurred to him to signal for her in some way, but he knew better than to speak.

"Alright, dinner's over!" Atlas grabbed Johnson by the arm with the rope in his other hand.

Dragging him closer to Margret, he tied them together back-to-front, the rope around their waists and her hands around him. He laid them down under a tree; gnarled roots dug into Johnson's shoulder and hip.

"Best get ta bed, big day tomorrow," he said as he stood up. "Them beans warm yet?" he asked, walking back toward the fire.

"Warm enough."

"Goddamn, alright."

Johnson barely heard him walk away over the rustle of the leaves blowing on the trees.

"You gonna be alright?" Johnson whispered to Margret.

"No," she replied. Tears welled in her eyes as she clasped him tightly. "I just want to be away from here."

Johnson said nothing as she sobbed, her tears wetting the back of his neck as she held him close. He considered trying to make an escape once the bandits fell asleep, but he was incredibly weary and knew he'd have trouble even if Margret hadn't been tied to him.

Boom! They both flinched as an extra-loud thunderclap raged above them. Escape was not likely.

Chapter 9

Johnson was jostled awake. In a daze, he heard screaming and was pushed repeatedly from behind, but it all seemed so slow and confusing. Another quick jerk. What was happening to him?

I don't have time to work, Burt, he thought in a cloud of haze. *What is he yelling about?*

Then he realized that his eyes were open, but he couldn't see! In a panic, he sat up and attempted to rub his face.

Thump! He fell back to the ground, struck in the head.

"Lay down, darkie!"

It came back to him as the screams continued. Margret's screams. She had been cut loose from him by one of the two bandits. He tried to focus, but his head spun even more as he felt a warm trickle running across his forehead.

"Please, no! Please!" Margret cried as she was dragged farther away.

"Shut up, cuuun—*ahhhh!*" Margret's screams were suddenly replaced by her assailant's.

Another dull thump. This time from the direction of their struggle. Margret went silent and Johnson could hear her body being dragged across the ground.

"What? You fuckin' gillard!"

"You were ready to do the same!"

"Bastard!"

"*Oof!*"

Johnson heard a new struggle ensue through repeated grunts and groans, the two men cursing at one another as their fight pushed them farther from the camp.

"Margret!" Johnson hissed, trying not draw attention.

There was no reply. Again, Johnson attempted to sit up, resting his back against the nearest tree. His feet weren't tied. A careless oversight by the bandits. Pausing to listen, he could hear the men wrestling on the ground several yards away. Removing the blindfold with his tied hands, he blinked, allowing his eyes to adjust. Margret's figure lay still in the dim light of an early cloudy dawn.

"Margret!" he repeated, trying to stand. He lifted himself against the tree, the bark digging into his back as he rose. Though he couldn't see them, Johnson knew the men weren't far and he had to hurry. Taking a step, he became dizzy and spilled forward onto the ground.

Splash! The men had taken the fight to the stream. Johnson could hear them as they wallowed around in the shallow water. Wet fists hit flesh, but their frequency began to wane. Head pounding, Johnson rose on all fours and tried to gather himself.

He crawled to where Margret lay. She, too, was bleeding from a blow to the head. He took off her blindfold and held it against the wound. He couldn't let her die.

Not this time, he thought to himself. *Not again.*

The blame would be his, and even if he survived, it wouldn't take long for someone to make a connection to what had happened in Saint Andrews.

"You'll be alright," he said nervously looking around.

Able to fully examine his surroundings for the first time in the dim light, opportunity presented itself. Whichever man had grabbed Margret must have dropped his knife during the fight. Scrambling toward it, Johnson froze when he realized the fight had gone silent: no splashing or blows, only the trickle of the stream. His heart pounded heavy in his chest. Still no movement. This was their chance to escape.

Turning the knife upward, he carefully ran the rope binding his wrists across it, freeing his hands, then crawled back to Margret.

"We gotta go!" he said, shaking her.

Opening her eyes, she slowly sat up. "Where are they?"

"Got into it by the creek. We gotta go!"

She looked around in a daze; he could tell she was barely conscious.

"Come on now," he said as he helped her to her feet.

He remained vigilant as he hurried her back to the horses, prepared for one of the bandits to emerge from the creek at any moment. Steadily the dawn grew, covering everything in a dark blue haze, as Johnson sat Margret down next to Atlas's bay horse.

"We gotta take the horses. Can you ride?"

"It's been a while," she replied, touching the wound at her brow.

"I mean, do you feel well enough?"

"I'll be fine, Mr. Johnson."

He had to convince himself she would be as he stood.

He rushed to Mildred and untied her from the tree. It saddened him to leave her behind, but she was no help to them now.

"I'm sorry," he said as he gave her one last brief pat on the nose. The old mule stood in the same position as if she was unaware that she had been freed.

When he turned around, to his surprise, Margret was folding a blanket to lay over the bay. The horse stirred and snorted when she approached but didn't protest as she carefully placed it on his back. Johnson hurried over to her and rifled through Atlas's things, looking for anything useful. He found another knife, a few dollars, and an extra pair of long underwear, but that was all.

"Bring the saddle before he gets too restless," Margret said, gently rubbing the horse's dark brown neck.

Johnson bent down to lift the saddle and revealed a .38 revolver hidden beneath it. He set the saddleback down again, his heart leaping as he examined the gun, slowly taking it in his hands.

"Mr. Johnson!"

The sound of hooves clomping arose in the distance.

"Hurry!" Margret yelled to him.

"Don't move!" J. T. yelled with his revolver drawn. "That'll be ol' Jester and the gang comin' our way."

His left eye was swollen shut and blood dripped from his mouth as he took heavy, labored breaths. His back to the bandit, Johnson carefully tucked the revolver in his waistband as he squatted, gambling that he hadn't seen it.

"Go ahead an' stand up. Real slow."

Johnson put his hands in the air and gradually rose.

"That's right," J. T. said as the sound of the hooves drew nearer.

They waited, listening for the sound of more horses, but a lone figure appeared in the distance.

"What the—Jester! That you?" he called out in confusion.

No response. Daylight had yet to fully set in, making it impossible to identify the rider from a distance.

Johnson swallowed. Was it Jester Wells? Where were the other members of his notorious gang?

"You'd better pray it's your man!" Margret yelled at J. T. "Because I assure you, you will hear no pleas for mercy from me!"

"Shut up, little bird!" he yelled. "I'll taste you yet!"

The rider drew closer.

"It's surely a lawman!" Margret yelled. Her voice was frantic.

"I said quiet!"

Bang! Margret flinched as J. T. fired in the air.

"Alright!" he yelled. "Reveal yourself 'fore you get any closer!"

The rider continued forward.

J. T. took aim.

Johnson held his breath as the man came into view.

"What do we got here, boys?" came the gravelly voice. "Looks like someone's got a story fer me." The rider wore a black hat and had a black beard and a visible scar on his right cheek. Johnson recognized the unmistakable face of Jester Wells as the outlaw slowly approached the camp.

A sly smile crossed J. T.'s bloody lips and he lowered his gun. He grimaced and clutched at a pain in his side. "Jester, I got a big surprise for you!" he said.

"Ho!" Wells yelled as he pulled his horse to a halt in front of them. "We made good time, eh?"

"I'll say," J. T. replied, moving closer. "Did you ride through the night? We wasn't expectin' ya 'til later."

Turning back the way he had come, Jester bellowed out at the open prairie, "Lay down here for the night!"

His words echoed as they all stood silently.

Margret gave Johnson a dire, questioning stare. Johnson returned it with a look just as confused.

"Boss, you alright?" J. T. asked as Jester dismounted.

Jester snapped his dark gaze to him. "The fuck's that sposed ta mean?" His demeanor turned sharp.

"I dunno, you're actin' funny," J. T. replied with caution.

"Bahahahaha!" Jester threw his head back, laughing madly, turning back again. "Boys, this'll be a good night!"

J. T. limped his way to Margret, grabbing her by the arm. "Boss, where's the rest of the gang?"

Jester turned to face him, the bloodstains suddenly visible on his clothes.

"They're all here," he replied coldly. "Nice of you to join us!"

Bang!

A bullet ripped through J. T.'s forehead. His body went limp and he fell to the ground. Margret cringed but remained standing. She took a deep breath, then slowly closed her eyes. When she reopened them, Jester was pacing back and forth, shaking his head as he mumbled to himself. She turned to Johnson with another look, but his focus was on the crazed man.

Jester's horse whinnied hysterically when he struck it. The beast took to the prairie in a sprint.

"Yer good and goddamn right I do!" Jester yelled, becoming increasingly wild. "Ya'll better fuckin' get one thing straight! None o' you'd be worth the buffalo shit one o' these strands o' grass grow on if it wasn't fer me, so ya'll can start actin' like yer listenin' to what I'm sayin' or ya can walk right back into that town! Or if ya'd rather, I'll save ya the time and put ya in the fuckin' ground myself!"

Johnson reached for the revolver.

"You!" he froze as Jester turned his gun on him. "Wanna join my gang? I got an opening!"

Jester smiled as he pulled the trigger. *Click.* No shot came.

Before Johnson realized what had happened, Jester Wells threw down his gun and charged at him, full sprint. It felt instinctual as Johnson raised the revolver and took aim. Staring down the barrel at the man running wildly toward him, he pulled the trigger. *Bang!*

The gun wanted to jump out of his hand as Jester continued his drive, untouched and unphased.

He had missed.

"*Oof!*" Johnson hit the ground hard, tackled onto his back.

The blows came so fast that he took two of them before he understood that he was being struck in the face. He followed the third with his eyes as the fist sunk hard into his left cheek. Swinging madly in defense, Johnson landed a blow to the side of Jester's neck and raised his right hand to block another fist. He grabbed at the outlaw's throat and tried to push him off. Jester jabbed him repeatedly in the gut. Another blow to the face. Johnson's vision was going blurry. He threw another desperate punch, this time striking Jester in the eye.

"*Bah!*" Jester yelled, raising up and putting a hand to his face.

Bang!

Another shot rang out, echoing across the landscape. Jester arched his back and exhaled in agony. "*Uhhhh.*" Then he collapsed, lifeless, on top of Johnson.

Johnson rolled the man's body to the ground beside him. Crimson red bled through the front of his shirt, blending with the existing bloodstains. Johnson looked up to see the blurry figure of Margret, both hands on the revolver. She breathed heavily as she held it steadily aimed at the bandit.

Johnson's head fell back limp as he allowed fatigue to take over. He stared at the gray mass of sky until his vision went dark.

"Mr. Johnson.

"Mr. Johnson, you need to eat this," Margret's voice came through to him as he slowly opened his eyes. It was dark. He could hear the crackling of a fire and turned to see its orange glow on her face as she held a spoon to his mouth. He tried to move, but his whole body ached, so he opened his lips instead. They were the best beans he had ever tasted. Lying on his back, he ate several spoonfuls that Margret fed him. When he finished, she rose to gather more wood. He watched the stars that dotted the clear black sky before finally passing out again.

Johnson woke again to the smell of smoke. It was daylight. Sitting up, he rubbed the sides of his head and looked over to see a pile of ashen branches smoldering a few feet away. Taking a deep breath, he stretched his arms, then recoiled when he rubbed his face. It was badly cut and bruised.

"Finally," came a man's voice.

Johnson sat up in surprise. He had not expected what he saw.

"Don't worry, Mr. Johnson," Margret said, standing next to Marshal Bradley. "The marshal arrived with a group of men a few hours ago."

"What?" His mind was still a fog of confusion. Margret and the marshal were present, but no other men. Even the bodies of the bandits were gone.

"Most of the party have already left," she replied.

"Miss Herston has been makin' us wait on you. You sure took a lick," Bradley said.

Margret shot Bradley a displeased, tight-lipped look before rushing to help Johnson as he moved to stand.

"Well, we should get him movin'," Bradley said, tucking his shirt in around his fat belly then adjusting his tin badge.

"Marshal, the man has only just awakened," Margret said indignantly. "Can we not afford him some time?"

Johnson's heart raced at the idea of going anywhere with the marshal. He looked around frantically for an escape. Noticing his trouble coming to grips with the situation, Margret laid a hand to his shoulder. "Why don't you sit back down, Mr. Johnson?" She motioned to a log away from the fire. "The marshal is only guiding us back to Flatridge." She turned to Bradley. "Marshal, will you kindly gather us some more wood while we wait for Mr. Johnson?"

Bradley started to protest. "You sure it wouldn't be better to—"

"Mr. Bradley!" she replied, putting hands to her hips.

"Alright, alright," Bradley said, bending over to pick up sticks.

Margret's interest in delaying their travel wasn't solely for Johnson's well-being. She herself was not quite ready to return and face a town full of people after being subjected to such violations. Emotionally, she was a disaster. It was all she could do to keep herself together in front of the rest of the men in the posse. Inside, she felt as if she were being ripped open. She wanted to scream until her voice gave out.

Johnson turned to stare at the stream, getting lost in the golden glow of reflected sunlight on its surface. His head was spinning and throbbing at the same time. It felt like the worst hangover he had ever had.

Burt and the others must have realized their absence quickly. More than likely, it was Margret who motivated their haste. Young, rich, white women always held a special place in people's hearts. Still, he wished Burt had come instead of the marshal. He wished he could tell him the truth.

He felt guilty. He had stolen from the one person who'd given him a chance. Was he really all that different from thieves like J. T. and Atlas? If they hadn't crossed paths with the bandits, he might've just as easily ended up dead just like them. He'd gotten lucky.

If you can call it luck, he thought to himself.

"Here," Margret said, handing him a canteen.

He looked up, gave her a slight grin, and took a drink.

"How do you feel?"

"Probably about how I look," he said, handing the canteen back to her. "How long was I out?"

"All of yesterday. After you passed out, I pulled you closer to the fire and you hardly even moved," she said with a slight laugh of relief.

"That bad, huh?"

Stepping over the log, she sat down next to him and took her own quick swig of water. "I wasn't sure you would make it."

"Me either," he replied, staring back at the stream. "Thanks."

"You are welcome," she said.

For the first time, they sat comfortably in silence together, listening as a warm breeze blew across the leaves. Then Margret rose to help Bradley with the fire.

Johnson ran his fingers through his hair and thought about what would be next for him. He had no choice but to return to Flatridge.

Would Cole Charles be waiting there for him? The man had been ready to gun him down at their last meeting. What could he expect when he came face to face with him again?

"Oh, come now, Mr. Bradley," Margret said, reprimanding him for his poor attempt at starting the fire.

"I don't need a woman to tell me!"

"Don't be so damned childish!"

Throwing his stick to the ground, Bradley huffed and folded his arms.

"Wait, where's Mildred?" Johnson interrupted them, looking for any sign of the mule.

"Oh," Margret said, looking around confused as if she expected her to be right next to them the entire time. "She must have wandered off in the night."

Saint Andrews, Indiana
June 1876

Frederick Boyd sat grinding his teeth in furious contemplation as he watched the deep orange sunset reflect over the water. Twirling his mustache between his fingertips, he paused to take a heavy sip of brandy then slammed the glass down, spilling much of it on the wooden desk.

"*Er-hem*," his spectacled assistant uttered as he carefully opened the door.

"Yes?" Boyd replied.

"I do hate to intrude, sir; I know how much you value your private time."

"Out with it!"

"Right, an urgent message has come for you from Mr. Pinkerton."

Boyd rushed to grab the letter from the man's outstretched hand and ripped it open. A wicked grin framed by the curls of his mustache spread across his face as he read.

"Good news, then, sir?"

"It appears one of their agents has stumbled across him in Kansas."

Chapter 10

Flatridge, Kansas
June 1876

Humid gusts blew debris down the road through Flatridge as Johnson and Margret sat on horseback at the edge of the town examining the damaged buildings. They had been gone only a few days, yet the town now seemed almost unrecognizable to them.

"Storm did a number on the place," Bradley said in response to their astonishment.

Next to them, the roof of the church was stripped to its wooden joists, and the grounds that had been neatly maintained just days before looked as though they had been neglected for months. Signs and shop windows were broken, and pieces of wood and glass still littered the ground in some areas. Large sections of the wooden awnings that covered the walkways were missing. Most of the rooftops were missing or damaged in some way, and some of the smaller structures were almost completely toppled. Only the Flatridge Inn appeared to be undamaged. Aside from the banner and some large pieces of siding that had gone missing, it remained in surprisingly decent condition, and people bustled in and out, using it as the center for the rebuilding efforts.

As the extent of the damage fully hit him, Johnson began to worry. "Is Burt alright?"

"Shit," Bradly replied begrudgingly. "Not sure anything could kill that old bastard."

"The station?"

"Fine. The barn's completely flattened, though. Burt's been busy rounding up horses that got away."

Guilt ate at Johnson. It had eaten at him the entire ride back. After losing Mildred, he had decided that he needed to tell Burt the truth. Now he didn't know if he had the guts to do it. To lay his transgression on Burt and expect forgiveness at a time like this made him feel even worse.

Johnson felt as if he were on display for his crimes as they made their way through the town, passing people working to rebuild their lives. Fixing roofs and reframing doors and windows, the townspeople were too busy to notice the trio riding by.

"My word," Margret uttered as she looked at the destruction.

"Marshal Bradley! Marshal Bradley!" the doctor yelled frantically as he rushed toward them from down the street. "I'm afraid Mr. Charles has taken a turn for the worse."

"How bad?" Bradley asked.

"I told him he needed to take it easy, but he hasn't listened," replied the doctor, breathing heavily. "I had to—*gasp*—amputate earlier this morning."

"Aw, shit." The marshal's tone suggested he was more bothered about having to deal with the situation than concerned about the condition of the man.

"I insist you come with me to the inn immediately!" the doctor said.

"What the hell do you need me for?"

"He is not well! Someone must help to sort his affairs!"

Johnson watched the interaction between the doctor and the marshal with interest. Amputate? He couldn't believe what he was hearing! It couldn't have been a more fortunate turn of events. Johnson desired to see Cole Charles broken. Not only for his peace of mind, but for his personal satisfaction in the knowledge that such a man had gotten a fate he deserved. He had to confirm it for himself.

Johnson spoke up, "Marshal Bradley, I'll come with ya to the inn. I want to help Ms. Herston back to her room."

"Why, thank you, Mr. Johnson," Margret said with a tired smile.

"If you would, please?" the doctor steered them back down the street.

"Alright," Bradley replied.

Johnson made his way with them to the inn, body warmed with a new confidence. If Cole Charles truly was in such bad shape, that meant

Johnson might be able to stay in Flatridge, or at least remain long enough for Rex to return so they could move on to Texas. Was his luck finally turning?

No one stood at the bar when they walked in through the double doors. The bartender was nowhere to be seen. The room was darker than usual and far dingier without its lively base of customers. A group of men huddled around three tables were the only other people in the room. Johnson recognized some of the local businessmen sorting through printed layouts of the town's buildings and conversing about the best course of action. The men broke from their conversation only when one of the waitresses emerged from the kitchen with a fresh pot of coffee.

"Ms. Herston!" one of the men called out in a heavy German accent. "I can only say that I am overjoyed to see you have been safely returned to us." Adjusting his bow tie, he smiled, motioning her to the front desk.

Margret forced a smile. "Thank you, Mr. Helm," she said. "I have Mr. Johnson here to thank for that." She trailed off when she realized he had abandoned her to follow the doctor and the marshal upstairs.

The doctor climbed the stairs. "He's caught fever. If it doesn't turn, I don't expect he'll live out the week," he said, scrambling up to the second floor. "Please do hurry, marshal."

The marshal huffed as he waddled up the first few steps, clinging to the railing, then slicked his hair back as he paused at the landing to rest.

To his disappointment, the doctor wouldn't allow Johnson to enter Cole Charles's room. Instead, he stood in the hallway listening at the door, pressing his ear hard against the wood. He found it impossible to separate their words or voices as they quietly conversed. He wondered how bad off Cole Charles truly was. What other reason would they have for speaking in near whispers? The floorboards creaked behind the door, and he jumped back when the marshal cracked it just enough to poke his head through.

"He's asked to see you, Mr. Johnson," Bradley said.

The warmth in his chest turned to near burning and sweat pooled on his brow. Although he had wanted to see Cole Charles, he had not expected this. Johnson nodded and the marshal opened the door wide enough for him to enter.

Cole Charles lay still on his bed. A pillow had been placed beneath the bloody, bandaged stump of his left thigh to keep it elevated, while the rest of his body was covered in blankets. He turned his head to acknowledge Johnson, but he made no indication that he was in any pain.

Johnson swallowed hard at the sight of the man. He had expected the meeting to feel triumphant as he stared down at his defeated enemy, but as Cole Charles glared back at him with his dark smile, Johnson knew he'd made a mistake.

"Mr. Johnson, good of you to visit," Cole Charles said in a sickly voice that sent a shiver down his back. "Come closer. I do have something to tell you."

"He's delusional from the fever," the doctor said from his chair in the back corner of the room, his lips a tight frown.

Cole Charles raised his left arm from under the blankets and beckoned him closer. Johnson carefully crouched next to the bed. Heat from the candle on the bedside table flickered at the back of his neck as he leaned in to listen.

With a ghostly exhale, Cole Charles whispered into his ear. Finding it hard to focus on any one thing as he processed the words, Johnson's eyes darted around the room while he listened. When he pulled back, Cole Charles gave him his most wicked grin then turned away, half cackling in a coughing fit.

Johnson tried to rise and calmly exit the room, but he stumbled when he moved. His heart raced. Brushing past the marshal, he ignored his inquiring look. Hand shaking as he grabbed the knob, he opened the door then slammed it shut behind him.

He leaned forward over the balcony railing, closing his eyes and trying to breathe normally. Inside, he cursed himself for his foolishness.

"There you are!" Margret's voice from down the hall made him jump.

"Oh, yeah." He exhaled nervously, staring down at the gathering of men huddled around the tables.

"Is that all you have to say?"

"Sorry, I guess."

"I thought we were past this," she replied, stretching out her hand. "Come now, Mr. Johnson, walk me to my room."

Casually, she approached him, taking his hand. Her touch was calming enough to make him momentarily forget why he was so worked up as she led him to the next set of stairs. The jumbled echoes of the men's voices faded as Johnson and Margret ascended into the silence of the third floor.

"Mr. Helm has informed me that the last stage to ever leave here for Wichita is supposed to depart in a few hours," she said with a smile, though her tone suggested she was anything but pleased. "If I don't leave today, I may never have another opportunity. I thought I wanted to see more of the West, but now I'm unsure."

"What do you mean?"

"Didn't Burt tell you?" She looked at him raising an eyebrow. "They are ending stagecoach service west of Flatridge."

"No, he didn't."

"Well," she looked at him, heavy in thought, "do I continue west or do I return home?"

"I thought west was the plan?"

"It was." Margret paused as they stopped at her door. "I still want to be a writer, Mr. Johnson. It's just . . ." Margret's tone grew serious. "Can I be honest with you?"

"I suppose."

For the first time in their acquaintance, she avoided his stare, rubbing a large stain she had noticed on her dress. The same dress she'd worn through the events of the past few days. "Ugh, this dress is ruined."

"That all ya needed to tell me?"

"No, don't be facetious." Taking a deep breath, she brought a hand to the side of her face. "These past few days have been quite traumatic for me, and it has made me painfully aware that, well . . ." she trailed off, looking at the ground. A door opened down the hall and a short, old white woman emerged. To avoid scrutiny, Johnson pretended to stare at a painting of a sailboat on the wall while Margret feigned unlocking her door. The woman quickly descended another set of stairs at the other end of the corridor.

Johnson had grown impatient. "Well, what?"

She snapped back at him, "Frankly, this is not easy for me!"

"Us talking about it? Or what happened?"

"Both!" she said. "This is not at all what I had expected, and it is hard for me to admit my naivete!"

"Well, if it's a bit rougher out here than ya thought, maybe ya shoulda thought about that before ya came," he said. His voice was strained, irritated. "Not everybody gets ta just come and go. If you can't handle it, maybe ya should leave!"

She burst into tears.

Johnson felt instant remorse for how he'd spoken to her. "Oh, no, no, no," he said awkwardly, trying to comfort her. He didn't know what to do. Both of her hands now covered her face; he attempted to gently touch her shoulder.

Softening his tone, he said, "Look, I'm sorry."

After a moment, he decided it was best to say nothing else. He waited uncomfortably for several minutes, hoping no one else would come upon them until she calmed down on her own.

"I'm sorry," he repeated.

She allowed her brown eyes to look into his. "Mr. Johnson, the finer points of gentility continue to elude you!" she said, swiping her tears away with the sleeve of her dress.

"Are you gonna be alright?" he asked, trying to sound as sincere as possible.

Taking another deep breath, she tightened her lips. "Father wasn't keen on my coming out here, nor on my choice of profession for that matter. He still expects me to be a proper lady married off to a man of status."

"Do you regret it?"

She paused, thinking for a moment. "I don't think I do." Unlocking her door, she turned back to him. "I apologize, but I must go."

"But?"

"Goodbye, Mr. Johnson."

Margret turned, opened the door to her room, and shut it behind her, leaving Johnson alone in the dimly lit hallway.

He stood there silently trying to work through what had just happened. He wished he had acted differently, but it was all too much for him with everything they'd been through during the last few days. He wanted to knock on the door and call her back. He needed her to make him forget about Cole Charles again, but standing there, he couldn't bring himself to do it.

Tightly clenching his fists, he paced in a circle for several minutes hoping she might reemerge on her own. When she did not, he gathered himself and decided it was finally time to return to the station.

As he came down the stairs, the men were arguing loudly among themselves.

"Don't you see? This is it! The beginning of the end!"

"It don't have to be. That's the point of this. That's why we're rebuildin'!"

"Precisely! Things will get back to normal in no time!"

"Not if that train passes us for New Pittsburg. Might as well all close up shop!"

"We cannot just abandon the town!"

"What reason do we have to stay anymore?"

None of them seemed to notice as Johnson moved across the room, threw the double doors out of his way, and exited the building.

A train. It was starting to make sense.

Mounting his horse, he took off at a gallop, ready to put the town and everyone in it behind him.

When Johnson passed the jail, he slowed to examine what remained. It was in dire shape. The eastern corner and the roof had collapsed almost completely, and the front door was hanging from its bottom hinge. Next to the door, secured to what was left of the front wall, the now half-torn poster of Jester Wells fought hard in the wind. The image of his face was missing but his name and "$250 reward" were still clearly visible as the paper rippled in the heavy gusts. Johnson continued to the station.

The barn wasn't flattened. It didn't look great, though. Johnson stared at the hayloft he had slept in for months through the exposed wooden beams. He was glad he hadn't been sleeping there during the storm. The roof, siding, and walls were mostly gone, and the remaining skeleton of the structure leaned eastward. Several horses wandered loose within the pen, and as he approached, they stirred, chuffing in apprehension when he dismounted. He gave them a quick whistle, but it only drove them farther away.

Tying his horse to one of the posts, he looked around for any sign of Burt. The stagecoach was there, but neither Burt nor the teamster were present.

He went into the station office and checked the time—10:23 a.m. If the stage was to leave that day, normally Burt would want it to be no later than noon, which meant he was running out of time. Johnson tried to sit patiently and wait for Burt's return, but after barely ten minutes it felt like he was going crazy.

All he could think about were the words Cole Charles had spoken to him, repeating them over again in his mind. Even when he tried to think about Margret, he couldn't shake the feeling of Cole Charles's warm breath in his ear. He gripped the revolver in his waistband. The cold metal didn't make him feel any better but gave him a new sense of security. If it came down to it, he knew he could put up a real fight now. Cole Charles would live. There was too much life in his words for any other alternative.

The sound of horses drew him up.

He didn't have to look; he knew it was Burt. Though he couldn't make out his words, he could hear him chattering in the distance over the hoofbeats breaking on the ground.

He stepped outside when he heard them moving horses through the fence.

"I wondered," Burt said with a smile. "Sam, go ahead and start getting the coach ready. I'll be there in a minute."

Johnson remained on the porch, waiting as Burt walked over.

"Sorry I wasn't able to come with the search party," Burt said, slowly taking the first step. "Come on, let's have a seat."

Johnson recognized how much of a struggle it had become for the old man as he labored his way up.

"I'm sure the good marshal was entertainment enough for you though," he said.

Johnson exhaled. "Yeah."

"By god! Look at your face," he laughed, motioning him back into the office.

"I finally met Jester Wells," Johnson joked.

"And I'm sure Bradley proudly finished the job he started."

"He had a little help."

"Looks like it," Burt pointed to the gun at his waist. "Pick that up on the way?"

"Long story."

"You can spare me the details. I'm just glad you're alright. The woman too?"

Johnson nodded.

"Good," he said falling heavily into the first seat inside the door. "I guess this place really does go to hell when you're not around."

Johnson forced a smile. Opening his mouth, he tried to find the courage to tell Burt the truth: that he'd planned to steal Mildred and run away. Burt gave him a look that suggested he was already wise to him. Instead of words, Johnson made a short guttural sound. It was like there was a pit in his stomach that swallowed everything he wanted to say before it could come out.

"You look lost," Burt said to him.

"Probably am."

"Figured as much, Any man who needs Bradley to come find him is bound to get lost sitting in a familiar place."

Johnson gave a weak laugh that turned into a groan as he looked around the room. From what he could tell, it hadn't changed at all, but somehow it seemed different to him. He turned back to Burt with a serious expression. "Why didn't you tell me about the stage?"

Burt returned his look apologetically. "I was afraid you'd leave. I can't hardly live on my own out here anymore." He stood up again, walked behind the front desk, and gave a long sigh. "The company was already talking about shutting us down. That's what the meeting I was supposed to go to was about. Turns out they made their decision without me."

"I'm sorry, Burt," Johnson said.

"Don't worry about me. I'm old," he replied. "Besides, this is my daughter's doing."

Johnson shot him a curious look.

"Yeah, she's married to Douglass, one of the owners. Been begging me to come back and live with them for years now."

"Didn't know."

"Why? Bad at reading minds or something?"

"Must be," Johnson smiled.

Burt exhaled. "It's probably about time anyway," he said, crouching down as he scrounged through the bottom drawer of the desk. "These storms have been testing my mettle for a while now. Knew it wouldn't be long before one got the better of me."

"You don't have to go back East," Johnson replied, trying to reassure him. "What if we go someplace together? I've been thinkin' about Texas."

"Ah-*ha*," Burt said, pulling something from the back of the desk drawer. He set a gun belt onto the desk and pushed it toward Johnson. "Look, I'm not slow. It's obvious you're running from your past. Trains are taking over and every day it's getting easier for more and more people to come west, and soon whatever it is you're running from will find you."

Johnson stared blankly at the desk. If only Burt knew, it had already found him.

"Don't just stare at it. I want you to have that," he said with a young man's excitement. "Believe it or not, this used to be a much wilder place."

Johnson put his hand on the belt, then looked at Burt.

"No, I'm not going to Texas. But if you're planning on it, you shouldn't linger. That Cole Charles has been asking a lot of questions," Burt replied.

"I know," Johnson said. "I don't plan to be anywhere near here come sundown."

"Smart."

Johnson picked up the gun belt and slipped his revolver into it.

"Well, I better go finish helping Sam," Burt said. "I would say you should gather your things while you're waiting, but I noticed you'd already done that."

Johnson twitched, hot with guilt and shame.

"Relax, you're always too tense," Burt said as he stepped out the door.

The last stagecoach to leave Flatridge for Wichita pulled out of the station just before noon. Johnson watched as it faded into the town then turned to stare out at the hills. Slinging his pack over his shoulder, he stepped down off the porch, hat tilted at an angle, gun belt wrapped around his hips, and walked toward Burt, who was standing next to his horse.

"Nice mount you got yourself here," Burt said, petting the bay's nose. "You pick this up on your trip, too?"

"It was one of the bandits'," he replied as he mounted the horse. "Probably stolen."

"You know horse thieving's a murderous crime out here," Burt said with a laugh, shaking his head. "Where is Mildred, anyway? Would've just told you to go ahead and keep her."

Johnson adjusted his hat then looked down at him. "She wandered off."

"Probably for the best," he replied as if he were talking about a long dead friend. "Can't say I'll miss waiting on that daggone mule."

Johnson shot him a curious look. "Daggone?"

"Ah, you know how these eastern types are more sensitive," Burt said with a grin. "Got to start watching my language."

"Goodbye, Burt," he said with a smile, bending down to shake his hand. "Thanks, and if ya see Rex again, let him know I'm headed for Texas."

"I'll let him know."

"Thanks," he repeated. "For everything."

"No, thank you, I guess," Burt replied, "for putting up with someone like myself."

Johnson gave him a nod then, with a loud whistle, turned his horse and rode off.

"Allan Pinkerton tells me that for years you have been one of his top agents." Frederick Boyd's words were sharp in the dim flicker of the candlelight. "It's a shame you have sustained such a crippling wound. I don't see how you could conduct a manhunt in your current condition."

Cole Charles spat. "I assure you I am far more than just what my body has to offer."

"Good," Boyd said with a cruel smile. "I intend to provide you with any provisions necessary to help you find this man."

Cole Charles leaned back against the pillows propping him up and closed his cold, dark eyes. "There has yet to be a man that I haven't been able to find."

PART II

Chapter 11

The Mississippi River
March 1876: Three Months Earlier

Whoooo—whooooooo!

The deep roar of the whistle came with a great whoosh of steam as Johnson frantically shoveled coal to fuel the boiler of the *Queen Bellamy*. Back and forth he turned in the hot, stuffy air, loading as much as he could with each scoop before tossing it into the burner.

"Thought I already told ya, you gonna kill yourself workin' that way," Abraham said to him as he walked up.

Johnson looked up from behind the grated steel door of the burner, skin darkened from the smoke and the coal dust, and shrugged, "I just get into a rhythm."

"Rhythm's fine, just find yourself a slower one, or go easy on how much ya load," he replied. "Somethin' or other, just not both."

Abraham, the head engineer, was heavy and muscular. His large build combined with his prudent personality made him the kind of person people naturally heeded.

Johnson leaned onto the handle of the shovel and used a forearm to wipe soot from his brow, revealing a patch of brown skin on his forehead. He nodded.

"Don't worry, your back'll thank me later."

Standing up straight, Johnson stretched, rubbing his lower back, "How soon 'til next port?"

"Two days."

Two days. He had two days left before new passengers came on board—and any one of them could be looking for him. They had come into port only once since he'd joined the crew, and he was still on edge, worrying about who might have boarded then.

It had been two weeks since the night Jimmy Perkins had helped Johnson escape the posse of men looking for him back in Saint Andrews. He'd sent him off in a rowboat with Abraham, and now Johnson's plan was to go west, just like Jimmy had suggested. Still, the gripping fear that anybody could be hunting for him hadn't disappeared.

"You even hearin' me?" Abraham asked, snapping him out of his thoughts.

"*Uh* . . . how's that?"

"I said, Sylvester Roy, best negro card player on the river."

"Right, yeah." Johnson had never heard of the man but tried to play it off like he had.

Abraham gave him a look that confirmed he knew what Johnson was about. "Look, we're playing a game in the quarters tonight. I get you like ta keep to yourself, but some of the crew already been askin' questions. Least ya could do is get ta know 'em a bit."

"I'll think about it," Johnson replied.

"Ya don't gotta worry," Abraham said, trying to reassure him. "They're a good bunch."

Johnson nodded again and turned back to the pile of coal, taking a large scoop then dumping about half of it out before throwing it into the fire.

Currently on a return trip from Cincinnati, the *Queen Bellamy* was a luxury steamboat out of New Orleans. Complete with a grand ballroom and high-stakes gambling hall, she was an impressive boat spanning almost four hundred feet in length with a thirty-foot paddle wheel that vigorously churned the river at its stern. Its five decks were outfitted with the finest accoutrements to satisfy its mostly high-class passengers, who were served whatever they required or requested by the black crew and service staff. Rarely did passengers purchase tickets solely for transportation; they sought to indulge in the best of life's pleasures as the steamboat made its way up and down the river.

Johnson rested his elbows over the railing and closed his eyes as spray from the paddle wheel hit his face. He wiped away as much of the grit as he could then dried his hands on his soot-covered shirt. Leaning forward again, he stared out over the dark river and fought the tight, uncomfortable feeling that grew as he thought about associating with the other men.

It wasn't that he didn't like them. Abraham was right; he didn't really know them, but that was part of the problem. He was afraid of letting his guard down. He continually reminded himself that he couldn't fully trust anyone. This made it hard to enjoy the simple pleasure of being in a space where others could relax, because for him there was always a sense of insecurity.

Taking a breath, he turned back inside and descended the stairs.

The engine crew's quarters were below the main deck in the center of the hold. Firm rules had been put in place by the captain, which restricted them to certain corridors on the main deck and rarely allowed them to venture above it. This was to minimize the likelihood that passengers would be bothered by the sight of them while they enjoyed their leisure time. Service staff dressed in the appropriate uniform were the only non-white personnel permitted on the top four decks, so the crew met in their quarters for most off-hour gatherings.

Light from the room flickered as it spilled into the dark hallway, and Johnson already could hear the buzz of lively talk. He paused just outside the doorway to listen.

"—an' he come runnin' outta that room so fast with her after him! Damn near shot his head off clean! Boy kept runnin' so hard with a grin on his face so big I thought he'd never stop! But when he finally did, and I asked him what he done ta get her so riled, know what he says? He says, 'I tried ta put two silver dollars in her mouth!'"

The whole room burst into laughter.

Standing in the dark, Johnson quickly pieced together the bits he'd missed from the doorway. He didn't want to join them—and part of him even considered staying in the dark hallway—but he knew getting caught eavesdropping posed a much more awkward situation than going in. Tensing his muscles, he turned the corner.

The quarters were dank and cramped with just enough space for the average person to avoid hitting his head on one of the wooden joists that supported the main floor above them. Abraham and three other men were grouped in the center of the room, sitting in chairs and bunks around a center table that had been set up for a game of cards, though no playing cards were present. Their amusement was evident and Johnson almost said something friendly to agree with the mood while they laughed, but in his nervousness he decided against it.

"We thought you was gonna work all night!" exclaimed the older man who'd told the story.

"I was just cleanin' up," Johnson replied.

"Probably got whistle bit," laughed a man with rusty hair. "You can take my shift if you like working so much."

"Sure, I suppose," Johnson said to play along, hoping they would change the topic of conversation. He took a seat in the nearest chair.

"Better stand your ass back up!" the man snapped at him, sending a chill through the room. "What do you think you're doing?"

Rattled, Johnson's eyes went wide and he sprang up. "Sittin'?"

"How you going to work sitting here?"

"What?"

"Go on, best get back to the boilers!" the man exclaimed, pointing to the door. "My shift starts in ten minutes—*ha!*"

Again, the men burst out in laughter, rolling back into their seats. Johnson stood tensely and said nothing, unsure of how to react.

"Relax," Abraham said, handing him a beer. "James's just givin' ya hell. And he'll catch some, too, if he don't get ta workin' on time!" He turned to James with a raised eyebrow.

"How about you talk the captain into letting it slip for the night?" James replied with a mischievous grin.

"That captain's a fool," Abraham said. "Already told him I got the boiler barely patched together, but he insists we keep pushing it anyway." Frustration colored his voice. "Ain't no way he'll look past one of my men skippin' a shift. Now go on and get *your* ass down there."

"Damn. Worth a try," James said. Finishing the rest of his beer, he stood and smiled at Johnson as he walked out. "Don't win too much money without me."

Still standing, Johnson swallowed nervously as he looked at the bottle in his hand. Abraham hadn't said anything to him about money. He hadn't even been paid yet. Surely the engineer knew that.

"Go on, sit back down," Abraham said to him reassuringly. "We just like ta have some jokes."

"Right," he replied rigidly. Popping open the bottle and returning to his chair, he took a large swig as Abraham introduced him to the other men.

"Johnson, you've met Willie, and that one over there who likes tellin' stories, that's old Henry," he said, gesturing across the table at the other two men. "I know y'all seen each other around, but it's a formality. This is Johnson, he'll be with us 'til at least New Orleans."

Johnson had crossed paths with Henry a few times, but they'd never exchanged words. He had never seen James until that night. Willie, Abraham's young apprentice, had worked with Johnson on a few shifts. Abraham had put the two together on Johnson's first day because he thought it would be good for them to get to know each other. He figured that it would help Johnson become familiar with the work and hoped that the chance to supervise would give Willie a little motivation. The boy didn't seem much interested in either conversation or working, as he was prone to daydreaming for long periods. Johnson couldn't blame him; it was normal for someone his age to wish he was elsewhere. Johnson did.

"I got 'em!" exclaimed a man in a dress shirt and vest as he burst through the doorway with a carton of beer. "An' some extra bub, too, for each of ya."

"'Bout damn time!" replied Henry. "What took so long?"

"There was a good game goin' upstairs. They liked the way I dealt."

"Shit, I don't!" Henry laughed, laying a hand to his belly.

Ignoring the comment, the newcomer set the carton on the floor next to Johnson then threw a deck of cards to the table.

"How you doin'?" he said, rubbing his hands together before extending one to Johnson. "Walter Brown, or Walt."

"Johnson," he replied, completing the handshake.

"You play?"

"Not real sure."

"What's to be sure about? You either do or ya don't."

"I know euchre."

"Oh, lord," Henry spat.

"Nobody comes here to play euchre," Walt replied. "Poker."

Willie smiled at him from across the table.

"Never played," Johnson replied.

"We'll show ya," said Abraham. He opened the deck and began to shuffle. An alertness came over the men at the sound of cards flipping together and being rapped onto the table in Abraham's hands.

"Is it hard ta learn?" Johnson asked.

"Nah. High cards, pairs, and such," Walt replied. "Real easy."

After a short explanation and the first few hands, Johnson couldn't decide how true that statement was. He quickly picked up the card play but found the betting a much more complicated aspect of the game. He wasn't certain when to call or when to raise, and after getting drawn into escalating a bet further than he'd intended on a pair of aces, he lost big to Walt, who had a full house of queens and fours. From there he resolved to play it safe.

"How many ya need?"

"Three," Johnson replied to Walt, sliding his cards over to him.

"Three for me, too," Abraham replied.

"I'll take two," Willie said.

"Just one," Henry replied. "One is all I need to beat you fools."

Johnson looked at his cards—king of hearts, three of hearts, five of clubs, jack of hearts, and jack of spades. "Check," he said hesitantly.

"Five," Abraham replied.

Willie slouched low, his eyes half-hidden behind the cards fanned out in his hands. "Alright."

"Fifteen," Henry said confidently.

"I'll do fifteen," Walt replied, putting his bet in.

Johnson looked at his cards—a pair of jacks. He felt uncertain. It didn't seem like a bad hand, but fifteen was a lot, and he didn't want to risk it. "I'll fold."

"Another fold?" Walt asked. "How am I supposed to take more of your money if you keep folding?"

Impatient to show the cards, Henry looked to Abraham and Willie. "Alright, let's see 'em. You in or not?"

Both men put in to complete the bet.

"Triple sixes," Abraham said with a smile, neatly laying down his cards.

"Damn," Henry replied as they all laid down their cards and pushed them toward Johnson for the next deal.

Each of the other four men was well-practiced, leaving Johnson far outskilled. The one advantage he did have was that since he didn't have any money, they allowed him to put his share of the beer in the pot in exchange. As the game went on, he was the only player still sober whereas the inebriated men's decisions became increasingly impaired.

The men had gone quiet in suspense as Johnson's stare shifted between the five cards in his hand and Henry across the table, his lone opponent still in the game. His careful strategy of folding until he had a strong hand had paid off, as Henry had knocked out Walt, Abraham, and Willie for him.

Henry leaned back, rapping his fingers over the five cards laying face-down in front of him. As Johnson studied his opponent, the grinding sound of a bottle rolling back and forth across the floor filled the room as the boat pitched side to side.

Saying nothing, Johnson pulled two cards from his hand and placed them facedown on the table, slowly holding up two fingers. Henry drew two cards from the top of the deck and expertly slid them to Johnson. His eyes lit up as he took them into his hand—two kings to go with the pair of fives and the ace he already had!

"Everything."

"All in?" Henry asked with a slight grin.

"Yeah, all in."

"Alright, what you got?"

Johnson laid his cards down, revealing his two pair.

He held his breath as Henry revealed his cards—ace, four, two, jack, eight.

His heart raced! He'd won! Excitedly, he began to grab the coins in the middle of the table.

"No," Abraham said, jarring him to a halt.

"Why?" he replied confused.

"He got a flush," Walt replied.

"A what?" Johnson asked before looking at the cards again. Each of Henry's cards was a spade.

"Dammit, I forgot." Johnson was deflated.

"It's OK, kid," Henry laughed. "Did well first time out."

"Don't let him butter you up," Abraham said.

Tension dispersed from the room with the conclusion of the game, and the buoyant manner of liveliness returned.

"Better than euchre, huh?" Willie said, stretching back on the bunk he'd been sitting on as Walt and Henry cleaned up.

"Different."

"We'll play again in a few days," Abraham said, standing to stretch his legs and moving some chairs to the side.

"Will that Sylvester Roy fella be playin' with us?" Johnson asked.

"*Ha!*" Walt laughed, shoving the cards back into the box. "Sly wouldn't bother playin' with us. He'll play the tournament with all them folks at the grand salon upstairs, and I got a plan for how we can watch it."

"And what might that be?" Abraham asked him in a stern voice.

"Y'all just have to wait!" he replied before putting the deck of cards in his pocket and darting out of the room.

"What kinda damned fool idea has he cooked up now, you think?" Henry asked, looking at Abraham.

"Don't know."

"Kid, you be careful around him," Henry said shaking his finger at Johnson. "He's liable ta get you in some kinda trouble."

"Aw, he ain't so bad," Willie replied. "You know we all wanna see Sly play."

As they settled in for the night, Johnson conceded to himself that Abraham was right: The poker game had worked. He did feel more comfortable, and now, after learning the game, he wanted to see Sylvester Roy play. Despite his lingering fear that he might be recognized, he wanted to see what a *real* card player could do, especially against the rich, white passengers who frequented the *Queen Bellamy*. As he lay there, he wondered how Walt planned to get them onto the upper decks without getting into trouble.

Chapter 12

"Sure ya don't wanna come with us? Abraham asked Johnson as the crew got ready to head for shore. They had made port earlier that morning in a small city someplace in Missouri inside a great bend in the Mississippi.

"C'mon, Abe, why you even askin'?" Henry called to Abraham. "Let's get goin'. I'm tryin' ta call on Miss Maybellene!" He began singing the woman's name as he stepped out into the hallway.

"I'm fine," Johnson replied, staring at the wooden slats of the bunk above him, hands cradling the back of his head.

"Want me ta get ya anythin'?" Abraham asked. "Food? Beer? Whiskey?"

Johnson perked up at the thought. "Think ya could grab me a newspaper?"

"Newspaper?" Abraham studied him with a curious look. "Sure."

"Thanks," he said. Closing his eyes, he turned to face the wall.

Abraham shrugged. "Alright."

As Abraham turned and walked into the dark hallway, Johnson heard his heavy footsteps head toward the stairway at the stern. A separate gangway was placed there for the crew to disembark away from the passengers.

Johnson lay there and fantasized about what he might be doing if he'd gone ashore with the rest of the crew, particularly Henry's mention of calling on a woman. He would've liked to visit a whorehouse, but he knew it wasn't worth leaving the boat. No, if he were going to take risks, they had to be worth it, which is why he'd decided he had to stay.

Closing his eyes, he tried to sleep but the muggy air below deck was stale and suffocating. Johnson laid there sweating uncomfortably for several minutes. He replayed the previous night's poker game in his mind to distract himself from the heat. Just as he'd finally drifted off, the sound of approaching footsteps woke him.

"Heard ya didn't wanna go ashore, so I was hopin' you could help me with somethin'," Walt said, walking in with a server's uniform draped over his arm.

Johnson raised an eyebrow and motioned to the clothing. "What's that for?"

Walt smiled a big toothy grin. "It's how we're gonna see Sly."

Johnson sat up tall with excitement. "What's your plan?"

"Put these on," Walt said, handing him the uniform. "We're going for a walk on the upper decks."

Johnson's heart sunk. He'd overheard some of the crew talking about a man who was caught out of place above deck just days before Abraham had brought him on the boat. They didn't mention any specifics, but there was nothing comforting about the tone of their voices.

"I-I can't," he said, shaking his head.

"It'll be fine. If you look like part of the waitstaff, no one will ask any questions," Walt said reassuringly. "You'll blend right in."

Johnson looked at the server's uniform. He thought about how easily Walt moved throughout the entire boat and how he'd been trapped in the muggy hold for weeks. Johnson was keen to taste the fresh breeze, and if he was going to see Sly play, he'd have to go above deck.

"Alright, but let's be quick," Johnson said, unbuttoning his soot-stained shirt and replacing it with the clean white one.

Johnson's heart raced as he and Walt ascended into the open air. The ornate features of the main deck were a far cry from those in the hold. Its exposed corridors were framed by intricate woodworking and decorated with flowers and colorful banners donning the doors and railings. The whitewash coating every wall, rail, and pillar gave the floating resort a lavish sense of elegance.

"C'mon this way," Walt said, leading him up the next flight of stairs.

Sucking his lips in, Johnson nodded, too afraid to say anything. He tensed his neck and shoulders as they reached the top and saw that passengers' rooms lined the corridor of the second deck.

"Relax," Walt said from the side of his mouth as a heavyset woman came out of her room.

Johnson did his best to smile but kept his eyes down.

"Good day, ma'am. I hope you are enjoying your stay," Walt said.

"Oh, it's been lovely. Thank you," the woman said with a smile as she passed.

Walt turned to Johnson and adjusted his vest. "See? All ya gotta do is be polite and nobody'll know the difference."

Johnson loosened his shoulders. Walt was right. To the passengers, he was just another black man there to serve them. They walked toward the bow, and Johnson stopped to look out at the brick buildings lining the edge of the river. Hidden behind layers of cobblestone, the riverbank led down to the docks, where longshoremen moved cargo along the wharf. Leaning his elbow on the railing, he watched an older woman wearing a large, feathered hat board the main gangway, followed by a young man with her luggage.

Then Johnson's muscles froze. A group of eight policemen marched down the cobblestone bank toward the dock. Counting and then recounting them as they approached, his eyes trained on their every movement, he watched as they stepped across the wooden planks. The group stopped and huddled together in conversation at the edge of the gangway, conferring with each other and shaking hands before sending a single man onboard. He was broad shouldered and had a very large nose.

"Johnson. Johnson!" Walt shook him, motioning with his eyes down the corridor. "We need to get back to work."

Turning, Johnson noticed a man in a green suit coat wearing a top hat walking past them. "Good day, sir." Johnson struggled to get the words out smoothly.

Saying nothing, the man narrowed his eye at him then touched the brim of his hat and kept walking.

"You're right. We should get back to work," Johnson said.

—◦—

Abraham had expected to feel more relaxed after enjoying time away from the boat, but upon his return, he was greeted with the unpleasant news that more passengers than expected had been taken onboard, and it left him fuming.

"We just took on twenty-four, supposed to take another twenty in Memphis," Abraham said as he walked up the gangway.

"We got too many damn people on this dinghy as is. How are we going to handle all that?" James asked, looking out at the water through the slats of the giant red paddle wheel.

"That's what I keep tellin' him! He don't listen," Abraham replied, referring to the captain.

Henry was not as bothered by the news because he had come to expect such circumstances. "That captain ain't nothin' but a Mister Charlie. Y'all are fools for even trying to reason with him," he replied as they walked. "I'm a bigger fool for stickin' with you fools. Shoulda caught a boat back to Louisville."

Their mood was sour as they descended into the hold, and they continued to squabble about the captain. His shortcomings had become one of their favorite topics of discussion.

"He also wants us each to start double cleanup shifts before we leave this port," Abraham said as he approached the room.

"What for?" Willie asked with disdain. "If you clean it once, why you gotta clean it again?"

As they trudged into their quarters, the conversation was interrupted by Walt's voice, booming like a ringmaster. "Gentlemen!" he greeted them with outstretched hands.

"Oh no!" Henry lamented as the other men shuffled through the door, excited to hear what Walt had to say.

"Oh yes indeed!" Walt replied. "I told y'all I had a plan to see Sly, didn't I? Tested and proven!"

He directed their attention to his left where Johnson stood, dressed in a server's uniform. Johnson still wasn't completely sold on the idea, though they had walked right through some of the main corridors past guests and even a white crew member. He was certain the dirt and nervous look in his eyes would make it obvious that he didn't belong. He felt even more uncomfortable now as the other men stared at him on display.

"So, we show up to the card game like we supposed to be serving drinks?" James asked, scratching at his rusty patch of sideburns.

"Just walk right up," Walt replied, motioning with his fingers. "Who'll know the difference?"

Standing in the back, Abraham crossed his arms.

"This a bad idea," Henry said, moving closer to examine Johnson. He brought his face close to the breast pocket of the vest and sniffed. "Where you gonna get all them uniforms?"

"He's got a point," replied Willie. "It'll be tough finding enough for all of us."

"Don't worry," Walt assured them, "I'm in good with some of the laundry gals."

"*Hah!* We'll see about that," Henry laughed. "Last I heard Mary ain't been too keen on you calling on her girls."

Walt's demeanor suddenly turned surly. "Well, I guess your hearin' ain't too good then."

"My hearing's fine, and I'll tell you right now only a fool would come up with this."

"It's not a bad idea," James replied, drawing a grin from Walt, "but he's right; it's no real plan neither."

Walt's grin faded as quickly as it had appeared. "What does he know?" he replied, chest thrust outward. "He's just an old man!"

"Better watch what you say to me!" Henry snapped, throwing a finger in his direction.

"You won't do nothin'!"

Quicker than any of them thought was possible, Henry leapt at Walt, throwing all of his body weight forward and knocking Johnson over the table as he violently grabbed Walt's throat. Johnson tumbled into Willie, sending both of them to the floor as Walt and Henry tussled in the cramped quarters. As quickly as the fight started, Abraham and James intervened, each man holding back one of the combatants.

"Alright, alright, that's enough!" Abraham yelled, doing his best to hold on to Henry's right arm while he flung his left in Walt's direction.

Johnson scrambled to his feet and helped Willie up. The boy tried to grab Henry's other arm, to no avail.

"Boy's gotta learn some respect somehow!" Henry yelled.

"It ain't worth it," Abraham replied. "You're twice his age."

"And twice his mettle!" he yelled, struggling to break free. "I don't need ta take no shit from the house nigger!"

A chill went through the air that tempered the mood. Everyone went silent.

"C'mon, we don't need that," Abraham chided him.

Walt stopped struggling against James but said nothing. Instead, he straightened his uniform and gave Henry a taunting, cynical smile.

"*Humpf*," Henry exhaled heavily.

"So should I inquire about a uniform in your size then?" Walt asked him.

"No, you have your fun," Henry retorted, catching his breath. "I think I'll just stay put and laugh when this all falls apart." He ripped his arm from Abraham's grip and stepped away from the group.

"Can ya really get more, or is this gonna be like your last plan?" Willie asked. "'Cause I'm too tall for what he's got," he said, tugging at Johnson's pants.

Johnson brushed at the smudge of dirt where Willie had grabbed him. They weren't his clothes, but it was nice to be wearing something clean for once, and it annoyed him that Willie had dirtied them so carelessly.

"Ya just gotta trust me," Walt said, heading for the door.

"We've heard that before," James yelled after him as he disappeared.

"Fool," Henry snorted, taking a seat and popping open the clay jug of whiskey he'd bought in town.

"The St. Louis plan worked alright," Willie said in a hopeful tone.

"Yeah, well, that was a while ago now," James replied.

Walt had a long history of scheming. His plans tended to be fueled early on by excitement, but as he hit barriers during preparation, that excitement often waned and led him to cut corners when it came to the execution. As it was, this plan was particularly sensitive because it involved defying the captain's "colored rules," something they had yet to challenge in the way he was suggesting.

Abraham paced slowly across the room like a general examining his troops. "You know I don't really like the idea of you goin' along with his plans," he said with his hand to his chin, almost as if he were thinking out loud rather than talking to them. "But I ain't gonna stop ya neither. If ya wanna see Sylvester Roy play that bad, it's your ass if you're caught."

"Well, I'd do worse ta see Sly play," Willie said, falling into his bunk with a hopeful smile.

"That's on you," Abraham replied. "I'm jus' tryin' ta get back home ta see my boy quick as possible."

"Shouldn't we get to those double shifts?" James asked, noticing how everyone seemed to be settled in.

"If the captain can take on extra passengers, I expect we can take a couple of extra hours to skip a little cleanup," Abraham replied. Picking up the newspaper from the floor, he walked over to Johnson. "Here."

Johnson grabbed it from him. Poring over its pages, he searched for any information about wanted men, fugitives, or recent crimes. To his relief, he found nothing related to Saint Andrews, but when he glanced up, he realized that every man in the room was staring at him curiously. Had he given himself away looking through the images of wanted men? The warm sense of camaraderie he'd started to feel with the men was replaced by a sudden rush of fear as James pointed a finger at him.

"Can you actually read that?" James asked him, eyes wide in surprise.

"Yeah," Johnson replied with nervous relief.

"Damn, really?" Willie sat up on his bunk excitedly. "How'd ya learn?"

Finding someone who could read who wasn't some kind of boss or rich man was scarce enough, let alone a poor working black man like him, and in the moment, Johnson realized how much he'd taken the ability for granted. The other men waited expectantly for his answer.

"My mother was a schoolteacher," he replied, hoping they wouldn't inquire any further.

"My daddy was a sharecropper, so I didn't get any schooling. Too busy helpin' in the fields," Willie said.

James came over and sat down next to Johnson on his bunk. "How do ya do it?" he asked intently. "Is it hard?"

Uncomfortable with his proximity, Johnson leaned away from him. "I dunno. I just do."

They all fell silent for a moment, mostly disappointed with the answer.

Sitting deep in his chair, Henry corked his jug and set it on the ground. "Well, go on," he said. "Read us something."

Johnson was surprised by the request. He hadn't expected to be put on the spot. Rarely did he read aloud, and he found it even more difficult with an audience and such dim lighting. With all the men's faces staring at him, his face grew warm.

"What should I read?" he asked.

"Whatever's on the front page," Abraham replied. "That's the most important, right?"

Johnson turned the pages back to the front.

"What's that say?" James pointed his finger at the main headline in bold text—"White League Riot!"

Johnson scowled. "Maybe I should read somethin' else in here."

"Nah! Skip that boring shit," James said. "You got to read us the big news."

All the men leaned in with interest.

"Alright, here goes," Johnson replied. Clearing his throat, he squinted. "Um, eleven dead and sixty wounded in a clash between the White League and the New Orleans Metropolitan Police force for control of the city." He read slowly to avoid any embarrassing mistakes, carefully enunciating each word.

"We already *heard* about that when we went into the city," Henry said unenthused. "Read something we didn't hear."

Carefully skimming down the article, Johnson came to a passage that caught his attention. "Alright, listen to this: 'Therefore, we enter into and found this White League for the protection of our own race against the daily increasing encroachment of the negro. You know that before the emancipation of the colored race we occupied toward them a patriarchal relation. The negros should receive the protecting care of those who were formerly his masters. I tell you my countrymen, the truest and best friend the negro ever had, or ever will have, were once their masters and owners. Left to himself, he will become a savage and an idolater.'"

"*Piiiisshhh!*" Henry said. "That's some Mister Charlie horseshit."

"Ain't that something?" said James leaning back.

"Abe, what kinda rag you buy him?" Henry asked.

"Like any other paper would say different?" Abraham said.

"There's gotta be a black paper in town," Henry said.

"He asked for a newspaper, not a church bulletin," Abraham replied.

Each of them was dissatisfied with the article, and for a moment, it reminded Johnson about the policeman he had seen get on the boat earlier in the day. He felt uneasy.

"White League," Johnson said, rereading the headline. "I'm not sure if New Orleans is the place for me."

"Oh, it ain't *that* bad," Abraham reassured him. "There's plenty of black folks. They just trying to make those whites feel more comfortable. No different from any other town."

"There ain't no town out there that's really good for us," Henry said.

"You know what I mean," Abraham replied, "just gotta know the rules."

"Right," Johnson replied skeptically.

"Kid, don't worry about what the papers say is going on in New Orleans. There's far worse places to avoid going just by their name," Henry said with a laugh. "Now Lynchburg, *uh-uh*," he said, shaking his head. "A negro don't wanna get caught in *no* town called Lynchburg."

They all had a quick laugh.

Despite making light of the situation, Johnson wondered if going all the way to New Orleans was his best option. The paper hadn't said anything about him, but he knew that didn't mean he was safe. Plenty of wanted men didn't make it into the news, just the *most* wanted. Though it was good to know he wasn't there just yet.

"Readin', damn," Willie said with wonder, still amazed at the skill. "Would it be hard ta teach us?"

"I ..." Johnson trailed off. He wouldn't have known where to start and really didn't want to anyway.

"Is there some kinda trick to it?" James pressed him.

"Ya gotta know your letters," Abraham said to James with a smile. "Maybe Ms. Stride will let ya take up some lessons next time you visit her."

James pursed his lips. "I can't learn from a whore, even if she is a madam."

"Why not?"

"What would I tell my wife?" James asked. "That I'd been goin' to school?"

"Ya don't have ta poke any whores," Abraham replied.

"Like she'd believe that."

"Why not?"

"You don't have a wife; you wouldn't understand. Besides, why would you go to a whorehouse and leave the whores alone? Not for reading."

"Well, I ain't too worried about reading," Henry spoke up. "I made it this long and haven't needed it. Ain't like it's life or death. Nobody I knew who couldn't read died any sooner because of it."

"Maybe if you could read you wouldn't be here," James responded. "Way I see it, anything that helps me get ahead is worth it."

The men sat and talked about other topics and drank for the next few hours into the night. Eventually, Johnson found some more pleasant articles in the paper and kept reading to the men. Henry passed out, sitting in his chair, the whiskey jug in his lap. Abraham listened, lying back on his bunk, relaxing with one foot hanging off the side while Willie and James played a game in which they tried to bounce corks off the table and into a bowl. Willie was about to throw his last cork when they all heard footsteps from down the hall.

Johnson stopped reading and Willie's cork badly missed, rolling under one of the beds. A young white man dressed in a sailor's uniform entered the room. Tension filled the space, and every member of the crew stiffened with his presence, save Henry, who remained asleep in his chair.

"*Er-hem*," he nervously cleared his throat. "Captain wants to know the status of the cleanup," he said slowly examining the room. He seemed even younger as he talked. Johnson guessed he was probably close to Willie's age.

Abraham sat up. "You can tell him he ain't got nothin' ta worry about. Cleanup is goin' just fine."

"Certainly," he replied with a rigid nod. "I'll let him know." He promptly turned and left the room, obviously eager to leave as soon as he could.

"Well, looks like we'd better do some extra-good cleaning tomorrow," Abraham said, lying back down.

Henry snorted loudly but didn't wake.

Chapter 13

Johnson turned away and coughed as a fresh supply of coal fell down the shoot and stirred up a plume of black soot. He did his best to wave the cloud away and shoveled the coal into a pile closer to the burner.

"Goddammit, this ain't in no good shape." Abraham cussed as he adjusted the pressure on the boiler. "If the captain thinks he can keep this up much longer, he's crazy."

"What'll happen if it ain't fixed?" Johnson asked, taking the opportunity to give his back a rest. He walked over to where Abraham was adjusting a large valve with a wrench.

"Well, you're feedin' that fire to boil all this water," Abraham replied. The metal clanged loudly as he tapped the side of the boiler with the wrench. "That turns it to steam pressure for the big wheel." He pointed to the main steam line that led to the giant crank arm and the other different copper lines leading off separate valves throughout the entire boat. "If the pressure ain't properly maintained, we got a problem."

"What kinda problem?" Johnson asked.

"Let's just say when we get ta Memphis, you'd better get comfortable with bein' there," Abraham replied. "If this don't get a real fix, we're all in trouble." He took a seat and exhaled deeply. "Wish I could be back with my son instead of dealin' with this piece of junk."

Johnson didn't like the sound of that. He had no intention of getting stuck in any one place for too long, not in the South, anyway. He had already decided that as soon as they arrived in New Orleans, he was going to get passage on a boat that would take him to Galveston, Texas. He hadn't forgotten the advice Jimmy Perkins had given him the night he'd left—go west. Johnson didn't know much about Texas or how far

Galveston was, but he knew it was in the West, where there were fewer people likely to be looking for him.

At the end of his shift, Johnson tried to wash as much excess dirt from his face as he could. It was the night of the poker tournament, and he was still uneasy about the plan. Excited as he was to see Sylvester Roy and to experience a real high-stakes poker game, he knew they would be surrounded by unwelcoming bodies.

Later that evening, James, Willie, and Johnson met Walt in a service closet on the main deck just outside of the gambling hall. True to his word, Henry wanted nothing to do with the plan and stayed in their quarters drinking whiskey. Abraham had agreed to work James's shift for him. Even if he had wanted to take part, he was too recognizable a figure on the boat to try and pass as one of the service staff. It didn't bother him to miss out; he had seen Sylvester Roy play in New Orleans several times and would be satisfied with hearing the news of his success in the tournament.

As it turned out, the uniform Johnson had worn was the only one Walt was able to get, which meant that two of them would have to take turns waiting in the closet while the third went out to watch the game.

"Y'all just have to share," Walt said to them. At least he had brought in some chairs and candles for whomever waited in the storage closet.

"I knew it," James replied.

"It's probably better this way, anyway," Walt reassured them. "Just take your turns. You'll be fine."

"There's no way I won't stick out with my trousers ridin' up like this," Willie bemoaned as he pulled on the pants. A good six inches of his lower leg showed beneath the hem.

"No one will be payin' you any attention," Walt replied. "They only give a shit about the cards."

"You always pull this kinda half-assed shit," James said. "How're we supposed to trust you?"

"Way I see it, you boys owe me for this one," Walt replied. "I let Jo deal tonight so I could tend bar. That way I can help y'all."

"Bet you're still getting a cut of his tips, though," James replied.

"So what if I am?" Walt said. "We all wanna see Sly and *I'm* the one makin' it happen. Are you in or not?"

"Yeah," Willie replied.

Johnson nodded.

"I guess I'm in," James said, looking around the dim, candlelit room where they'd gathered. Its shelves were filled with extra linens and table settings for the ballroom.

"Alright then, here's the plan," Walt said, glancing at each of them. "I'll be behind the bar. Most guests come up and order drinks, but the players get theirs delivered. That's your job. Each of ya will get to take drinks right up to the table where you can stay and watch for a bit, but ya can't linger too long. Got it?"

They smiled and began to get excited. Suddenly the plan didn't sound so reckless. They would be able to get right up to the table, and no one would think anything amiss.

"OK, I'll give it to you," James said. "This is a pretty decent plan after all."

"What did I tell ya?" Willie said, slipping the vest over his shoulders and buttoning it up. "He knows what he's doin'."

Walt grinned big and motioned for Willie to follow him out the door. "You two wait here and I'll send him back in about an hour."

As Johnson and James waited in the storage room, their excitement turned to impatience. Neither of them had any means of keeping time, and with each moment they were certain an hour had passed long ago. They spoke little as they waited, except to comment on how much time they thought had passed. When Willie finally returned, he was brimming with enthusiasm.

"The man is somethin' else!" Willie said to them excitedly as he took off the server's vest. "Even their best players can't keep up."

"What are they playing?" James asked as he helped him take off the shirt.

"Stud," Willie said as he stepped out of the pants.

"Five or seven?"

"Five, one in the hole," Willie said. "I'll tell ya, what a game!"

Johnson was confused. He hadn't realized that there were different kinds of poker and was lost by their phrasing.

"Look, I'll go next," James said, quickly pulling on the pants and throwing the vest around his shoulders. "He can stay here and explain."

James buttoned the vest and scrambled out the door, tucking in the shirt as he moved down the hallway. Willie, still high with excitement, paced around the small room for several minutes, talking about how great Sylvester Roy was. Using terms Johnson only understood somewhat, the boy gave him a play-by-play of each hand. Eventually, Johnson was able to sit him down and have him explain the difference in the rules. He was intrigued that the first card dealt was facedown while the rest were shown.

"Wouldn't that make it easier for the other players?" he asked.

"Nah, it's all even. They see what you got, you see what they got, and there's no tradin'," Willie replied. "That's why ya gotta be good, and Sly is good."

"Must be why they call him Sly."

"Exactly, the man gets it all. Money, clothes, women." Willie added, "Who doesn't want all that?"

Johnson had to agree, though more and more it was looking like a prospect he would never see. He still felt lucky to have gotten out of Saint Andrews alive, let alone to be working hard, shoveling coal on a luxury steamer. Once it was his turn to see Sly play, he decided he would enjoy every moment. He deserved it. Sly's luck ran better than most, and it was like watching him play for those who would never become anything. It felt like he played for every black man.

When James came back, he was just as excited as Willie had been. "You're lucky Walt is keeping track," he said. "He damn near had to drag me out of there, or else I would have stayed all night."

Johnson dressed and left the room. He was astonished when he entered the gambling hall. All the windows were stained in dark glass, creating images of playing cards, dice, and roulette tables. The floor was carpeted with colorful, intricate patterns, and the ceilings were lined with beautiful chandeliers that lit the room so perfectly that it was impossible to tell the time of day. At each end was a balcony and in the center of the room was the main table. Smoke from cigars and cigarettes filled the air along with lively chatter and the sound of glasses clinking together. Every man and woman were dressed in their most elegant garb.

Walt was mixing a drink at the bar, which sat under the nearest balcony. At first, Johnson moved carefully, nervous about looking out of place since he was the third server in as many hours. But he quickly realized that Walt was right: No one seemed to notice his presence. Almost everyone in the hall was focused on the main table, watching as each card was dealt. Even in the balcony, men and women leaned far over the railings trying to get a better glimpse of the game.

"You're just in time. One of the players just ordered a drink," Walt said as Johnson walked up. Walt stirred the cocktail with one hand while wiping the bar with the other. "Take this up to the table, grab the empty glass, then stand back and watch a few hands. But don't stay too long."

Before Johnson had time to say anything, Walt handed him the drink on a tray and urged him to leave. Johnson tried to protest: Walt hadn't told him who ordered the drink.

"Just take it!" Walt said, whipping a bar rag in his direction.

Johnson reluctantly turned away, anxious about how foolish it would look not knowing where to deliver the drink. He made his presence known and was surprised by how willingly people parted so that he could reach the table. As he moved through the crowd, the spectators reacted to something, clapping and even cheering.

"It was a good play," a voice said.

Sly sat across the table across from Jo, the dealer Walt had switched jobs with. Sly was in a lively mood, wearing a wine-colored suit jacket with tan pants and a black vest. He had a joyous presence that seemed to excite everyone around him.

Smiling big as Johnson walked up, Sly motioned to him. "Looks like you've got Officer Birchman's drink there."

Sly pointed to his left. Johnson looked and realized that Sly was referring to the police officer with the large nose who had boarded the boat two days earlier. The man raised his hand in acknowledgment but was so focused on his cards that he didn't look up to see who delivered his drink. Johnson set the cocktail down next to him, carefully taking the empty glass as Walt had instructed.

"I thank you, sir," Sly said to him, "and if ya don't mind, I would like another one of these myself." He shook his glass and the half-melted ice cubes rattled around the bottom.

"Absolutely," Johnson said with nervous excitement, turning back toward the bar.

There was a sudden gasp from everyone who was watching the game, but Johnson didn't turn back. He intended to get Sly his drink as quickly as possible.

"Sly wants another," Johnson said in response to Walt's questioning look.

Walt nodded and set a glass on the bar. He turned to grab a bottle of rye from the ornate wooden shelf behind him. Filling the bottom of the glass with ice, he poured the whiskey over it then added a dash of bitters. In the mirror behind the bar, Johnson saw people pushing closer to the table, and he worried he might have missed something important.

"Here, go," Walt said, quickly handing him the drink.

The sudden change in the game made the crowd less willing to allow him in, so he had to push his way through, careful not to spill anything. As he got closer, he heard Sly talking to the other players.

"Look at him, do you think he's not gonna raise? He'll raise, so I'll go ahead and make it harder for him: three hundred."

"Five hundred to stay," Johnson heard the dealer say as he reached the table.

"Fold," Birchman replied, pushing his cards forward in frustration.

"You were too easy!" Sly said with a laugh. "You had a pair, I had nothing," he said, flipping over his hole card—the three of diamonds.

The room erupted in applause.

"Ain't over yet, folks," Sly replied, almost scolding them. "Ah, my drink. Thank you, sir," he said, handing Johnson his empty glass and a tip.

Johnson lit up. He hadn't even considered that he would make any money. Standing back to watch the next deal, he glanced at Birchman, who remained completely focused on the game. He watched the faces of the other two players, both absorbed in their cards. Only Sly seemed to be enjoying himself as he interacted with everyone around him, feeding off their energy.

"Brother, watch this," he said leaning back to Johnson as he was dealt the two of clubs.

Birchman was given the nine of diamonds, and the other two players the three and ten of clubs.

"The bring in is twenty to Mr. Roy," said Jo.

Sly lightly placed his chips in front of him and grinned at Jo.

"Your bet, Mr. Poole."

"Fifty."

"Too low, too low," Sly replied, "raise you one hundred."

Saying nothing, Birchman threw in his chips to call.

"Mr. Logan?"

"I'll call."

"Me too," replied Poole.

"Third street," Jo replied, "the five of spades to Mr. Birchman, the king of clubs to Mr. Logan, the jack of diamonds to Mr. Poole, and the three of spades to Mr. Roy. The bet is to Mr. Logan with the king."

"Two hundred."

"Raise one hundred," Poole quickly replied.

Sly sat back and stroked his thin goatee, looking at Poole's hand. "Jack of diamonds is a dangerous card," he said, touching his chips. "Fold."

Whispers rang out from the crowd. Birchman folded as well, and Mr. Poole bought the pot on the next round.

Flipping over his hole card after the play, Sly revealed he'd had a pair of twos. "Don't worry; we'll get 'em next time," he smiled.

The more hands Johnson watched, the better he understood the game. Now he realized why this kind of poker was better suited to spectators. It allowed everyone to follow the action of each play and created a much more entertaining environment as the crowd reacted to the turn of each card. When he finally made his way back to the bar, he felt more at ease. The police officer was the one person he'd been worried about, and he was completely occupied by the game. Johnson could stand back and enjoy without having to worry.

"You took a little too long," Walt said as he walked up. "Watch it."

"Sorry," he replied, "I just lost track."

"Yeah, well, you don't wanna lose more than that."

Walt handed him another drink and Johnson went back into the crowd.

———

Abraham quickly threw a scoop of coal into the burner then leaned the shovel against the coal shoot. Yawning, he rubbed his face and stretched his arms as he sauntered over to check the main gauge. The boiler pressure was high, but that was normal for its condition, and with the way the captain insisted on running the engine, Abraham didn't expect that condition to change anytime soon. He was worn out from the extra hours, and as he was about to sit down for a break, he heard a high-pitched hissing sound. Concerned that they had blown a seal in one of the valves, he cursed the captain. He stomped around the corner but stopped short as hot steam jetted out of a broken pipe. Before Abraham could scramble away, another pipe exploded, shooting a rivet into the side of his head and killing him instantly.

Pressure continued to build with no one to maintain the boiler.

———

"Officer, it is still to you," Jo said to Birchman, who had the seven of diamonds, king of clubs, and four of clubs showing.

Birchman sat for a moment, spinning his facedown card, "Check."

"The check is to you, Mr. Logan."

Logan showed six, queen, and seven, all of hearts. At first, Johnson thought the flush would be highly improbable, but looking at all the other hands, he realized that there were no other hearts showing. Assuming his hidden card was hearts wasn't bad odds.

"I'll check as well," Logan replied.

"One hundred," Poole said before Jo could address him.

His hand seemed the least impressive to Johnson—ten of spades, queen of clubs, five of diamonds. Sly, on the other hand, appeared to be one card away from a possible straight, holding the seven of clubs and the eight and nine of spades.

He grinned, took a drink, then shaking a finger, threw in his chips to call. "This is too good not to try it," he said, turning to Birchman. "I know you'd try it."

Birchman scowled and threw in his chips. "I'll see it." He rubbed his big nose.

Whispers traveled in pockets around the room. Unless he was hiding another king, it was a clearly brash move. It reminded Johnson of when Walt had goaded him into a poor bet.

"Well, we've made it this far," Logan replied, "let's see it. One hundred."

"I like your attitude," Sly said, slapping the table. "You two should take lessons accordingly." He sat back, meeting the eyes of his other two opponents.

"How about we just see the next card," Birchman said to the dealer with an impatient tone.

"Certainly, fifth street," Jo replied dealing the cards. "The seven of spades to Mr. Birchman to make a pair of sevens showing."

The crowd began to talk a little louder, curious to see what card would be dealt to Logan, wondering if he could draw another heart. As Jo flipped the card, everyone gasped when they saw red, but their excitement turned to disappointment.

"The jack of diamonds to Mr. Logan."

Logan sank down in his chair, visibly defeated.

"Five of spades for Mr. Poole."

Poole smiled. The five gave him a pair. Though it was still weaker than Officer Birchman's pair of sevens, he seemed confident that he held the upper hand. Sly smiled, too—right at Mr. Poole.

"The ten of diamonds to give Mr. Roy a possible straight."

Loud chatter rose from the crowd. Johnson couldn't believe it. Seven, eight, nine, ten. Could he have it? Most of the crowd seemed to think it impossible. His hidden card needed to be a jack or a six and there was one of each already on the table.

"Now this is interesting," Sly said joyfully. "I have to say I really didn't expect this."

"Keep bluffing," replied Birchman.

"It's to you, sir," Jo responded to him.

"Five hundred," Birchman said, throwing down his chips.

"Wonderful, he's got some brass balls after all," Sly said, drawing laughter from some in the crowd.

To no one's surprise, Logan folded. Piling his cards, he slunk back, defeated.

"I'll raise you two hundred," Mr. Poole said staring at Birchman as he pushed his chips to the middle of the table.

"Seven hundred?" Sly asked over the noise of the crowd. "Seven hundred is a lot."

"You can always fold," Poole replied, stone-faced.

"I said it was a lot, didn't say it was enough," Sly responded. "I'll raise you another two hundred." He turned and shot a smile to the people around him then to officer Birchman, who silently rubbed his nose.

"The bet is now nine hundred," Jo said to Birchman.

"You don't have it," Birchman said to Sly. He stared at his hidden card. "I'll raise you another five hundred."

Jo turned to Mr. Poole, "It is another seven hundred for you to stay."

Taking another peek at his hidden card, Poole pulled the chips from his stack, setting them neatly in the middle. "I'll play."

"All in," Sly said without hesitation.

This time, the crowd erupted with excited cheers, and some men even started making bets among themselves about whether Sly really had the straight or not.

"I still say you're bluffing," Birchman replied. "All in."

More excitement from the crowd.

Something in Mr. Poole's eyes changed. Having played the entire night without betraying any insight into his thoughts, he looked less confident, and Birchman, Sly, and everyone watching knew it. His hand hovered over his stack of chips; he paused, then he wavered.

"Fold," he said with a great exhale, turning over his cards.

All eyes focused on Sly, who appeared calm as ever, taking a sip from his glass.

"Mr. Roy, it is you to show."

"Oh—right," he replied as if he had lost track of what was going on.

It felt as if the whole place might explode in anticipation. A jack or a six—Johnson could visualize the cards Sly needed so clearly. He stood there, heart racing, nervous and tense, and in that moment nothing else mattered to him. He wanted Sly to win so badly. It was a high of excitement that only could be satisfied fully with the winning card.

Rubbing the side of his chin, Sly stared at Birchman. Stretching out his hand, he turned over his card—the ten of clubs.

Everyone went quiet. It was like the air had been sucked out of the room. He didn't have the straight! Johnson's heart sank. There was a lull among the crowd, and it took a moment for everyone to realize what Sly did have—a pair of tens!

"No!" Birchman yelled as he flipped his card and slammed it face up onto the table.

"Mr. Birchman has a pair of sevens ace high. Mr. Roy wins it with the pair of tens!" Jo announced loudly.

The whole room cheered and clapped. Even those who had lost their side bets were awed. It was a masterful performance. Sly had played it brilliantly all the way, convincing one player he had the straight and another that he was bluffing. Johnson was elated.

"Thank you, ladies and gentlemen, but we still have two opponents remaining," Sly reminded them as Birchman angrily stood and walked away.

Everyone toasted each other to celebrate such an entertaining game, and normal conversation began to drown out Jo as he called the next deal. After a long night, the crowd realized the most exciting moment of the game had passed and lost interest in the three remaining players. Intent on watching the conclusion of the game, Johnson was annoyed as the movement of the crowd obstructed his view. He tried to move closer to the table but was pulled back.

"Johnson!" Walt yelled angrily, tugging on the back of his vest.

Johnson turned with an innocent look on his face, but it was no use. Walt dragged him toward the door.

"I told you not to linger!" Walt scolded him.

"I just wanted to watch the game."

"Well, one of the passengers complained you was blockin' his view," Walt said. "Now he wants an apology. You're lucky it ain't worse!"

"Wait, what?" Johnson started to sweat. "No, no! I can't!" he begged as they approached the door.

"You have to or we're all gonna get it," Walt replied. "Do you want him to go to the captain?"

Walt opened the door and pushed Johnson into the hallway, shutting the door behind him before he could protest further. The gas lamps that lit the corridors were dim compared to the chandeliers in the gambling hall, and it took a moment for Johnson's eyes to adjust.

"Mr. Johnson, correct?" said the man leaning against the railing. "You joined the crew in Saint Andrews?"

He lit a cigar revealing his clean-shaven face and the outline of his short top hat. Blowing a large puff of smoke, the man stepped into the light, and Johnson instantly recognized his green coat. It was the man he and Walt had passed while they were testing the server's uniform. Johnson cursed himself.

"Well?" the man asked. "No use in lying; your friend already confirmed it for me."

"What do you want?" he asked.

"Don't play dumb," the man said. Holding open his coat he revealed a Pinkerton's badge. "You're coming with me."

Johnson moved to strike him but stopped short when the barrel of a revolver was shoved into his face.

"Do not test me," he said, pulling back the hammer and motioning him down the hall. Johnson stepped in front of him and raised his hands. "Put your hands down. I'm not trying to make a scene."

As soon as he said it, two crewmates came running down the nearest stairway straight toward them. Johnson and the man in the green coat jumped out of the way as they darted past and dashed into the gambling hall. *Boom!*

The explosion rattled the windows and Johnson and the other man crouched as it shook the whole boat. A moment of stillness followed. The boat had stopped moving. Trying to understand what had just happened, they slowly got to their feet, then the doors of the hall burst open and the guests streamed out in a frenzy. In the commotion, Johnson grabbed the man's gun, and they wrestled for control. A hysterical passenger knocked into them, and Johnson fell against the railing. His right arm hung over the side, holding him up while his left hand still grasped the man's wrist as he held the gun.

Johnson glanced down at the river below. His left arm shook with fatigue while his right tried to gain a better grip on the railing to keep him from being pushed to the ground. The man grabbed Johnson with his other hand and pulled the gun toward his head. Johnson tried to kick the man but couldn't find leverage to strike back. Looking out over the edge of the boat, he noticed an orange glow reflecting over the water. Then came a push. Johnson fell backward onto the floor and heard a splash. When he realized what had happened, Walt was helping him to his feet.

"C'mon!" Walt yelled, "We gotta get off this boat!"

Walt ran toward the bow and Johnson did his best to keep up as screaming passengers scrambled into the corridor. Smoke surrounded them, adding to the chaos, worsening visibility, and making it harder to breath. Diving into an entryway, Walt flung open the door. They ran across a large empty room, ripping the door open on the other side and nearly colliding with Willie.

"Where's James?" Walt asked him.

"Dunno," Willie replied. "He ran one way; I went the other."

Walt looked out at the riverbank. "We gotta jump."

"I don't swim too good," Willie said apprehensively.

"You probably don't burn too good, neither," Walt replied. "You think these white folks are gonna save you a buoy?"

Johnson walked to the railing. The screams of men and women scrambling to escape surrounded them. He took hold of the nearest column and climbed on top of the rail. It wasn't a long drop, but the water was dark and unsettled. It was still a better alternative than burning to death. He looked back at Walt and Willie. Taking a deep breath, Johnson leapt off.

Chapter 14

Johnson dragged himself up the muddy bank, collapsing onto his back and coughing between heavy breaths. As he looked across the water at the riverboat, flames raged from its smokestacks, illuminating the night. "*Queen Bellamy*," painted on its side in bold red and white letters so that all could recognize this grand example of maritime achievement, burned. Smoke billowed as passengers continued to scramble to escape, many of them leaping into the water as he had.

Johnson slowly stood up as he caught his breath. He discarded his wet vest to relieve himself of its extra weight and walked along the bank in search of Walt or Willie. As he walked, he called their names. The voices of passengers who had managed to safely board the lifeboats and those who had abandoned ship, floating on whatever they could find, echoed back and forth. The burning riverboat continued to float downstream, shrinking until it became nothing more than an orange glow in the distance and eventually disappeared around a bend. Eventually, the yells of the passengers dropped off until the only voice resounding through the night air was Johnson's.

After a few hours of scrambling over rocks and around trees, he finally found Walt unconscious in a patch of tall grass. He tried to wake him but received only a heavy groan in response. It was good enough for Johnson, who sat down next to his sleeping companion and stared out over the dark water. At least he wouldn't be alone.

Arkansas
April 1876

During the few weeks after escaping the *Queen Bellamy*, Walt and Johnson traveled through Arkansas from town to town, scrounging and begging for odd jobs to survive. Walt always had a scheme up his sleeve, but as time went on, their options grew scarce. The longer their stomachs stayed empty, the more desperate his ideas became.

"Wasn't able to find another one, but I found this," Walt said as he handed Johnson a branch in the shape of a revolver.

Johnson scowled. "What am I supposed to do with this? It doesn't even point straight!"

"Just put it under your shirt like ya don't want nobody to see," Walt replied. "It'll be fine, I have mine." He waved the rusty cap-and-ball revolver he'd dug out of an old wagon the day before. They didn't have any ammo for it, but it probably wouldn't have fired even if they had. "You'll just be the lookout anyway."

This was Walt's most ambitious plan yet, but it was so hurriedly planned that if it hadn't been for the burning hunger in Johnson's gut, he wouldn't have gone along with it. The lonely little mining camp had only a bank and a general store with a small bar attached to it. Since there was no jail or marshal, Walt surmised they could run in, rob the bank, and then escape into the woods, where it would be hard for anyone to find them.

Walt explained the operation while drawing a crude map in the dirt. "We put our masks on and sneak up from the back, so nobody sees us," he said, pointing at the square representing the bank. "You stand by the door and I'll go in and get the money."

"I don't like this."

"Don't worry, it'll be quick," Walt reassured him. "In and out."

"What if someone shows up with a real gun?" Johnson asked.

"Tell me and point yours at 'em."

"I'm not tryin' ta get shot!"

"No one 'round here is gonna come. Ain't no law."

"But what if someone—"

"Then tell me about it and *you* can go ahead an' run off ta leave me there!" Walt replied with heavy sarcasm. "Now let's hurry, we already wastin' time."

As they left the cover of the forest, Johnson was relieved to find the camp mostly empty. Other than a few shacks with smoke coming out of their chimneys, there was no sign that anyone was around. Masked in strips of burlap tied around their noses and mouths, they carefully snuck around to the front of the bank and scrambled up the porch. In a rush of adrenaline, Walt took hold of the handle and tried to throw open the door, but the door didn't budge. Again, he tried shaking the handle and throwing his shoulder into the door.

"The bank's closed!" Johnson yelled, pointing to a sign in the window. Pulling off his mask, he stopped Walt from making a bigger scene.

"How was I supposed to know that?" Walt asked, taking off his mask and shoving it down his shirt. "Why would a bank be closed during the day?"

"I don't know," Johnson replied. "What day is it?"

"Monday," Walt replied, biting his lip as he thought about it. "I thought it was Monday."

"Well, it's obviously Sunday or they'd be fuckin' open!" Johnson said, throwing his branch to the ground. "C'mon, let's get out of here before somebody sees us."

Running off, they decided it was best to abandon the plan altogether and keep moving on to the next town.

It was a chilly morning, so they kept a brisk pace to stay warm. A few miles down the road from the camp, they noticed a large white tent that had been pitched in a clearing among the trees. As they got closer, a preacher emerged from a wagon with a wooden roof and walls. Seeing them approach, he became animated, throwing his arms wildly in the air. Bidding them to come closer, he shouted scripture.

"I tell you my colored brethren, you may have been freed by your earthly masters, but the only way you can truly be free from the chains of your sins is through Jesus Christ!" he addressed them as they walked to the tent.

"Says who?" Walt asked, stopping in front of him.

"C'mon, let's go," Johnson said to him, trying to ignore the man.

Holding his Bible high in the air, the preacher orated. "Says so right here in the good book!"

Walt stood there, hands on his hips, and gave him a skeptical look. "Seems like if God's in a book an' I can't read, God just ain't meant for me," he replied, "but Johnson over here reads real good."

"What do you say?" the preacher asked, turning to Johnson with a hopeful glimmer in his eye.

"I'll pass," Johnson replied and continued walking.

Holding out his hands and shrugging at the preacher, Walt turned and followed.

"Just know that the eternal flames await those who do not repent!" he exclaimed to their backs before turning into the tent.

"Hey, ya know somethin'?" Walt asked, catching Johnson before he could get too far. "I bet the preachers got some o' that bread and wine."

"I don't wanna sit through that just for a small bite."

"No, I'm sayin', we just take it," Walt replied excitedly. "He's gotta have plenty in his wagon."

Johnson thought about it for a second. He didn't like the idea of stealing from a preacher, but his stomach groaned at the thought of food. "Alright."

Creeping up to the wagon, they were careful not to make any sudden movements that might draw the preacher's attention as they slid inside. There wasn't much, just a bedroll and a few pots and pans, but in the back, cradled against the wall, Walt found a small cask.

"Think I found the wine," he said, bending over to pick up the cask, but it lifted too easily to contain any liquid. He shook it with disappointment. "Empty."

"Found something," Johnson said. Unfolding a cloth lining a small basket, he revealed a few pieces of hardtack. "Let's go." Grabbing the basket, they climbed out of the wagon.

"You bastards!" the preacher yelled as he exited the tent and saw them running into the woods. Pulling out a revolver, he wildly fired two shots in their direction.

"We're sorry!" Johnson yelled over his shoulder, his voice echoing off the trees as he scrambled down into a shallow ravine.

Texas
July 1876

Emmett Siddens wasn't surprised to find another man sitting at the table with his wife when he arrived home after a long day of work for the Texas Central Railway. They were prominent members of the Deep Ellum freedman's community, and his wife regularly invited men to their house who'd recently arrived in the area and were unfamiliar with the local black codes. The Freedman's Bureau had never been reliable, so they had taken it upon themselves to find jobs for those who came to town. Having worked his way up with the railway, he'd earned the favor of the stationmaster, an easterner who had a certain level of sympathy for their cause. His "in" with the stationmaster allowed Emmett to quickly offer a man an unskilled position long enough to avoid being arrested as a vagrant and forced into unpaid labor by the law. Many places in the West offered a black man the freedom of movement he rarely found in the East; Texas was not one of them.

Taking off his hat, he ducked under the doorframe. "A smarter man might worry his woman was being unfaithful to her husband," he said in his deep soothing voice, "bringing in so many strays as such."

Johnson shot up from his chair. "I promise my intentions are honorable."

"Sit down, sir," Hassie Siddens laughed, setting a bowl of stew in front of him. She wore her hair pulled back in a tight bun and her face held a comforting smile. "Emmett knows I'm too old to go finding a new husband. Besides, he's the spittin' image of John Henry; that is, if John Henry had worked on the telegraph lines instead of hammerin' away in some cave."

Smiling, the middle-aged Emmett walked over and gave her a kiss before unbuttoning his plaid vest and draping it over the chair across from Johnson. His hair and mustache held a tinge of gray, and he was so tall his hat would've hit the ceiling if he hadn't removed it. Sitting down with a bowl for himself, he introduced himself to Johnson. "I assume you came here for work?" Emmitt asked, taking a spoon in his hand. "I could get you a job working here for the railway."

It had taken Johnson a little more than a week to ride from Flatridge to Deep Ellum, and during that time, he'd found security in the open prairie. Fewer people meant fewer chances of being found by Cole Charles.

"I was hopin' for a job out on the range," Johnson said.

Emmett paused to take a mouthful of stew.

"Looking to become a buckaroo, huh?" His words were heavy on the vowels. "It's tough work on the plains. I can't offer you anything less demanding, but at least you'd have a roof over your head most nights."

Johnson paused to dip his spoon into the bowl. "It is a generous offer, but mostly I prefer bein' on the move."

"I won't fault you for that," Emmett replied. "Society's ills are far less present on the range. Society is far less present in general. Hard for a man to settle down or have a family."

Johnson slurped at the broth. "Been on my own so often I'm starting to grow accustomed to it."

"It don't have to be that way," Hassie spoke up. "We have a safe community here with a good church. Emmett can get you good work and you won't hardly be bothered."

"Don't want to seem like I'm insultin' your hospitality, but I have no intentions of stayin' here," he replied.

"I understand," said Emmett.

"Do you know where I might find work on a cattle drive?"

Emmett looked at his wife and then finished his bowl. "Yes, you'd have to go to Fort Worth. Only about half a day's ride west of here, but I suggest fording the Trinity River to the north of Dallas to avoid the toll bridge. You don't want to get caught vagrant, and they'd surely stop you for questions there."

"If you would like, you're more than welcome to stay here for the night," Hassie said. "It would be safer for you to leave in the morning anyway."

"I'd appreciate that, ma'am."

"I'll go make up a bed," she said and left the room.

Johnson finished his stew, placed his spoon in the empty bowl, then leaned back in his chair. Emmett looked him over, his eyes darting quickly as if he were reading him like a book. Scooting back from the table, he extended his long legs and rubbed at the soreness in his knees.

"Working on the telegraph lines," he said, "you can't have no fear of falling when you're climbing a pole."

"I would expect not," Johnson replied.

Emmett stood and walked over to a cabinet. He pulled out a bottle of clear liquid. "What I am saying is a man must do what he can to survive, and if he intends to survive, there is no place for fear or doubt."

Johnson rubbed the scruff on the side of his face and considered the older man's words. He was sure that out on the range away from most people was the best way to evade Cole Charles.

Setting the bottle down, Emmett returned to his seat. "Would you like some gin?"

Grinning, Johnson leaned forward and reached for the bottle.

———

Johnson arrived in Fort Worth late afternoon the next day with no trouble. It was an easy ride, but longer than he had expected, and after stabling his horse, he decided to go for a drink. He hoped that he might be able to find someone who could get him onto a cattle drive in one of the local saloons. When he came to the main drag, he was drawn to the first bar he saw; it had a large sign above the door that said "Saloon" in bold letters and "The Well" just below them.

The room wasn't packed, but there were plenty of patrons to keep the place busy. The bartender, a bald man with a thin mustache and a bow tie, wiped his bar after each drink and kept the glasses organized into perfect rows. Lively music rang out as a man pounded the keys of a piano in the back corner, accompanied by a banjo player. Several tables were occupied by groups of men playing cards, and almost as soon as he walked in, Johnson heard laughter erupt from the closest table.

To his surprise, he looked over and found Margret seated there. Her hair was fashioned into a bun and she wore a low-cut dress. She leaned against the man next to her as she laughed, lifting a tall-booted foot into the air and allowing her skirt to ride above her knee. She was the only woman in the saloon, and several men had gathered around the table to watch her.

Margret composed herself. Wiping a tear from her eye, she examined her hand. "I'll take two," she said, sliding her cards into the middle.

"Two fer the lady," the dealer said with a wink.

A smile crossed her face as she received their replacements. "I raise."

"Yer already out of chips, though," the dealer reminded her with a sly smile.

"Oh, I am," she said playfully. Removing a dangling silver earring with a red jewel at its center, she placed it on the pile. "There is my wager, gentlemen."

"I'm in," replied a young man to her left.

"Please," she said, grabbing his arm to stop him, "before we continue, I will need another drink."

"Of course!" He sprang up to go to the bar, pushing some of the other men out of the way.

"Oh, and this time—" she stopped short when she looked toward the door. "Mr. Johnson!" she cried, rising from her chair as she saw him. "Come, sit with me."

The other men turned, curious to see who had caught her attention. She held out her hand, covered in a white glove to the elbow, and led Johnson to a separate empty table. Seeing this, the man getting her drink at the bar curled his lip. He stomped over to their table, set her drink down hard in front of her without saying anything, then returned to his cards.

"What about your hand?" the dealer asked annoyed.

"Just play it and cash me out," she replied, dismissing him with a wave.

Clearly unhappy, the group of men mumbled to each other as the bets continued. Johnson knew they were likely as upset by the color of his skin as they were the loss of Margret's attentions.

Margret folded her hands and laid them on the table. "How have you fared these past weeks, Mr. Johnson?"

"Fine," he said, shooting a nervous glance at the men.

"Is that all you have to say to me?" she asked. "After all we've been through?"

"It is good to see you, I suppose."

"Well, I am glad to see you haven't changed," she replied with heavy sarcasm. "I mean, after having saved your life and all."

Johnson grinned.

"There," she said with a smile, "was that so hard?" Margret took a sip from her glass, tightened her lips, and slowly blew out. "Here," she said to Johnson, pushing him the drink. "I fear I've had too much already, and it would be most unbecoming if I were to end up top-heavy upon our reunion." As she said this, she pulled a small glass bottle with a red flower printed on the label from a deep pocket tied around her waist. She took a sip.

Johnson raised an eyebrow at her and pointed to the bottle. "What's that then?"

Margret returned the bottle to the pocket and patted it. "Oh, it's only laudanum. Nothing but a medicinal drink."

"Medicinal for what?" he asked.

Margret's gaze dropped toward the table. "You know. The ordeal in Flatridge," she said lowering her voice.

Johnson tensed, realizing her discomfort. He decided to change the subject. "Have you been writing?"

Margret lit up. "I have been. How sweet of you to remember," she said, touching his hand.

Warmth coursed through Johnson's body. He smiled at her and took a drink.

A groan arose from the poker table. Margret pulled her hand back and sat up straight, her expression sober. The man dealing the cards walked over to them and set a large stack of chips on their table. "Here," he said, handing her the earring.

"Thank you kindly," she replied, "and I do apologize for not giving you a chance to win it back."

Grunting something under his breath, he sniffed and turned away.

"Here, come with me to the bar so I might cash these," she said to Johnson as she carefully hung the earring in place.

He followed her to the bar, where she handed her winnings to the bald bartender. Then she sipped from the bottle of laudanum again.

"You do look well," Johnson said.

"I struggled for a while but have overcome it," she said, playfully shaking the bottle.

"The medicine helps that much?" he asked.

A tight grin came to her lips. "It gives me a golden feeling. Pushes out the dark thoughts."

The bartender returned, handing her several banknotes and a silver dollar. Johnson ordered a shot and quickly downed it, sliding the glass back down the bar and ordering another.

Counting the money, Margret folded it and stuffed it into her cleavage, leaving the silver dollar as a tip. "I'm sorry, Mr. Johnson, but I do have to be going."

"But I just got here."

"And I was glad to see you," she said, patting his hand, "but I have to see a woman about a story I've been working on."

He raised an eyebrow at her. "All this wasn't part of a story?"

"Heavens no! Can't a lady be allowed to have some fun, too?"

Johnson remembered their previous lesson in assumptions. "I suppose so."

"Will you be in town long? Perhaps we could meet another time?"

He shrugged his shoulders. "I'm not sure. I'm lookin' for work on a cattle drive."

"Well, if you do stay, leave a message for me at the inn." Margret kissed her hand and touched it to Johnson's cheek. Turning to the door, she gave one last enthusiastic farewell to all the men in the saloon and exited.

As soon as Margret left the room, Johnson felt the tension in the air increase. Glares from the other men in the saloon proved how much his presence was detested. No sooner had he finished his second drink than he noticed two figures moving toward him from the corner of his eye. Throwing his money on the bar, he turned to leave before they had a chance to insist. Having only just arrived in Fort Worth, he didn't need any sort of trouble, especially after Emmett's warning about how dangerous it was to be unemployed.

He stepped from the doorway, and in the dry heat a breeze moved across the town. Dusk was approaching quickly, and the streets looked hazy. Heavy dust filled the air and stuck to the beads of sweat that ran from his brow.

Just find a spot outside of town to put down for the night and try again in the mornin', Johnson decided to himself. *No need to take chances.*

It occurred to him that he might find a group of cowboys camped along the river. If that were the case, he wouldn't have to worry about coming back anyway. Satisfied with this plan, he straightened up tall and let himself enjoy the warmth of the small, though not insignificant, amount of liquor he drank at the saloon with Margret. Thinking of her, he smiled and whistled as he walked. If he didn't find work, maybe he could see her again.

As he turned a corner, the metal jingle of spurs accompanied by footsteps caught his ear. His muscles tightened and he picked up his pace.

You shoulda known better goin' into a place like that and gettin' friendly with a white woman, he berated himself. While deep in thought about Margret, he had aimlessly rambled. "Just keep walkin', just *keep* walkin', don't look back," he muttered under his breath.

Now he moved like he had a purpose to avoid drawing any further attention to himself. Left turn down an alley. Right turn past the back door of a shop. He tried to stay calm as the backs of shops and saloons gave way to rundown shacks and storehouses. Coming upon an empty intersection, Johnson paused to listen.

Silence. No one was around.

He slowed his pace again. Only the wind made noise as it blew through the darkening streets.

Maybe they weren't followin' me, he thought, *never hurts to be too careful.*

The steps resumed from down another alley as the spurs struck their violent rhythm even faster. A chill shot through his nerves as he heard the voices.

"I know that negro is 'round here somewhere," shouted a man.

Panic got the better of Johnson. In the dark, he had no idea where he was, and now he was in an area of town with few people. He cursed himself again, this time quite audibly.

"Think I heard somethin' over there!" he heard another man say.

You idiot!

He brushed his jacket away from his gun belt to gauge how quickly he might get to his revolver. Fewer people meant fewer witnesses if things went poorly, and he knew all too well what happened when a black man found himself in the wrong situation with too few witnesses. Especially if those witnesses were white. The steps behind him drew closer; he was out of places to go. He could see the end of the alley opened into an empty clearing.

Then, he realized: *the livery!*

It was just around the corner. It should've been the first place he headed, but Margret and the alcohol kept him from thinking clearly. His heart raced. *Just a few more steps*, he thought to himself. He took a quick half breath and held it as he approached the intersection. Then it came. The jingle. It closed in behind him.

"How ya do, cowpuncher?"

Johnson froze. It wasn't either of the voices he'd heard before. Slowly, he turned and confirmed his suspicion.

"What's the problem?" she asked, half laughing. "Ain't ya never seen a woman before?"

Throughout his entire life, he'd never seen a woman like this. She was a rough sort. Tall with dark brown hair, she wore pants and a single-action Colt .45 hung low from her hip while a tin flask and bowie knife rested high on her belt. If he hadn't heard her talk, he might not have thought she was a woman at all.

"There he is!" one of the men yelled, running out from a different alley before Johnson could respond. He wore a gray bowler and had scruffy, unkempt sideburns. "Where d'ya think you's going?"

"Don' let him get off nowhere!" yelled the younger man who had bought Margret a drink as he ran up from behind the woman. He was more handsome than the other man, sporting a white vest with liquor stains on it. "I'm gonna have to insist he come with us."

The woman's face twisted into a scowl. "Y'all don't look like the law," she said, turning to him.

"No, ma'am, but we aim ta hand him over to the law promptly," replied the man in the bowler, grabbing for Johnson's arm. The smell of alcohol was heavy on his breath.

Johnson took a step to the side, easily resisting the drunkard's attempt to detain him. Stumbling forward, he lost his bowler hat, revealing a bald patch on the top of his head. Propping himself against the nearest wall, he struggled to catch his breath.

"No sense resistin'," replied the younger man, trying to move past the woman.

Taking a step to block him, she stood firmly between him and Johnson and rested her hand on the hilt of the Colt. She scoffed, "Ya ain't got no right takin' him in, far as I can see."

"He's vagrant. Ain't sposed ta be no coloreds vagrant," he replied. "They cause too much trouble."

"Not sure I appreciate y'all talking that way 'bout my cowhand here," she replied leaning toward him. "Don't see no one here vagrant 'cept you two fools, got nothing better ta do than sit drunk all day waiting for the first chance ta gull everyone ta thinkin' ya got more than just twigs between yer legs fer a pecker!"

"What'd you say, you bitch?"

"Said I reckon I got a bigger prick than you! How 'bout ya put on a dress and come dancin' with me?"

His eyes bulged in anger as he reached toward his gun belt. "Ya got a mouth!" he yelled, red in the face. "Ya better watch—"

The words were cut short as the butt of her gun collided with his lips. "Least my mouth got teeth!" she yelled.

Blood burst from his face as he hit the ground in a heap. Picking up his bowler, the other man scrambled over. "And don't call me ma'am!" she added, kicking him in the backside, causing him to topple over onto the younger man.

As the two men struggled to their feet, she fired a single shot in the air, and they turned and scampered off. The shot echoed off the buildings through the alleys, yet no one seemed interested enough to investigate its origin.

"Thanks," Johnson muttered. Shaken by how quickly everything had happened, he continued toward the livery. He wanted to get out of the town as soon as possible just in case the men had gone straight to the law.

"Ah, he was too pretty for his own good," she replied, holstering her gun. Realizing where he was headed, she chased after him. "Hold up there. Where ya headed, partner?"

He paused and stared at her blankly for a moment, unsure of what to say.

Staring back, she cocked her head at him like a curious dog. "Don't speak much, do ya?"

"I guess I'm just not used to being called that," Johnson responded, finding his words, "especially by someone who looks like you."

She took a second to work out what he meant, dismissed it, then threw out her hand.

"Edna B. Nowles!" she said. "But you can call me Eddie."

"Johnson."

"Glad ta meet ya," Eddie replied as she shook his hand with enthusiasm. "So, where ya headed?"

"Nowhere, I suppose," he replied. "I was lookin' for work here on a cattle drive, but that was before I ran into trouble."

"Then that's twice ya got lucky with me tonight," she said with a grin. "I'm looking for new hands. 'Bout ta start a drive southwest of here, little town where the Concho rivers meet called San Angela. If yer interested, we can head out tonight."

Johnson smiled at his fortune. Then his heart sank as he thought of Margret. Deep down, he knew he would never have a real chance to be with her. "I'm ready to go when you are."

"Ever been cowboyin' before?" Eddie asked.

"Nah," Johnson replied apprehensively, "but I'm decent with horses."

She slicked back her shoulder-length hair and tucked it behind her ears before placing the flat-topped, wide-brimmed hat hanging down her back onto her head. "Well, fer the most part, it's pretty dull music, but it has its excitin' moments an' pays decent enough."

"Sounds like my kinda work," he replied.

"Alright then, what say we get to the horses and let's drift?"

Chapter 15

Arkansas
April 1876

Fort Smith, Arkansas, was the kind of town that never slept. During the day, its streets were filled with people and covered wagons pulled by oxen. Migrants gathered and packed supplies for their long journeys. Women kept busy trying to restrain children who impatiently ran about playing games and causing mischief. Stores bustled as men traded goods, assembling their final necessary provisions before they settled the lands west in Indian Territory and beyond. And each day more came.

By night brothels and saloons kept the town bright and lively. Whores and card sharks plied their trades liberally, taking advantage of corruptible travelers and often leaving them penniless, requiring them to sacrifice some of their wares to cover their debts. It wasn't uncommon to find men prepared to trek west who had gotten so drunk and fallen prey to such a bad hand of cards that they were forced to abandon their plans entirely and return home.

Cold rain poured down the night Johnson and Walt wandered into town. Tired and hungry, they were lucky enough to find a stable to sleep in for the night. The stable boy had agreed to not tell anyone that they were staying there if they did his work for him the next day.

Covered in mud and straw up to their knees, they wandered the overcast backstreets like the living dead by midmorning, both so hungry they had barely said a word to one another. The air smelled of wet clay and animal droppings. Turning down an alley, two mangy cats darted from under a shack. Pausing to stare at the men, the cats abruptly turned back to the shack and pawed at the door.

"This one here," Walt said, coming alive from his weary state, shaking the old, locked door to the little storage shed.

Johnson walked up and threw a heavy kick at the rusty latch, but as soon as he did, three more cats emerged from under another shack. The cats surrounded them, meowing loudly.

"Shoo," he said, trying to quiet them, but the cats only grew louder which attracted more of the creatures. Kicking at the door again, Johnson cursed as another cat appeared. "*Shoo!*" He hissed at them in frustration, but they would not be deterred. Finally, Johnson kicked one of the cats. With a loud shriek, it scampered off, along with two others.

"Here, watch out!" Walt exclaimed as he wound up to strike the latch with the butt of his rusty revolver.

"I'd think twice before doing anything stupid in this town." The heavy voice came from behind them.

Suddenly, all the cats ran off. Surprised, both men turned to see who'd caught them. They relaxed somewhat at the sight of the man. He was black, short, and stocky but wore a blue army uniform, which kept them uncertain.

"We were just pickin' up some resupply for the store," Walt said in his most charismatic tone.

"Judge Isaac Parker isn't too keen on thieving," the man replied. "They call him the Hanging Judge."

"Surely he wouldn't hang anybody for stealin' food?" Johnson spoke up.

"Out here, the law's thin," the man replied, "so he's gotta set a standard somehow."

"Please don't turn us over to the marshal," Walt begged. "You know how the law treats us negros."

"Don't worry, I'm not gonna give you to the marshal," the man said softening his tone, "though I wouldn't expect Marshal Bass Reeves to treat you any differently, seeing he's just as black as you or I. That said, if you two come with me, I can forget about this."

Despite not knowing where he might be leading them, both Johnson and Walt agreed.

"Well, c'mon," he said to the pair, quickly turning out of the alley and toward the main thoroughfare. As they caught up to him, he introduced himself in an official manner. "Sergeant Francis Sherman, Tenth Cavalry, Company T, United States Army."

"They let you be a sergeant?" Walt questioned him with a laugh as they passed a group of pioneers changing a broken axle in the deep mud.

"I earned it," Sherman replied coldly. "If you work hard enough, it doesn't matter the color of your skin."

"You really believe that?" Johnson asked.

"I've lived it," the soldier turned to him stone-faced. "Some men are satisfied to sit idly and wait for their chances." The whiskers in his beard were white on his chin but black leading from his mustache to his sideburns, giving him a striking appearance. "I make my own."

"Fightin' for the army?" Johnson scoffed. "Seems more like ya just made yourself a different kinda slave."

Sherman pointed to the insignia on his shoulder. "Say what you will, but you see this? This uniform gives me power. I get respect. No one asks questions, no one calls me 'boy.' I have a salary, a pension, and I don't have to steal to survive."

Johnson had no reply. Sherman turned to look at Walt, who didn't say anything, but he wore a smile reminiscent of when he had a plan.

"C'mon," Sherman said picking up his already brisk pace.

As they approached the edge of town, it became clear he was leading them to the cavalry's camp near the Arkansas River. Blue cracks pierced through the overcast sky as the regimental flag flew high over the neatly organized rows of tents. Just beyond, what looked to be a few hundred or so horses were roped off and grazing. Soldiers were scattered around the camp doing their rounds, loading supplies, cleaning weapons, and standing guard around the horses.

There wasn't a single white soldier in the outfit.

"This some kinda special unit?" Walt asked with excitement, examining the men.

"Call us the Buffalo Soldiers," Sherman responded proudly as he led them to the main tent. "Get these men some food," he ordered one of the soldiers.

They sat at a table under a large open tent, and two plates of warm beans and cornbread were laid in front of them. Mouths watering from just the smell, they dug in. Sherman sat silently and watched as they ate.

After a few heavy spoonfuls, Johnson spoke. "We expected to join up now, is that the deal? You don't turn us over and you feed us; now we're supposed to be grateful to the army?"

"Not necessarily. I'm offering you the opportunity for a better life," Sherman replied. "It's your choice."

"So, what are y'all gettin' ready for?" Walt asked around a mouthful of beans.

"We're preparing to pursue a rogue band of Indians who refuse to settle in the Indian Territory. I won't lie; they are a dangerous bunch."

"We saw a few Indians livin' just outside town on our way through," said Johnson. "They didn't seem so dangerous." It was the first time he'd seen Indians, but they didn't look wild like the stories people told about them suggested. They just seemed poor.

"That's 'cause they've already had the savage beaten out of them. They've been tamed," Sherman replied. "The Indians we're going off to fight are Comanche. They don't have that kind of quit. They'll fight until either they're all dead or we are."

To Johnson's surprise, Walt's excitement only seemed to grow with these words. "I'll join."

"Good," Sherman smiled. "And you?" he asked turning to Johnson.

"I'll think about it," Johnson lied. He had no intention of getting killed. The whole reason he'd come west was to stay alive, and he wasn't about to ride off with the army just so he could die lying in the grass with his scalp missing.

Mounted on a large gray horse, a white officer with a thick broad mustache that curled at the ends approached the camp from town. Immediately, every soldier in the vicinity stood at attention, holding a stiff salute.

"Lieutenant," Sherman said.

"Ease," the lieutenant replied throwing a quick salute to the men. "Recruits?"

"Yes, sir," Sherman replied.

"Good. When they're finished, send them to my tent. I'll ready the paperwork." He turned his horse and trotted off but abruptly paused. Turning back to them he said, "Oh, and sergeant? You'd better come along too if they can't read."

"Sir," Sherman acknowledged with another quick salute as the lieutenant rode off.

Still got a white master, Johnson thought cynically as he chewed up a piece of cornbread.

He was certain at that point that the cavalry was not a good fit for him. He would miss Walt's company but not his half-cocked plans. They were well overdue in finding their own separate paths; it was only a matter of time before they were unlucky enough to be caught and hanged.

"What are you gonna do now?" Walt asked later that day. In his hands he held a fresh, neatly folded blue uniform with a new pair of boots under his arm.

"Dunno," Johnson replied, looking out over the river. "Keep movin', I suppose. Missouri, maybe Kansas."

Texas
July 1876

Eddie talked a lot. Johnson quickly gathered that she was the kind of person who would keep talking regardless of whether anybody actually listened. She just couldn't seem to stand the sound of silence. Whether it was speaking or singing the same few songs horribly out of tune when she had nothing left to say, she was rarely quiet. They traveled into the night under the light of a moon just a few days past full, and while they rode, she provided him the rundown of the cattle operation, nonstop, often repeating herself.

"We actually got two bosses. Most drives work outta one ranch, but Mr. Howe and Mr. Caldwell have two smaller ranches."

"So, they pool together for one drive?" Johnson asked, catching on.

"I work for Howe," she said, not stopping. "He's got the larger of the two, twelve hundred head."

"It's a decent-sized operation," she continued. "Two thousand head total."

This he repeated with her in his mind. It was the third or fourth time she'd mentioned the size of the herd to him that night.

"Earl Howe's an older fella. He don't go on drives no more. S'why he hired me. I act on behalf of his interests," she continued. "We gotta good crew though, 'bout half Caldwell's men, half Howe's."

"How many total?"

"Fourteen includin' you an' me," she replied. "Unless Caldwell hired new hands. I only hire for Howe. Couple Tejanos, some other negros, too, an' we're meetin' up with another hire when we get into San Angela tomorrow."

"What's this town like?" he asked.

"Well, we're really goin' out a few miles west o' San Angela, not much ta the town 'cept Fort Concho. 'Fore I left, a small group o' Buffalo Soldiers had just come in from a fight with the Comanches. Apparently they took some heavy casualties."

A somberness came over him. "Is that right?"

"Rest o' the place is mostly old Tejanos and cowpokes."

Johnson yawned and adjusted his hat. "We ridin' through the night?"

"Figured we'd go 'til I find a decent spot ta camp," she replied squinting in the moonlight. "Hell, looks like a spot good as any up yonder." Breaking into song, she rode ahead. Her long brown duster draped over the large pack behind her saddle, which made it look as if she had a giant hump. She sang into the darkness: "*Oh, I'm gettin' old an' feeble and I can't work no more . . .*"

The next day, they arrived in the little town of San Angela. It was a dusty town on the edge of the plains with only a few trees growing along the river. They met up with Eddie's final hire in a small café, a light-skinned black man named Ned Moss. He was only a few weeks past eighteen but looked all of twenty-five, yet his most striking feature were his deep hazel eyes.

They didn't linger, as Eddie was adamant that Mr. Caldwell was an impatient man, and when they arrived at the camp, he was already waiting for them. The camp sat between two grassy hills. It reminded Johnson of

Kansas, but with more scrub and shorter yellowish-brown grass instead of green. Several horses roamed free, mostly sticking to a lusher patch of grass that grew down the center of the valley. A large chuckwagon sat in a worn path at the base of the north hill. Smoke from a cooking fire billowed into the blue sky as a chubby black man stirred a large pot; the burning smell of dried cow patties filled their noses. Mr. Caldwell walked out to them from the wagon as they approached.

He was a middle-aged white man with deep lines in his face that told the story of a life spent on the range. A large mound of chewing tobacco was wadded in his lower lip, and he regularly spat thick, sludgy, brown saliva.

"You been in Fort Worth?" he asked Eddie, turning to spit on the ground next to him.

"No, been in a hot air balloon," she turned and spat mockingly. "Where do ya think I've been?"

Though visibly irritated, he chose to ignore her comment. "These them?"

"Yep, this here is Ned, an' this is Johnson. Boys, Mr. Lucas Caldwell."

Johnson sat awkwardly in his saddle as Caldwell studied them individually. He was standing on the ground, but it didn't make him any less intimidating. "Look pretty green to me, Eddie," he replied skeptically. "What d'ya two know about driving cattle?"

"Ah—" Johnson opened his mouth to speak, but Eddie interjected before he could answer.

"If ya don't like who I hire, take it up with Mr. Howe."

"These are my cattle, too!" he reminded her, angrily thrusting a finger in her direction.

"Look, I ran up and down the Chisolm with 'em each a few times, alright?" she lied. "Good enough for ya?"

Caldwell exhaled what was more of a growl than a breath and turned back to the men. "This ain't no quick, easy poke up the Chisolm Trail," he said to them with frustration in his voice. "Most o' the Indians were cleaned out of that part of the country years ago. We still got bands of Comanche, maybe even Apache to worry about."

"I promise ya they're both excellent marksmen," Eddie sarcastically replied.

Ned sat coolly with his hands crossed over the horn of his saddle and seemed content to let her say what she wanted.

Johnson swallowed hard. "I helped bring down a gang of stagecoach robbers back in Kansas."

"There ya have it," she said with a smile. "Now, can I get these two settled in?"

"Fine." Spitting again, he waved them on before walking back to the wagon. "Don't forget we're leaving in the morning!"

"Gonna be hard to now," she said throwing her hands out.

"Cookie, you got those beans soft yet?" he yelled as they trotted toward the horse herd.

"What's his problem?" Ned asked when they were out of earshot.

"He's always got a stick up his ass," she replied with a chuckle, "feels like he gotta overcompensate 'cause the money used ta run his ranch is actually his wife's."

"Seems like a poor excuse for bein' red-assed," Johnson said.

"Aw, he ain't so bad, an' he knows what he's doin'," she replied. "Better than havin' a perfect saint that don't know shit."

Eddie climbed off her horse and began to lead it; Johnson and Ned followed suit. Two more men walked toward them, both Tejanos, though one was older and the other almost a boy.

"Hola, miss," the younger said excitedly as they walked up.

"Hey there, Tony, how ya doin', partner?"

The boy turned to the older man and spoke rapidly to him in a mix of Spanish and English.

"*Buenas tardes*, Eddie," the older man replied, "he is doing well and much excited for the trip."

"Good ta hear." She smiled at Tony and gave him a pat on the shoulder. "Boys, this here's Cecilio García Sanchez and his son Antonio García Cordero," she struggled through the proper pronunciations. "Cecilio's been workin' fer Mr. Howe fer twenty years or more, and this'll be Tony's first drive."

"Mucho gusto," Cecilio replied, tipping his large straw hat to them. Upon hearing this, Tony smiled widely and took his hat completely off in order to bow, then pushed his long dark hair back and returned the hat to his head.

Johnson nodded and touched his brim.

"Pleasure," Ned responded.

"Ol' Cecilio scouted fer Sam Houston himself. Couldn't stand Texas bein' part of Mexico."

At the mention of this, Cecilio stood tall and proud. "This is true. I was named for St. Cecilia, who refused to worship the Roman gods. I refused to worship a Mexican emperor."

"Where's the rest o' the boys?" Eddie asked him.

"They camp near the cattle tonight," Cecilio replied.

"Where are the cattle?" Johnson asked. As often as Eddie talked about the size of the herd, he had fully expected to see them everywhere, but all he saw in the valley were horses.

"Oh, don't worry," Eddie replied, pointing to the north hill, "they're up over that ridge yonder, but you'll mostly spend yer time with the remuda."

"Alright," he muttered, unsure of what she meant.

"Said yer good with horses, right? Figured we could use another good wrangler. You and Ned here can show young Tony the ropes."

"But he don't even speak English!" Ned replied.

"He understands more than he can say," she reassured him, smiling at Cecilio. "'Sides, he's gotta learn somehow."

"Correct," Cecilio agreed, "it is how I learned."

"Alright, best get you two acquainted with the rest o' the crew. Cecilio, Tony," she said touching her brim, "afternoon."

They remounted and turned north up the hill. Johnson felt the steps of his horse change with the pitch of the hill and adjusted his weight accordingly. The smell of dry grass and smoke from the fire wafted in the air as they rode, the late afternoon replete with all the vibrance of the land.

"How far we goin', anyway?" he asked her.

"Goin' all the way ta Wyomin'," she replied with excitement. "I guess they found a special buyer there."

Why-o-ming, he thought to himself. "Where's that?"

"Oh, 'bout eight hundred miles north o' here," she replied as if it were just over the next hill. Her response was accompanied by a chorus of guttural animal noises. "Here we are, boys!"

Johnson was awed as they crested the hill. A wave of smell hit his nose that was unlike any animal scent he had experienced before, and the sea of longhorn cattle were spread out across the plain. They stood around as one large living mass of brawn breathing, bellowing, pissing, and shitting wherever they pleased. He had never seen so many animals in a single place. Until that moment, he had not realized how large the cattle were. Pale and brown, each stood about five feet tall, and their large horns stretched just as wide, some even wider. A dark *HC* was branded onto their hind quarters to identify them with the drive. They slowly trudged in groups grazing every blade of grass available, leaving nothing but dirt and dust in their wake.

Four men lounged on a small plateau just above the herd, their horses hobbled and grazing nearby. Riding over to them, Johnson became anxious as he remembered what Rex had said about driving cattle: It's a sink or swim business. Johnson wasn't a cowboy, and it wouldn't take them long to realize that. He dreaded the thought of being left behind if he was ultimately deemed useless.

Eddie introduced Johnson and Ned to the lounging cowboys. "Where's the rest of Caldwell's boys?" Eddie asked, displeased as she examined them.

A white cowboy in his mid-thirties named Herb Drake stood up. He had scruffy black stubble and shorter, slicked-back hair. "Said they was checking for strays."

"Fair enough, I suppose," she said as she dismounted.

"They's restless," Wendel Freeman spoke as he lay there, "just ready to go." He was an older black man with a full beard on his lined face, and he wore an old Confederate soldier's hat.

This intrigued Johnson. He'd seen plenty of southern whites who continued to don the gray uniforms, but it was the first time he had ever seen a black man in the colors of the South. He wanted to ask how he'd acquired it but decided it should wait until they were better acquainted.

The next two men were also black. The first had hair twisted into thick locks that hung from under his large white hat. The last man was the tallest of them all, but he hunched as he stood. Their names were Jesse Fur and Pokey.

"Well, those other boys better be back shortly," Eddie said, looking out over the cattle for signs of their return. "It'll be chow time soon enough."

They chatted for a good half hour as they waited for the other men to return. Johnson mostly stayed silent as he tried to learn as much as he could by listening to them talk about driving cattle. Pokey and Drake were both drag riders who followed the herd, whereas Jesse was a flank rider just in front of them. Wendel was a swing rider toward the front of the herd and occasionally the lead rider. Johnson had gathered Cecilio was a kind of scout who rode far ahead to look for the best route, searching for good water, river crossings, and easy land for the cattle to graze without straying too far. Eddie, along with Caldwell, seemed to fill in where needed, everywhere except on the drags.

When they tired of waiting on the other men, all seven of them decided to head back to the valley to help the new wranglers get acquainted with which horses were preferred by each rider. The sun was getting low when Cookie called them in for food, and the other men still had not returned.

"Think it's 'bout time we fix a party ta go lookin'," Eddie said as she finished her plate.

"Yeah," Caldwell agreed, looking over the valley. The sun hadn't quite touched the horizon yet. Standing, he began to bark orders at them. "'Cilio, have Tony stay here and help Cookie clean up. Drake, I want you, Jesse, Wendel, and Pokey to stay and watch the herd while the rest of us go out." He turned to Johnson and Ned with a stern gaze. "Now's the time to prove your mettle. Load up."

Saddling their horses, the two new wranglers rode off with the small crew. They were each given a rifle and a holster to strap to their saddles, and as they thundered off through the plains following Cecilio's lead, Johnson couldn't help but feel excitement flowing through him.

Chapter 16

"This way," Cecilio said, touching the ground. The grass was trampled in a way that he could easily read. "A. J. and the others. They were chasing something."

He remounted and let out a high-pitched whistle, sprinting off along the tracks. The rest of the party followed close on his tail. They were a few miles past the herd now, and Johnson could tell by the seriousness of their demeanor and the speed of their gait that they suspected the problem was more than just a few strays. He tried to question Eddie about it, but she only said to keep an eye out. For what, he wasn't exactly sure.

The sun was about halfway visible on the horizon when they came to a small canyon only thirty feet deep. It was surrounded by brush and low, rocky outcroppings. The western sky was an orangish yellow; where the moon was rising in the east, it faded from bluish purple to dark.

"Look yonder!" Eddie pointed to the bottom of the canyon. "That their horses?"

"Appears to be," Caldwell replied pulling his rifle from its holster. Climbing from his saddle, he crept to a large boulder for a better look.

Three horses stood unattended on the canyon floor, though they were difficult to see in the dying light. Johnson wouldn't have noticed them at all had Eddie not said anything.

Crack! A gunshot echoed off the rocks.

The riders who were still mounted jumped down, taking cover wherever they could. Johnson and Ned fell prone in the dirt while Eddie and Cecilio scrambled to another large boulder nearby. The shot took them all by surprise, and none of them was able to grab their rifles from their horses except Caldwell.

Her back against the boulder, Eddie forcefully whispered to Caldwell, "Could ya tell where that came from?"

"No," he spat back while taking aim across the way. He saw nothing. "A. J., that you?" he called out. Another loud shot rang out in reply. This time, it skipped off the rocks in front of them. Caldwell fired back at a pile of rocks across the canyon, then cocked his rifle and fired again.

"Don't waste your bullets!" a voice called out from below them. "We hit one earlier, but they got us pinned down!"

"A. J.?" Caldwell asked. "You three alright?"

"Yeah, just fine. Waiting for it to get too dark to aim proper."

Caldwell fired off two more shots in quick succession. "Y'all are lucky we ain't found you in the fucking daylight!" he yelled at their attackers.

The attackers fired another shot, this time sparking off the side of Eddie and Cecilio's boulder.

"Jesus, Caldwell, they're only shootin' 'cause you are!" she shouted at him.

"*Tranquillo, señor!*" Cecilio said.

"It ain't worth it!" A. J. shouted in agreement.

Fearful of catching a stray bullet, Johnson and Ned both crawled to an outcropping surrounded by scrubby brush and took cover. A breeze kicked up and whistled through the brush, blowing dust over them. Johnson squeezed his eyes shut. When he opened them again, a bright white light cut through the dark half of the sky as a shooting star raced into the orange glow of the sunset.

"Oh, *Dios!*" Cecilio cried out.

Johnson had seen nothing like it before. The heavens suddenly showered onto the backdrop of an already colorful sunset. The canyon fell silent under the brilliance of falling stars, and the entire crew found themselves lost in the sky.

When it finally ended, the sun had sunk beyond the horizon. The loud scream of a horse echoed from the canyon followed by several gunshots from below. Both Eddie and Caldwell called to the men. Johnson tried to make out what was happening amid the chaos of gunfire rattling off the boulders. Looking over at Ned, Johnson saw an unfamiliar silhouette creeping behind his companion.

"Look out!" Johnson warned as the figure closed in behind him.

Ned snapped up and drove the attacker into the ground with a thud. A shot rang out and Johnson covered his face. The bullet sunk into the dirt next to him. There was an audible gasp, and Johnson leapt up to see the figure rising to his knees as Ned writhed on the ground. Johnson aimed and fired. A wheezing, gargling noise followed the shot that dropped the assailant.

Scrambling over the ground through the smell of burned powder, he helped Ned to his feet. "Are ya hurt?"

"I'm fine," he replied taking a deep gulp of air. "Just took my wind."

The shooting had ceased from within the canyon, and Caldwell began to make his way down. "Still alright?" he called out to the men frantically.

"All good," replied A. J., "but they've got one dead, and we're down one horse."

"Two dead," Ned called out as he examined the body lying next to him.

"You an' Johnson both alright?" Eddie asked.

"We're fine," Johnson said.

"Quite the shot," Ned said to him as he put two fingers in the pool of blood pouring out of the bullet wound and onto the dirt.

"Lucky."

"Lucky for me. Here, help me with this." He grabbed the body under the arms.

Johnson walked over and stared into the moonlit face of a dirty young man with shaggy hair. He'd been shot clean through the neck and gazed lifelessly into the distance; blood covered his neck and shirt. It almost felt as if someone else had dealt the fatal bullet. Johnson only recalled firing at a shadowy figure. Crouching, Johnson lifted the man's legs and they carefully carried the body over to the horses, where Eddie and Cecilio were waiting.

"He's heavier than he looks," grunted Ned as they dropped the corpse to the ground next to them.

"Ya mean 'she,'" Eddie said.

Johnson looked at Eddie in disbelief. "She?"

Again, both men crouched low. Sure enough, when they reexamined the body, what they had at first mistaken for a young man with shaggy hair was, in fact, a woman. Her shirt and pants were similar in style to what they wore, and her hair wasn't much longer than any man who'd let his hair grow to his ears. She was young, albeit older than they had first thought when they'd mistook her for a man.

Johnson's thoughts raced, and he felt the urge to puke. He took a few steps away from the group.

"How could you tell?" Ned asked Eddie curiously.

"I got some experience with these kinda things," she replied.

"Don't know how I feel about killing a woman," Ned said in a remorseful tone. He scratched at an itch on his back.

"Shouldn't feel no different than if you'd killed a man who was tryin' ta kill ya."

Johnson was already rationalizing this in his mind before she said it, but his thoughts kept returning to the girl in Saint Andrews. It was as if the nightmare of his past kept returning to haunt him. Hands on his knees, he bent forward, taking deep breaths.

"Ya OK there, partner?" Eddie asked him, concerned.

"Just need a minute," he replied, kneeling to the ground.

"Here," she said, handing him her flask, "take a drink."

Opening the lid, he took a large swig. The burn caught him by surprise, and he coughed.

Slapping his back, she helped him to his feet. "Ya be alright."

He returned the flask. The liquor rushed to his head and helped calm his nerves. "Thanks."

Eddie took a large swig before safely tucking the flask away in her belt.

Cecilio was already tracing their path back to camp in the dark. After finding their tracks leading in, he mounted and rode out, then returned.

When Caldwell came back up the slope, he was leading one of the horses. Behind him followed another man who led a horse with a body laid across its saddle. He called out behind him to two more white men on either side who were steadying the body, warning them of a patch of unstable ground. Johnson could tell by the man's voice that this was A. J. Navigating the last few rocky steps at the top of the canyon, they weaved through the brush and rejoined the rest of the crew.

Caldwell dropped the reins of the horse he led and walked to his own. Silently taking an old bandanna from his saddlebag, he wiped down his rifle and placed it in its holster then patted his forehead and returned it to the bag. A. J. gripped his reins as he tried to make out the rest of the party in the pale moonlight. None of them had spoken a word in several minutes, and it was making Eddie itch with impatience as the crickets chirped a chorus in the night air.

"No need ta start tellin' us all at once what happened down there," she joked. "Y'all forget where ya were headed or what?"

"Got ambushed by a couple of rustlers," A. J. replied. He was similar in age and stature to Caldwell but had long wiry hair with thick gray streaks. "We chased 'em down into the canyon where they had a rifleman waiting for us and—"

"Jesus, A. J., after the last incident, I figured ya knew better," she interrupted. "What happened ta yer other horse?"

"Let me get to it!" A. J. snapped. "They tried to sneak off with two of our horses while we was watching the sky, but one of 'em spooked and crushed this poor bastard," he said jerking his thumb to the body over the saddle. "The other got away. Took some shots, but they was too quick."

"Shoulda never gone down there," she scolded him again.

"What, and you woulda just let 'em get away?"

"I wouldn't've acted like no goddamned fool!"

"Settle down, you two!" Caldwell's booming voice quieted them. "It's late and I wanna get back. We're still leaving in the morning."

"Right," A. J. replied. Tucking a strand of hair away from his face, he turned to the other two men. "Slim, you're gonna have to ride on the back of Bill's horse."

Bill was skinny and the clothes he wore were ratty and torn. He was an older-looking man who walked with a slight limp, but it was hard for Johnson to determine just how old. Slim was anything but what his name suggested. He was a large bearded man who walked with his toes pointed outward and whose belly protruded forward far enough to hide his belt buckle. Johnson felt bad for the horse that had to carry both him and Bill.

Walking over, Caldwell stood by the body of the dead woman. "You two seem like you'll check out just fine," he said matter-of-factly to Ned and Johnson, nudging the body with his foot. "Load 'em up."

"Let's put this one on yer horse there, Cecilio," Eddie said motioning to the body. "I'd say these two have seen enough of her fer the night."

Just as before, Cecilio led the group back to the camp but this time with less urgency. Caldwell rode next to him, followed by Bill and Slim, then Ned and Johnson. Eddie and A. J. purposefully lagged as they unsuccessfully attempted to clear the air.

"What's this, you only hire negros now?" A. J. prodded her. He pushed his long hair behind his ears. "Gonna start bringing on more women, too?"

Ned caught this and darted a glance at Johnson who returned it. He shook his head to dissuade Ned from saying anything unnecessary.

"So what if I do?" she snapped back. "I'd reckon the boys I hired could do twice the work yers can!"

"Wanna put a wager on it?"

"Wager on what?" she asked. "I ain't fallin' fer yer horseshit."

"No tricks this time," he assured her. "I'll bet you that when I'm running point, my guys get more miles than when you or one of your men runs the point," A. J. said with a smug voice.

"What's the wager?"

"Half wages."

"Ha! Yer willin' ta part with half yer wages? Ya must really be in a bind." Her laughter caught the attention of the men at the front of the party who looked back at them inquisitively.

"Sure am."

"Well, you may be, but I ain't," she replied. "'Sides, I'll make almost twice what you do." Adjusting her hat, she stared forward looking out over the dark shadow of the plains.

A. J. waited for a counteroffer, but as her silence dragged on, he grew impatient.

"Fine, a third."

"A quarter."

He extended his hand with a toothy grin. "Deal."

Pausing for a moment to stare at him, she cocked her head downward, spit a great amount of saliva into her hand, and shook. When she released, he wiped his hand on his pants.

"How about the wranglers?" he asked.

"I'll make sure it's kept fair," she replied, "though I can't speak fer you."

Grinning again, he snapped the reins and rode forward to catch up with Bill and Slim. As he drew up to Johnson's right side, he turned toward him and lightly touched his hat as he passed.

"You catch any o' that?" Eddie asked them as she rode up.

"Yeah," Johnson replied, scratching under his hat.

"You two are gonna have ta draw lots."

"Draw for what?" asked Ned.

"See what team yer on," she replied. "He'll try ta pay ya both off in his favor otherwise. Probably still might."

"What about the other men?" Johnson asked.

"Well, Jesse an' Wendel'll be with me. Pokey and Drake don't matter so much in this, Slim, neither, 'cause they're all on the drags. Front of the herd's what determines how far we get. The back just follows," Eddie explained to them as if she was only just working it out herself. "But since you two gotta bring us fresh horses once a day, makes a difference if yer favorin' one side or another."

"I supposed that's a fair assessment," Johnson replied with a nod. He was still struggling to keep straight who did what in his head.

"Let's not worry 'bout it 'til tomorrow." Taking another sip from her flask, she offered it to them. They both obliged. "'Sides, he'll probably run inta someone lookin' ta collect on an old debt 'fore we even get back ta camp," she joked. "It'll all be for naught then."

Johnson didn't know what to make of Caldwell's men. They had yet to be formally introduced, but he already felt a strange, if not comfortable, kinship toward them. Considering the wager, he didn't know how to prepare himself if he were to draw with their team. He hoped he wouldn't be the one yoked to A. J.'s men, but neither did he wish it on Ned. The competition only seemed to create animosity among the crew and left little room for the new hands to comfortably assimilate.

A wolf howled into the night some ways off in the distance. Its call was so close that it startled Ned.

"Aw, it ain't gonna hurt ya," Eddie reassured him. "Just lookin' fer some company." She playfully attempted to yodel an old cowboy tune to accompany the wolf's cries; her garbled voice carried lightly over the warm air of the plains.

They rode steadily until the sounds and smells of cattle resumed, and they could see the faint flicker of a campfire in the distance. The night sky was abundant with stars and the waning gibbous moon had risen high above them, lighting their path.

Chapter 17

Earle Gregory Howe was a bright, comforting man in the later years of his life. Seated next to an old Mexican woman with dark hair, he drove a mule-led wagon along the broad, dusty trail that led into the cowboys' camp. They arrived amid the bustle of the crew's morning preliminaries and pulled alongside Cookie's chuckwagon as Johnson, Ned, and Tony packed for the long journey. The woman descended first then carefully helped Howe down. The old man was energetic, yet his body had failed him, and despite how lively he still felt, he could no longer move as freely as he wished.

"Edna, it looks as though you've picked a fine crew," he called out, greeting her as she and Caldwell rode down from the hill to meet them.

"Howe," Caldwell acknowledged him with a handshake as he dismounted, but his features were rigid.

"I trust everything is in order?" Howe asked his partner as he looked over the valley. Once again, the sky was clear, and the low, early morning sunlight cast long shadows over the yellow grass.

"Had a bit of trouble last night, but it's all been cleared up."

"What kind of trouble?" Howe inquired. "None too serious, I hope."

"Just a couple o' rustlers who thought they could sneak off a few cattle 'fore we'd notice," Eddie replied. "Caught 'em at a canyon a few miles yonder."

"You'll have to send for the marshal to collect the bodies." Caldwell motioned to the two blanket-covered corpses lying several yards to the east at the bottom of the north hill. Two vultures circled high above them, dark spots in the blue sky waiting for the party to depart.

"Nonsense," Howe replied. "Have them loaded onto my wagon. Adelita and I can save the marshal the trouble."

The bodies of the two rustlers were moved into the back of the wagon by Johnson and Ned while Howe made his way up the hill with the help of Adelita, Eddie, and Caldwell. There, he looked out over the herd, examining the heart of his enterprise. Dust filled the air as the rest of the hands rounded up cattle on the outer edges of the herd and drove them toward the middle. Their calls carried over the grunting and mooing of the animals.

Holding onto Adelita's left arm for support, Howe removed his hat and spoke to them with a longing to join them in his voice. "Enjoy this while you can. Time only affords you so much freedom in this life, and it's a shame to waste it."

A warm wind carried the dust high into the sky and created swirling bands of brown clouds above them. The cowboys circled and hollered, their faces covered with bandannas to keep the dirt from their mouths, and wide-brimmed hats kept the sun off their heads. Caldwell raised his hand high, signaling to A. J. in the distance. In acknowledgment, A. J. gave a loud whooping yell and began to drive the cattle at the front of the herd forward. The rest of the cowboys fell in, pushing the herd after them.

"I trust you'll send word should anything go awry," Howe said to them.

"We'll do our best to send you updates from Denver and Cheyenne," Caldwell said.

"Good," Howe replied. Holding tightly onto Adelita, he turned to Caldwell and Eddie. "Pray you have a safe ride."

Caldwell mustered an awkward reply. "Yes, um, well, best get to it."

Again, they helped the aging man back down the hill and into his wagon. Their farewell was brief. With a quick brush of his mustache and a tip of his hat, Howe coaxed the mule into action, turning the wagon back toward San Angela. The pair watched them until the wagon sank below the yellow ridge of the south hill.

"I never know how to act proper around that man," Caldwell confessed to Eddie as he double-checked his saddle and provisions.

"How's that?" she asked.

"Always been peculiar; used to be more so."

Eddie scrunched her face as she tried to conjure memories that fit this report. "I never found him so peculiar."

"Well, he hired you, for one," he said, putting his foot into the stirrup and throwing himself over his horse.

"You've never been one fer jokes," she said unimpressed. She stood with one hand on her hip and stared at him sharply from under her hat.

"I know," Caldwell replied stone-faced. Spitting out his tobacco, he pulled out his snuff pouch and placed a fresh pinch in his lower lip. "Better hurry up 'fore they get too far."

"I'll catch up. Let me get my boys laid out."

"Fair enough." He circled his horse around her in a broad orbit then cantered off up the hill.

Bending low, Eddie picked three strands of grass. Carefully trimming two of them into different lengths, she placed the third in her mouth and walked over to the chuckwagon. The wranglers and Cookie had just finished packing everything neatly into the back when she approached.

"Pick a strand, boys," she said enthusiastically to Ned and Johnson. Holding her fist upright, the two pieces of grass appeared identical in length. "Short one stays with me."

"Go ahead," Johnson nodded to Ned.

He tried to tell himself he didn't care about the outcome, but his heartbeat quickened as he watched Ned take the strand to the left. It was the strand he would've grabbed. His stomach churned when Ned pulled it out; it appeared short. Ned didn't say anything as he examined it, and Johnson held still as he focused on the blade of grass in Ned's hand.

"*Ahem,*" Eddie cleared her throat, giving Johnson an urgent look to take his turn.

Stepping up, Johnson took the other strand of grass and looked at it. They compared the two.

"Well, looks like me an' Ned won't be seein' much of each other durin' the day," Eddie said, brushing her hands together. "Ya better ride up and talk ta A. J. 'fore he gets too far ahead."

"Right," Ned replied. Dropping his piece of grass to the ground, he walked to his horse, mounted, and rode off.

Turning to smile at Johnson, she looked over the flat spots in the grass where their packs and bedrolls had once been laid out, then back to the loaded wagon that was ready for the long journey. The smell of the prairie breeze caught her nose and filled her with exhilaration. "Let's hit leather, boys!" she exclaimed with fervor. "This is gonna be one fer the ages!"

Johnson sat atop his horse and looked out over the plain from the ridge. Where there was once a mass of noisy, smelly animals, only trampled dirt, cow shit, and emptiness remained. The remuda began to fill the void left by the cattle as they streamed down the other side of the hill, pushed on by him, Eddie, and the wagon. A large column of dust rose high into the sky several miles ahead of them where the cattle herd was, and he could see a lone rider heading their way in the distance.

"*Yah!*" Cookie yelled as he drove the mule leading the chuckwagon down the slope of the plateau. Seated next to him was young Tony, who excitedly asked him as many questions as he could with what little English he was able to muster. Cookie was patient with him and happily did his best to converse with the boy. He knew some Spanish words but was limited in his understanding and vocabulary.

"*¿Has visto Indians?*" Tony asked.

"Indians? What about them?" he asked, looking around with concern.

"*¿Los has visto?*" he put his hand over his brow and mimed looking out over the land at oncoming riders then pointed to Cookie.

"Oh, no. I ain't never seen any on the plain," he replied shaking his head.

"*¿Dónde?*"

"Well," he said scratching his head as he thought, "seen a few in Fort Sumner an' a few other towns."

"We go to Fort Sumner, *sí?*"

"Yeah, should be there in a week or so."

"*Muy bien,*" Tony replied with a smile.

A wind from the west picked up, stretching the great column of dust for miles and dropping it to the earth in streaks like brown rain.

Eddie squinted as the approaching rider got nearer. "Yep, that looks like Ned comin' back." He was still a way off, but Eddie had been giving Johnson some much-needed pointers on the maintenance of the remuda in his absence. She seemed keenly aware of his lack of basic knowledge when it came to the open range but recognized that he had the raw skills necessary for his task. When supplied with a rope, she was impressed that he already knew how to fashion it into a lasso.

"Where'd ya learn that?" she asked.

"Friend from Kansas."

"Well, let's see what we can do with this."

Taking it in her gloved hands, Eddie separated one of the straggling horses of the remuda and drove it off to the side. Riding close on its right, she swung the lasso overhanded and loosed it. Sailing in the air with a fluid motion, the rope perfectly dropped around the animal's neck and pulled tight, almost in a whiplike motion. The horse immediately stopped and turned around to face her. Slowing, she freed the knot and sent the horse back on its way, recoiling the rope as she returned.

"Try it just like that," she said, handing him the lasso. "There's a few more easy ones near the back of the pack. Make sure ta keep it wrapped tight around yer saddle horn or they'll pull ya right off yer horse."

Moving ahead of her, Johnson chased down a large dark horse with tan around its eyes and snout, but when he came upon its side, the animal quickly glanced back at him and jumped into a full sprint. Determined to prove his worth, Johnson blew a high-pitched whistle and his horse took off. They raced across the trodden land, where each footstep looked like a flash of smoke from a small blast as the dark horse's hooves hit the dry ground. They weaved past stands of brush and uneven ground, and Johnson's horse began to gain. Taking the rope in his hands, he swung it high and released, but the lasso fell short, hitting the horse's back. The dark horse's lead grew after this failed attempt. Drawing in the rope, Johnson pushed his horse forward again. Catching up within a few strides, he waited until he was almost even with the horse. The dry air rushed across his face as he swung the rope in a circle. This time, he aimed for where the horse was going instead of where it already was.

"*Yah!*" he called with excitement as the loop dropped over the horse's neck. He pulled the rope tight, wrapping the excess around the horn of his saddle as Eddie insisted. Instantly, the dark horse turned about-face as he pulled. It chuffed, trying to shake the rope, but Johnson held tight.

Whistling softly as he rode up, the horse calmed. He patted the side of its long neck then turned and led it back to the rest of the herd.

"Just keep practicin' like that, an' ya be ropin' 'em easy in no time," she encouraged him when he returned.

In the distance, Ned watched Johnson make a daring chase after one of the horses, catching it on his second try. Johnson continued to chase down, rope, and then release different horses as Ned approached. He must have caught seven or eight before Ned finally reached the lead horses at the front of the oncoming remuda. Circling wide around the herd, he flanked Eddie and Johnson, then fell in next to them.

Eddie questioned him about A. J. "What'd the good Andrew Jackson Stern have ta say?"

"Says he would prefer for you to bring him his next horse," Ned said to Johnson.

"What'd I tell ya?" Eddie replied without surprise. "Make no mistake, he's gonna try ta buy ya."

"What should I say to him?" Johnson asked her.

"That's up ta you," she replied. "Gotta ask yerself where yer integrity lies. Won't blame a man fer takin' some extra coin, but I ain't got much respect fer cheaters neither."

"I'm no cheat."

"Fer my sake, I hope not," she replied. "Any other word from up front?"

"Nothing far as I could tell."

"Horseshit. Those boys are always up ta something when I ain't around," Eddie said. She squinted ahead as if she could already detect their mischief. "'Bout time I head on up, I reckon."

"When should I bring up fresh horses?" Johnson wanted to get as much information as he could before she left.

"Don't worry, Ned'll help ya figure out the schedule," she reassured him. "Boys." Touching the brim of her hat, she rode off.

"You haven't ever been on a drive before, have you?" Ned asked him bluntly as he watched Eddie cut through the plain.

"No," Johnson admitted with slight embarrassment, "but I did work for a stagecoach company."

"I watched you roping those horses. You've got what it takes."

Johnson took off his hat and wiped his brow. "Hope I do."

Several hours passed and boredom sat heavily upon him. The drive didn't seem to be any different from traveling across the plains from Kansas to Texas, only now he was getting paid.

Not a bad consolation.

He squirmed restlessly in his saddle and passed the time as he always did now while traveling; he thought of Margret.

The sun had risen high in the sky, warming the air considerably. In the distance, the heat shimmered over the land and made it almost impossible to see more than a few miles. Johnson wouldn't have known where they were going if it wasn't for the great amount of dust that was thrown into the air by cattle, but Ned and Cookie seemed untroubled, so he didn't worry.

Ned mostly sat quiet. Occasionally he chased down a stray horse or gave the task to Johnson, but that was the extent of their communication. Cookie and Tony took exchanging vocabulary in their respective languages, pointing out features of the land or different animals.

As they rode on, Johnson recalled Eddie's description of a cattle drive. "Dull music" was a good way to put it. He began to count the horses, and once he'd counted the horses, he counted the number of steps they took before reaching a stand of brush, and when they reached it, he kept on counting just to see how high he could count.

Eventually, Ned perked up as a low, dry wash became visible through the heat in the distance. It was lined with bright green mesquite trees.

"Let's run the horses," he said, riding over to Johnson. "They'll try and stop to eat if we don't."

Johnson nodded and pushed his hat down tight over his head.

"You take the left flank, I'll go right, and the wagon can stay center."

It didn't seem like much, but Johnson was all for some action to break up the monotony of the day. Riding alongside the chuckwagon, Ned informed Cookie and Tony of their plan and took his position. Swinging wide, Johnson held the reins of his horse tight. He nodded to Ned, who loudly hollered and snapped his horse into a sprint.

The horses thundered as they descended into the sandy wash, splitting into different paths between the trees. Most of the horses funneled through a broad opening that was regularly traversed, but a group of three veered left through a thick cluster of trees. Chasing after them, Johnson ducked low when he approached the mesquite, shutting his eyes as the branches whipped at his body, tearing at him from all angles as he pushed through the thicket until his horse wouldn't go any further. His right shoulder burning with pain, he dismounted.

Cookie pushed through the wide opening to the wash, urging the mule faster than necessary at the behest of young Tony, who cheered the chase enthusiastically. The bulk of the remuda crossed the wash quickly and slowed when they reached the other side. Speeding down the slope, the mule was in a near sprint. Then, without warning, the right front wheel struck a rock and the wagon popped into the air, throwing Tony airborne. He floated above the wagon like a ghost, then crashed back down onto the bench. The wagon came to a dead stop, nearly throwing both Tony and Cookie over the front and onto the mule.

"Shit!" Cookie examined Tony with concern. "You alright?"

With a giant smile, Tony rubbed his tailbone. "*¿Otra vez?*" he laughed, which drew a hearty laugh from Cookie.

Johnson walked his horse to a small clearing in the mesquite. Taking out his bandanna, he examined his bloody arm where one of the thorns had ripped his sleeve. Folding the bandanna into a long strip, he tied it tightly around the wound then went to look for the stray horses. Their hooves had disturbed the sandy ground and he found the first two not far away, nibbling on the bean pods of the mesquite. The trees gave off a pleasant smell of moisture in a way the dry grass and scrub didn't. Allowing his horse to eat, he grabbed his rope and left all three of them there while he searched for the last horse.

The tracks split off into a tributary branch, where he found an extra set of hoofprints leading upstream. He wasn't sure if the tracks were the missing fourth horse or if they were made by a different rider altogether. Watchful, he continued. The wash began to cut into the ground until there was almost four feet of a rock wall lining the left edge with the trees growing above. A solid floor of stone lined the dried-out streambed, which kept the mesquite growing at a distance and made the trail harder to follow. Several yards ahead, the eroded path took a sharp turn to the left, and as he got closer, he heard shod hooves on the rock and the voice of a man.

Crouching low against the wall, he drew his revolver and listened. The words were hard to make out but grew clearer with every step. The man was heading in Johnson's direction.

"We'll get at 'em," the voice said as it rounded the bend.

"Don't move!" Johnson yelled.

"Whoa, hold on now!" Herb Drake said as he sat atop his horse with his hands raised. His right hand held a rope encircling the neck of the missing horse that Johnson had been searching for.

Johnson lowered his revolver, relieved. "Sorry about that. Didn't expect you."

He was covered in a thick layer of dust from his hat to his boots and his once orange bandanna was now a dusky brown as it hung around his neck. "Seems you might've lost something," Drake said.

"Yeah, it got away from me." Johnson briefly explained how the horses had all scattered when they tried to cross the wash. "What are you doin' here?" he asked. "Aren't you supposed to be with the cattle?"

"Horse tired out. Wouldn't go with 'em no further, so I rested her then started heading back this way."

Johnson nodded, motioning back from where he came. "Well, the rest are over this way."

They gathered the remaining horses where Johnson had left them and joined up with the rest of the remuda. All the horses were now stopped and grazing on the mesquite at the west bank of the main wash, just as Ned feared they would, and they found Ned, Cookie, and Tony still at the large crossing, changing the broken wheel on the chuckwagon. Almost everything had been unloaded to relieve its weight and was scattered about the ground.

"You'd better go ahead and take A. J. his horse," Ned grunted to Johnson as he and Cookie struggled to lift the wagon so that Tony could put the spare wheel into place.

"I'll head back up with you," said Drake, taking off his hat and smacking it against his leg to remove the excess dust, which plumed into the air and left a distinct mark on his pants.

Helping Johnson single out a horse for A. J., Drake picked out a black-and-white mare for himself and they rode off toward the herd. Johnson led A. J.'s horse, and Drake rode at his side as they followed the trace made by the cattle.

"So, where'd you say you worked on a drive before this?" Herb asked as they rode.

"Chisolm Trail."

"So that's how you came to be fighting off bandits in Kansas?"

"I suppose."

"Must've been good pay to go looking for a fight like that," he said squinting through the heat shimmers in the distance. "How many did you kill?"

"None."

"Took 'em alive? That's mighty diplomatic of you," Drake laughed.

"They all died," Johnson replied. "I didn't kill any of 'em. Never shot anyone 'til . . ." he trailed off as he thought about the dead woman at the canyon.

"I've never shot no one before," Drake spoke up. "Been shot at and fired back, but never hit nothing, far as I know."

"Hope ya never have to," Johnson replied solemnly.

"I appreciate that," Drake joked. "So what brought you back to Texas?"

"How do you mean?"

"Said you rode the Chisolm? Starts in Texas, don't it?"

"Right." Johnson hadn't known that. He thought for a moment before he replied. "Wanted to get back to the range."

Drake gave him a curious look but didn't question him further.

As they got closer, they could see Slim's fat belly and Pokey's towering frame through the heat and dust at the tail end of the cattle drive in the distance. Pointing him in the right direction, Drake gave Johnson a wave then lifted his bandanna over his nose and headed toward the other two men on the drags.

Riding wide to avoid most of the dust, Johnson took a path that cut up a small brush-covered ridge. From there he could see the herd stretched out for miles. The cattle resembled a stream of water cutting through loose soil as they moved in different packs, separating and joining together again. Their pace was slow but steady, and each of the riders kept to the outside, driving any that strayed back toward the main group.

As he caught up to the front, he saw that A. J. was tailing at a distance a large bull leading the drive. It wasn't the biggest animal in the herd, but its horns were the widest Johnson had seen by far. Appearing to be seven feet or more from tip to tip, one of the horns pointed almost downward while the other curved up and out, making the bull look as if it had a bent horseshoe coming out of its head. Riding back down the ridge, A. J. saw his approach and promptly turned to meet him.

A. J. addressed him as he rode up. "Johnson. Trust you're well."

"I suppose. Yourself?"

"Can't complain."

"I've got your new mount," he said, coaxing the horse closer to them.

"I see that." Departing from the unnecessary formalities, A. J. said, "How would you like to make some extra money on this drive?"

Johnson was resolute in his reply. "Don't think I'm interested."

"Hold on," he said. "You haven't even heard me out. We're talking close to double your pay."

"Still don't think I'm interested, but thanks," Johnson repeated. "Your horse?"

"Aw, c'mon now. What Eddie don't know won't hurt her, will it?"

Johnson paused for a long moment and thought, watching the cattle slowly pass while A. J. sat with a satisfied smirk on his face. Finally shaking his head, he remembered Burt. "No, I'm done goin' back on folks who gave me a chance."

A. J. lifted his bandanna over his nose. "Suit yourself."

He drew his revolver and fired two loud shots into the air. Easily startled, the cattle nearest them cried out and began to run wild, crashing into the others, creating a chain reaction of disorder. In a matter of seconds, the whole herd became a thundering stampede. Frantically, A. J.'s new horse reared violently against Johnson's grip. Not trying to fight it, Johnson released the rope, and it took off running through the dusky clouds kicked up by the chaos of the stampeding herd. Johnson turned his own horse and escaped to the safety of the ridge with A. J. following closely at his side.

When they reached the top, A. J. removed his hat and brushed his long greasy hair back from his face. "This is your fault," he said, pulling down the bandanna. "I saw you spook them cattle and any damages will come outta your wages."

"Fuck you!" Johnson yelled. "You're not gonna pin this on me!"

"Already have," A. J. replied with a smirk. "Who's gonna believe you over me?"

In the distance, Eddie sprinted up the ridge on her horse to meet them.

"What the hell happened?" she asked over the thunder of hooves.

"Your new hand spooked the cattle, that's what!" A. J. replied. "Shouldn't even be on this drive far as I'm concerned. Now I gotta try and get 'em turned!"

He yelled and chased back down the hill after the running cattle.

"He's lyin'," Johnson replied angrily. "Told him I wouldn't help him win the bet. Now he wants to pin this on me to force my hand."

Eddie sighed and looked out over the running chaos. "I believe ya, but it'll be hard ta convince Caldwell," she said handing him her flask. "Would say this is a new low for A. J. but he's tried this kinda shit before, an' he's got Caldwell's ear."

It took a good hour before the cattle ran themselves out. A. J. insisted that he'd tried to turn the herd in on itself, but he claimed it just wasn't possible with how worked up they'd been and decided the best course of action was to just let them run. He relayed this to the crew, most of whom had regrouped around the chuckwagon about a mile west of the wash. They were worn out, smelled of dirt and sweat, and looked as if they had just emerged from battle. The drive was done for the day. After the stampede, there was no way the herd would move any farther. Caldwell and Cecilio were still out counting, assessing whether any major injuries had occurred, while the remainder of the crew waited on Cookie to finish stewing the rabbit he'd managed to catch earlier that day.

Johnson sat anxiously on his saddle with the rest of Eddie's team. By then it was late afternoon and low cloud cover had rolled over them, threatening rain. Johnson knew the blame would fall to him. Eddie assured him that he needn't worry about losing any pay; she would see to it, but he wasn't convinced. He glanced at where A. J. was seated between Bill and Slim. Smirking, A. J. raised an eyebrow toward him then lay back on the ground, pulling his hat over his face.

It was evening when Caldwell and Cecilio finally returned, and Caldwell was on a tear, violently cussing in the darkness and spitting as they approached the camp. The crew had grown accustomed to his foul temperament, but this was beyond his usual unpleasantness. Even Cecilio was riding several yards away to avoid his ire.

Johnson wished he could make himself disappear as they rode in.

"A fine start this turned out to be!" Caldwell bemoaned as he swung his left leg off his horse and dismounted. Turning, he looked at the rest of the group. When he saw Johnson's face in the flickering light, he stormed across the camp. Unheeded, he stepped right through the fire, sending a burst of red-hot embers into the air.

Johnson took a deep breath and stood, determined to face the man down.

"One full day! Couldn't even make it a full fuckin' day 'cause o' you!"

Eddie intercepted him with her arms out. "Hold on now, Caldwell." She was a good head taller than he was, but that didn't stop him from putting a finger into her chest.

"His carelessness could've ruined us today!" he yelled at her. "Four cattle! We lost four, Eddie!"

"And I'm willin' ta let ya take the damages outta my wages."

"That's good!" he replied with fire in his voice. "Cause he ain't getting paid nothing to take it out of!" Angling his body around her, he looked at Johnson. "You're done!"

"He's my man and ya ain't got no right!"

"Do I look like I give a damn?"

"I can have him 'round regardless what you say," she said, stretching to her full height. "Ya can't fire my men. They don't work fer you."

Stepping around Eddie, Johnson tried to defend himself by setting the record straight.

"Look—"

Caldwell's fist laid him on the ground before he could finish speaking. "We leave at dawn!" he yelled as he turned and walked several paces away from the camp.

Chapter 18

Colorado
July 1876

> *Dearest Father,*
>   *Will you be home soon? I miss you terribly. Auntie Isabel is help-*
> *ing me to write this letter. My schooling is going well and soon I might*
> *be able to write you all on my own. Every day cousin Thomas and I*
> *play catch with the baseball you sent for my birthday. I am eager for*
> *your return so that we might play together. Surely it will be soon?*
>   *Your loving son,*
>   *Phillip Charles*

Cole Charles laid the letter down in front of him, rereading it several times in the dim flicker of lamplight. Taking a deep breath, he hunched forward and rested an elbow on the knee of his new wooden prosthetic leg and sat in contemplation. On the edge of his desk a pile of letters from his various contacts of detectives and informers sat unopened. Turning to stare at them, he exhaled. Neatly folding his son's letter, he placed it in the breast pocket of his coat and took the letter on the top of the pile into his hands. The sooner he finished his work, the sooner he could be reunited with his son.

Texas
July 1876

Johnson's heart thumped in fear as he looked out across the cloudy brown water of the Pecos River. Old cattle bones were scattered over the muddy banks where thousands had previously crossed. He shifted nervously in his saddle; this would be his first major river crossing of the drive. Almost a full week had passed since the stampede, and he had done everything he could to avoid Caldwell during that time. Luckily, nothing else had gone awry to further Caldwell's displeasure—not as if that improved the man's overall demeanor toward him. Still, Johnson did not wish to further damage their rapport, and he was unsure about this crossing.

Though the rains had not reached them, storms on the northern horizon had raged two days prior, elevating the water level significantly. The waters of the Pecos had become swift and eerie. The river danced, stretched, and churned as it curved through the desert landscape, the wet smell of mud and decay fresh in the air.

Johnson swallowed, and as he adjusted his hat, a pale object in a tree to his left caught his attention. Cracked and bleached by the sun, a horse skull hung from the branch of a mesquite that grew from the bank of the river.

"Horsehead Crossin'," Eddie said, riding up from behind with Ned as Johnson stared at the skull. "Only spot ta get across fer miles."

"Water seems high. The cattle crew made it safe?" Johnson asked her.

"The water's gotten higher since they crossed, but I've crossed worse," she replied.

Johnson turned his gaze to the opposite bank. "I haven't."

"The horses know what ta do. Just keep 'em steady and you'll be fine," she reassured him. "I'll take point, you come second. Ned, take up the rear."

Johnson nodded. Turning his horse, he and Ned climbed the bank where the remuda was waiting.

"Should we wait for the water to go down a bit?" Johnson asked Ned as he stared back toward the river. "Think Eddie is hurryin' us 'cause of this competition?"

"Don't really care. I ain't worried about no teams," Ned replied. "I only wanna get through this job so I can get back home."

"Missin' your family already?"

"Not exactly . . ."

Johnson's focus shifted from the river to Ned. "You got a girl you're sweet on or somethin'?"

Ned's gaze shot to the ground and with an embarrassed grin he said, "I suppose I'm sweet on her. She let me steal a kiss before I left."

"Gotta be careful when it comes to women. They can be difficult."

"Women like Eddie?" Ned joked.

"No, I mean womanly women."

"So definitely Eddie, then," Ned said with a chuckle.

"Just don't get yourself in any trouble."

"They're just women. How much trouble can they really be?"

The horses stirred as the two of them crested the bank and rode into the fold of the herd. Again, Johnson's thoughts drifted into a swirling muddle of worry as he focused on the crossing.

"You ain't worried about the river?" Johnson asked again. "Cookie and Tony are gonna wait."

"What's there to worry about? It's just water."

The horses didn't hesitate as they descended into the river. The splashing of hooves quickly turned to swimming as Eddie led them across. Their heads bobbed just above the surface as they reached the deepest point in the middle, then raised up again when they returned to shallow water on the other side. Johnson's pulse raced. His eyes were glued to Eddie as her lower half reemerged, water falling off her horse as they climbed onto dry land.

With gritted teeth, he clenched the reins and drove his horse into the river. As they plunged in, the water took his breath, filling his boots and reaching above his waist. He had not expected it to be so cold. Staying downstream of the horses, he kept careful watch as they swam diagonally upstream to avoid being swept away in the current. He was relieved when they reached the other side faster than he had expected and with no problems.

As they emerged from the water, Johnson looked back to see Ned enter. When Ned's group reached the middle, one of the horses struggled. Dunking its head underwater, it began to drift. Quick to act, Ned directed his own horse toward the struggling one, which panicked as Ned got close. In an instant, the horse threw its head, knocking Ned into the cold, brown current.

"Eddie!" Johnson yelled. Throwing his hat to the bank, he snapped into action, driving his horse back into the river as soon as Ned hit the water.

Ned's arms flailed desperately as he tried to keep his head above the surface. Johnson floated downstream in pursuit, cold waves lapping at his sides. Pushing his horse to swim faster, Johnson stretched himself as far as he could without losing balance. Aided by the current, he closed the gap. Taking hold of Ned's shirt, Johnson pulled him across the front of his saddle and tried to turn his horse back toward the bank, but the current had become too strong for the horse to handle two riders.

Grabbing his lasso, Johnson scoured the bank for anything he might be able to rope.

"The tree! The tree!" Eddie yelled as she chased them on horseback along the bank, dodging boulders and weaving through scrub. A large tree stretched out over the water close enough for Johnson's lariat to reach it. He had to be perfect. Several yards beyond the tree, four large boulders formed a series of dangerous rapids.

Johnson wiped water from his face and swung the lasso above his head. Concentrating on the largest branch, he released. His whole body gripped as it looped around the branch. Taking Ned by the arm he yelled. "Grab on!"

In fatigue, Johnson's horse sunk below the surface, taking the pair under before they could reel themselves in. Still clasping both the rope and Ned, Johnson peered through a lens of muddy brown water. The current pulled at him, and Ned flailed as they both tried to get back above the surface.

With little breath in his lungs, Johnson's whole body ached. He was about to release the rope and attempt to swim when he felt a tug and realized they were being pulled toward the bank. His tight chest struggled for clean air. Stretching his feet toward the river bottom, Johnson was desperate to feel the ground and fought to stay alert as darkness seemed to take over his body.

His foot touched the muddy bottom. Thrusting upward out of the water, Johnson sucked a deep breath. There, standing knee-deep in the water under the tree, Eddie pulled them toward her with all her might.

Having slipped into unconsciousness by the time they reached shallow water, Ned was limp. Eddie grabbed Ned from Johnson with both hands. Dragging him up the bank, she laid him on his back in the sloppy mud at the edge of the water.

"He ain't breathin'," she said to Johnson as she leaned over to shake him.

"What do we do?"

"Stand back!"

Eddie turned Ned onto his side and punched him hard in the gut. His eyes sprung open as he coughed up a mouthful of dirty water. Taking a deep breath, he convulsed with a coughing fit.

"There. Looks like ya made it," Eddie said, slapping him on the back.

Drenched and gasping for breath, Ned looked up at them weakly. "Yeah?"

Extending her hand, Eddie helped him to his feet. "Figure ya owe me for that one."

"Bullshit," he said, nursing his bruised stomach. "I was almost drowned working for you!"

"Fair," she replied with a smile. "How 'bout I buy ya both a drink in the next town and we call it even?"

Johnson grinned and climbed to his feet.

A loud chuff caught their attention as Johnson's horse climbed out of the river and shook off, saddle and reins still attached.

Eddie produced her flask and took a deep swig. "Well, now that we've all had a nice swim, we best get movin'."

From that point on, Johnson and Ned saw more of Eddie. Whereas before she might visit them for a couple hours every few days, now she was riding with them regularly for whole days at a time. Johnson didn't mind the company since Ned was mostly quiet and Cookie and Tony often lagged, but it also worried him. He couldn't decide if she questioned their ability to do the work, if she worried about their well-being, or if it was something else entirely.

Passing into New Mexico Territory, they followed along the Pecos. Caldwell might have warned about the danger of the Comanches, but the closest they had come to an encounter with Indians was a lone brave who watched them from a distance for an hour or so before moving on. The Pecos was a far more threatening danger in Johnson's mind, having tried to take his life once already. Every time he looked out over its waters, he felt like it was watching him, almost as if it knew it had been robbed and still was waiting for what it was owed.

Competition wasn't just rife among the men from the two different ranches, but among the individual hands themselves. Wagers had become key to passing the long hours of boredom. Wendel and Jesse Fur especially were locked in a never-ending rivalry.

On one occasion, Johnson brought Jesse Fur a fresh horse while the two were arguing about who could run the fastest.

"You couldn't get a sniff of me," Wendel said as Johnson rode up to them.

"Go ahead, keep lying to yourself," Jesse Fur replied.

"Who's lying? Johnson's here. He can watch the horses. I say first to that scrub!"

Before Johnson knew what was happening, both men had dismounted and taken off afoot over the plain, leaving him with their horses.

"*Ha!* What'd I tell ya?" Wendel yelled in triumph.

Hunching over to regain his breath, Jesse Fur brushed back his locks and protested, "The ground weren't even!"

"We can go again," Wendel replied, gripping his side.

"Ah, ain't worth it. I know I can beat you if things was fair."

"Ya saw it," Wendel said, walking back to Johnson. "He got beat by an old man."

"We're the same damn age!" Jesse Fur yelled, snatching the reins of his new horse from Johnson.

Lightning struck in the distance as dark clouds moved overhead.

"Welp, pretty soon it's gonna sound like a cow pissing on a flat rock," Wendel joked, dusting off his hat and adjusting it low on his head.

Chapter 19

Despite Johnson's determination to stay loyal to Eddie, the competition between the cattle crews quickly became a lopsided affair regardless. They'd almost reached Fort Sumner, New Mexico, and A. J.'s team was ten miles ahead. Eddie suspected that A. J. might have paid off someone else but, in reality, she'd drawn a run of bad luck. Poor weather would strike every time her team was leading the cattle herd, slowing the pace of the whole operation. If Johnson, Ned, and the rest of the horses hadn't seen enough water crossing the Pecos, they saw plenty of it during the storms that followed.

Johnson couldn't remember being so wet. Unlike the other cowboys, he had no rain slicker to protect him. Drenched to the bone, the only way he could sleep at night during a downpour was to lie under the chuckwagon. On the nights that Cookie and Tony lagged, he slept with his head under his saddle to block the rain.

A week after crossing the Pecos, the drive settled just southeast of Fort Sumner. Johnson, Eddie, and Ned arrived with the remuda by early evening with the chuckwagon following close behind. They were worn out from the continual storms and ready to spend some time indoors. Most of the cattle team had already set out for town, but Caldwell remained in the camp.

"What took ya so damn long?" Caldwell asked. He sat alone on his saddle by a small fire and gave Johnson a nasty glare as they rode up.

"Our pace has been more than satisfactory an' if ya gotta problem with it, you can drive the horses yer goddamned self!" Eddie replied.

"You ain't even supposed to be with the remuda, Eddie!"

"Oh, I'm certain y'all are makin' out fine without me."

"I don't give two shits about when you show up, just them." Caldwell motioned to Cookie and Tony, who began unloading the chuckwagon. "If they'd get here quicker with the chow, I wouldn't have to worry about all my men going off and coming back stone-drunk!"

"They'd be getting drunk regardless and ya know that," Eddie said turning her horse away from him. "Matter of fact, I think we're fixin' ta head that way ourselves. C'mon boys."

Caldwell spit then pulled up a clump of grass and thrust it into the flames.

On their way into town, they passed an abandoned military fort, then dropped off their horses at a livery run by an old Apache man. The Apache was the first Indian Johnson had ever met up close, though he was dressed not as an Indian but a normal man. Johnson wondered how the man came to run a livery stable and why he didn't live the life of a renegade with the rest of his people, but the old Apache hardly spoke as it was, so he did not ask.

As they headed for the saloon, Eddie paused in the middle of the road. Putting her hands to her hips, she looked up at the clouded sky. She was deep in thought and Johnson worried something might be wrong until she turned back toward them.

"Ya know, you boys seem like you could be wantin' for some company," she said in a way that suggested she intended to change their plans.

"What's that supposed to mean?" Ned asked.

"Well, what say I get ya a couple o' whores instead of that drink I promised?"

The faces of both men lit up. Surprised by the suggestion, they were eager.

"Is there a good whorehouse around here?" Ned asked.

Johnson prodded him in the back. "Thought ya already had a sweetie?"

"Ain't like we're wedded!"

Eddie turned and continued walking down the street. "Well, if you fellers are comin', there's a place 'round the corner that's got some nice girls."

The brothel was a single-story adobe brick building with a small awning over the front door. When they entered, a pleasant smell of potpourri filled the entryway—a sharp contrast to the mix of body odor and livestock that exuded from the three of them. They were met by a well-dressed woman of Mexican descent with long, tight curls that hung down over the back of her silvery silken dress. She introduced herself as Madam Felina and smiled at Eddie.

"*Buenas noches*, Ms. Eddie. How might we serve you?"

With an air of politeness, Eddie removed her hat and tucked her long hair behind her ears. "Three of yer best sporting girls please."

"Three?" Johnson asked, interrupting. "Who's the third girl for?"

Eddie looked at him in disbelief as if he were asking how to use his own manhood. "Well, she ain't for you!" She smacked him with her hat.

Johnson flinched and went hot with embarrassment. "I didn't realize!"

"These are proud workin' women and I aim ta give 'em some business," Eddie said turning her attention back to the madam.

"Three girls, please."

"Of course," the madam replied. Clapping her hands three times, a line of three girls made their way into the room. The first two were white, one quite large with reddish-brown hair and the other short and blond. The third was a petite Mexican no older than twenty with long hair braided into two buns. Each of them wore little more than a large, receptive smile.

"Buyer's choice," Eddie said to Johnson and Ned. Walking up and taking the Mexican girl by the hand, Eddie was led down the hall into a private room.

With a childish grin on his face, Ned stepped forward. "I'll take the blond."

"Will you now?" the blond girl replied, turning away from him and disappearing down the hall.

Uncertain about what to do, Ned stood there as he watched her slow walk.

Noticing he hadn't followed, the blonde girl looked back at him over her shoulder and called in a soft yet commanding voice, "Are you coming?"

Ned nearly tripped over himself, running after her.

"I guess that just leaves us," the last girl said to Johnson, taking him by the hand.

Her grip was strong, cold, and rough. Not like Margret's.

Denver, Colorado
July 1876

The streets of Denver's Hop Alley were lined by tall brick buildings that cast towering shadows in the moonlight. Several of the buildings had lights in their upper windows, but few people were present along the main street as Margret walked along the storefronts. Her movements were stiff and anxious, and she counted each alleyway she crossed until she arrived at the ninth one. Pausing, she peered down the darkened lane and saw a dim light glowing from a small doorway at the bottom of a set of stairs. Glancing back in the direction she came, Margret took a deep breath and entered the alleyway.

A man in a dingy saloon had told her where to go. She'd all but abandoned writing as her habit consumed her. The laudanum had stopped being enough weeks ago, and since arriving in Denver she'd been unable to afford a doctor who could prescribe her morphine.

Light from the cracks of the door revealed a distinct haze. As she reached the bottom of the steps, she knocked four times in a specific pattern. A moment passed with no answer. Margret raised her hand to the door, but just as she was about to knock again, the sound of footsteps approached from the other side.

A lock unlatched, the door slowly cracked open, and the small silhouette of a man spoke to her in Chinese, but she couldn't understand.

"Please, opium," Margret said.

The man replied, but again Margret did not understand.

Producing a silver coin, she repeated herself. "Opium, opium."

Nodding, the man spoke again and then opened the door. He was short with a thin mustache and round glasses.

Margret was immersed in the smell of the flavored smoke as the man led her into the room. The walls were lined with cushioned seats occupied by languid men smoking from long pipes. Oil lamps with low flames burned on small tables in front of each seat. Stopping at an empty seat, the man turned to her and spoke, holding up two fingers with one hand and an open palm with the other.

"Here," Margret said, laying two coins in his hand.

Smiling, he motioned for her to sit and walked into a small back room. When he returned, he carried a lamp and another long pipe. Handing her the pipe, he set the lamp on the table in front of her, lit it with a match, and adjusted the flame.

Margret's body ached as she watched him fiddle with the lamp. Coming to Chinatown was not her original intention but she was desperate. She'd gambled away almost all of her money in pursuit of her habit. It was the only way she could cope. Closing her eyes, she could see the dark image of a man pushing himself onto her. When she opened them again, her ears rang as though she had fired the shots into Jester Wells. It didn't matter if she was awake or dreaming, the events haunted her continually.

The man motioned to signal that the flame was ready, and she held the pipe over it. She felt clumsy with such a long apparatus, but as she took the first few puffs of smoke, a wave of euphoria suffused her whole body, and she sank back into the depths of the cushioned chair. She inhaled again, the length of the pipe allowing her to remain reclined.

Smiling again, the man gave her a shallow nod and returned to the back room.

Margret was unsure of how long she had been sitting there when white men burst into the room and began smashing lamps, overturning tables and chairs, and dragging smokers into the street.

"If you like to smoke with the Chinese, then I got just what you need," a man with a thick curled mustache and tobacco stains on his shirt said to her. Grabbing Margret by the arm, he pulled her up and took her outside.

"Where—where are you taking me?" she asked. Her mind was still hazy as they reached the street. Chinese men, women, and children fled through the streets as their shops and storefronts were destroyed by the white men.

"You're gonna work for me now," the man said gripping her arm tighter. "If you behave yourself, I'll get you all the dope you want."

Fort Sumner, New Mexico
August 1876

"They ever give you trouble, the rest of the crew?" Johnson already had been curious about Eddie, who was unlike any woman he'd met, but after seeing her visit a whore, he felt extra inquisitive.

"They know better," Eddie replied. "You seen that limp old Bill's got?" Johnson and Ned both nodded.

"Well, he didn't always have it. I shot old Bill. That's why he's got his limp. Came at me one night all liquored up. Said he wanted ta see if my parts still worked. So I put a bullet in his hip."

Ned's face went blank at her words.

"I suppose that gave them some pause," Johnson said.

"You could say that," Eddie replied. "It's why Bill hardly comes 'round me, and the rest don't mess with me neither."

The sky was still clouded but the night air was dry as Johnson, Ned, and Eddie headed for the saloon.

Light and the sounds of festivity spilled into the main street of Fort Sumner as men congregated outside, some of them lying passed out in the road. A raucous chorus of men's voices emanated from the saloon as the three of them made their way to the main entryway. The smoky room was packed with a mix of men. They sang songs together to the accompaniment of a piano and fiddle. A circle had formed in the middle of the room where several of the men danced with each other wildly, surrounded by others who clapped and stomped along. Between each song, the men in the center switched out with those from the edge of the circle, and when the music began again, it was met with cheers and the occasional bottle thrown against the wall.

"Well, this is quite the paradise of bachelors! Hope you boys brushed up on yer Walt Whitman!" Eddie exclaimed, playfully hitting Johnson on the shoulder and pushing her way into the room.

Johnson and Ned squeezed through the crowd after Eddie, but they were separated by other men pushing through the room. Were it not for her height, they would've lost her entirely.

As they shuffled forward, Herb Drake appeared in front of them headed the opposite direction.

"Drake," Johnson said to him.

"Got some business to take care of," he said, continuing past them.

"Probably going to see Madam Felina," Ned said to Johnson with a smile.

The entire length of the bar was three men deep, with men jostling and fighting for the attention of the bartender. When they caught up to Eddie, they realized she had found the crew. Wendel, Jesse Fur, Slim, and old Bill stood in line as Eddie talked with A. J. nearby.

A. J. prodded her and suggested that they call the bet early for half the prize. "I already got twenty miles on your boys."

"It ain't that much and you know it!"

"Alright, ten, but still!"

"No deal. If yer gettin' my money, I'm gonna make ya work for it!" Eddie turned away from him and pushed closer to the bar.

The fiddle player carved a winding solo that came to an energetic finish. A great cheer of whoops and hollers erupted from the crowd as dancers exchanged partners and a wave of thirsty men moved toward the bar.

Two white men pushed their way in front of Johnson at the bar.

"Hey!" Johnson yelled at the man and tried to retake his spot.

"Shove off," the man said. He was a scruffy blond and well intoxicated.

A. J. grabbed him by the arm and moved him out of the way, allowing Johnson through.

"You fixin' for a fight!" the man yelled at A. J.

"Just trying to associate with my man here," A. J. replied over his shoulder.

"Best watch yourself!" the man said, almost falling over.

A. J. turned and pushed a strand of hair from his face. "You'd better run home to momma 'cause it seems it's past your bedtime."

Several of the crew and other men around them laughed. As A. J. turned around, the man lunged at him but was stopped short, grabbed by old Bill and Slim. Using Slim's large frame to push through the crowd, they tossed the drunken man out onto the street to a bevy of cheers.

Johnson watched A. J. look on with an approving smile. When A. J.'s focus returned to him, Johnson was unsure of his intentions.

"I know I put you in a spot with Caldwell, but business is business," A. J. said. There was little remorse in his voice.

Johnson resented the statement. "Ain't much consolation if Caldwell don't want me around."

"Don't worry about old Caldwell," A. J. reassured him. "He don't hardly like nobody. Been that way for years."

Before Johnson could respond, something heavy struck him in the back of the head. In a daze, Johnson touched the back of his skull and turned to see that the scruffy blond man had returned. Judging by the shock in the drunken man's wide eyes, Johnson had not been the intended target of the bottle he had thrown. Wendel's fist struck the man before any words were exchanged. Another man jumped in to try and grab Wendel, but Jesse Fur struck him.

Seeing two black men attacking whites, several of the other white patrons went for Wendel and Jesse Fur, but A. J. and old Bill were quick to come to the defense of their fellow cowhands. Angered and poised for a fight, other white men came at Johnson and Ned, but Slim fended them off.

The bartender went into a frenzy, loudly cursing at them. "Get them darkies outta here!"

Eddie jumped over the bar and knocked the bartender out cold. The music stopped and the whole saloon fell into a chaotic brawl. Punches, bottles, and glasses were thrown as the members of the cattle crew came together to fight their way out.

Old Bill and A. J. fought back-to-back, exchanging blows with a group of men while Ned grabbed the arms of a man on top of Jesse Fur. Johnson ducked as a large man threw a punch in his direction. Slim struck the man who missed Johnson, but then he was tackled by two more men. Johnson grabbed one of the men from Slim's back only to be blindsided and knocked to the floor. When he was pulled up by the scruff of his shirt, he flinched in anticipation of the strike, but was relieved to see it was Slim helping him to his feet.

One of the men sitting at the bar turned and pulled a revolver. Seeing this, Eddie grabbed a half-empty bottle of whiskey and struck the man over the head, who slumped face first onto the bar, blood running onto the wooden countertop. Jumping back over the bar, she pulled his barstool out from under him, sending the man to the ground. Cussing at everyone, she swung the barstool in a wide berth to make room, crashing into the crowd and pushing her way toward the door.

Scrambling to grab whatever unbroken bottles of liquor they could, Johnson, Slim, A. J., old Bill, Ned, Wendel, and Jesse Fur all filed in behind Eddie, covering their heads from incoming blows as she cleared a path. When they reached the door, Eddie tossed the stool back into the crowd, and they all ran for the livery.

"Ain't raised that kinda sand in a while!" Eddie yelled as they ran.

A few of the men in the saloon gave chase, but too drunk or too tired, they trailed off, satisfied to throw whatever was handy at the fleeing cowhands.

Bruised and drunken, the crew reached the livery with labored breathing. Slim, who was the last to arrive, nearly fell over as he vomited in the street.

Eddie was irritated with this display. "Ya couldn't spare us by havin' a spit in the alley?" she chastised him.

Wiping his lips with his sleeve, Slim had no reply and instead washed his mouth out with the bottle of whiskey he'd grabbed.

"Well, don't waste it!" Jesse Fur yelled, grabbing the bottle and taking a hefty swig.

"Where's Drake?" A. J. asked. Realizing he was not among them, he did his best to take stock of everyone in the dark.

"Thought he came with you lot?" Eddie said, banging on the stable door.

"We saw him leaving the saloon as we came in," Ned replied.

Opening a window, the old Apache stuck his head out and looked at them but said nothing. He closed the window again, and after a few moments the stable door swung open.

A. J. pointed to the black-and-white mare Drake had been riding. "His horse is still here."

"Should we wait for him?" Johnson asked as they grabbed their saddles.

"If he can't make it back on his own, he ain't worth havin' 'round," Eddie said as she carefully slid the bridle into her horse's mouth.

Johnson went quiet. He knew Herb Drake was a far more competent hand than he and was surprised she would be so willing to leave him behind. Surely, she would have more loyalty toward him?

"Don't worry," she reassured him, mistaking his silence as concern for Drake's well-being, "he'll show up."

"I must be crazy 'cause I swear I heard this mule say something," Jesse Fur said, drunkenly staring at a mule in the stable.

"That was me," the old Apache standing behind him said. "Pay and leave."

Before the crew reached the old fort at the edge of town, all the alcohol had been consumed, and they joyously recounted the specifics of their scrap. Johnson's head buzzed with pleasure as they laughed at how Eddie had held off the whole room with a barstool.

Silence fell over the group as the cloud cover that had been following them for weeks broke, and a broad display of stars hung over the open prairie. Wendel hummed a low tune and almost as soon as he caught it, Jesse Fur joined in, followed by Ned and Eddie, who harmonized. Jesse Fur started a verse and the rest followed with a chorus in a call-and-response pattern.

"Gonna saddle my horse and hit the range."

"Almost time for roundup."

"Gonna spend my days where the cattle play."

"Almost time for roundup."

"Almost time, almost time,"

"Almost time for roundup!" They all joined in the last verse of the chorus with enthusiasm.

Catching on to the tune, Johnson whistled along as they continued with three more verses.

As expected, Caldwell expressed intense dissatisfaction with their state of battered drunkenness, but after what A. J. had told Johnson, Caldwell's anger didn't hold as much weight as before. His heavy gaze, on the other hand, still made Johnson uncomfortable.

Chapter 20

Herb Drake did not show up the next day. True to her word, Eddie was adamant that they leave him behind, and she insisted Johnson take his place. At first, he was excited to move up to the cattle crew; it meant he was doing a good job—and an extra $2 pay. But before long he questioned if $2 was enough. Johnson was put to work on the drags at the back of the drive. It wasn't hard, but after the first day he couldn't tell where the dust ended and he began.

Slim and Pokey, his fellow drag riders, assured him he would get used to it, but after three days in the dry heat, covered in dust from head to toe, he almost longed for the nonstop rainstorms they'd gone through during the weeks before. On top of that, Eddie was so determined to catch up to A. J.'s crew that she made them drive through the night to make up the miles. Over the course of three days, he got maybe nine hours of sleep total.

On the fourth day, Johnson was so tired he kept falling asleep on his horse. Once, after dozing off, he shook awake in a panic and it took him a moment to realize where he was.

"You alright?" Pokey asked him in his deep voice.

Johnson squeezed his eyes closed and slapped himself in the face. "Yeah, I'll be fine."

As he peered through the brown haze toward the western horizon, it seemed as though his wish for rain might come true. A long row of dark clouds stretched for miles at the edge of the plains.

"Looks like another storm is comin'," he said to Pokey.

Pokey just looked at him and laughed. "Them ain't clouds."

Johnson blinked several times and looked again. "What am I lookin' at then?"

"Ain't you never seen mountains before?"

He squinted hard with his tired eyes in disbelief. "Mountains?" Turning his horse west, Johnson rode toward them. It seemed impossible that anything could be so massive.

"Hey, where you going?" Pokey asked as he rode off.

Ignoring him, Johnson rode until he was past most of the dust, but even in the clear air, it was hard for him to comprehend what he was seeing. The mountains pushed higher and farther than any mass of land he had ever seen. It was like a great wall. How could anyone possibly cross them?

Over the next few days, the mountains grew larger.

"Just wait 'til we get ta Denver. It's quite a sight from there," Eddie said to him while they sat around the fire later that night. "An' we'll be there in time for the annual rodeo!"

"You fixing to join?" Wendel asked her.

She gave him a disconcerted look. "Would, but I got the fuckin' cramps."

"We all got cramps," Ned said.

Eddie picked up a smoldering stick and threw it across the fire at him. "My womanly cramps! Mind yer own self!"

Wendel and Jesse Fur laughed as Ned flinched and did his best to turn away. He jumped up and brushed at himself as it hit him, fearful of catching fire.

Stretching his feet to the fire, Wendel took off his gray Confederate hat and set it next to him on the ground.

Seeing it, Johnson found his opportunity to ask about it. "So, you kill a reb for that hat?"

"No, always been my hat," he replied as though he'd answered the question a thousand times. "Back in Louisiana, near the end of the war, my master said he'd free me if I fought. Never saw any action, though, and when I realized there was no chance of winning, I fled the first chance I got."

"A slave fightin' for the South," Eddie said.

"Didn't fight for the South. It was for my freedom," Wendel corrected her.

"Well, I left New Orleans soon as the war started," Eddie replied. "The French side o' me didn't want ta go, but I'm glad I did."

"You're no Frenchie. You don't even speak French!" Wendel exclaimed.

"Half French Canadian!" she shot back at him. "Just 'cause you don't speak no African don't make you any less negro. We are what we are."

Still patting at his shirt, Ned spoke up. "My mother is from Sweden, but nobody would say I'm a Swede."

"That's different," Eddie replied.

"Different how?" he asked. "'Cause I'm half negro?"

"Well, it's just different is all."

Johnson leaned forward and stared into the fire. "There's no half. When you're part negro, you're a negro. White men don't even care which negro you are. We're all the same to them."

Eddie took an apologetic tone. "I didn't mean it like that."

"Sounds to me as if you've had a run-in or two with the 'white man's law,'" Jesse Fur joked.

Johnson went quiet and pulled his face back from the fire.

Realizing he had struck on something Johnson didn't want to talk about, Jesse Fur stood, stretched out his arms, and turned about looking at the endless dark prairie. "No need to worry. We've all been pushed around by a lawman for something or another, but out here it's just us, and we're telling stories. I know I've been caught vagrant and had to cut town more than a handful of times." Sitting back down he pushed his thick locks away from his face and looked at Johnson. "So what's your story? What'd they come after you for?"

Johnson didn't want to say anything but feared staying silent would make him seem more suspicious. His mind raced as he scrambled for something to say. He was blunt with his reply. "They said I stole from a rich man."

"Is that all? Did you do it?" Jesse Fur asked.

"Doesn't really matter. Color of my skin says I did."

"Well, out here it's about collateral. If you got money or you're with a white person, it's safer than being on your own."

—◡—

Colorado
August 1876

Crickets chirped in the dry night air as two men dismounted their horses and entered a small wooden cabin. Tall and trail hardened, the first man led Herb Drake into a dark windowless office that was dimly lit by the glow of a kerosene lamp.

The whole building smelled musty, as if it had gone unoccupied for many years. As he sat and listened to the words of a man sitting at the desk across from him, Drake shifted his gaze uncomfortably—the lamp, an empty bookshelf, the badge on the man's chest that read "Pinkerton National Detective Agency."

"Andrew here tells me you might be privy to the whereabouts of the negro man I am searching for," Cole Charles said.

Drake swallowed hard, avoiding the man's piercing gaze as he answered. "Said he came from Kansas. And I was told I'd be paid if I heard of any negros coming from Kansas."

"How would you feel about getting paid more to aid in his capture?" Cole Charles asked him. Opening a drawer, he produced a large Colt revolver and placed it on the desk, then next to it he placed a tall stack of paper banknotes.

As Herb Drake looked from the money to the revolver, he could no longer avoid the crooked grin on Cole Charles's face. The reflection of the lamp's flame danced in his eyes.

<hr />

Denver, Colorado
September 1876

Denver's annual rodeo coincided with the end of the cattle-driving season, since most of the drives ended there before the cold weather set in. The rough outskirts of the town became even rougher as hundreds of dusty cattle hands with heavy pockets flocked to the saloons of the growing western hub.

After spending the morning hours drinking at one of the more popular saloons, Johnson, Eddie, and the rest of her crew migrated toward the stock-trading yards to watch the rodeo. The event represented the best and most skilled of their trade competing against one another to prove their prowess on the range.

"Gotta be among the toughest," Eddie said to Johnson as they moved through the crowd of people toward the grounds. Taking a swig from her flask, she passed it around to the rest of them.

The rodeo was held in the largest of the stock pens, a circular enclosure fenced with a bulky gate that led to the biggest, whitest barn Johnson had ever seen. Two stories high and almost one hundred feet long, horses and cattle were being led in and out of the barn for the event. The fence of the enclosure was lined with spectators—men, women, and children—packed in a tight crowd, anxious to catch a glimpse of the action. Johnson did his best to get closer as several cowboys took turns riding a wild bronco bareback while the crowd cheered them on. One after another, men stepped up to see how long they could ride an untamed bronco, many of them thrown after just seconds.

Johnson didn't particularly wish to ride a bronco, but every time a rider was bucked, he was able to move closer as another rider stepped up from within the crowd. This went on until he was right against the fence.

After each rider, a short man wearing a buckskin suit and a large hat entered the pen. His manner was heavy with theatrics, using broad gestures to emphasize his words.

"What man still wishes to try his hand? As yet, we've seen none up to the task of beating the record!"

Standing next to Johnson, a well-built white man with sandy hair and a thick beard raised his hand and called out.

"Do y'all think this man has what it takes?" the announcer asked the crowd.

Some in the crowd responded with cheers while others clapped.

Held steady by three handlers, a midnight black bronco was brought over, and Johnson watched intently as the sandy-haired man climbed onto the top rung of the fence.

The animal's eyes stared white hot with defiance at the man and it gave a great snort.

Leaping onto its back, the man grabbed the horse by its mane, and the three handlers released it and ducked for the safety of the fence. The bronco jumped up and down in a violent display. Loudly cheering, the crowed was impressed. The man hung on longer than any previous rider before him.

For a moment, it appeared as if the bronco was slowing down, or at least the man thought as much. He leaned back to give a cocky wave to the spectators, but as soon as he released one of his hands from its mane, the bronco leapt and threw him into the air.

Everyone heard the snap when the full weight of the man's body came down on his right arm.

Several women gasped. The three handlers rushed in to help the man, and a rider wearing a clean white suit with tassels was let through the gate. He quickly roped the angry bronco and pulled it back out the gate. Chatter burst from the crowd when a stretcher was brought in, and Johnson's sweat went cold when he saw the unnatural angle of the man's forearm as he was carried away.

The rider with the white suit performed rope tricks to distract everyone from the gruesome incident. Standing while his horse ran the loop of the fence line, he twirled his lasso above his head, down around his body, and back up. The distraction worked. Cheers from the audience were quick to resume. Johnson was impressed. He had never seen such skill with a rope.

"Quite the show already!" Eddie's voice came from behind him. "Bet that big fella thinks twice 'fore addin' an extra joint to his other arm."

"Would you have tried to ride that horse?" Johnson asked her.

"Nah, bronc ridin' ain't for me. I prefer ropin' steer," she replied. "That's up next."

After the trick roper was finished, the man in the buckskin suit returned to announce that the next event was in fact steer roping.

"Fastest man to take down a steer and tie up its legs is the winner!"

Johnson and Eddie sat right on the fence with several of the crew behind them. They watched in excitement as the first man easily chased his steer down on horseback and tied it up in quick succession. The next man was just as impressive.

"You should have a go," Eddie said to Johnson when the announcer ran out again.

Johnson nodded sarcastically. "Why not?"

"Who thinks they're faster than these men?"

"He does!" Eddie pushed Johnson off the fence and into the pen.

Almost losing his balance as he hit the ground, Johnson ran forward to stay on his feet, and when he stopped, the announcer was standing right in front of him with a horse and a rope ready.

"This young buck looks tough!" the announcer said, handing Johnson the reins and the rope. The crowd applauded.

Johnson froze for a moment. He didn't want to look like a coward in front of such a large audience by running off, but he also didn't want to embarrass himself if he was unsuccessful.

"Go on an' rope 'em!" he heard Eddie yell, and when he looked up he saw both her crew and A. J.'s had gathered at the fence.

Swallowing hard, Johnson mounted the horse. He rode it around the pen a few times so they could get a feel for one another, and the cattle crew cheered him as he passed. This gave him the confidence he needed.

"Ready?" the announcer asked.

Wiping the sweat from his brow, Johnson nodded.

The steer was released from behind the gate. It took off and Johnson went after it. The crowd rejoiced wildly.

Chasing down the steer, Johnson clenched all his muscles tightly, but when he got close and swung the lasso high above his head, he was able to relax. He realized he'd done it so often now that it felt natural. With a confident smile on his face, Johnson tossed the rope and easily looped it over the neck of the animal.

The crew whooped and shouted encouragement. "Get 'em! Tie 'em down!"

Johnson slowed his horse and pulled tight to stop the steer, but he was too familiar with horses trained to submit. He hadn't expected the steer to resist. Instead of stopping, the steer jerked the rope right out of his hands.

Johnson's stomach sank as people in the crowd laughed at him.

The steer stopped, looked back at him, then shook its head.

"Ya ain't done 'til he's licked!" Eddie said to him.

Johnson exhaled. Hot with determination, he turned his horse back to the steer. He wasn't going to let it make a fool of him in front of everyone. The steer took off again and Johnson watched as the length of rope around its horns trailed in the dirt. He pushed the horse faster until he'd caught up alongside it.

The crowd went silent, unsure what he intended to do.

Johnson didn't think, he just acted. He sprung from his horse. Flying through the air, he landed atop the steer and grabbed it by the horns. Pulling back with all of his weight, he wrestled the beast to the ground, took hold of the rope, and quickly tied its legs together as he had seen the previous men do.

Johnson stood in triumph.

The crowd exploded with excitement. No one had seen anything like it before.

The whole cattle crew invaded the pen and lifted him up in celebration.

"Johnson, yer a shinin' jet black negro of splendid physique!" Eddie said.

The announcer and the handlers ran in to usher them all back out of the pen, and the crew carried Johnson to the fence. He felt a rush of admiration he'd never known before. Not just from his crew, but from all the people watching as well. He was overjoyed. It had been a long time since he truly felt good about himself.

The crew stood Johnson on the fence and he held out his fists in triumph.

"It may not have been the fastest, but it sure was something!" the announcer said to the spectators.

Johnson scanned the crowd and saw Caldwell, who, for the first time that Johnson had ever seen, had a smile on his face. To his surprise, Herb Drake was standing right next to him. Before, he would've worried that since Drake had returned, he would take back his position on the drive, but after what he'd just done, Johnson was confident his spot was secure.

Johnson was struck by an even bigger surprise, though, when he spotted another familiar face—one with bright red hair.

"Rex!" Johnson called out. He climbed from the fence and pushed through the throng of people.

"Looks like ya learned a thing or two without me," Rex said, shaking his hand. His beard had grown out long and unkempt, and he wore the same clothes he'd had back in Flatridge, only they were much dirtier.

"Ya look a little rough," Johnson said to him.

"You must not've seen a mirror lately yer damn self then," Rex replied with a laugh.

Johnson smiled. "Let's get a drink and you can meet my crew."

"I never been the kind to pass on a drink," Rex replied.

Just then Caldwell and Drake pushed their way through the crowd.

"I have to say that was mighty impressive," Caldwell said to Johnson.

"Taught him damn near everythin' he knows," Rex said, pushing Johnson's hat lower on his head.

"Drake, where've you been?" Eddie interrupted them. "Never mind, it don't matter. We got celebratin' ta do!"

Wrapping her arm around Johnson's shoulders, she walked him to the saloon down the street with the rest of the crew in tow.

"So, you must've ridden the Chisolm Trail with Johnson then?" Caldwell asked Rex as they followed.

"Chisolm? Can't say that I have. Didn't think he'd been on a drive before."

Caldwell raised a brow. "That so?"

"Er . . . that's not to say that he didn't after we went our separate ways," Rex replied, realizing he'd said something he shouldn't have. "He's one of the hardest workin' men I've known, I can say that."

Caldwell narrowed his eyes at Rex.

Rex sucked in his lips, tipped his hat, and sped up to catch Johnson as he and Eddie made their way into the Red Dog Saloon with some of the other men.

The room wasn't very wide, but it stretched back thirty feet or more and had about twenty patrons. The bar was against the left wall with tables and chairs in the middle. A few men played cards at a table in the back corner while the rest stood at the bar. Ned, Slim, Pokey, Wendel, and Jesse Fur all swarmed the bar as soon as they walked in.

Seeing Rex step through the doorway, Johnson introduced him to Eddie. She squeezed Rex's hand so hard he thought it would break.

"Pleasure," Eddie said. "Now, let's get y'all a drink." Turning to the bartender, she startled half the room with her booming voice, "We got a champion steer roper here who needs some whiskey!"

"Quite the odd stick," Rex said, rubbing his crushed hand and taking a seat.

"She takes some gettin' used to, but you can always count on her," Johnson said as they each took a chair at the nearest table.

One of the men who'd ridden the bronco during the rodeo walked up and set a shot of whiskey in front of Johnson. "That was somethin' special, what I seen ya do. Ya got sand, that's fer sure."

Taking the drink in his hand, Johnson nodded to him, swallowed it, and raised the empty glass to the man.

Doing the same, the man turned and walked away.

"Yer makin' good friends in this town," Rex said.

"I suppose," Johnson replied. He knew it was stupid to attract notice, but he'd be back on the range tomorrow and deserved to be celebrated for once.

Eddie came back and slammed a bottle and some glasses down on their table. "On me!" She uncorked the bottle, poured herself a shot of whiskey, and downed it. "Ah, this is the good stuff." Pulling out her flask, she finished what was left inside and refilled it from the bottle. "Well, I reckon it's been too long since I tried on my poker face. Don't you two go sneakin' off ta whisper sweet nothin's!" And with that, she strutted over to the table of men playing cards and sat down.

Rex gave Johnson a questioning look. Johnson took the bottle and poured them each a drink.

"So where ya been since Kansas?" Johnson asked. What he really wanted to know was if Rex had any news about Cole Charles, but he was careful not to ask outright.

"Oh, mostly 'round here," Rex replied.

"Done bein' a teamster?"

"Fer the stage lines, I am. Mostly hauling supplies between here an' the mines now."

"Thought ya wanted to go back to Texas?"

Rex shrugged. "I thought about it, but then I got offered this job and it's good pay."

"So you didn't make it back to Flatridge?"

Rex took a drink. "No, I did. That Cole Charles was still there. Tried ta push me 'round about gettin' at you.

Johnson's blood went cold.

"How'd he look?"

"Mean as always, had a bit of a limp."

A limp? How could he walk after losing a leg? Johnson finished his glass and tried to remain calm. The liquor helped.

"Where'd he end up?"

"Couldn't tell ya," Rex replied. "He damn near questioned the whole town 'fore he up and left. But I guess he's got big money behind him. Offered me a pretty sum."

Johnson was taken aback by this. "You—you didn't take it?"

"I might've considered it," Rex said with a laugh, "if I'd known any-thin' 'bout where ya was. You were smart ta leave when ya did!"

"And Burt?"

"Burt was gone by the time I came back through."

Johnson flinched as someone slapped his back.

"What a feat that was back there!" the man who had slapped him said, setting another shot in front of him.

Forcing a half smile, Johnson downed it, only with less enthusiasm this time.

"Where'd ya learn that?" the man asked.

"Dunno, just did it."

"What a thing!" Giving a hearty laugh, he slapped Johnson on the back again and went back to the bar.

A loud cheer erupted from the poker table. "Don't mind me, folks," Eddie said in a joyous tone, "just doin' some honest work."

Johnson looked over and saw that A. J. and old Bill had joined the game, but judging by their faces, they hadn't fared so well.

"Quite a day," Ned said, pulling up a chair next to Johnson and Rex.

Pushing his half-empty drink to Ned, Rex stood up. "And I wish I could stay longer, but I'm due for Golden in the mornin'."

Johnson stood, too, looking Rex in the eyes as he held out his hand.

Rex pulled him in for a hug. "Reckon this is probably farewell. Least fer a while."

Pulling away, he scratched at his scruffy red beard, tipped his hat to both of them, then walked out.

Ned had a puzzled look on his face. "How do you know him?"

Johnson didn't answer, and before Ned had a chance to ask again, both Wendel and Jesse Fur scrambled over to their table from the bar. Both were in good spirits.

Jesse Fur playfully grabbed Ned by the shoulders. "You boys staying outta trouble?"

"Best we can," Ned replied.

"Say, how many full glasses you think are left in this bottle?" Jesse Fur asked. Closing one eye he leaned up close to assess the half-full bottle of whiskey sitting on the table. "I bet six shots at least!"

"You're a fool! It's no less than eight!" Wendel exclaimed.

"I've had about enough of you for the day!" Jesse Fur replied.

"You've had enough? I gotta put up with you day in an' day out and you've had enough?" Wendel stared down at the bottle again. "Definitely eight glasses!"

Jesse Fur grinned. "There's only one way to find out!"

"I say nine!" Ned weighed in with a guess.

"How much y'all trying to put on it?" Jesse Fur asked them.

Overhearing them from the bar, Pokey and Slim were excited by the prospect of betting and joined in. One at a time, they went around the table stating how many shot glasses they thought could be filled and how much each man was willing to wager that he was the closest to having the right answer. Jesse Fur was set on six, Pokey said seven, Wendel and Slim both bet eight, Ned guessed nine, and Johnson ten. In the event of an uneven glass, they all agreed that anything above the original guess was a bust.

Each of them was silent as Wendel poured out the first glass, and the second, and the third, but when he got to the fourth, Jesse Fur began to lament his guess of six. It was obvious that there was more than two shots left.

"Dad-gummit!" Pokey yelled after the seventh shot was poured and liquor still remained in the bottle.

"*Ahhhhhh!*" Wendel yelled as the whiskey reached the rim of the eighth glass.

Slim snapped his fingers in disappointment.

"Here we go," Wendel said as he shook what little bit was left in the bottle.

Setting another glass in front of him, he poured slowly.

Johnson watched in intense silence while Ned muttered, "C'mon, c'mon, c'mon."

In the background, voices rose from the poker table but all the men were glued to the shot glass.

Wendel poured even slower. The liquid approached the top of the glass, stopping just short of the rim.

"Yes!" Ned cheered as Wendel turned the bottle completely upside down and shook it.

"Looks like we have our winner," Wendel said, setting the bottle down. "Only one thing to do now!"

Each of them grabbed a shot of whiskey with a big smile, touched their glasses together, and downed the shots.

With Cole Charles still in the back of his mind, Johnson immediately grabbed another shot and drank it.

Jesse Fur wrapped his arm around him. "I'll have to take ya to my favorite saloon when we get to Cheyenne." He leaned in close and lowered his voice, "Has a spot in the back where you can get some nice girls."

Johnson smiled at the thought. Cheyenne, Wyoming, sounded like the right kind of place for him to hide away from Cole Charles.

The rest of the time became a fuzzy blur of singing songs, dancing, and cheering as the whole crew celebrated late into the night. At one point, he saw Eddie put a man into a headlock over a disagreement about the poker game. Johnson stood by and laughed as she let the man go and pushed him to the floor. He was disappointed when they had to rush out afterward. He was having a good time and wanted to stay longer.

Chapter 21

Johnson was so hungover when he awoke that he nearly puked. He didn't hear the gunshot; his ears rang sharply and his head throbbed as if it were getting beaten like a drum. Drawing his revolver, he ducked behind the chuckwagon, where Eddie, Cookie, Tony, and Cecilio had all taken cover.

He cringed in agony as Eddie fired a shot in return.

"What's goin' on?" Johnson asked, trying to keep his stomach's contents inside of him.

"Ain't sure," she replied, motioning to a low hill to their northwest. "Shot came from over yonder."

Johnson rubbed at his temples with one hand under his hat. "Everyone alright?"

"Don't know 'bout the others. Got us here, an' Jesse's back there pissin' on his boots."

Johnson turned to look behind them, and sure enough, there was Jesse Fur, out in the open, still so drunk he was wobbling left to right. A stream of urine crossed back and forth over each foot as he garbled out an old church hymn.

"What's he thinkin'?" Johnson asked. "Jesse! Get down—" Gagging, he nearly puked again.

"Ya can't cheat yer bladder and ya sure as shit can't cheat a hangover," Eddie said, gently patting him on the back as she peeked around the wagon toward the hill. "Cecilio, my eyes are bad this mornin', you seein' anythin'?"

"Two, maybe three men moving on the hill," Cecilio replied.

"Probably some o' them chuckleheads still red-assed from losin' money last night," Eddie said. "Cookie, think if ya jus' make 'em some biscuits it'll send 'em on their way?"

Another shot was fired, and they all took cover.

Jesse Fur hit the ground.

There was a quick rustle of feet and Caldwell and Drake came running around the chuckwagon with rifles.

"Fur, you alright?" Caldwell yelled to Jesse Fur, but there was no response.

"Where's the rest of the boys?" Eddie asked Caldwell.

Caldwell pointed to their left. "The others are pinned down in that gulch."

Johnson saw a shallow ravine with some scrub but couldn't see any of the men.

"I'll take Johnson and we can try to go around 'em," Drake said, drawing a crude map in the dirt.

"Good idea." Caldwell cocked his rifle. "Cilio, grab Fur while me and Eddie give cover fire. Go!"

Crouched low, Johnson followed close behind Drake as Eddie and Caldwell raised up and opened fire on the hill and Cecilio ran to Jesse Fur.

Sliding low onto the ground next to where Jesse Fur lay facedown, Cecilio saw that Jesse had taken a bullet in his upper back.

He shook him firmly. "Yesse! Yesse!"

No response.

"He is not well!" Cecilio yelled to Caldwell.

"Dammit!" Caldwell fired and one of the men appeared to go down.

Several more shots came from the hill.

Climbing the hill to their south, Johnson was relieved to reach the other side, where he was out of the line of sight. The pops of gunfire echoed as they moved toward a small wash. As the adrenaline wore off, Johnson's mouth watered. Dropping to all fours, he couldn't hold it in any longer. The vomit burned as it expelled from his mouth and through his nose. He tried to take a breath, but the smell triggered his stomach again. Johnson coughed and blew bile from his nostrils.

"Hate to give a man trouble when he's feeling so poorly, but I'm gonna have to ask for that revolver."

Johnson wiped a long glob of spittle from his face, took a breath, and looked up into the barrel of Drake's rifle.

"Hurry it up, those men will hold them off for only so long," Drake said, motioning with the rifle.

Johnson cursed, slowly sliding the revolver out of his gun belt and tossing it to his feet. He should've known.

"How much ya gettin' paid?"

"It's enough. C'mon," Drake said.

Waving him across the wash, he picked up Johnson's gun and led him down to a thicket where his black-and-white mare was hobbled and saddled along with another horse.

"You takin' me ta Cole Charles?" Johnson asked.

"Didn't give me his name, just a price," Drake replied. "Get on that horse. We don't have much time."

"Suppose I refuse?"

Drake cocked the rifle. "You're still worth money dead, but I prefer to get the full bag."

"Thought ya said you'd never killed a man?"

"Don't mean I ain't ready."

Nodding, Johnson exhaled and climbed the hobbled horse as slowly as he thought he could get away with.

Putting his rifle in its scabbard, Drake kept Johnson's own revolver trained on him as he unhobbled the horses then pulled a rope from one of his saddlebags. "Lemme see your hands."

Johnson did as he was told, holding out his wrists several inches apart from each other.

Drake raised the revolver higher, "Closer."

Johnson glared at him as he touched his arms together.

Drake's grip on the revolver was loose in his right hand as he handled the rope, and as he came closer, Johnson took his chance. He hit hard with his fists, knocking the revolver away.

Drake leapt to the ground and grabbed hold of the gun, but Johnson was too quick. He jumped from the horse and kicked his hand. The gun went flying. In desperation, Drake grabbed Johnson's leg and bit hard into his calf. Johnson screamed as he awkwardly struck Drake's face several times with the side of his fist.

Drake released, blood pouring from his nose. For a moment, his eyes went dull, then he fell to the ground.

Johnson clutched at his leg. A patch of crimson bled through his pants. Trying to stand, more vomit rushed into his mouth. He squatted back down and spat toward Drake, who had managed to rise to his knees and then his feet.

Blood ran down Drake's face as he lumbered closer and towered over Johnson. Johnson's eyes went wide and he dropped prone into the grass covering his head.

A rifle shot echoed as it tore into Drake's left shoulder.

Looking through the blades of tall grass, Johnson watched Drake clutch the wound and slump back to the ground then turned to Eddie and Caldwell, who were racing down the hill toward them on horseback.

Johnson called to Drake. "You dead?"

A low groan came from the man.

Caldwell jumped off his horse as soon as he got there and kicked Drake onto his back. "You snake!" he yelled, hitting him in the stomach with the butt of his rifle.

Eddie knelt next to Johnson. "You alright?"

"I'll be fine." His breath was heavy and tasted sour. "How'd ya find us so quick?"

"Them cowards gave up almost soon as ya left," she replied. "Guess ya shoulda paid 'em enough ta fight harder, Drake. Or at least enough not ta talk!"

"I hate Pinkertons," Caldwell said, glaring down at Drake. "Them and anyone in their employ are good-for-nothing scum."

Taking the rope intended for Johnson, Caldwell tied Drake's hands behind his back, leaving him on the ground.

Brushing his hands together, Caldwell turned to Johnson. "Time for you to come clean. Why were they after you?"

Eddie interjected. "Caldwell, he's proved his worth. Does it really matter?"

He turned a stiff finger toward her. "Eddie, just 'cause I hate Pinkertons don't mean I'm still signing on to your story about the Chisolm Trail."

It should be obvious by now why I wanna know I can trust those working for me."

"A rich businessman paid men to come after me," Johnson replied. "He thinks I took somethin' away from him."

"Did you do it?" Caldwell asked.

"No." Johnson's mind raced as they stared at him. He couldn't bring himself to tell the whole truth of the matter. He worried they wouldn't give him the benefit of the doubt if he explained the whole story about the woman.

"He's one of us now, Caldwell, and he needs our help," Eddie said. "Safer with us than on his own."

As Caldwell paused to think, a large amount of brown tobacco sludge shot from his lips. "Fine, we'll protect you, but once this drive is over, I make no guarantees. If Eddie wants to stick with you, that's on her. And I don't wanna see no slack. You still work!"

"Yes, sir," Johnson replied.

They laid Drake over the back of the black-and-white mare then headed back to camp.

Cresting the hill, Johnson could see the rest of the crew in a circle, and his heart sank when he realized that they were standing around the spot where Jesse Fur had gone down.

"Oh, no," Eddie lamented at the sight as they got closer.

Wendel crouched over Jesse Fur's body. Tears ran down the wrinkled lines in his face as he wept. Reaching for the inside pocket of Jesse's vest, he removed a folded piece of paper and put it in his own vest pocket.

Walking up, Caldwell laid a hand on his shoulder. "We'll make sure he's sent back to his family."

In between sobs, Wendel cleared his throat. "He was born a slave; he had no family left."

As Johnson helped the other men dig a grave, Eddie and Caldwell took Drake and the other three men back over the hill. When they returned an hour later, it was just the two of them.

Once again, the crew circled up, this time around the fresh grave of their companion.

No one spoke. A warm breeze blew down the hill to their west and cut across the plain.

"Someone should sing somethin'," Eddie said, breaking the silence.

Wendel took his bandanna and wiped his tears. "Jesse was the one who sang best."

PART III

Chapter 22

"Mr. Herston, I assure you there is nothing to fear on my end," Frederick Boyd said as he thumbed through a pile of legal documents on his desk while his gray-haired business partner sat across from him. "The loss of the *Queen Bellamy* was a setback, but the insurance we recovered from the fire has allowed us to cover our debts, which have been piling up because of the success of these damned trains!"

Herston raised an eyebrow. "Our new livestock venture relies heavily on those trains."

"You think I am unaware of that fact?" Boyd asked. Standing, he turned to look out his window. "I question if this is even the right course of action daily."

"Come now. San Francisco is a fast-growing city; the people need meat. We stand to make a fortune," Herston said.

Sitting back at his desk, Boyd opened a fresh bottle of brandy and poured himself a glass. "The fee I had to pay the Stock Grazier's Association just to start this operation was exorbitant. Governor John Allen Campbell made certain of that."

Herston crossed his legs. "You should be careful when dealing with their organization. They have a hand in most everything that goes on in that region."

"They're nothing but crooks as far as I am concerned," Boyd replied.

"Nonetheless, we have to put up with them."

Boyd twisted the end of his mustache. "Yes, I have had to put up with quite a lot these past months. The money I've been paying the Pinkertons is no small fee and they've yet to find the man who soiled my daughter's honor."

"At least you still have your daughter. Mine decided to throw her life away with the foolish notion that she could become a writer then ventured off to God knows where."

"From what you've told me about her, it could have been worse had she stayed," Boyd said with a smirk. "She might've become one of those outspoken suffragettes. Think how that would have reflected on your reputation."

Herston grimaced. "Still, it's been some time since I've received any communication from Margret. I'm beginning to worry."

"I would suggest you hire the Pinkertons to find her, but my faith in them has waned considerably."

Putting on his hat, Herston stood. "She's just trying to spite me is all."

Boyd exhaled. "Yes, I know the feeling."

"I hope you have safe travels. Send word as soon as you arrive," Herston said then turned and walked to the door.

As Herston walked out, Boyd's spectacled assistant came in and stood hunched in the back corner.

"Have we received any more communications from Cole Charles?"

"No, sir."

There had been several weeks of silence. Boyd threw his glass across the room.

His assistant flinched as it shattered against a bookshelf.

Boyd began to pace back and forth in front of the tall arched window in his office. "I have lost too much! To fire, to the Union Pacific, to that nigger who stole the innocence that was my daughter!" Looking out the window, Boyd pinched the bridge of his nose. "I had really hoped to have this matter cleared before we made the move out West."

***

Colorado
September 1876

Jesse Fur's death set the whole crew in poor spirits. Conversation that once dominated their time around the fire at night had dwindled to near silence. Even Eddie found little to say. Gray cloud cover had returned, casting dull tones over the landscape of rolling hills covered in gnarled scrub, which made their days driving cattle even more unpleasant and gloomy.

Despite Caldwell's promise of protection during the drive, for Johnson, the thought of Cole Charles so close on his trail brought a resurgence of anxiety. Johnson wasn't certain what the rest of the crew members knew about why Drake had tried to take him, but at this point he didn't care. His thoughts raced when he was around them. He continually worried about how to avoid revealing anything. Even while he was around Eddie or Ned, whom he trusted the most, he kept quiet. Had it not been for Eddie's insistence that he was safest with them, he would've taken a chance and gone on alone.

Tense from staying on such high alert, Johnson wore himself out by nightfall each day and barely ate before falling asleep. Each night he slept with his revolver across his chest.

The only solace Johnson found was in the few moments he had to himself when he woke with the sunrise each morning and could still feel his dreams about Margret.

There was little wind and the clouds seemed to hang over the plain as they drove the cattle north. The days felt long.

"We're getting close to the end now," Wendel said to him one morning as they mounted for the day.

How far are we from Cheyenne? is what Johnson wanted to ask, but he feared it might lead to questions about where he would go afterward and what he planned to do next. "I suppose," was all Johnson said as he rode off.

By the time they were only a few days from crossing into the Wyoming Territory, the mood of the crew had mostly returned to normal. The thought of being so close to the end of the drive helped. They knew it meant their big payday was within reach.

"Last I checked, it's neck an' neck!" Eddie shouted at A. J. from across the fire one night.

Throwing down his empty tin plate, he shouted back, "You must've lost track then, 'cause I'm ahead!"

"Didn't say you wasn't. Just said we're close is all!"

"Close to losin' your money!"

"We'll see how yer feelin' in Cheyenne!"

Johnson finished his plate and walked away. He didn't care about the competition anymore. Now that he was on the drags, he wasn't much a part of it anyway. Unraveling his bedroll, Johnson checked his revolver before lying down. All he knew was that once he got his money, he would use it to find a place to lay low.

As Johnson, Pokey, and Slim rode amid the great cloud of dust the next day, the cattle were on edge. Several strayed and had to be recovered. Clear skies had returned, but the fall weather had turned hot, drying the landscape into an arid scene of crisp, yellowing vegetation.

Despite the bandanna fixed tightly around his face, the dirt that concentrated at the rear of the drive still managed to invade Johnson's body. He continually dug grime out of his nose and ears, and as often as he could remember, he tried not to breathe through his mouth while working. This left him vulnerable to the smell of the cattle, a stench he'd yet to completely grow accustomed to.

"Look, antelope!" Slim shouted as a group of about fifteen pronghorns bounded away from them over a hill to the east.

Johnson turned to view the orangish, deerlike creatures. He had never before seen pronghorn and found them striking. They ran in a pack just as the cattle did during a stampede, but they did so with such grace and control that it was hard for Johnson to believe they were wild animals.

"They's nervous like the cattle. Must be 'cause we comin' up on the Platte River," Pokey said.

This caught Johnson off guard. Was there a danger to the Platte he wasn't aware of? "Why would the river make them so nervous?"

"Ghosts." Pokey smiled. "Ain't nobody told you about the death ship of the Platte River?"

Annoyed by such a foolish answer, Johnson exhaled and scratched under the brim of his hat. "No."

Riding his horse closer, Pokey told him the old cowboy tale. "It's a ghost ship that rolls in with a thick cloud of fog. Folks say it's all covered in frost. Sails, masts, crew, everything. Even in the dead of summer. They say there's always someone hanging from the bow and whoever sees 'im first dies that very day."

Johnson rolled his eyes. Did Pokey really believe in ghosts? He had always found him kind of slow and thought it strange to bring the subject up so soon after Jesse's death. "Why are you tellin' me this?"

Pokey shrugged. "Dunno. It's a story every cowpoke tells. Besides, you looked like you needed a story to help take a load off."

"I need ta get out of all this dust," Johnson replied.

No sooner than he said it, a group of four cattle broke away from the herd and started running east toward the same hill the pronghorn had disappeared over.

Without a word, Johnson sent his horse into a gallop, catching up to them easily, but as he turned the strays back toward the main group, what he saw on the western horizon made his eyes grow wide. A low, thick cloud raced toward them. Swirling through the air at great speed, it grew larger as it moved to overtake them. Johnson couldn't believe it. Was this the fog? Could Pokey have been right?

As the dark mass got closer, it covered the sky. A deep drone emanated from within. More cattle broke off from the herd and ran, but Johnson froze. He couldn't move.

Could it be the death ship?

"Take cover!" Pokey yelled to him, but Johnson remained immobile.

The whole herd now ran as the cloud engulfed them. Johnson's horse bucked, sending him to the ground.

Dazed and with his head pounding, Johnson clenched his eyes shut. If it was the death ship, he didn't want to be the first to see it. Sweat covered his body. He listened as the drone transformed into a loud buzz then became thousands of separate buzzes. Something struck his face. It felt strange and alive. He was hit again, only this time, sharp thorns dug into his cheek.

Opening his eyes, Johnson sat up and grabbed at the creature on his face. A locust! He looked up—millions flew through the air. His eyes raced from one spot to the next as he examined them. There were so many that only specks of blue sky could be seen through the mass of insects. It was just like the Bible stories he'd heard as a child. Had they been sent as a plague by God to punish him?

Johnson waved his hands in front of his face to bat them away as he moved toward a small gulch to wait them out. This only added to his ever-growing list of bizarre experiences. Maybe it was a sign?

The locusts swarmed several hours before the sky was visible again. Even after the large mass had gone, the ground still was littered with the winged brown bugs. With each step, their bodies crunched under the weight of feet and hooves.

"What a stroke of luck! Ain't no way A. J. can beat me after this!" Eddie rejoiced as she and Johnson tracked down stray cattle. "I ain't never seen that many before."

"Does it happen often?" Johnson rubbed the spot where he'd hit his head. It was still tender.

"They usually swarm 'round this time o' year," she replied. "Give more hell ta the sodbusters than us, but that sure was somethin'."

Johnson looked over the plain at the locusts covering the grass. "I'd say."

He still felt on edge, but the swarm helped to ease his anxieties. It made him realize that all manner of natural phenomenon occurred regardless of what he chose to do. He never hesitated in the face of rivers or storms, which could kill him just as easily as any man could. Johnson wrapped his fingers around his revolver and squeezed. He had a better chance of defending himself against another man than he did wild nature, and he had people who had committed to help protect him.

Letting go of his revolver, he turned to Eddie. "When the drive is over, what do you plan to do next?"

Eddie gave him a smirk that suggested she knew what he was getting at. "Oh, hadn't really put much thought to it. Why ya askin'?"

His heart beat faster and seemed to push into his throat. Why was it so hard for him to get this out? He took a deep breath. "Could—would you help me find a safe place to go after this?"

"Was wonderin' when you'd ask fer my help. You'd kept too quiet fer too long," she replied, tucking a strand of hair behind her ear. "Don't worry, I'll help ya."

A wave of coolness came over him. He nodded in relief and thought about how much Eddie had done for him. She'd kept him from being caught vagrant, given him a job on the cattle drive, and saved him from Drake.

"You stuck your neck out for me since the beginning. Why?"

Eddie pulled her horse to a stop. Her face muscles relaxed with a look of raw sentiment. "Ya know, I was sittin' in that saloon in Fort Worth when ya walked in that first night we met. Like everyone else there, I watched ya talk with that white woman. Every man in that place was madder than hell that a negro had stolen her away, but I saw what they didn't care ta see. *You* loved that woman. Loved her an' ya couldn't be with her. I felt for ya. Nobody knows like I do what it's like ta have folks tryin' ta say who ya can an' shouldn't be with. So when I saw them two fellers follow ya out, I wasn't gonna abide them pushin' ya 'round."

"But what about the Pinkertons?" Johnson asked.

"I ain't never been too worried 'bout what ya may have done nor where ya came from. We've ridden the trails together now, we've communed over drinks, and we've fought together. You been far more loyal ta me than most o' these yahoos has ever been. Far as I'm concerned, that makes us pards."

Smiling, Johnson stretched out his hand and Eddie shook it.

"There's a new camp in the Black Hills. South Dakota Territory. Supposed ta be a good place to disappear an' start over," she said. "We can head there soon as we leave Cheyenne if ya want."

Johnson nodded then rubbed at his head again. He caught a whiff of a funny smell and sniffed at the air. He looked around and when he couldn't pinpoint it, he sniffed at different parts of his clothes.

Eddie watched him like he was a dog biting at a tick. "You fall in somethin' foul?"

"Nah, hit my head and now everything smells funny, like horse piss."

Leaning over closer to him, she took a big whiff herself then recoiled. "*Ugh!* Nah, I think yer horse just pissed on ya 'fore it ran off!"

"Huh?"

"Ya might need ta burn them clothes 'fore this is all over."

They both shared a laugh at his expense then continued their search while Eddie sang one of her old cowboy tunes.

**Colorado
September 1876**

> Mr. Charles,
> I require an update as soon as possible. If you are not a man fit for this job, then I will find one who is.
> F. Boyd

Fury rose in Cole Charles as he read the note. "*Ahhhh!*" he screamed as he swiped everything off his desk. The lamp that had been sitting on it shattered when it hit the ground. Sending oil across the floor, it ignited all the papers that were now strewn about the small office.

Rising from his chair, he turned to grab his coat and gun belt then limped out of the room as the fire spread. The burning cabin sent flames into the late afternoon sky while he saddled his horse, the smell of tarred pine heavy in the smoke.

His trail-hardened associate, Andrew, ran toward him in a panic from a small grove of trees. "I was down by the crick and saw smoke! What happened?"

"I am leaving for Wyoming. If those I hire cannot help me find the negro, then I will find him myself!"

Andrew's heavy jaw went slack. "Leaving? Well, I'm not going to Wyoming."

"Then I will find help elsewhere," Cole Charles said. Placing the foot of his good leg into the stirrup, he lifted himself and sat sidesaddle, then adjusting his prosthetic into the stirrup, swung his good leg over the other side of the horse.

"But what about my money?" Andrew asked.

Cole Charles looked down on the man as if he were a varmint. "You've been no help to me. I owe you nothing."

"Wha-what? You fucking crook!" Andrew yelled, arms held out in disbelief.

Disinterested in his grievance, the Pinkerton did not see fit to reply and rode off without another word.

This disrespect enraged Andrew even further. "You ain't leaving until I get paid!" Drawing his gun, he fired a shot in the air to get Cole Charles's attention.

Andrew's vision blurred as he watched Cole Charles turn around in the saddle. He fell to his knees as an ache burned red-hot in his chest, and when he squinted to focus, he saw Cole Charles place his large Colt revolver back into its holster and ride off.

Chapter 23

Wyoming Territory
October 1876

The cattle drive came to its dusty conclusion on a Saturday morning on the prairies of eastern Wyoming. The grit in Johnson's teeth felt even thicker as they pushed through the last few miles, and when they came to a shallow valley in the plains, Eddie was there waiting for them. Tall and proud atop her horse, she was mounted next to Caldwell and Cecilio, who watched the herd pack in.

"You did good, boys," Caldwell said as they rode up. "Just gotta get them to the stockyards and we'll be finished."

Eager to lay claim to victory over A. J., Eddie blurted out, "Got any idea how far back Cookie is? I wanna check that roadometer an' see how many miles I won by."

Caldwell huffed. "We didn't come all this way for your games, Eddie. Worry about it when the job is done!"

"This ain't no game! I'm 'bout ta be owed money."

"Well, I don't have time for it. We're supposed to contact Howe and then meet the buyer in town."

"Go on without me," she replied. "I'll stay an' help with the cattle."

Caldwell huffed again then spit. "Fine. But be quick about it." Turning his horse, he rode off.

"In a mood, as always," Eddie said as she searched the plains for signs of the chuckwagon. In the distance, a dust cloud signaled that it wasn't too far behind. As she took in the view, her curiosity turned to A. J., who had yet to show up. "Slim, ya seen A. J. 'round today?"

"*Huh?*" Slim replied, too preoccupied with dusting off his large belly to pay attention.

"*A—J?*" she drew out the letters.

"Oh." He looked up and thought for a moment. "No."

"Fine help as always there, Slim," Eddie replied with annoyance in her voice. "Well, he's up ta somethin'. No good, likely."

She wasn't surprised when A. J. rode his horse in alongside Cookie and Tony with the chuckwagon.

A. J.'s face flushed at the sight of her. "You must have tampered with the meter!" he yelled at her. "You couldn't have gained almost ten miles so quick!"

The smile on Eddie's face was so big it almost cut to her ears. "The numbers can't lie!"

"Bullshit!"

"Don't gimme that! You're the one who tried ta pay off my hands against me!"

"*Ahhh*, bullshit!" Rattled with anger, A. J. couldn't seem to produce any other words.

"I expect payment 'fore we cut out tomorrow. Now get goin'. There's work ta be done," Eddie said, waving him on his way.

Still cursing, A. J. rode off.

Putting on a face that meant it was time to get serious about work, Eddie turned back to Johnson and the other men and began barking orders. "Well, guess we all best get ta cowpunchin' then. Wendel, Slim, start roundin' up ta go into town. Pokey, you stay an' keep things together here with Cecilio. Johnson, yer with me."

They were quick to step to their work, rounding up the cattle into groups as Eddie made her way south with Johnson following at her side.

"Where we headed?" Johnson asked.

Removing her hat, Eddie ran her fingers through her dirty hair. "Wanna check on Ned. We'll make sure the remuda is good, then head into town with the rest o'—*ah!*" she cut her words short, frustrated as she worked a tangled knot from her hair. "Ya know, A. J. better not try ta stiff me. I worked hard ta win that bet."

Johnson was glad Eddie had won. He hadn't forgotten that A. J. had almost gotten him kicked off the drive, and Johnson wanted to see him lose because of it. Still, he was curious how Eddie had managed to pull ahead so late in the competition. "Did those locusts really set A. J. that far back?"

"Hell, no!" Eddie replied with a laugh. "I jacked up the chuckwagon last night and spun the wheel 'til I thought the counter looked good. Wasn't gonna let him be the only one ta cheat."

They came upon Ned just a few miles away. His shirt was soaked with sweat as he hammered metal stakes into the dry ground, setting up a makeshift barrier of rope that surrounded the remuda. The horses stirred at their approach, neighing and chuffing as they sought their intention.

"Yer workin' too hard. Them horses ain't goin' nowhere," Eddie said to him as they rode in.

A bead of sweat rolled off Ned's nose as he looked up at them. "I'd hate to lose one right at the end," he replied.

"Fair," Eddie tucked a strand of hair behind her ear. "We ain't got much time, so I'll get to it. Me an' Johnson are headin' to the Black Hills after this. Don't know what you were thinkin' next, but if ya wanna ride with us, yer welcome."

Removing his hat, Ned wiped his brow with a quick brush of his sleeve and then placed the hat back onto his head. "I appreciate you wanting to throw in with me, but Caldwell already said he'd pay me to drive the remuda back to Texas."

"Guess that ain't a bad deal," she replied.

"Nope."

Johnson nodded and smiled at Ned. "Gotta get back to your girl, too."

An embarrassed grin peeked at the corners of Ned's mouth. "Yeah, I suppose there's that, too."

"Can't keep the heart wanting for too long," Eddie said, "Or the loins. That's how a young man gets himself in trouble."

"I'd be more worried about trouble coming after you two," he said to Johnson more than Eddie.

Johnson stiffened, almost as if the words spoken out loud would draw Cole Charles nearer.

Eddie sat up straight in the saddle. "Ain't nothin' we can't handle."

"I'd rather avoid talking about any trouble altogether," Johnson said, scratching at the back of his neck.

"What'd you do to get people chasing ya all the way out here anyway?" Ned asked him. "Couldn't have been no stealing."

Johnson's heart jumped, but Eddie interjected before he even opened his mouth. "That's none o' yer damn business!"

"What?" Ned asked with an innocent look on his face that reminded them both of how young he was. "I don't care. Just curious is all."

"If he wanted ya ta know, don't ya think he'd have told ya already?"

Ned turned to Johnson with a wanting look, his strange, brownish-green eyes begging for an answer.

Johnson swallowed. A wind brushed across the land, and the sound of the tall grass rustled over the noise of the horses. "Maybe if we ever see each other again, I'll tell ya someday."

Ned's face twisted in confusion. "Ain't I gonna see you tomorrow?"

"That's what we're tellin' ya," Eddie said. "It's likely we're cuttin' out before tomorrow."

Ned looked skyward and scrunched his nose as the sunlight hit his eyes. "Ah, well, damn. Guess this is goodbye."

Eddie laid her hand on the crown of his hat as if she were leaving a pet dog behind. "Goodbye, Ned. If I never see ya again, it was good ta know ya."

Johnson rode closer and Ned adjusted his hat, which Eddie had pushed down over his brow.

His eyes were wide with disappointment. "You saved my life twice and I never got to repay you."

"Then I guess ya still owe me," Johnson said, extending his hand. "Go find your girl and settle down somewhere nice."

Shaking his hand, Ned smiled. "If I still owe you, that means you gotta stay safe to collect."

"I suppose it does," Johnson replied.

Colorado
October 1876

Cole Charles tore across the plains northward. He'd exchanged his tired horse for a fresh one in Denver and was now only a day out from Wyoming. Hard riding caused more pain in his leg, but that pain didn't outweigh his desire to finish his job so he could return home. Patting the letter in his vest pocket, he had already decided that this would be his last commission for Pinkerton.

He was tired of working long hours to maintain contact with incompetent men who were beneath him, half of whom couldn't successfully complete a simple task given to them. Still, despite his physical ailments, he would not concede defeat and allow another man from the agency to take control of his assignment. If he had to track down Johnson on his own to bring him in, he would.

Squeezing the leather reins in his hands, he spurred his horse in the side to push it faster. No, he would be the one to bring Johnson in, dead or alive.

Chapter 24

Cheyenne, Wyoming Territory
October 1876

Cheyenne, Wyoming, wasn't as impressive as Johnson had expected. Part of the reason for this was due to the way the crew had talked. The other part was because it was their final destination, and he'd built it up in his mind that it would be as big and lively as Denver, but it wasn't even close to half its size. Like Denver, it was set against the backdrop of a large range of mountains to the west and plains to the east, but Cheyenne was made up of mostly single-story wooden buildings and seemed to be populated by only a handful of people.

Leaving the main herd on the plains, the crew split the cattle into smaller groups and drove them to the train yard south of Cheyenne in waves. Iron track and telegraph lines stretched in either direction for miles. Extra rows of track detoured off the main line, where a string of cars sat at the stock pens ready to be loaded with cattle. Each car had a layer of hay on the floor and gaps in the wooden slats that made up the walls. The guttural sounds of the animals were concentrated as they were packed in, and the whole place smelled of cattle, grease, and coal smoke.

Moving the cattle from the plains onto the train cars was a rigorous process, and Johnson was impressed with how every step of the operation functioned together. He waited at the gate of a holding pen while Eddie, Wendel, and Slim herded the cattle in. Once Johnson closed the gate behind them, A. J. and Bill pushed the cattle through a narrow fenced path and onto the cars. Cattle were crammed in tight, their long horns often protruding through the gaps in the walls. When the car was full, the train pulled forward and the process started over again.

"Why come all this way?" Johnson asked Eddie as they herded a group in. "Couldn't we have sold the cattle in Denver?"

"Ain't no easy way ta go west o' Denver. Guess the buyer here is payin' top dollar so he can ship 'em across the mountains ta California," she replied.

"What's in California?"

Eddie shot him a look like he'd asked her which way the sky was. "Gold! Whole mess o' people been goin' there fer years ta strike it rich."

Johnson paused; he was intrigued. *Strike it rich with gold?* "Do they?"

"Hardly. In my experience, its only rich people who make any money off the gold mines, an' most don't even need ta own a mine."

"How do they get rich without a mine?"

Eddie held out her hand and motioned to the cattle. "Selling beef ta all the poor souls who're hungry."

"Huh," Johnson replied.

Eddie pointed as they approached the train yard. "Better man yer gate."

As Johnson moved into position, he realized he hadn't made the connection before. He knew that the cattle would ultimately be slaughtered for food, but he hadn't grasped how his work played into a larger operation that profited off the needs of people. He'd been so focused on using the cattle drive to hide himself, he'd never considered what he was doing beyond the daily work.

Caldwell approached from the across the tracks with two other men on horseback. One rode beside him while the other lagged; both men were dressed in clean suits that looked out of place among the cowboys.

The man who lagged wore spectacles and held a handkerchief to his nose to block the smell of the cattle. As he passed the engine, a quick spray of steam was released and startled him so much that he almost fell off his horse.

The man riding next to Caldwell was ominous. His short graying hair was slicked back and matched his waxed mustache. The suit he wore was a deep navy blue, ornamented with gold buttons and a pocket watch chain that draped from his lapel to the watch hiding in his breast pocket. His garb was far more elegant than what his counterpart wore, which made the man appear even more out of place amid the dirt and grime of the stock pens.

"As you can see, Mr. Boyd, we are working diligently to have them all loaded by the end of the day," Caldwell said, his lip full of tobacco. Turning his body away, he spit neatly into an old pouch rather than on the ground like he normally would, hoping to appear more respectable.

As they rode closer, Boyd looked over the operation, watching the movement of the cattle. To him, the crew and the operation appeared unruly and chaotic. Squinting, Boyd focused on Johnson mounted at the open gate. He scowled. "I didn't realize so many niggers were used to drive cattle."

Caldwell paused to gather his words. "We hire competent men, I assure you."

Boyd looked toward Eddie. "That appears to be a woman."

"She is Mr. Howe's hire."

"I see," Boyd said, turning his gaze back to Johnson. "Unsightly creatures, aren't they?" Boyd said to his assistant.

"Yes, very much so, sir, and dreadfully foul smelling," his assistant replied through the handkerchief.

"I have seen enough. I'm returning to my railcar."

Johnson was uneasy as he watched Caldwell and the two men slowly ride by to observe. It felt as if he were some animal on display for their entertainment, and he was relieved when they moved on. The well-dressed man with the mustache made him particularly uncomfortable as his face did not deviate from its dissatisfied arrangement.

"Who was that?" Johnson asked Eddie as they disappeared behind a line of passenger cars on a parallel set of tracks.

Eddie turned her horse in a circle on the spot but kept her gaze locked on him. "I know you ain't that thick."

"That was the buyer?" He looked back toward where they'd disappeared. "Don't see why a man dressed like that would come here."

Now Eddie chided him. "Sure is funny to think he'd wanna have a look at his product."

"But a rich man dressed like that, you wouldn't expect him to come down here."

"No? I forgot how much experience you had with the dos and don'ts of high-society types."

"Just seems strange is all."

"Why? They're his cattle. He bought 'em, didn't he?"

"Alright, I take your point," Johnson said. Turning his horse, he headed back out for another group of cattle.

By the time they had loaded the last of the cattle, the sun was low, casting shadows from the mountains that stretched over Cheyenne. Every member of the crew was exhausted from the long day of work, yet having finished gave them new vigor. A. J. and Wendel talked at length of getting a drink, while Bill and Slim were eager to find a brothel.

Caldwell was in the best spirits Johnson had ever seen him. Once the door to the last car was closed and latched, Caldwell cheered and rode several laps around one of the pens with a huge grin on his face. "This is our best haul yet!"

Johnson scratched under his hat and looked at Eddie. "What's got into him?"

"He's always like this once we finish," she replied. "Just lets loose. It's a load off fer him."

"Wish he'd been more like this during the drive."

"Well, think now, the man's got a lotta responsibilities. Anythin' that goes wrong ultimately falls on him, an' half the cattle are his. It ain't no easy task getting two thousand head this far."

"But we still lost several cattle." Johnson lowered his eyes. "And Jesse."

Eddie patted him on the shoulder. "I've gone shorter distances and lost more."

Caldwell finished his laps and rode over to where they'd all gathered outside of the pens. "Let's head to the saloon," he said to the group with a smile. "Eddie, have you made a decision yet?" He looked at her, then to Johnson. Caldwell's face wasn't as rigid as usual, but his eyes still looked hard.

Johnson did his best to stare back at him with confidence.

"We're headin' out soon as we're paid," Eddie replied.

"Surely you have time to grab a drink with us?" Caldwell asked, still staring at Johnson. "It'd be bad manners not to at the end of a drive."

"Well?" Eddie turned to Johnson.

Breaking his stare with Caldwell, he turned to acknowledge her. "I suppose we wouldn't want to be rude."

Eddie grinned. "Alright, we'll come then. But we can't stay long," she replied. "A. J., I expect my money."

Grunting, A. J. forced a smile that made him look as if he were struggling through a bowel movement.

The saloon was as quiet as it was empty. When the crew entered through the open doorway, there wasn't even a bartender behind the bar, and only a few of the oil lamps sitting on the tables were lit, which made the space dark and hard to see in.

"Anybody even here?" Eddie loudly asked as she walked across the wooden floorboards to the bar. She turned back to the rest of the crew. "This place even open?"

Johnson gave her a nervous shrug.

A loud creak came from the back of the room, then a door was thrown open and slammed into the wall.

All of them grabbed at their holsters and drew as a man entered the room.

"Whoa! Hold on!" the man yelled. "Don't shoot!"

"Get yer hands up then!" Eddie yelled.

"I'd oblige were it not for my hands being occupied."

"Well, come into the light a bit then," Caldwell commanded.

Carefully, the man stepped forward next to one of the lit tables. Short, black, and wearing an apron, he was obviously the missing bartender. Holding a crate of liquor bottles with both hands, he asked them, "Would you mind if I set this down? I'd rather not drop it."

"Why ya tryin' ta scare us for?" Eddie asked, putting away her revolver.

"Didn't hear ya come in."

"That seems unlikely, loud as Eddie is," Bill said.

"Bill, ya better watch what comes outta yer mouth unless you're lookin' ta get more than a limp from me!"

Bill took a deep breath, but A. J. put a hand to his chest to stop him. Letting out the breath in a huff, he pushed back his white hair and scrunched his wrinkled face into a scowl. "Can we get a drink or what?" Bill asked.

"Sure," the bartender replied. He waddled behind the bar carrying the heavy crate. "What can I get y'all?"

Nearly all of them replied in unison, "Whiskey." Except for Caldwell, who requested a beer.

After the crew was served, the bartender lit the remaining lamps.

"Alright," Caldwell said, sitting down at one of the tables with his beer. He set down a satchel he had carried with him and opened the flap. "It's time for what you've all been waiting for." Kicking the spittoon bucket out from under the table with his foot, he turned and spit. "Line up."

One by one, each member of the crew walked up to the table. Caldwell thumbed through a stack of banknotes, handed them their cut, and then checked their name off a list.

Johnson was anxious as he approached. Even though he'd managed to stay on after the stampede and seemingly gained Caldwell's trust, he was unsure if he was still expected to pay for damages.

Caldwell gave him his usual hard stare, counted out the money, and handed it to Johnson. "Count."

"Huh?"

"Count it to make sure it's all there," Caldwell repeated.

Johnson carefully thumbed through each bill and tried to keep track in his head—$95. He smiled. "It's right."

"Alright then," Caldwell said, dismissing him.

Johnson's head buzzed. He was ecstatic. It was the most money he'd ever made in his life. Walking over to where Eddie stood at the bar, he counted it again. "I wanna head out soon."

The sooner they left lessened the chance of someone deciding he'd been overpaid. He wanted to get away with his money and use it to find a place to put all this business of Pinkertons and Cole Charles behind him.

"Here's your damned money," A. J. said, slapping a stack of bills on the bar next to Eddie.

With her finger, she slid each bill off the pile, counting them one at a time. "Ya owe me more than that."

"Well, I ain't paying no more!"

Eddie swallowed a shot of whiskey. "If you weren't gonna pay up, you shoulda kept out!"

"How about we make another bet?" A. J. asked her. "One where neither of us can cheat."

Eddie sniffed the air like she was smelling for any hint of deception. "What is it ya got in mind?"

"Simple target shooting. Nothing special. Winner gets an extra fifty on top of the original wager."

"I shouldn't even be entertainin' the idea, but I know I can outshoot you any day. Twice on Sunday."

"But it's too dark for any shootin'," Johnson interrupted, a sick feeling growing in his stomach, "so shouldn't we just get goin'?"

"Nah, it won't hurt ta wait 'til dawn. It'll be quick enough," she replied. A. J. smiled as she said it. His greasy hair clung to his cheeks.

Any elation within Johnson died and a troubled feeling grew in its place. His heart raced. He wasn't comfortable staying any longer than they needed. He knew something bad would happen if they didn't leave soon.

<hr/>

The Railyard, Cheyenne, Wyoming Territory
October 1876

The confines of Frederick Boyd's private luxury car were similar to those of his office back in Saint Andrews. Ornately worked bookshelves filled with volumes, red carpet with an intricate gold pattern, and matching curtains. He'd even had the large wooden desk from his office brought along and placed near one of the windows. Still, it was too cramped and rough while moving. He hated trains and was ready to be back near the waters of San Francisco Bay.

Boyd dictated to his assistant, who sat on a couch across the room with a pen and notepad. "Furthermore, I request that distribution be handled through my business partner, Mr. Herston in Boston. You may contact him for any questions regarding—" Boyd cut his words short as a knock came from the back door of his car.

He sighed. "Go and see who it is."

Setting aside the notepad, his assistant rose and answered the door. "Good evening, Governor Campbell." This he said loud enough that Boyd could hear. "An unexpected visit, I might add. May I help you?"

"I know Boyd's in there, and we still have words to discuss."

"Just a moment, sir," the assistant said.

"I'll wait," Campbell loudly replied so that Boyd might also hear.

Shutting the door, the balding man looked to his employer for an answer.

"Go ahead and let him in," Boyd said.

His assistant opened the door again and moved out of the entryway to invite Campbell through. "Right this way, sir."

Campbell climbed the steps into the car. He was in his late thirties, with a full beard and thinning hair.

"Governor," Boyd addressed him without standing.

Walking over to where Boyd's assistant had been sitting, Campbell picked up the notepad, dropped it to the floor, and sat down. "Our last conversation was cut short before we could finish the discussion on additional fees."

"I cut the discussion short," Boyd replied sternly, twisting his mustache. "I have paid more than enough already."

"For the territorial tax, yes, but you are short on payments owed to the Stock Grazier's Association."

Boyd scoffed. "Those dues are tantamount to extorsion."

"They are owed nonetheless."

"And what will you do about it if I refuse to pay?"

"Me? Absolutely nothing. But I can't promise there won't be retribution from the Stock Graziers."

"Ah, yes. An organization that you head. It appears your old drinking buddy U. S. Grant has taught you a few things about politics," Boyd said, leaning back in his chair.

Campbell stood up. "This is my territory. I make the rules!"

"It is my money, and I won't allow you to squeeze one more red cent out of me with your corrupt tactics!" Boyd yelled back.

"I'm warning you." Campbell walked back to the door. He stuck out his finger and pointed it at Boyd as he grabbed hold of the handle. "You do not wish to cross the Stock Graziers!" He slammed the door behind him.

Boyd's assistant stood, nearly quivering, with his back to the corner.

"He thinks because he's the president of his little club that he can intimidate me!" Boyd said. He paced in front of his desk. "The bastard! I won't have it."

The next day Frederick Boyd sat stretched out on the couch reading a book in his private car as his train moved west through the low rolling hills of the plains west of the Laramie Mountains. He smirked at the thought of Campbell's attempt to use threats to coerce him. Boyd commended himself for knowing better than to fall for a tactic he himself had perfected.

Closing his book, he stood and walked over to the window, staring out at the endless landscape. He squinted, taking notice of a figure riding in the distance, followed by another rider, then another. His face twisted into a scowl when suddenly a whole band of men on horseback closed in on the train.

"You godforsaken Stock Graziers!" he yelled, shaking his fist.

Before Boyd had a chance to call for his assistant, he was thrown to the ground as the train came to a halt. His head pounded when he sat up, and he heard the voice call to him from outside his car. "Frederick Boyd, come out here so we can have a talk with you!"

The Laramie Mountains of eastern Wyoming loomed dark as Cole Charles rode. He cut through the early dawn fog that pooled in the low areas of the prairie like wisps of clouds scattered along the ground. Pushing his horse to near exhaustion, he arrived in Cheyenne just as the sun's first light peeked over the horizon and lit the mountaintops.

The first person he saw was an old white man in overalls, sitting on his porch, lighting a pipe.

"Where is the sheriff's office?" Cole Charles asked the man.

Taking a long puff, the man stared at the warm glow of the embers then slowly blew out the smoke. "Sheriff's office is near the capitol building. Need to report a crime?"

"No, I am searching for a man who has come to the city."

Squinting, the man stared at Cole Charles's badge. "Pinkerton, huh? Well, you could talk to the sheriff, but I'd suggest ya go to the Stock Grazier's Association first. Not much happens in this town without their knowing about it."

Cole Charles's face twisted into a satisfied look.

The office manager at the Stock Grazier's Association was a young man wearing black slacks and a vest with a white shirt underneath. His feet dragged across the floor as he walked, letting Frank Wolcott know he was coming before he was even at the door. "There's a Pinkerton detective here asking questions."

"Thank you, Ronald," the portly Wolcott said from behind his desk, stroking his long mustache. "You can send him back."

Before Wolcott had finished speaking, Cole Charles limped through the doorway and into his office.

"Frank Wolcott, business secretary of the Wyoming Stock Grazier's Association," he said, standing and extending his hand. "To what do I owe the pleasure of a visit from a member of such an esteemed organization as the Pinkertons, Mr. . . . ?"

"Cole Charles."

"Mr. Charles," Wolcott repeated.

"It seems you have quite the operation," Cole Charles said, gazing around the room at the framed images of men shaking hands in front of fenced-in cattle and charters hanging from the walls.

Wolcott smiled. "We are a growing organization, but our president is also the governor of this territory."

Cole Charles smirked. "How fortunate."

"Indeed. Now, how can I help you?"

"I am looking for a negro on a large cattle drive, two thousand head. Cheyenne was to be their terminus."

"Running a bit late then, eh?"

Cole Charles grimaced. "They're already gone?"

"Pulled out of here about three days ago," Wolcott said. Resting his chin on his fist, he thought for a moment. "Though they had quite the dustup among themselves before leaving."

"Dustup?"

"Yes, some disagreement over money. A bet."

"And the outcome?"

"A man was shot."

Cole Charles's eyes narrowed. "Dead?"

"No, still quite alive but awaiting trial in the custody of the sheriff."

"For what?"

"Attempted murder," Wolcott replied. "He was shot in self-defense."

Cole Charles took a deep breath through his nose and exhaled. "Is your sheriff a reasonable man?"

"He can be." Wolcott paused. "If he is told to be."

"And what do you need from me to make that possible?"

"As I have said, Mr. Charles, our organization is growing. A favor from the Pinkertons would be invaluable."

With an awkward movement, Cole Charles balanced on his right leg and pivoted slightly to better face him. "What kind of favor?"

"The buyer of the two thousand head you asked about? There was a disagreement between our organization and his." Wolcott met Cole Charles's gaze with a coldness that rarely matched the Pinkerton's.

"That is not our kind of work."

"You misunderstand me, Mr. Charles. The man has been taken care of. All we desire from you is for one of your agents to manufacture an alibi and determine that there was no foul play."

"I see."

Cheyenne Jail, Wyoming Territory
October 1876

Shirtless, A. J. pressed a hand to the bloody bandages at his side and groaned as he sat up. The sheriff and a man with a Pinkerton's badge pinned to his chest stared at him through the black bars of his cell door.

"Your presence is no longer necessary, sheriff," Cole Charles said after the sheriff had unlocked the door.

The sheriff shot a quick glance toward A. J. then turned and left without a word.

Slicking back a strand of hair from his face, A. J. watched the man cautiously.

Cole Charles did not sit when he entered but instead stood favoring his left leg.

A. J. was about to ask who he was, but Cole Charles held up his hand and stopped him.

"I don't need you to talk. You don't need to know who I am," Cole Charles said, examining A. J.'s bandages to assess his mobility. "I know your type. Your penchant for making wagers has put you in a dangerous position. You were desperate enough to try and kill one of your associates to pay off a debt, but your desperation made you sloppy."

A. J. groaned. "Clearly."

"I need to find one of your crew members. A negro."

Despite the pain burning in his side, A. J. leaned back against the cell wall and laughed. "Johnson," he said as he gathered himself.

Cole Charles nodded. "I will get you out of here on the condition that you help me hunt down this man."

Standing, A. J. grabbed his shirt. "I'll help you find him. He's the bastard that did this to me."

Chapter 25

Dakota Territory
October 1876

The Black Hills were unlike any of the mountains Johnson had seen before. Trees thickly covering their peaks created a striking contrast against the bald cliffs of gray granite and rock spires that extended through treetops.

"You sure we're going the right way?" Johnson asked Eddie. They had been traveling several days without seeing any sign of civilization.

"If ya wanna lead us, go right ahead," Eddie replied.

Johnson pulled his hat lower over his brow.

"Good idea. Best ya leave the singing ta me, too," she said, raising one of her usual tunes.

A gust of wind picked up off the mountains and the sweet smell of pine hit them in the face while they rode. The chill in the air stung Johnson's nose and ears. He closed his coat tighter around him. Whistling along with Eddie for a time, he eventually became too cold to continue.

"How much farther do we have to go?" he asked, interrupting her mid-song.

Humming, Eddie pulled a ragged map from the pocket of her duster. Looking out toward one of the distant peaks, she examined the lay of the land leading to it. "I'd say we should be 'bout there. Maybe another day?"

Low cloud cover had gathered over them for the past few hours, and Johnson worried about how miserable it would be if it rained. "There'd better be a warm place to stay once we get there."

Pulling out her flask, Eddie unscrewed the top, took a swig, and then handed it to Johnson. "The saloons better be warm, 'cause I'll be huntin' down a game o' cards soon as I can."

Several inches of heavy white snow padded the ground when they finally reached the sign for the town of Deadwood the next day. Neither of them had expected the snowfall when they had gone to sleep the night before, and they found it impossible to warm up once they woke covered in the icy powder. Snow continued to fall as they rode into town.

Deadwood was tucked in a mountain valley at the convergence of two creeks. Most of the hills surrounding the town had been stripped of their pines to build the houses and structures scattered around the main thoroughfare, and several more buildings were in the process of being erected.

The smell of burning pine filled the air as smoke rose from the chimneys of every building. The thought of a warm fire caused Johnson and Eddie to shiver violently as they approached the livery. They each had at least two inches of snow piled on their hats.

"C'mon in and get warm," the old stableman said, scrambling to take the reins of their horses. "Right in there by the fire."

Teeth chattering, they dusted themselves off and hurried into the warm building where a large stone fireplace sat in the back wall. A small pile of logs blazed inside.

"That ain't gonna do," Eddie said. Walking over to where the wood was stacked, she grabbed three more logs and placed them on the fire then scraped up as much sawdust and bark as she could and threw that in as well.

The fire swelled up. Johnson sat in front of it, removed his boots, and stretched his lifeless toes so close to the flames that it looked as if his feet could have been burning.

Eddie sat next to him and did the same.

The stableman returned a few minutes later. "You two must've had a hell of a trek in this weather."

"Startin' ta see why not many people make it up this far," Eddie replied.

"Mostly miners and miscreants," the stableman said, removing his coat.

"Get many lawmen in these parts?" Eddie asked.

Johnson's heart jumped and he shot her a stern look.

"Nope. We don't even have a marshal ourselves."

"Then the job's open," she joked, slapping Johnson on the back. "This one here has grown adept at shootin' down criminals."

"Well, I figure there's no marshal 'cause that's the way people here want it," the stableman replied. "Lots of folks here prefer to avoid the law."

Eddie turned back to Johnson. "That's too bad. Looks like yer out of a job already."

As Johnson massaged his feet back to life, he began to feel good about the decision to come there. If this was what winter was like in the Black Hills, surely he would have a few months of safety before Cole Charles was able to make it to him. Then he could be gone again.

The Black Hills, Dakota Territory
October 1876

The heavy snowfall made travel difficult for Cole Charles and A. J. They had spent only two days in the icy, mountainous terrain, and Cole Charles was tired of hearing A. J. ramble on about Johnson and the woman he was traveling with.

"They both think they got me! I can't wait to see the surprise on their faces." A. J. wiped away the snot running from his nose.

"Stay focused," Cole Charles insisted. "I need to know more about each of them."

A. J. sniffed, scrunched his face, and cocked his head back slightly as he thought. "He's always strange acting. A quiet type. And Eddie never shuts up. She'd have a better chance of hitting a hare with a rock than hitting a note!"

"I am not interested in her singing ability," Cole Charles replied with little inflection in his voice. "Tell me something important."

"Well, she ain't scared of nothing, how about that?"

"Neither am I." Cole Charles stared out at the snow-covered peaks. Dusk was setting in, leaving the land in a winter glow.

"Know this at least," A. J. said, feeling at his wound through several layers of clothing, "that Johnson might seem unassuming, but he's quick."

Cole Charles shivered as a strong gust blew at their backs. The bitter cold increased the pain in his leg. Stopping in order to relieve himself, he dismounted and made sure he'd be well hidden behind a patch of snow-covered brush. Lowering his pants, steam rose from the ground where his urine hit snow. Finishing, he tightened the leather straps of his hollow wooden prosthetic. His thigh was almost burned where the cold metal buckles touched his bare skin. Taking his handkerchief, he tucked it under the metal. He was still growing accustomed to the replacement and hadn't anticipated the effects of the frigid weather.

In the following days, A. J.'s condition worsened with the weather as well. This frustrated Cole Charles even more, since it cut their travel days short and required him to gather extra kindling to build a fire big enough to keep the fugitive warm each night.

Cole Charles planned to use A. J. as a distraction, which might allow him to take Johnson and his companion by surprise. In the past, when he'd had two good legs, he would've left a man in A. J.'s condition behind regardless of whether he was needed.

His reliance on such a lowlife meant he was going soft. Where once the thought of such a thing would have burned inside him, that sentiment was replaced with the desire to watch his son grow to become a man. It served as a reminder that he was ready to put the life of a Pinkerton behind him.

The pair had set up camp for the night under a large pine without any low branches. A. J. sat propped up against its trunk.

Helping him to change his bandages, Cole Charles saw that the skin around his wound had become infected and was turning black. "It does not look good."

A. J. leaned his head back. He was becoming delirious. "I'm gonna kill him," he said, wincing. "It was like he knew. Like he saw it coming before I had time to get a good shot at her."

"So you've told me," Cole Charles said, tying the bandage and pulling down his shirt.

"She didn't see it coming, but he did." A. J. repeated. "I'm gonna kill him."

Cole Charles woke the next morning to find A. J. blue in the face and lifeless. Saddling his horse, he gathered the rest of the provisions, packed them onto A. J.'s horse, and left his body lying in the snow.

The loss of A. J. would make the task more difficult, but now at least he wouldn't have to listen to him rambling on.

❦

Deadwood, Dakota Territory
October 1876

Johnson opened his eyes and was blinded by the bright light shining through the window of his room. Jumping up, he realized he was late. Dog Patch had expected him at Jim Ricket's place by nine o'clock. His card shark employer was a forgiving man, but this was the third time he had been late that week.

Rushing to get dressed, he threw on a shirt and strapped on the Colt Navy revolver Dog Patch had given him to use while he was on guard.

Johnson was glad to have found employment, even if it was as a roughneck. It wasn't the most honorable of jobs, but it was better than shoveling coal on the *Queen Bellamy*. He wasn't starving, like when he and Walt traveled through Arkansas. Plus, he was able to enjoy watching card games while he worked.

As he made his way down the stairs and out of the inn, he wondered how Walt had fared with the army. *Is he even still alive?*

Johnson stumbled into the snow-covered street. Trying his best to stay upright as he walked, he realized that he was probably still somewhat drunk from the previous night.

Before he even walked through the front door of the saloon, Johnson heard Dog Patch's heavy British accent and knew his employer had already found his first mark of the day.

When Johnson entered, Dog Patch was at the bar talking to the tallest woman he had ever seen. At first Johnson thought he was mistaken, but when he heard the person speak, sure enough, this was a woman. "People call me Eddie," she said.

Tall with long brown hair and wearing a duster, she was loud when she spoke. Too loud for his aching head. Beside her stood a black man with a scruffy beard and a black hat.

"So, yer from jolly old England, huh?" Eddie asked, poorly mimicking Dog Patch's accent.

Dog Patch gave her a devilish smile as he fixed the cuffs of his coat. "That's right. London, love."

"Don't go thinkin' yer gonna sweet talk me with that shit!" she said. Straightening her spine, she towered over the well-dressed Englishman.

Johnson double-checked the buckle on his gun belt to make sure it was tight then walked over.

"Ah, Gnat, you finally made it," Dog Patch said, acknowledging Johnson as he made his way toward them.

Gnat. Right, he remembered. Dog Patch gave everyone nicknames, but after a few months, he still wasn't comfortable being called Gnat.

"This is Eddie," Dog Patch said, motioning to the tall woman. "And this here is Johnson. Just like you, innit? Remarkable. Two Johnsons. Might even say you look a bit similar."

Gnat was taken aback as this man, this other Johnson, stared at him in shock like he'd known him from somewhere before.

Standing next to Eddie, Johnson couldn't believe what he was seeing when Dog Patch introduced him to Gnat. "It was you," Johnson said to Gnat. "You were there!"

"What's he on about?" Dog Patch asked, turning back to Gnat.

"Ain't sure," Gnat replied, touching his Colt. "You've seen me before?"

Johnson nodded. "Saint Andrews."

Gnat squeezed the handle of the revolver. "You with the law or somethin'?"

"Well, that's a stupid fuckin' question," Eddie said, staring him down. "Would ya expect us ta say if we was?"

"Then I suppose they've been after you, too. The Pinkertons," Johnson said.

Now Gnat wore a surprised look. "Who are you?"

Johnson scratched under his hat. He thought back to the small tavern he'd always gone to for a drink after work in Saint Andrews. Remembered the surprise he and everyone else had felt when a rich white woman came in. She was looking for some exotic excitement, rebelling against her strict father. The other Johnson—now known as Gnat—was there, talking with her throughout the night. That was the night everything had changed and sent him fleeing to Kansas where he met Rex and Burt, then on to Texas with Eddie, who had brought him all the way here.

"I was there that night in Mill's Tavern," Johnson said to Gnat.

Slack jawed, Gnat's eyes went wide. That night had upended Gnat's entire life. The narrow escape from Saint Andrews with Jimmy. Joining the *Queen Bellamy* with Abraham, starving through Arkansas and leaving Walt with the Buffalo Soldiers. Gnat had been through so much and now fate had reunited him with his past here in Deadwood. This Johnson also must have been on the run and facing blame for what happened to that woman.

"I—I was drunk, so I don't really remember much from that night." Aware of being in mixed company, Gnat was careful not to say too much.

Johnson decided not to push the matter further. "That's in the past. Doesn't really matter now, I suppose."

Producing a comb from his coat pocket, Dog Patch slicked back his dirty blond hair. "Right then. Now that you two have apparently caught up, shall we continue with business?"

"I should hope so," Eddie replied as she unrolled a stack of bills and set it on the bar. "Hope this ain't too strong for ya, neither."

"Not at all," Dog Patch said. He turned to the stocky man behind the bar. "Mr. Ricket, might we use your back room?"

Jim Ricket crossed his arms. "That's fine."

"Well then. What do you like to play?" Dog Patch asked turning back to Eddie.

While Eddie talked with Dog Patch, Johnson focused on Gnat. It seemed unlikely that the two of them would cross paths. Was he really being chased as well? Could this be a trap set by Cole Charles? Johnson rested his left hand at his hip just above his revolver.

Gnat seemed similarly concerned about Johnson, and both men exchanged several searching glances trying to read one another.

Eddie and Dog Patch settled on five-card draw at $5 a hand. "Shall we?" Dog Patch motioned to the private back room.

"There's only one other thing I wanna do in this town," Eddie said, walking toward the door with a smirk, "but that won't involve you."

Windowless and lit by wall-mounted lamps, the room was just large enough for a card table and a few people. Both Johnson and Gnat stood back from the table in different corners, watching as Dog Patch shuffled the deck and dealt out the first hand.

"Not a bad first deal," Eddie said, looking at her cards.

"I assume you are a talker, so I'll be satisfied to listen quietly while we play." He placed his chips in the middle.

"How gentlemanly of you," Eddie replied in a fake accent, laying one card on the table, "but I can be quiet when I wanna be."

Johnson watched Gnat from the corner of his eye. Dog Patch's hired gun stood firmly at attention with his hands ready at his sides.

Though Johnson wasn't there to settle disagreements with his revolver, neither Gnat nor Dog Patch were aware of that, and he did his best to appear intimidating. Standing tall, Johnson kept his face tight, and his lips pursed.

"*Ha!*" Eddie yelled, laying down a full house. "Thought ya had me there, didn't ya?"

Dog Patch smiled calmly. "Indeed."

Collecting the pot and then the cards, Eddie shuffled. "I have a good feeling about this game already." She turned to look at Johnson. "We're gonna make this one quick. Hope ya got yer carrot stick ready 'cause I'm buying!"

The two of them played back and forth for nearly two hours. Johnson's feet ached from standing upright in one spot for so long. He could no longer maintain his air of toughness, but he refused to leave the room. Instead, he rocked heel to toe and shifted from one foot to the other.

Gnat's posture remained unchanged, and Johnson wondered how he kept his feet from hurting.

"Dammit!" Eddie threw down her cards. Dog Patch's straight had beaten her two pair. "Quite the run of luck," she said, pushing the pot toward him.

"Mm-hmm," Dog Patch nodded, holding out his hand for the deck. "My deal."

Collecting the stray cards, Eddie set the deck down in front of him instead of into his open hand. "Ain't got me whipped yet."

Smirking, Dog Patch picked up the deck, shuffled and offered her a cut.

Eddie waved him off. "I trust ya."

Dog Patch raised an eyebrow. "What say we raise the minimum by ten?"

Eddie fingered her pile of bills. "Fine by me."

This made Johnson nervous. He was not normally interested in poker, but he'd witnessed Eddie's reaction in the past when things didn't go her way in a low-stakes game.

Dog Patch passed Eddie her last card. She always waited for her final card to be dealt before she even touched her hand.

Barely lifting her cards from the table to see what she had, Eddie threw in $60 and said nothing.

Johnson gritted his teeth.

Dog Patch laughed. "Now you're trying to bluff me?"

"Just ready to end this game," Eddie replied.

"I'll see it," he said, putting in his money without any hesitation.

Gnat watched the game more intently, too. Putting a hand to his chin, it was the first time Johnson had seen him shift position.

"Give me three," Eddie said.

Gnat's eyes widened briefly, and Johnson caught it. Did he see something Johnson hadn't?

Quietly, Dog Patch passed her three cards, then laid down three for himself.

Eddie picked up her cards, placed them in her hand, then carefully rearranged them. "Wonder what two ya already got there," Eddie mused out loud as she watched him pick up his three new cards and examine them.

"I suspect you'll know soon enough. Your bet."

Laying her hand facedown on the table, she pushed everything she had into the center. "All in."

Johnson and Gnat leaned closer.

"Just remember, you're the one who wanted to finish this," Dog Patch said as he put all his money in as well. "What you got?"

Eddie cupped her cards in her hand and smirked. "Well, damn. Was really hoping you wouldn't bite." Laying them down, all she had was a pair of jacks.

"How 'bout that?" Dog Patch replied, his devilish smile returning. He flipped his cards face up one at a time—all four aces showed.

Eddie's face tightened in fury. "*Ya didn't have no four aces!*" she stood and screamed.

She drew her Colt .45 in a flash and fired a shot right into Dog Patch's chest.

Thrown back in his seat, Dog Patch clutched the wound with wide eyes. Blood poured out of the hole, spilling from between his fingers. Looking down at his bloody hands he fell onto the table.

Stunned, neither Johnson nor Gnat moved. Then Gnat drew and fired into the back of Eddie's head. Eddie fell face forward.

It was like a chain reaction. As soon as Gnat pulled the trigger, Johnson put a bullet in his gut. Gnat collapsed in the corner.

Smoke from the discharged powder filled the small room, and a sharp ringing was all that Johnson could hear. As he pulled opened the door, Ricket and another burly man stood on the side, guns drawn. Splattered with blood, Johnson dropped his revolver and raised his hands.

With their revolvers aimed at him, the men barked questions, but all Johnson could do was point to his ears and repeat to them that he couldn't hear.

Ricket motioned for him to exit. Johnson obeyed and was led to a seat at a table. The burly man stayed with his revolver drawn to make sure Johnson didn't go anywhere while Ricket went back into the room to examine what had happened. He returned soon after.

Ricket put his hands to his hips and addressed Johnson. "Can you hear yet?"

Johnson stuck a finger in his ear, which was still ringing, but he could hear. "Yeah."

"C'mon in here and see this."

The smoke had cleared from the room. The bodies of Eddie and Dog Patch lay hunched facedown onto the table, and Gnat lay dying on the floor. The cards and chips were scattered across the table, covered in a pool of sticky blood.

"Look here," Ricket said. Holding up Dog Patch's left wrist, he pulled back the sleeve and revealed a metal device holding three cards strapped to his forearm.

"Did you know he was cheatin'?" Johnson asked.

Ricket crossed his arms. "I suspected, but it meant a bigger cut for me, so I didn't care."

Johnson furrowed his brow and scowled at the man. Turning to look at Eddie, he quickly looked away. He couldn't bring himself to stare at her in such a mutilated state, so he turned to Gnat instead.

Eyes closed, Gnat was mumbling quietly. Johnson put his ear low and tried to listen.

"That night. I remember it was that night—she."

Johnson's heart jumped. "In Saint Andrews? What about her?"

"I didn't do it. I didn't. . . ." No more words came from Gnat's mouth as he exhaled his final breath onto Johnson's cheek.

"What was that about?" Rickets asked.

Slow to stand, Johnson ignored the question. He gathered his revolver and turned to the man. "You accusin' me of murder here?"

Rickets shook his head. "Not necessarily. There aren't many people who'll mourn his passing," he said, sticking a thumb toward Dog Patch. "You looking to make any claim on that money?"

Johnson turned and looked at the other man standing in the doorway then back to Rickets. "No, you can have it."

A large grin revealed Ricket's dirty, yellowing teeth. "Well, looks like self-defense to me then."

Holstering his revolver, the man in the doorway stepped aside. Johnson left without another word.

Chapter 26

The wind was bitter. Johnson couldn't keep his thoughts in order as he trudged through the snowy street. His only friend was dead—*What was she thinking? I'm all alone. Eddie is gone. What do I do now? I'm not safe.*

He spent the day getting drunk in the back of a dingy bar trying to numb his feelings. When it didn't work, he decided to find the nearest brothel.

"Don de roat. Don de roat." The scruffy bartender's foreign accent was hard for Johnson to understand.

Turning an ear to the man, Johnson opened his mouth as if it might somehow help him to hear better.

Irritated, the bartender pursed his lips, moved toward the door, and pointed to his right. "Dat way. Don de roat."

"Oh, sorry," Johnson replied as he discerned the words in his head. *Down the road.*

He paid the man and returned to the now darkened street, rubbing his hands together as the cold invaded his body. Johnson hoped the warm touch of a woman could console him, even if only for an hour.

The moon was just a sliver, outshone by the brilliance of stars that sparkled in the wintery sky. Their light reflected off the snow was bright enough for Johnson to make his way to the edge of town where the buildings thinned. The backdrop of mountains created a dark line where the sky ended and left everything below in darkness.

Light from the brothel was like a beacon. The two-story structure was built of freshly cut wood, and as Johnson ascended the front steps, an unkempt white man waited inside the doorway to greet him.

"Welcome to my house of ill repute," he said with a toothy grin. Flecks of brown tobacco were stuck in his teeth and tobacco juice stained the front of his shirt. "Call me Mr. Albert. I assume you've come to partake?"

Johnson was curt with his reply. "I want a girl for the night."

Still grinning, Mr. Albert motioned him inside. "As you can see, we have the ability to accommodate. Come in, stay awhile."

Tipping back his hat, Johnson examined the room.

It was an open space occupied by eight or so scantily clad women playing cards around a table and laughing with one another. A set of stairs led to a balcony that overlooked the lower floor with a line of private rooms visible behind the banister. The whole place smelled of fresh pine and a strange oily smell Johnson couldn't quite place.

Mr. Albert motioned to the girls. "Take your pick. We treat negros here as good as any white man."

There were two other men present. One was working behind a small bar, picking under his fingernails with a knife. The other man was in a corner with a woman on his lap. Her clothes were revealing yet ragged. She whispered into his ear, and a wily smile grew across his face. The woman stood, took him by the hand, and led him upstairs toward one of the rooms.

"That one is obviously not available," Mr. Albert said.

Johnson examined the table of women, all of whom either played cards or stood around and watched the game. They wore men's shirts that had been cut and torn to make them scant.

"C'mon away from the cold." Mr. Albert directed him out of the doorway. "What kind of girl are you looking for? White, I would suppose," he said with a laugh.

The fresh floorboards creaked as they moved toward the table of women. They were a mix of appearances: skinny, fat, tall, black, white.

One of the white women kept glancing at him then quickly looking away to see if anyone else had noticed. It was as if she didn't want the others to know she was looking at him.

"Stop being rude!" Mr. Albert stamped his foot. "Game's over. We have another guest."

Indignant, the women threw down their cards, pursed their lips, and faced Johnson.

Mr. Albert grinned. "That's better."

Johnson briefly looked at a few women, but his focus was taken by the woman who'd been glancing at him since he'd walked in. She was now staring at him with wide-eyed intensity. There was a bruise on her left cheek and her long brown hair was tangled.

Johnson squinted as he stared back into her eyes, and she nodded rigidly to him like she expected him to recognize her.

His heart jumped. He couldn't believe it—Margret!

He hadn't recognized her dressed as she was and so dirty. He took a deep breath to calm himself. He was wary of what might happen if Mr. Albert learned that they were acquainted.

"What the fuck is wrong with your face?" Mr. Albert demanded, noticing Margret staring at Johnson. "I oughta—" With heavy steps, he moved toward the table.

Margret flinched as he approached.

"No, its fine!" Johnson protested. "I'll have her."

Stopping, Mr. Albert turned back to him. "You sure? You haven't spent any time with the girls yet. Plenty to choose from."

Margret looked away.

"I ain't picky," Johnson said. "I just want a girl."

"Well, alright then. Easy customer," Mr. Albert replied. He waved Margret over and she joined them without speaking.

Mr. Albert gave Johnson an hourly price. He found it high but didn't care.

Margret took Johnson's hand and squeezed tight. Despite the roughness of her appearance, her hand was just as soft as he remembered. Without a word she led him to the stairs.

"Better enjoy it on a cold night like this," Mr. Albert laughed.

Johnson gave the man a fake smile and nodded to him as they walked to the farthest room.

As soon as Margret closed the door behind them, she embraced him tightly. "My God, Mr. Johnson, you have to get me out of here." She was careful not to speak too loudly.

"What happened?" he asked. "How did you get here?"

"I need help. I am sick from morphine and he has me trapped." She was frantic. Her motions were erratic, and she paced from the window to the front of the bed. "You have to help me escape!"

Grabbing her by the shoulders, Johnson gently brought her to the edge of the mattress and seated her. "It's OK. I can get you out."

"Thank you!" she said, releasing a heavy breath. "It seems that we are destined to keep running into one another." As she said it, she pulled him close and placed a kiss just above the scruff on his cheek. "Your appearance is so much wilder than when we first met," she said with a smile, "though I suppose you think the same of me."

"I'm not worried about that right now," he replied. He stood and looked around the room. Aside from the bed, there was a small dresser, but that was all. "Do you have much to take?"

Margret shook her head. "Just some extra clothes."

Johnson walked over to the window and looked out. There was a thin roof that ran along the second-story windows. "I will have to come back."

Margret tensed. "What do you mean?"

"I can't take you now, but I have an extra horse."

"Can't we just go now then get the horses?"

Johnson shook his head. "It'll take too long. We'd be caught before we got to the livery. Probably before we left the building."

"Please, I must leave this dreadful place!"

Walking back to where she stood, Johnson wrapped his arms around her. She squeezed him tightly.

"I'll come back."

Tears wet his shirt where Margret buried her face in his chest.

Johnson descended the stairs after only a half hour. "Quick poke," Mr. Albert said to him with his toothy, tobacco grin. "Thought I might get an hour out of you."

Buttoning his coat, Johnson nodded to the man and pulled his hat low as he walked out into the cold. He could feel his pulse beating in his head as he ran through the snow toward the livery.

"Sorry, to hear 'bout your friend," the stableman said as he led Johnson to the horses. "Probably is time this town gets a lawman."

"What's the nearest settlement outside here?" Johnson asked him.

"That'd be a place they call Scooptown. You'll wanna follow the pass east. It's at the edge of the mountains," he said, pointing out into the darkness where the two peaks came down in a V shape and revealed the starry night sky. "Wouldn't you rather travel in the morning? You could stay here for the night."

Johnson tipped his hat to the man as he took the reins of the horses. "Thanks, but I'm in a rush."

When Johnson returned to the edge of town, he dismounted and walked the two horses up to the brothel. There was less light coming from inside than when he'd left. He tried to be as quiet as possible while approaching, but the snow crunched with each step. As he snuck around to the side of the building, Johnson examined all the other windows on the second floor. They were dark, but that didn't mean he wasn't being watched.

Margret was waiting in her room, staring through the window. She had put on the only other dress she had left and a tattered coat over that. Sliding her window open, she tossed out a makeshift rope made from bedsheets. The end was tied to the bed and it ended about seven feet short of the ground. She motioned for Johnson to come closer, careful not to make too much noise.

Remounting, he positioned Eddie's horse beneath Margret's rope.

Grabbing hold of the twisted bedsheets, Margret took a deep breath and crouched in the windowsill. She turned around and extended her right foot in a careful step and leaned out. The snow on the roof gave her footing little purchase, so instead of taking another full step, she shuffled her feet backward, gripping the rope as tightly as she could.

Johnson's heart raced as he watched, his gaze shifting from window to window, afraid they would be heard. When Margret got close to the roof's edge, she squatted low.

Dull light shone through one of the windows three rooms down as a lamp was lit within.

"Hurry!" Johnson hissed, waving Margret closer.

"I am doing my best—" The snow at the edge of the roof gave way beneath her boot. Margret fell face-first on the shingles, legs dangling over the edge.

A woman holding a lamp peered through the window at the scene.

Johnson's muscles tensed. Gritting his teeth, he stood up in his saddle and took hold of Margret's legs. Still gripping the rope, she lowered herself onto the other horse with Johnson's help.

Margret grabbed the reins, wiping the snow from her face with her forearm and adjusting her seat in the saddle. "Let's go!"

Turning their horses toward the road, Johnson looked up and saw the woman still watching them. Her face looked blank as if she were unsure of how to react. Nodding to him, she turned away and extinguished the lamp. Johnson let out a sigh of relief.

They didn't slow for nearly an hour, following the creek that ran east through the pass, but as the adrenaline wore off, the cold began to get to Margret. With her legs bare, she shivered uncontrollably.

"I cannot go any further like this," she said through chattering teeth.

Pulling the horses to a stop, Johnson grabbed the blankets and laid them across her lap. "Is that enough to keep goin' for a while?"

"I believe so. Thank you," she replied, still shivering. She looked back the way they had come and let out a loud shriek. "I hope never to return to that wretched place!" Tears streamed from her eyes, and she hung her head.

Johnson placed a hand on her cheek to console her. "It's alright now. You're safe."

"Safe from there, yes, but I can feel my sickness building inside. My body aches. It has been too long." Despite the cold, her face was wet with sweat and she could not sit still in the saddle.

"You sure ya can keep goin'? It's not much farther."

She wiped the tears from her eyes. "I will try."

They made it another few miles before Margret vomited and nearly fell off her horse. Johnson helped her down and they moved deeper into the pines where there was less snow covering the ground. He found a spot where several fallen trees had created a shelter from the wind, and Johnson laid Margret down and started a fire.

Once the flames burned steadily, he sat down next to Margret, whose face looked sunken and frail in the firelight.

"Do you need anything?" he asked, tucking the blankets around her legs.

Margret shook her head. "Will you please lie with me? I'm so cold."

Nodding, Johnson's pulse raced. He crawled behind her and pulled her against his body.

Turning her head back, she stared at him from the corner of her eye. "I meant under the blankets, Mr. Johnson."

"Oh, right."

She lifted the blankets and invited him under. He tried to appear confident as he pulled them around his body to join her. Heat radiated from him as she snuggled into his chest. Wrapping his arm around her waist, he held her close. The last time he'd held her this close, they were held captive. He had been powerless when she was wrenched away against her will. In the end, it was she who saved his life. This time he was saving her. Johnson felt for his revolver nearby. He wasn't going to let anything bad happen to Margret. They lay there for several minutes listening to the flames crackle and pop. Nearby a great horned owl let out its ghostly call—*whoo-whoo, whoo-whoo.*

As they lay there in silence, it was the first time Johnson's mind had a chance to slow all day. Despite their current danger, all he could think about was Eddie, not Margret. *I should've seen it coming. I knew she could be erratic. If I'd just been faster . . . I should've been faster!*

"Are you alright?" Margret asked looking up at him. "You're shaking."

"Huh? I didn't realize." He looked down into Margret's eyes and watched her warm breath as it left her lips as a cloud. He'd dreamed every day of holding Margret in his arms, but he hadn't imagined feeling so much fear and uncertainty.

She continued to stare into his eyes. "You cannot fathom what I have been through, what I have done to cope with everything that has happened to me. It's hard for me to believe it myself, yet here I am with you. Thank you."

"Margret, I—"

She leaned forward and kissed his lips. When she pulled away, Johnson's face burned with excitement. Pressing a hand against his chest, she could feel his rapid heartbeat.

Johnson's head spun. He wanted so badly to tell her how he felt, but like always the words were somehow stuck in his throat. Instead, he just smiled and laid his head on top of hers. Tomorrow he would tell her. He would make himself say the words—*Margret, I love you.*

Closing his eyes, he was lulled to sleep by the comfort of her body and the sound of the pines blowing in the wind.

—◦—

Margret waited until she was certain Johnson had fallen asleep. Careful not to disturb him, she unwrapped his arm from her waist and slid from under the blankets.

All that was left of the fire was the smoldering glow of red embers, so she had to crawl on the icy ground in the darkness, feeling her way to where Johnson had set down the saddlebags. Lifting the leather flap, she fumbled through each one until she found what she was looking for.

Tears rolled down her cheeks. "I'm so sorry, Mr. Johnson," she whispered.

—◦—

Deadwood, Dakota Territory
October 1876

The corner of Cole Charles's mouth twitched as he listened to Mr. Albert describe the events at his brothel the night before. He had already questioned most of the town and he was growing impatient.

"It had to be that negro that she ran off with. They were both acting out of the ordinary as soon as he showed up. Picked her straightaway. Most men at least make a little small talk first."

"And this was the same man involved in the killings at the saloon?" Cole Charles asked.

Mr. Albert wiped tobacco juice from his lip with the front of his shirt. "I can't say for certain; I only heard about that from Eustace Braseale."

"The stableman claims he gathered his horse and left around two o'clock."

"Who, Eustace?"

"No, the negro," Cole Charles said through gritted teeth.

"Oh, well, that would make more fucking sense," Mr. Albert laughed.

"Is two o'clock near the time you suspect the girl left?"

"Can't rightly say." He grinned. "I was occupied around that time. Didn't realize she was gone 'til this morning."

"I see."

"Make sure you bring her back here. She still owes me a debt."

"That is of no importance to me," Cole Charles said. Turning away, he went around the side of the building to examine the hoofprints in the snow. The tracks led out of town. He was getting closer.

Chapter 27

Johnson shivered when he woke and felt for Margret. She wasn't there.

Dawn had yet to break above the mountains. It was a dull morning, the chill lingering. Johnson sat up, rubbed the sleep from his eyes, and looked at the charred pile of ashes next to where they'd slept. *Maybe she is gathering wood?*

The horses were still tied, yet Margret didn't seem to be nearby. Examining the ground below the surrounding trees, he noticed a set of footprints in the snow that led up the hillside. *Has she gone to relieve herself?* Then he realized the saddlebags had been left open. When he looked inside to see what was taken, a tight pinch grew in the pit of his stomach.

"Margret!" he yelled, racing after her footprints through the pines.

Sweat ran from his brow as he trudged through the ankle-deep snow, his chest pounding. "Margret!" Johnson fell face-first onto the ground. His foot had caught something that set him off balance. The snow had gotten into his coat. Kneeling, he unbuttoned the coat to clear it out and brushed at his chest, frantic to keep moving.

When he looked up again his heart stopped.

No.

Margret lay on the ground in front of a small bluff.

Johnson jumped to his feet, scrambling toward her, but when he got close, he froze. Her body was limp and lifeless. Around her neck was the rope Johnson had used so many times to wrangle horses and cattle on the trail. The other end was wrapped around a large branch that had broken when she tried to hang herself. Instead, Margret had fallen to her death, dropping thirty or more feet from the bluff and hitting her head.

Tears welled in Johnson's eyes as he approached.

Crouching over her body, he carefully removed the rope from around her neck and brushed the tangled locks from her face.

Wind blew through the trees and the chill cut through him. He shook as he lifted Margret's body in his arms and carried her back to the camp.

Johnson's mind felt empty, his chest hollow. He didn't think, he only acted. Laying Margret on Eddie's horse, he pushed on, continuing toward Scooptown.

Everything was a blur as he rode. Trees, the mountains, the sounds and smells. It all muddled together. Several hours could have passed, and he wouldn't have noticed the difference when he rode out of the mountain pass. It led to a wide-open valley bordered by another low ridgeline of bluffs on the other side. The sun was high and the air grew warmer the farther he got from the mountains. The ground was wet and muddy.

In the distance, Johnson saw a small wooden church with a bell tower above the front door. Set apart from the rest of Scooptown, the structure was new, though there were already several graves in the cemetery that surrounded the church.

No one was present when Johnson stopped. He looked at the little bronze bell and saw several mourning doves huddled together beneath it, their distinct coos crying at his arrival.

Lifting Margret from the horse, Johnson carefully ascended the steps of the veranda and entered the church. He carried her body down the aisle past the rows of pews, laying her on the front pew.

Kneeling over her for several minutes, he wanted to cry but couldn't. He wanted to feel sadness but couldn't. He shook as a deep anger burned in his chest. After everything he'd been through, he'd finally gotten his small chance at happiness, and it was ripped away from him. Giving into his rage, he turned and flipped the pew next to where Margret lay, then kicked over the next one behind it. Grabbing a small side table at the entrance, he tossed it through one of the glass windows.

Once his anger subsided, Johnson walked back to the front and sat down next to Margret. He bowed his head and was silent for a long time, listening to the sound of his own breath, searching for any sign that he was still alive.

A strange rhythm of footsteps echoed from the veranda outside the front door of the church—a step, then a drag, followed by a crunching noise, step, drag.

Johnson raised his head and looked toward the pulpit.

"Has the good Lord answered your prayers, Mr. Johnson?"

The voice was as eerie as he had remembered. Turning around, Johnson saw Cole Charles standing in the doorway.

"I must admit, I did not think it would be this hard to track you down," Cole Charles said. His body pivoted over the prosthetic as he moved to step with his good leg—step, drag, the crunch of the pivot, then another step. He motioned to Margret. "You've left quite the trail of bodies."

Johnson's blood boiled as a rush of energy welled inside him. Drawing his revolver, he sprang up.

A shot from Cole Charles's large Colt ripped through his right arm.

Johnson ducked below the pew and crawled toward the wall away from his assailant.

Step, drag, crunch, step. "I was told you were faster than that."

Johnson set his revolver down and clutched at the wound. He could feel where it had gone through the other side of his arm. It burned but he could still move it. Grabbing the revolver, he sprang up again and fired two quick shots.

Cole Charles went down.

Johnson dashed through the pews toward him. Cole Charles was lying flat on his back, bleeding from his side. Johnson took aim to finish him as he rushed forward. *Click.* The revolver was empty.

Cole Charles flinched as Johnson pulled the trigger. When the firing pin hit the empty cartridge, his eyes shot to where he'd dropped his gun just out of reach. Johnson kept coming. Thrusting hard with his good leg, Cole Charles caught the onrushing Johnson in the stomach. He grabbed hold of the pew with both hands and awkwardly lifted himself onto the prosthetic.

Johnson didn't fall but the kick knocked the breath out of him. He tried to gather himself before Cole Charles could get back to his feet but he wasn't fast enough. Cole Charles grabbed him by the neck and shoved him against a row of pews, nearly throwing himself off balance.

Hopping on his good leg, he tried to find his footing with the wooden one. Grabbing one of the pews, Cole Charles caught his breath.

The small of Johnson's back hit hard on the edge of the pew. His vision blurred and he fell to the ground. He blinked. Cole Charles's Colt laid in front of him. Snatching it, Johnson rose to his feet. A hand grabbed his wrist. Cole Charles tried to pry the gun away. He struck Johnson in the stomach again.

Johnson hunched forward but still gripped the gun firmly. Cole Charles wound up another fist, but Johnson grabbed his arm before he could strike.

Muscles strained and bullet wounds burning, they struggled against one another. Each of them exhausted, each in pain.

"Did you run out of goons?" Johnson grunted. "Need another woman to do the job?"

Cole Charles scowled. "I don't know what you're talking about."

Johnson nodded toward Margret. "She was the one who killed Jester Wells."

Through a clenched jaw Cole Charles uttered, "Am I supposed to be insulted? You think that white woman loved you? She was just using you."

Fury rose inside Johnson. With all his weight, he pushed toward Cole Charles's prosthetic leg and threw him over the pews.

Cole Charles landed on his back between two of the rows. His eyes went wide as Johnson drew down on him. Tensing, he rolled under one of the pews.

Johnson fired through the seat and into the Pinkerton. Splinters went flying as the bullet ripped a hole into the wood. He stared down the barrel of the gun, keeping it trained on the spot.

Cole Charles did not move. Blood ran along one of the cracks between the wooden floorboards toward Johnson's feet. He exhaled a heavy breath and slid the Colt into his gun belt. It was bigger than his .38 but it fit.

Walking back to the front of the church where Margret lay, Johnson bent over and put his hand on her shoulder. A tear rolled down his cheek. He knew that she had cared about him. They had gone through too much together. He kissed her forehead. Standing, he wiped away the tear then pulled his hat low.

He turned and walked down the aisle and out the door.

A large cloud covered the sun, leaving the area in shadow as Johnson mounted his horse. His eyes glanced from the church to the graveyard then to Scooptown in the distance. Looking out over the scattered buildings, he could see people moving about. He returned his gaze to the church and peered through the doorway at the mess of blood, broken glass, and overturned pews.

Dismounting again, he walked to the door. A rope hung on the right side, leading up to the bell tower. Johnson gave the rope three solid tugs. The doves scattered as the bell rang out.

Nodding to himself, Johnson remounted his horse and headed back toward the mountain pass. He wondered if the Pinkertons would send another man after him. Johnson was ready if they did. A new vigor burned inside of him. He had come too far and lost too much to quit. Johnson had fought for his freedom and found his salvation. He wasn't going to give it up.

As he rode, he whistled one of Eddie's favorite tunes.

ACKNOWLEDGMENTS

MY EX-WIFE ONCE TOLD ME I COULD NEVER WRITE A BOOK. SHE WASN'T trying to be mean, but it stuck with me for years afterward, reinforcing this idea I had that writing was for writers. I was a parks maintenance worker when I got the idea for *Wild Salvation*. I told it to one of my oldest and closest friends, Nick Waterfill. I had always admired his ability to tell a story and thought he might want to do something with it. Instead, he encouraged me to write it. Nick, this book wouldn't exist without your friendship.

I can't thank Shola Jhanji enough for encouraging my wannabe cowboy side despite hating all the country music I listen to. Shola, you've always helped me to challenge my perceptions of the status quo. Our friendship made me want to write a Western that better represented the people in the old West so that more people now might see themselves in the stories of that time period, too.

I have to thank everyone in the fiction writers' group at the Indiana Writers Center in Indianapolis. I cannot begin to explain how helpful and supportive you have been to me throughout this process. Your feedback didn't just improve my book, but it helped me become a better writer. I could not have asked for a nicer or more fun group of people.

Once I started writing, I would not have been able to navigate this intimidating new world were it not for Maurice Broaddus. Maurice, I appreciate that you have always been available to answer any questions I have had despite your busy schedule.

I will be forever grateful to Sarah Parke for taking a chance on me and my work. This all came at me much quicker than I expected, but the book is stronger because of your guidance.

Katherine, I love you and I can't thank you enough for putting up with me, reading and rereading so many parts of this until you were sick of it and for giving me the time and space to become a writer.

And finally, to all my friends and family not mentioned by name who either read parts of this story or just encouraged me to keep going, I really can't thank you enough for being there for me.

ABOUT THE AUTHOR

ALFRED STIFSIM GREW UP WATCHING SHOWS LIKE THE *TWILIGHT ZONE* and *Bonanza*, which inspired the kinds of stories he likes to write. A 2014 graduate with a degree in history from Indiana University–Purdue University Indianapolis, Stifsim has worked at FedEx moving packages, served drinks as a bartender, and handled animals and led guided hikes for the Indiana Department of Natural Resources. Currently, he is an electrician with IBEW Local Union 481 in Indianapolis, Indiana. He enjoys sports, bugs, playing music, road trips with his friends, and exploring new places. You can find him on Twitter @AStifsim or at www.alfred stifsim.com.